TWISTED SOUL

A PARANORMAL REVERSE HAREM ROMANCE

CURSED LEGACIES
BOOK 3

MORGAN B LEE

READ BEFORE YOU READ

This book isn't wholesome or fluffy, and trigger warnings can be tough to gauge. If you're concerned about potential triggers not listed here, please feel free to reach out to me on Instagram, TikTok, or Facebook and ask me to spoil anything you're worried about. I will 100% spoil possible triggers because reading safely is extremely important.

With that being said, here is the series ~~check~~list:

- Death (on page)
- Death of a main character (don't worry, it doesn't stick)
- Drugs
- Female dominant/switch
- Group sex scenes (no M/M)
- Graphic violence
- Loss of a loved one
- Mentions of childhood abuse
- Mention of implied past cannibalism
- PTSD
- Somnophilia (prior consent given)
- Stalking (of FMC by MMC)
- Strong language

- Torture (on page)

This isn't an official trigger, but as a final warning before you dive in...this one really does end in a cliffhanger.

Yes, I promise there is an HEA in Book 4.

But you're allowed to hate me until then ;)

MEET THE GODS

Arati - The Queen
*Goddess of passion, love, anger, war, vengeance, and fire.
    Pronounced "Are-uh-tee"*

Galene - The Knowing
*Goddess of life, healing, prophecy, the arts, and history.
    Pronounced "Gay-lene"*

Koa - The Wise
*God of earth, riches, magic, truths and lies, knowledge,
    plants, and fertility. Pronounced "Ko-uh"*

Raan - The Serene
*God of water, moonlight, peace, storms, invention, discovery,
    and the oceans. Pronounced "Ran"*

Syntyche - The Reaper
*Goddess of spirits, fate, soul, time, dreams, darkness, and
    death. Pronounced "Sin-tick"*

Pheli - The Jubilant

God of air, sky, levity, hope, light, laughter, change, and second chances. Pronounced "Fee-lee"

Sachar - The Judge
Not considered part of the pantheon. Eternal judge of souls reaped by his twin sister, Syntyche, when she brings them to the Beyond. Pronounced "Suh-car"

PROLOGUE
MAVEN

THREE YEARS Ago

I sheath Pierce into my thigh strap as Lillian wraps another loaf of oat bread. As usual, I'm not in a chatty mood, but I can tell she's nervous because she can't stop talking.

"...which, of course, is just how the fae do things," she goes on, placing the loaf inside a bag she made from the scraps of old clothes.

A transparent, humanoid blur drifts in front of me, waving a wispy arm to get my attention. I know exactly who this one is. She's been following me for seven years, ever since the incident.

I make no reaction since my caretaker gets concerned whenever I interact with the ghosts.

Lillian starts working on the final loaf, blowing a strand of pale, curly hair out of her face. "And you know how I've told you about romcom movies? Those were my *favorites*, but Edgar wasn't a fan of them. I think it's because of the way he was raised since most fae families are so pragmatic. They work very hard to maintain their own culture. Edgar loved to say his family was the only one that remembered the correct way to make *real* fae mead…"

Uh oh. If she's blabbing about her ex-husband from her long-ago life in the human realm, she's more anxious than I realized.

She slips a wrinkled piece of parchment covered in fae runes and English translations into the bag and ties it shut. I step through the ghost to accept it from her, slinging the bag over my shoulder.

"Stop worrying. I'll be fine."

My caretaker turns gentle, concerned blue eyes on me and sighs. "I know saying this will make you uncomfortable, but this is a truly sweet and kind thing you're doing. It shows you care far more than you would ever willingly admit."

Me, sweet and kind? "Hardly."

"Oh, really? Then why are you risking your life for them again?"

"Can't risk something I don't have," I point out.

Lillian protests that she doesn't like when I talk that way before shaking her head. "I just don't think tonight is the best night to make another trip. You had a long, *horrible* day, little raven. I was forced to witness most of it, so don't even try to pretend otherwise."

My day was just like every other day has been ever since Amadeus ripped my heart out two and a half years ago: training until I literally dropped dead.

However, Lillian is right that today varied slightly since the necromancers strapped me down in their laboratory for more "reinforcement training." Dagon, the chief necromancer, carved my skin to test dripping acid on exposed veins—one drop for every brush of his skin against mine.

Even I must begrudgingly admit that method of torture was grotesquely artistic. I haven't screamed that much in a long time.

It was almost nostalgic.

But the necromancers healed me afterward, as they always do, without even a hint of scarring. So I'm fine—no need to waste time letting Lillian coddle me. Besides, I want this information sooner than later. Amadeus has been meditating on his revenge more than usual, and at the moment, he's extra pissed.

It's only a matter of time before I'm finally sent to the mortal world.

I glance out the glassless, shuttered window of the isolated hovel that has always been mine, located on the outskirts of Amadeus's kingdom near the twisted woods. Lighting is always weak in the Nether, but it's pitch black to mortal eyes at night. If I wait longer, I won't be able to find the entrance to the system of caves I've been secretly using to get to the nearest human compound for over a year —ever since I made a blood oath that I would get them out of the Nether.

"I'm going tonight. The food can't wait," I remind Lillian quietly.

The Nether is far from flourishing. Amadeus and his court, the monsters, the Undead, and anything else that haunts this hellish plane of existence are primarily carnivorous. Lillian has worked hard to cultivate wild oats and mushrooms, and Amadeus has captive humans tend to small farms around his kingdom to feed the captives, but food has always been a scarce resource here.

A few months ago, two of those farms burned down. Now, the only humans getting enough to eat are the servants within the citadel and those forced to fight to the death in the arena for entertainment.

The nearby compound is starving.

Lillian considers the situation and finally sighs long and slow.

"All right. I'll pray to all the gods that you make it there and back safe and sound." She sees the face I pull and raises a brow. "You might think praying is useless, but I promise it's not. The gods—"

"Forsook everyone in this shithole a long time ago," I finish for her, double-checking everything on my person one final time.

Weapons, check.

Bag of homemade and stolen food that we'll be punished severely for if it's found out, check.

Fae runes, check.

Needy ghost who is now trying to tap on my shoulder, check.

And finally, one mysterious, clear shard.

Check.

"Maven." Lillian's voice stops me as I walk toward the door.

When I glance at her, she looks more ardent than I've ever seen, as if she's trying to communicate something important but doesn't know how.

"The gods haven't forsaken us. That's why *you* are here. You are a long-awaited blessing—I wish I could tell you just how important you are, little raven."

Right. Because the freedom and lives of thousands rests on my doomed shoulders.

No fucking pressure.

I leave without another word. Two hours and several close calls later, I make sure the coast is clear before limping out of a cave mouth toward the misshapen, ancient stone buildings. By this point, I'm trailed by a handful of murmuring specters who gravitated toward me when I passed them in the twisted woods on the way to this compound.

No fires are lit here. The place appears silent and empty.

Amadeus doesn't bother posting guards at any of the human compounds because everyone knows that if they try to leave, there is nowhere safe to go. The fiends that run amuck in this realm will devour them long before they can make it to the Divide.

Even if they did make it that far, humans aren't strong enough to survive passing through that thick barrier of magic into the mortal realm—not without extreme magical interference from something like a lich. It will have to be thinned and weakened significantly for the mortals to get through when the time comes for my gambit.

In the meantime, they feel safest in their compounds, where the permanent magic wards keep out the wild dangers.

Not that "safe" actually fucking exists, but everyone takes what they can get here.

As I near a crumbling wall of stones, a shadow moves nearby. I whip out a dagger, expecting to behead a vampire or dismember another Undead, but the thin, one-armed figure steps forward so I can see it better.

Felix looks more gaunt than ever, which is saying something. I assume he's giving his scant portions of food to his sick mother. His father was devoured by the Undead six months ago after breaking his leg doing manual labor in the citadel, so now Felix is the unofficial leader of the humans here.

"If it isn't the *telum* herself," he greets. "Hi, there."

I bend to yank a severed claw from the back of my thigh, trying not to visibly grimace at the pain. Gods, that hurts. It's going to slow me down on the way back. I also have several gouges from harpy talons on my left arm, which haven't stopped bleeding.

The fun just never ends here.

"I know you avoid talking like the Undead avoid direct sunlight, but how about a simple hello? It's called small talk—and you'll have to use it to blend in after you're sent to the mortal realm," he points out. "Which means *speaking* to people, oh horror of horrors."

I drop the bag of supplies at his feet without a word. Felix picks it up, and the way his face brightens at once makes me wish Lillian could've been the one to deliver it. She's the one who secretly bakes things for the humans, and I'm sure she would appreciate Felix's look of pure gratitude far more than I do.

Shows of emotion aggravate the Undead and many types of shadow fiends—hence why, much like myself, Felix grew up suppressing his expressions. But right now, he's plain emotional as he hugs the bag of stolen food to himself with his one remaining arm.

"Thanks. Seriously, you have no idea what this means to us. To me."

Felix getting sappy is fucking weird. Things must be worse off for the humans here than I realized. I look away, waiting for him to compose himself so we can get down to business.

A couple of the ghosts whisper unhappily, trying to pass through me like I'm the solution to their restless fate. All I feel is the slightest chill. Felix doesn't see them, of course. He clears his throat and glances at my bleeding arm as he sets the bag down again, opening the top.

"I'm glad you came, but cover that up before the scent of blood lures vampires. You'll get the people I care about hurt if you're not more careful."

There we go. That's the Felix I know.

I rip a section off the bottom of my shirt to wrap the wounds on my arm. "Too bad you're not a necromancer, or you could heal me and be done with it."

He scowls, scanning the area as if the dead trees or bones littered outside the compound will overhear his secret—that magic manifested in his blood when he was six years old. Surprisingly strong magic, at that. If Amadeus finds out, Felix will be treated like all other manifested casters in the Nether: killed in a dramatic ritual and brought back to serve as a lich. Those fiends are a personal favorite of Amadeus's.

Felix has been carefully keeping his magic hidden for seventeen years.

"Thank the gods I'm not a necromancer," he mutters. "Nasty things. That type of magic is not for me or for anyone who happens to have these pesky things called *morals*."

Thank fuck I don't have those weighing me down anymore.

Felix pulls out the fae translations on parchment, and his face lights up again. "Send Lillian my thanks again for helping me learn fae. It's been unbelievably useful for figuring out complex healing magic for my mother."

"How is she?"

He blinks up at me, startled. "Uh...do you actually care? Not trying to be rude, I just didn't think that was even possible, considering your lack of heart."

Word spread quickly throughout the Nether about the way Amadeus decided to officially turn me into his *telum*. The monsters who come to take innocents away from the compound must have been gossiping because these humans know I'm no longer one of them.

Although they're still kind whenever I show up, they fear me much more now.

They're smart like that.

"It's called small talk," I parrot before moving on. Pulling the shard from my pocket, I hold it up.

He makes a face. "You brought a piece of glass?"

"It's not glass."

"Yeah? Looks exactly like it. How do you know for sure that it's not?" he challenges with a smirk.

"Because I pried it out of Amadeus's crown."

Felix's smirk dies immediately, and he swallows hard. "Are you serious? You must be insane."

"Yes to both."

He rubs his face. "Oh, gods. I'm not sure that was the wisest course of action. Isn't he going to look for it eventually?"

Amadeus is already looking for the culprit. If he finds out it was me, I'm sure my fate will be eternally worse than death. I almost admire how creative my self-appointed "father" is with punishments.

He keeps his intricate adamantine crown locked up in his extensive quarters behind several extremely heavy protective spells, which I tampered with so I would leave no trace when I left. Within the crown, three pieces of this substance were embedded.

When I saw it for the first time, I knew they couldn't be glass. Something about the transparent, flawless element drew me in, so here we are.

I toss the shard to Felix, who barely manages to catch it. "Tell me what it is."

He grumbles as he tries to study it in the dark lighting. "Not sure. Maybe if I could see it in the morning with a bit more light, I could figure it out. I mean, it wouldn't make sense for him to have clear quartz or something cheap stuck in his crown. It would have to be something incredibly precious, like—"

He cuts off suddenly, gawking at me. "Hold on. Hold *on*, what if…shit. That must be it. Oh, my *gods*, I can't believe it."

"I'm not the kind of monster who can read minds," I pointedly inform him.

Felix has forgotten about controlling himself again and is now animated with excitement. "Okay, I'll back up. Did you know this compound is made out of the ruins of a fae castle from thousands of years ago—from before the Entity came along and turned the Nether into a realm of death?"

"Did you know I didn't come here for a history lesson?"

"It's relevant, I promise. Over the years, I've dug up countless old, broken slabs of stone engraved with ancient fae writings and illustrations. I think they had an impressive library here long ago. That's what I've been studying to learn magic. There's so much to learn from the fae about agriculture, arts, diplomacy, folklore, and especially their unique ways of crafting minerals and—"

Gods. Who knew this guy had such a hard-on for knowledge?

My hard stare makes him trail off. "Right. Relevance. Gods forbid I say anything that isn't conducive to what you have your mind set on. You have an astronomical case of tunnel vision, you know that?"

"I'm blushing," I say flatly. "Cut to the chase."

"Okay, here it is. Fae craftsmen tried to incorporate *this*—" He lifts the shard. "Into their designs, but could find no way of working with the substance. It's called etherium and comes from Paradise. Supposedly, it can be endowed with extremely high levels of magic and enchanted to work in all manner of ways. The fae were fascinated by it but never used it much because only holy magic works on etherium. Oh—holy magic comes from the gods...so only their chosen saints, prophets, priests, and so on can use it," he tacks on.

In other words, this is utterly fucking useless.

Fantastic.

Felix tips his head thoughtfully. "But you know what? I doubt they ever tested *your* type of magic on it. Fae records said etherium was extremely rare. I wonder why it was in his crown. Then again, I guess no one really knows much about his background, huh?"

It's true. How Amadeus came to rule the Nether has long been forgotten—hence why I was poking around in his chambers, searching for answers.

I nod at the shard in his hand. "Keep that hidden. Maybe we can experiment with it to see if it could still be useful."

He nods but examines me. "You mean, if it could be useful to help you get us humans out of the Nether."

"Obviously."

"You're really going to try freeing us, aren't you?" he murmurs, his expression changing to something…*affectionate*. It's a touchy-feely, older-brotherly look, complete with a soft smile and proud, gleaming hazel eyes.

Gross. Any form of camaraderie aside from Lillian's has returned to haunt me, so I lift my chin.

"I won't *try*. I will. But if you ever look at me like that again, I'll gut you like a fucking fish and leave your rotting innards behind for the Undead to feast on."

Anyone else in the Nether would balk at my tone, but Felix sighs heavily.

"Seriously? Would it kill you to at least *pretend* to still have a heart? Your entire personality is like a damned thistle. May the gods have mercy on anyone who ever tries to get close to you."

Joke's on him. Only an idiot would ever try to get close to me, as he puts it.

He's correct. I'm heartless—and I intend to stay this way. The less I let myself feel, the less it will hurt when I complete my mission and finally join the other restless dead.

1

MAVEN

Fight or flight.

The former is all I have known since my entire life, and the latter has resulted in unbearable punishment.

Yet standing here, watching Silas unconscious and struggling to breathe, and knowing this is the calm before another storm…

Fighting is out of the cards. We need to run. It's cowardly, but that prophetess was right. Plenty of eyewitnesses escaped after seeing me kill Somnus, so every second that passes is another second that the truth is spreading like wildfire: the *telum* is in the mortal realm.

The Immortal Quintet will send hired killers.

The Legacy Council will send bounty hunters.

Others will try to end me for the hell of it.

I'm in grave danger.

I wish I could savor it more, but facing any fight head-on would risk Silas. He's too vulnerable right now. There's no telling when he'll wake up—and he *will* wake up, or I swear on all the fucking gods, I will drag his soul back from the Beyond myself.

Glancing down, I again study the dark House of Arcana emblem that begins a few inches below my jugular notch and ends at the top of my upper abdomen, a straight line down the center of my chest directly over my pale scar. It's a stark declaration that I've been bound to this cutthroat fae.

I like it.

But it still makes no sense. Was a mistake made? Is this a trick the gods are playing on me? I've made no secret of the fact that I think they suck ass, so I doubt they would toss a random blessing my way or some shit like that.

"Focus," I order myself out loud, turning to rummage through my dresser for new combat-friendly clothes that I quickly slip into, along with a new pair of gloves. Spotting my adamantine dagger on the dresser, I sheath it to my hip. Crypt must have collected that, too, before carrying me back here.

Time to get down to business. We have to get out of here ASAP and find somewhere safe to lay low while Silas transitions into a necromancer—which can sometimes take days.

Stepping out into the hallway, I nearly collide with a lean, pale, beautifully sculpted chest. Everett steadies me, his soulful blue gaze roving over me as if he's looking for any sign of damage. One of his cool hands cradles my face, and he exhales with relief.

"There you are. I had to see that you're okay."

My most meticulous match is still streaked with dried blood and dirt from First Placement. He must have just woken up from Pia's healing, which left him with no visible scars. I suppose I should have figured that my former supermodel match would look like this, but…

Damn. Talk about lickable abs, I muse distractedly.

Are my abs more or less lickable in your estimation, blood blossom? Silas's faint, slurred fae words drift back inside my head, growing faint at the end.

Oh, my gods.

I look wide-eyed up at Everett. His gaze drops to where my hand instinctively goes to cover the center of my newly marked chest, and he tenses.

"Shit—what's wrong? Are you in pain?"

"Is it her shadow heart again?"

Baelfire's voice startles me before the dragon shifter is suddenly beside us in the hallway, crowding this small space. He showered off the worst of the gore and dirt left behind from First Placement, but he's back in his combat clothes again. Obviously, he's as aware as I am that we'll have another fight on our hands sooner than later. Changing would be redundant.

"Are you all right, Raincloud?" he presses, brow furrowed.

I hold up a finger to pause their concern and peer inside my room again, expecting Silas to be sitting up in bed with a knowing smirk. But he's still motionless, propped up on the pillows that are now stained with dried blood and ash. His feverish, labored breathing is the only sound in the room.

Silas? I try to send to him.

There's no response.

I'm so perplexed that I actually yelp in surprise when Crypt appears in the room directly in front of me. Unlike Baelfire, he hasn't redressed from his shower yet, so I'm treated to a delicious display of his nakedness—the light and dark swirling markings covering most of his body, muscles dripping with water droplets, and piercings glinting in the afternoon light streaming in from the window.

The incubus frowns. "What's got you so jittery, love?"

I hesitate, glancing between the three of them. We really don't have time at our disposal, but this fluke on my chest pertains to all of us. There's no point keeping it a secret. Decision made, I strip off my black shirt. Rolling my eyes at Baelfire's whistle of appreciation, I lift my gray exercise bra so they can get the full picture of what's going on.

His whistle dies, and Everett visibly stops breathing. Crypt is equally stunned.

"How the hell is this even possible?" Baelfire finally manages, reaching out to gently run a warm finger over my new emblem. He catches my eye. "Does it hurt, baby? Do you feel any different?"

"I don't know, no, and not really." I pause. "Aside from hearing him inside my head, that is."

To my surprise, Crypt has the strongest reaction to that. He swears and turns an impressively murderous glare on the unconscious fae in the room as if he's about to pick a fight before Silas even wakes up.

"Right. Anyone else insanely fucking jealous now?" he bites out.

Baelfire agrees, but when Everett is silent, I realize he's gazing at the new emblem on my chest with unadulterated hope written all over his handsome features.

Our eyes meet. "Does this mean…his curse is broken?" he asks.

Gods, I hope so. Silas was barely hanging on. His curse was the one I was most concerned about—the one I was most determined to find a cure for. Does this fluke mean he'll wake up in his own head, sans voices?

"Maybe?" I hedge, replacing my clothing.

Everett swallows, stepping closer to me. "Then, if we can figure out how you broke Silas's curse…if we could end my curse before it gets the chance to hurt you more…maybe I could finally belong to you without ruining everything," he whispers, closing his eyes and resting his forehead against mine.

He's never gotten this close to me on his own, and the raw longing in his voice makes my stomach flip. The idea of hurting me clearly petrifies him. I understand that part of him. It's the same reason I pushed them away so hard at first. I was desperate to keep them out of the clusterfuck that my not-life is about to become.

Seriously, though, Everett's curse is the least of my concerns—not to mention, I have some doubts about this "prophecy" he received so long ago. It's something I should talk about with him later. Maybe he'll even let me read it myself.

But now isn't the time to dive into that.

"This conversation can wait," I say quietly, reaching up to brush a streak of dried harbinger blood off of Everett's jaw. That tiny bit of contact makes my heart pound, but it doesn't send my stomach careening anymore, a fact I'm still adjusting to. "Right now, we're too vulnerable. We need to get out of here and find somewhere to lay low."

Baelfire takes my hand from Everett's face, rubbing gentle circles on its back. He ignores the death glare that the ice elemental shoots him. "You mean we're going into hiding to wait for this shitstorm to blow over while your newbie necromancer recovers?"

That...and to set the stage for the next part of my plan.

My theory about Somnus's totem was correct. It wasn't glass at all —it was crafted out of etherium. Hearst's soul amulet was probably the same, which leads me to believe all members of the Immortal Quintet might have their souls tied to an etherium object. Perhaps the gods decided that the best way of sustaining the Divide through their life forces was by tying them to a physical anchor.

Meaning I need to hunt down three immortals *and* their anchors.

I also need to find more etherium.

Etherium became an integral part of my plan after Felix and I ran countless tests on it and agreed it would fix a significant flaw in my gambit to free the humans. Which is why, during my first two weeks at Everbound, I carefully sought out rumors of another black market dealer known to possess etherium. I don't have a location or a way to contact him, but I need to get my hands on that substance.

It's how I plan to keep the Nether at bay after I kill most of the Immortal Quintet. Without it, I'll fail.

And that's not an option.

"Yes," I finally reply to Baelfire. "But first, I need to see if Kenzie made it out of the maze. Wait here."

When I try to step around them, Everett's hands move to my hips and steel. His previously tender voice turns ice-hard.

"Baelfire told me everything. We nearly lost you today, and it's not happening again. Just stay here and keep an eye on Silas. We'll find your friend for you."

They nearly lost me? Tough fucking luck because I nearly lost *all* of them today. The more I think about it, the more dark fury starts to boil beneath my composure. That, combined with the residual power boost from killing Somnus, makes me feel like a ticking time bomb.

But I can't afford to tap into that monster's life force now stored within me as fuel. I need to save it until I get my hands on etherium.

I shake my head. "You're staying. I'm going."

"Oakley, please just—"

Before our argument can continue, a loud knock on the apartment's front door makes us all go still. Crypt vanishes, and a moment later, I hear a shriek at the front door, which he's obviously opened.

"Gah! Where the hell are your clothes? And why are your tattoos all—oh my gods, are those *piercings?* Oh, shit. I—I'm so sorry, I did *not* mean to look down, and I promise I so did *not* want to know that. I'm just looking for—"

Kenzie. Thank the fucking universe.

I rush out of my bedroom, followed closely by Bael and Everett. The lioness shifter is standing in the university hallway outside the front door, leaning against Luka. Her orange combat attire is ripped and charred in places. They're both covered in as much dirt, blood, and sweat as we were earlier. It looks like Kenzie got a nasty cut on her head at some point, gauging from the amount of blood staining her pale hair and crusting down the side of her face. The injury is gone now, thanks to her shifter healing.

She looks like hell and must be exhausted, but her bright blue eyes light up when she spots me.

"May! Thank gods you're okay! I'm so sorry to ask this, but—" she begins, stepping forward.

But the moment she tries to cross the threshold, she slams into an invisible barrier that knocks her back into Luka with a startled *oof.*

"Kenz!" The vampire levels us with a vicious glare like that was intentional. "What the fuck?"

For a moment, I'm confused about why she can't enter since she's not a siphon who would have to be invited in, but Crypt hums.

"I admit, that pointy-eared bastard's magic is reassuring."

Oh, right. Silas spelled this place with an imposing amount of wards to keep anyone except us from entering.

Come to think of it…how the fuck did Pia get in here earlier?

I see that same realization dawn on the others as Crypt tips his head curiously, Everett scowls, and Baelfire frowns.

"So much for reassuring," the dragon shifter huffs. "How the fuck did she get in here? I mean, she probably saved our lives and shit, but still. Maybe his old spells are weakening from his transition or something? Is that a thing with casters?"

I don't have answers, but I notice Luka checking over his shoulder at the hallway which is now filled with smoke and the distant echo of shouting from some faraway corridor. Clearly, Everbound University is in chaos after the Immortal Quintet ran off in the middle of a lethal test.

A chill runs down my spine, and my senses sharpen painfully. I look back at Kenzie. "There are shadow fiends in the castle."

She blinks. "Yeah, there are. How did you—oh, right! You can sense them, like that ugly-ass ghoul back in Halfton. That will be super useful getting out of here because when we finally escaped that stupid maze and made a run for the castle, a bunch of shadow fiends escaped, too. It's mayhem out there, and we were going to try to take cover in our apartment, but then Vivienne was swarmed by Undead and…"

Kenzie's voice breaks, and she takes a deep, shaky breath. Luka kisses the top of her head. I know she's trying to be strong for her quintet. At first glance, she seems bubbly and whimsical, which aren't traits that legacies see as ideal in a keeper. But I've observed her enough to recognize that she hides more of a backbone than most people might guess.

She lifts her chin. "Anyway, I know a good way of getting out of here. The catacombs."

What's this now?

"I mean, I thought I knew *everything* about this castle," Kenzie says quickly when she sees that she has my full attention. "But while we were running from other legacies and some Undead, I saw Harlow Carter leading a bunch of asscasters into this secret entrance in one of the courtyards, so we followed. It turns out there are these ancient underground catacombs that connect this place to those old ruins out in Everbound Forest. Dirk and Viv are waiting there. I think that's the quickest way to escape the university right now, so I really think we should all just group together and—"

I hold up a hand, my mind racing through the next steps to take to keep my quintet safe. "You had me at catacombs. Where exactly is this secret entrance?"

She rattles off a description of a tiny shed in the corner of the university's smallest courtyard that seems to hold garden supplies but hides a narrow stone staircase descending into the underground burial passageways. As she speaks, the hall fills with more smoke. More shouting and yelling echo throughout the castle.

I nod. "We'll go with you."

"Not to point out the obvious, but this could be *way* easier. Can't we just transport out of here with magic? Should be a fucking breeze for your magic prodigy boyfriend," Luka points out, glancing behind us like he's looking for Silas. "Huh. Unless he didn't survive the placement. Tough shit."

If he *doesn't* survive…

My stomach clenches with sharp dread. I'm positive I'm still controlling my expression to seem unbothered, but Crypt takes one look at me and fixes Luka with a stare that makes the vampire flinch.

"I distinctly recall promising to feed you your innards if you opened your idiotic mouth—"

"Threaten him later when we have more time," I interrupt to get away from this touchy topic, glancing at Baelfire. "Can you carry Silas?"

"Baby, I'm twice the size of that fucker. Of course, I can carry him."

"Good. I'm trusting you to get him to the catacombs unscathed."

Everett starts to say something but cuts off when all of Crypt's paler markings light up brightly. The incubus hisses in pain, staggering back from the door. I'm instantly at his side to help support him—and to stand in front of him since he's still naked, and as much as I trust Kenzie, there's no denying the Nightmare Prince's body is pure eye candy.

"Those damned wisps," Crypt rasps. His silver-flecked violet gaze settles on me, his jaw clenching. "Things are worse than we realized. Get your fae to safety, darling. I can follow after you once I've ensured those little bastards aren't endangering you any further. I'll be quick."

I want to demand that we stick together, but seeing the pinch of pain on Crypt's face reminds me that I have no right to be a possessive brat. He's the steward of Limbo. If there's turbulence there, it affects him.

When it comes to this, my hands are tied. And not in the fun way.

"You'll be *safe*," I amend firmly.

Crypt leans to kiss just behind my ear. "I'll be anything you like, darling. Just get away safely for me."

I loathe the emotions crawling up my throat, but I can't help it. My quintet hasn't had any time to recover from First Placement. They're exhausted. The idea of them leaping back into trouble puts me on edge.

I can bounce back from a good fight. I was made to take hits and come back stronger.

But if they get hit hard, they won't come back. Then I'd have no choice but to lose myself in vengeful fury, raining down hell on whoever took them away from me—and as fun as that latter part may sound in theory, my schedule is just way too fucking busy for another vendetta.

Crypt's weight disappears as he moves into Limbo. I take a deep breath and turn back to the others.

"Everett, watch Baelfire's back while he's getting Silas to the catacombs."

"I'll be watching your back," Everett insists. When he folds his arms, I see frost encompassing his skin just past his wrists. "Baelfire can protect Silas on his own, away from you."

Gods, his bare upper half is so distracting.

Bael snorts. "At least you're admitting how capable I am."

"This isn't about capability, Lizard Brain."

"Yeah? Then what's it about, Ice Prick?"

"It's because you're a godsdamned *liability*. Accident or not, the second you lose your temper—which is inevitable since you desperately need anger management training—you'll fucking burn her to death," Everett snaps, the temperature around us steadily dropping.

The dragon shifter snarls back, enraged now. Before it can come to blows, I shoot Kenzie a *bear with me* look and step between them.

"You're both wasting time. Who's the keeper here?"

Baelfire's golden gaze drops to me. "You are, Mayflower, but—"

"But fucking nothing. You two will work together to get Silas *safely* to the catacombs, and if I fall behind while I'm ripping out the hearts of anyone who gets in the way, leave me be because you'll only be ruining my fun otherwise. Got it?" I look between them.

It's like bartering with petulant toddlers. Neither is happy about it, but they don't argue.

I turn to Luka and Kenzie. "Stick with them. I'll follow behind you, but not too closely. If there's more fighting, there's a high chance I'll start...you know."

Kenzie's eyes widen when she catches my meaning. When I told her all about what they turned me into, I explained the berserking. She knows that I'm not myself when I lose it in combat—I black out, driven by bloodlust and the monstrous urge to take life. I won't be able to differentiate between friend or foe.

"Uh, no, I don't fucking know," Luka pipes up impatiently. "There's no need for this stupid drama. Just stick with us, asscaster."

Baelfire growls, but I speak to Luka in a saccharine voice. "If you don't want drama, get a head start before I join the fray, or I may accidentally pull your spine out of your ass."

"Fuck," Luka shudders. "She's scary sometimes."

"Yes, yes she is," Kenzie nods sagely, looking back at me. "Ready, May?"

"One moment," Everett grumbles, going to get a shirt while Baelfire gets whatever he'll need, plus Silas. I hurry to my room and grab the remaining nightshade root powder in its tiny bottle, a few more knives, an extra pair of gloves, two vials of kraken ink, and anything else I can reasonably stash in my pockets. When we reemerge, Kenzie sees Silas slung over Bael's shoulder, dirty, unconscious, and drenched in feverish sweat. She catches my eye.

Is he okay? she mouths, brow furrowed.

I nod because I really fucking hope he's fighting through the fever. As they move to leave the quintet apartment, possibly for the last time, Baelfire adjusts Silas on his shoulder and leans down to kiss the side of my neck, inhaling my scent.

"Be as safe as fucking possible, hellion. I know you love a good fight, but avoid one now if you can help it, okay? Please."

His gravelly plea does me in. I'm such a sucker for him saying please for me.

But he's right that I'm also a sucker for a good fight, and I doubt we'll get out of here without some bloodshed. It's deliciously unavoidable.

I kiss his cheek as reassurance. Once he steps away, I'm surprised when Everett leans down and pecks me right on the lips. It's chaste and abrupt, mostly because he pulls back immediately. When I arch a brow, the professor blushes profusely.

"I just wanted… I'm still not used to…sorry," he fumbles, adjusting his sleeve repeatedly.

Aww.

Kenzie also *awws* from the hallway, reminding me we have an audience and are on a time crunch. They leave the apartment. I watch my fae, who is fighting just to breathe, until they round a corner.

Then I stalk into Everbound Castle.

2

CRYPT

I slash through another wisp, but ten more pile onto my back and legs, their piranha-like teeth tearing into me. White-hot pain blooms all over as I send another wave of mania through Limbo to stun the rabid horde I'm battling.

I haven't seen this many wisps in one place for quite some time, and they're abnormally riled. They're acting nearly as savage as shades, which I'm sure have also gathered in this part of Limbo to lay in wait for me.

That thought pisses me off further, and I was already in a rotten mood after learning that *Crane* gets to whisper sweet nothings straight to my darling obsession's pretty mind whenever he pleases.

I've never experienced jealousy, let alone to this degree.

It's fucking unpleasant.

Still, at least one good thing came out of today: despite getting run through and the two full-blown heart attacks from practically losing my keeper *twice* within an hour, Somnus DeLune is finally, blessedly dead—and may he rot in eternal misery because that monster deserves no semblance of peace. Anything less than utter hell for him would be unacceptable.

Speaking of unacceptable things, Maven has been out of my sight for over thirty minutes.

I finish dispersing the remaining wisps and step into the mortal world to better survey my surroundings, ignoring the searing sensation in my limbs from switching planes. I'm in the grand entry hall of Everbound, where several legacy corpses lay. Bloodcurdling screams echo elsewhere in the castle, along with echoing shrieks that can only belong to shadow fiends. It sounds like several someones are getting brutally slaughtered.

From Limbo, I've observed the university go to shit. Whatever students survived First Placement are fleeing the school or fighting each other, more out of fear and confusion than for any other reason. The faculty is all but gone.

Lifting my sword arm, I watch my skin struggle and fail to close the thousands of tiny puncture wounds the riled wisps left behind. I'm not strong enough to heal at the moment. Although I grabbed a simple black T-shirt and jeans from the apartment before taking on the horde, everything is ripped to threads now.

Lucky for me, one of the nearby legacy corpses looks to be about my size. I only wish the poor sap was wearing a leather jacket when he bit the dust.

I've just dressed in the conveniently bloodstain-less clothes when the massive double doors of Everbound University burst open behind me, and a deafening snarl rips through the air. I drop into Limbo on instinct—which is fortunate because if I'd hesitated a moment longer, my head would have wound up down the throat of the massive hellhound that leaps through the air where I was just standing.

"Fuck. Pretty sure that was the Nightmare Prince," a voice grits.

I turn to observe the newcomers, pocketing my sword, which has shrunk to a lighter once more. The one who just spoke is a redhead almost the size of Decimus. He has the Legacy Council's bounty hunter tattoo on his jugular, while the others have it visible on the backs of their hands. From the looks of determination and distaste on their faces, the guns they're brandishing, and the trained hellhounds prowling into the room, it's clear they're not here for an alumni reunion.

One of the bounty hunters glances at the redhead. "You must've imagined it. Why the hell would the Nightmare Prince be here?"

The redhead uses his boot to turn over the corpse who just very kindly donated my new ensemble, minus his shoes and underwear.

"They didn't say in the official assignment, but my uncle was working here for the I.Q. and got a front-row seat when shit hit the fan. Just got a call from him warning me to watch out for the so-called 'lottery quintet,' which has the DeLune bastard in it, along with a bunch of other hotshots. He said their keeper is a *telum*, whatever the fuck that means."

I was just about to leave unseen to see why it's gone so hauntingly quiet in the castle. All the screams have mysteriously died out. But the mention of Maven makes me pause.

One of the other bounty hunters, a fae girl with pointed ears, snaps to attention with wide eyes. "What? That's impossible. Are you sure you heard him right, Asher?"

Asher. Hmm. Why does that name sound familiar?

"Yup."

"Oh, gods. Prophets have been warning us about the *telum* for centuries. My family used to say it was just a bit to scare legacies into behaving, but…" The fae swallows. "The *telum* is here?"

"Asher" pets one of the hellhounds as if it's a puppy instead of a monster with a strong taste for legacies. The Council has been selectively breeding them for decades to make them freakishly obedient to their bounty hunter masters. All they need is one taste of someone's blood, and they can track them within a thousand miles.

While he's petting the beast, I notice his green eyes are glowing as he scans the room.

Ah. This must be the Asher *Douglas* I've heard of—a bounty hunter notorious for his ability to track magic usage from great distances. A magic bloodhound, so to speak, who tracks down his targets based on their magic signatures. I must say, he doesn't resemble the other Douglas legacies much.

If he samples Maven's unique magic, he'll be able to hunt her easily.

"Relax. I'm sure this *Maven Oakley* chick will die just like any other legacy convict," he drawls. "And if she doesn't, we'll capture her and let the higher-ups deal with her. Dead or alive, there's one hell of a bounty on her head. And if any of you see the Nightmare Prince again, he's *mine*, got it? Now move in."

I watch from Limbo as they take formation to sweep through the school. On the one hand, I'm tempted to snap Douglas's neck for daring to speak my keeper's name in that tone. But on the other hand, slowly unraveling his psyche would be much more satisfying.

My markings light up in a blaze of angry purple. As usual, I feel a sharp tug in the direction where another swarm of wisps must be trying to get into the mortal realm. I grit my teeth, fighting the pull as I kick into the air, intent on finding Maven.

It doesn't take long.

I rise through the ceiling into the next floor of Everbound directly above the entry hall and stop midair. No wonder all the shouting and screaming has stopped.

Syntyche's scythe. They're all dead.

I drift above the massacre, which is a bit much even for me. Undead, battling rival legacies, and various monsters have been literally ripped to shreds. Their many bodies and innards now litter the floor or are impaled to the walls with daggers. Blood coats everything, splattered on the windows and dripping from various surfaces. Several hearts have been ripped out and scattered across the ground. It looks almost as bad as when a horde of wisps tears through a human town like a million faceless piranhas, leaving nothing but gore behind.

Is this the only hallway where this happened?

The gleam of something catches my eye, and I slip back into the mortal realm to withdraw Maven's adamantine dagger from the disembodied head of a small basilisk—a rare monster from the Nether that the Immortal Quintet must have stocked in First Placement.

I grin. So this is the macabre brushwork of my keeper, is it?

How frighteningly impressive.

But my smile drops away as a soft groan sounds in the otherwise silent hall—*her* groan. I rush to where I couldn't see her before, lying half-hidden behind a collapsed decorative hall table.

She's quite a sight, completely soaked in blood, and blinks groggily as I help her sit up. My gaze sweeps over her for any signs of damage. She's unharmed, thank the gods, but we both seem to notice the forgotten, still-beating heart clutched in one of her hands at the same time.

Quite the souvenir.

"I see you threw a party without inviting me, love," I tease, gently wiping blood off her pretty face.

Her unfocused attention drifts over the rest of the hall as she tosses the heart aside. "Oops."

"You berserked," I realize.

Maven rubs a spot on her abdomen as if checking for an injury that no longer exists. "I don't remember the fight, so yes. Pretty convenient that I bled out when I did because expiring is the only way to stop me once I lose it like that."

She's obviously still recovering from what she calls "*expiring*"— and I call my own personalized brand of hell. Perhaps I should be grateful that my keeper can return from a temporary death, but knowing I lost her even for those moments makes me want to massacre something myself.

Spine-tingling howls sound elsewhere in the castle, growing closer by the moment.

"Oh look, more party guests," she muses, making expectant grabby hands at her dagger, which I still hold.

I adore her, but she's in no condition for more of this. "Another time, love. If any of those hellhounds gets a taste of your blood, they'll be able to track you from here to Kansas."

She allows me to help her to her feet. I don't like how unsteady she is—she must be far more exhausted from reviving than she's letting on.

"We're not going to Kansas. Kenzie's family is in Nebraska."

I'd ask how that's relevant, but I can't focus on anything except getting my keeper away from here when the howls sound closer. Much as I dislike the risks, this calls for desperate measures.

"Might I take you for a waltz through Limbo, darling?"

"Only if you're waltzing me to the castle's smallest courtyard."

Her wish is my pleasure. As the hellhounds race up the nearby stairs, I turn Maven to face me and give her a serious look. "Keep your eyes closed. Limbo drives mortals mad when they're conscious, and I wouldn't want you to lose that deliciously dark mind of yours."

She smirks. "Too late. Let's go."

I grin in reply and pull her into my arms—and into Limbo—just as hellhounds leap into the hallway, followed closely by the bounty hunters. Their shouts of alarm and horror at the mess my keeper left behind quickly fade as I cover Maven's eyes with my hand and drift through the now-lifeless castle.

My heart is crashing in my chest, both from the thrill of holding Maven in my element and the increasing worry that we'll reemerge in the mortal realm with her mind in fragments.

"Nice heartbeat," she murmurs, where her head rests against my chest. "Can I peek now?"

I switch directions to move toward the courtyard that she requested, ignoring the flare of pain throughout my body as Limbo tries to pull me in another direction. "Do you fancy madness?"

"Since I 'fancy' *you*, the answer must be yes."

She's teasing, but I still find myself happily flustered. "Careful, love. I enjoy hearing that a little too much."

"You can move your hand. I've been in Limbo before and came out just fine."

I pause before the courtyard, glancing down at her. "When was this?"

"When I killed your father. He took me here to try disorienting me while we were fighting."

That obviously didn't work out in his favor.

She reaches up to remove my hand from her eyes, peering up at me curiously. I'm momentarily panicked that she's going to melt into a psychotic attack and shatter under the duress of this foreign plane, as I've seen happen to countless others.

Instead, she tips her head. "Why are your markings glowing?"

"It's to tell me that Limbo needs stewarding, or there will be tears between the planes of existence. But it will have to wait. You're feeling all right?" I check, fascinated.

Maven nods, glancing around as tendrils of her dark hair waft around her blood-streaked face. "Limbo is bizarre and otherworldly. Distorted. Some would call it disturbing."

"So you like it."

"That's what I just said."

I smile. It's unusual that Maven can withstand Limbo. Then again, she grew up in a far darker, unquestionably cruel plane of existence. Perhaps it's no wonder her mind can tolerate this dream plane more easily than most.

Yet the fact that she actively *enjoys* my domain pleases me more than I might have imagined.

Maven removes herself from my arms but takes my hand to pull me toward the exit. "Come on. The others are waiting."

"No need for doors here, darling."

I guide her through the castle wall and glance around the tiny courtyard. It's as it's always been, but Maven pulls me toward the old gardening shed. A moment later, we pass through a molding trapdoor into a claustrophobic, narrow, dark passageway. Catacombs, I realize. A dim light shines somewhere far down the hall, so we drift towards it, turning a couple of corners.

The light is from Dirk holding a torch. Their air elemental is unconscious and quite severely bloodied. Kenzie is fussing over her, while Frost and Decimus are scowling at each other as if they're in the middle of a heated argument—a surprise to no one, I'm sure. Crane lies on the dusty ground, drawing broken, ragged breaths. He looks awful.

"And I thought that fae couldn't possibly get any paler," I hum.

Maven crouches beside him in Limbo, tugging off her blood-soaked gloves. "Do you mind...?"

Right. I was enjoying our private little stroll through Limbo, but at least this part never gets old.

When I reappear, both my quintet members startle and swear about me scaring the shit out of them just as I expected. Decimus recovers quickly when he sees Maven also just appeared and is now testing Crane's forehead.

"Shit, did he just—were you just in—are you okay?" He fumbles in shock, pulling her up into his arms and burying his face in the side of her neck. He just as quickly jerks away, snarling, "Wait a fucking minute. Damn it, Boo, is this *your* blood?"

"Relax. Not all of it is." She pats his shoulder reassuringly. "Put me down. We need to get going before the bounty hunters catch up."

Frost tenses, looking at me. "None of their hellhounds got a taste of her, did they?"

I start to shake my head and then frown. She did bleed out in that hallway. Is there a chance they could pick her scent out amongst all that blood and death?

Kenzie jumps up with a smile to greet Maven when Decimus finally sets her down. "You made it! I was getting worried about— oh, ew. No offense, May, but you need a shower. And I mean more than the rest of us, which is *seriously* saying something at this point. Speaking of which, when we get to the ruins, are we just running or…more transportation magic?"

She looks as if she dreads the answer, but her idiotic vampire match pipes up as he turns to Maven. "Like I said before, why can't we just fucking transport already? You can at least do that much, right? Get us the hell out of here."

His tone toward her grates on my nerves, and I'm not the only one. Frost glares at him, and Decimus bares his teeth. If he weren't important to someone important to Maven, I would have removed this vampire's head from his body the first time he insulted my keeper.

"Unless you'd like me to perform a laryngectomy on you with my bare hands, you won't breathe another word around my keeper again," I warn him darkly.

Although Kenzie shoots me an exasperated look for threatening her match, I don't miss the way Maven's lips twitch in amusement when the vampire goes pale at my threat. Her enjoyment of others' fear is delectable and something I intend to explore in the future.

"He's right that it's practical to transport from here," Maven muses. "Kenzie, I'll need you for the spell."

"Me? Why?"

"Because we're going to your hometown."

"We are? Why—oh! You're trying to get me home because you know my parents are probably worried sick about me after everything that just happened here at Everbound, and since they haven't heard from me since before the university went on lockdown, right? Not to mention, you probably know how much they want me home for Starfall Eve, right? That's really considerate and sweet of you, May!"

My keeper wrinkles her nose. "Stop. I'm just taking you somewhere relatively safe. Since you're from the middle of nowhere, it will also be a good place for us to lay low."

"Uh-huh, yeah, sure. Just admit that deep, *deep* down, hiding under all that hardcore badassery, you're a total sweetheart."

"Keep insulting me, and I'll leave you here to be the hellhounds' chew toy."

Kenzie laughs and moves toward Maven, but I tense.

"Wait, love. Let's not do the spell so close to the castle, or Douglas will be able to track it."

Frost swears. "Asher Douglas is here? If they sent him, they're sparing no resources."

"Maven just offed Somnus fucking DeLune. Of course, they're freaking out," Decimus points out.

Luka's head jerks back. Dirk does a double take at Maven, his eyes perfectly round.

"What? She...*what now?*"

The temperature drops sharply as Frost pins him with a look. "So? What will it be? Keeping your trap shut, or death by hypothermia?"

"Enough!" Kenzie snaps with surprising fire. Even when I glare at her, she doesn't cower as usual. She just swallows hard and lifts her chin. "Of course, we aren't going to tell anybody, so there will be no more threatening my quintet, do you hear me? Everyone in here is exhausted and really fucking crabby, so how about you three keep *your* traps shut until you can calm your tits?"

Did she just raise her voice at me?

I should remind her why they call me the Nightmare Prince.

But Maven's laugh stops me from scaring an apology out of the blond shifter. The temperature returns to normal when Frost glances at her, and Decimus gazes at her like a lovesick puppy. The big brute has to hunch slightly because this tunnel wasn't built tall enough for him.

Kenzie huffs, embarrassed. "Sorry. I didn't mean to snap."

"You did. Don't apologize for it." My keeper looks at me. "Will this Douglas guy be able to track my magic from the woods?"

"Not nearly as easily as he'll track it if you were to cast it here, in such close proximity to him."

She nods, glancing down at Crane, who is looking worse by the minute. She's careful to conceal her emotions, as always, but her voice breaks slightly. "Okay. We need to get him somewhere safe, and you all need rest."

Decimus frowns. "You need rest too, Boo."

"I told you to stop calling me that," she mumbles as she starts down the tunnel, but there's none of the usual fight in her voice because the dragon shifter is right. Today has been taxing, especially for her.

We make quick progress through the catacombs. Luka holds the flashlight, Dirk carries their elemental, and although Decimus gripes about having to carry Crane's "nerdy ass" bridal style, he at least makes sure Maven doesn't hear his complaint.

After several minutes, I move through Limbo to emerge at Maven's side. When I glance down at my obsession, she has a frown on her beautiful face, her very biteable lower lip protruding slightly.

"Something the matter, love?"

"It's fine."

"Tell me."

Maven sighs. "Not one haunting whisper, reanimated corpse, vengeful spirit, or cursed coffin. These catacombs suck."

I laugh. It's absolutely adorable when she pouts.

3

MAVEN

MY VEINS ARE abuzz from fresh kills. I doubt there's anyone left alive in Everbound Castle. If I think about it long enough, I'll start feeling bad about it.

Then again, those shadow fiends, monsters, and legacies would have killed me without hesitation had the roles been reversed.

So fuck feeling bad.

When we emerge in Everbound Forest near the old ruins, it's disconcerting how quiet it is. The misty, dark forest typically conceals countless dangerous creatures and the occasional shadow fiend whose haunting cries can be heard in the distance. Maybe they got scared silent after First Placement.

For the hundredth time, I glance at Silas. He's still motionless in Baelfire's arms, but now his skin is a concerning sallow hue. His fingertips are blackened from using necromancy, but either Kenzie and her quintet haven't noticed, or they're opting not to say anything about it.

Silas, I try again. *We left Everbound. Call it an early graduation.*

There's no reply.

Dirk glances around nervously, adjusting Vivienne so he can scratch the back of his neck furiously. "Uh. Not to pressure you, Maven, but…"

Right. Time to transport.

I brace myself and remove my stained gloves, reaching toward Kenzie. "This might take a second to set up. Once the spell is ready, everyone must be touching someone touching me."

They position themselves as I take Kenzie's bare hands in mine. Immediately, my nerves clench violently, and I try not to cringe as the typical repulsion sweeps through me at the feel of her bare skin dragging so horribly against mine. Nausea curdles in my gut, sending my pulse into a panic.

What the fuck? I thought I was getting over this.

Maybe I'm only better when it comes to my quintet.

Amidst trying to get a grip, my gaze collides with Everett's light blue gaze, as gentle as feathers.

Are you okay? he mouths, brow furrowing deeply.

I nod and try to focus on anything but the physical contact. At least my voice sounds steady. "Kenzie, hold in your mind exactly where you want us to arrive in your hometown."

"Got it."

Shutting my eyes, I whisper the incantation I'll need to start the common magic spell. I'm overflowing with power right now, so much so that I'm not concerned about accidentally dipping into Somnus's life force with this. Soon, rune-like symbols surround us, humming with energy.

Howls split the forest air, and Kenzie's hands tense. "Are those hellhounds? Oh, my gods. They're so close. Shit, should we—"

"Spell's ready," I announce. "Everyone, hold on."

Five seconds later, the blindingly bright light fades, and Kenzie immediately yanks away from me to puke. Dirk looks green, Luka dry-retches, and Everett has to brace himself on his knees for a moment, but I'm relieved to see everyone made it with all body parts attached.

My relief stutters when someone shrieks a few feet away. Glancing over, I realize we're standing under some kind of stacked metal seating structure and just interrupted two teenagers who were getting hot and heavy, judging by their toplessness despite the bite of winter cold. They look terrified of us—but mostly me since I'm covered head to toe in blood and gore.

"Use protection," I advise helpfully, checking to make sure Pierce is still strapped to my thigh and I didn't lose him in the transportation spell.

They grab their discarded shirts and coats and run away, screaming.

Everett rubs his neck. "I'm pretty sure they think you just threatened them with that."

That explains the screaming.

I look at Silas for the hundred and first time. Any hope that the spell would shake him awake changes into alarm when I see that Baelfire has set the fae down and is checking his pulse.

"He's fine, baby," he says quickly, offering a warm smile. "Just wanted to double-check."

Thank the fucking universe.

Kenzie finally straightens, groaning as she takes in our surroundings. "Sorry, I didn't mean to send us under the high school bleachers. I just have a lot of fun memories under here when my parents didn't know I snuck into town," she tacks on with a wink.

That earns a teasing poke from Luka before he notices Silas. "Is he…sick or something?"

"Or something."

Kenzie looks at me with an expression I've seen on Lillian's face countless times. It's a mix of concern and hope.

"Look, now that we're out of the woods—literally—and you guys just need to lay low, do you want to come stay at my parents' place? It's pretty far out of town since you know all those pesky laws about legacies living outside official city limits, so they'll mostly be away from humans or whatever. It'll give you a place to rest."

I consider it, observing my quintet. Baelfire grins like he thinks it's a good idea. Everett shakes his head, and Crypt doesn't seem to care as he lights another one of his cigarettes, rolling one of his shoulders as if it's in pain. All of them are still in bad condition.

We need somewhere Silas can rest, where we won't be found. But as much as I like Kenzie, I don't know and therefore don't trust her parents. All I know is that they may belong to one of the anti-legacy factions. I doubt they'd be pleased if the *telum* showed up at their door.

By now, I'm sure most legacies have heard I'm in the mortal realm.

Aside from all of that...there was howling when we transported. This "Douglas" guy must be one of the bounty hunters and apparently can sense magic somehow, so he may have been close enough to feel my magic when we left. If that's the case and they're hot on our tail, I don't want to be too close to Kenzie or her quintet, or they might get dragged into the crossfire.

"Thanks, but no. We'll stay in this area briefly and move on as soon as possible," I decide. "Is there a hotel or something? And somewhere to get spell ingredients?"

"Spell ingredients?" Baelfire frowns. "What for?"

"You four are inconveniently high-profile and well-known." Not to mention, Everett will be especially easily recognized by humans, given his supermodel career in their world. "We'll need to change your appearances somehow."

Kenzie grins. "I would totally offer to help give your guys makeovers, but I need to stay with Vivienne. Plus, my family will *freak* when we show up, so I doubt I'll be going anywhere for a while. There aren't any stores around here that cater to casters or legacies in general, so I'm not sure about the spell ingredients...but there are a couple of nice hotels you could try."

Vivienne moans and grimaces, shifting in Dirk's arms. Immediately, Kenzie zeroes in on her, worry eclipsing her face. The lioness shifter rattles off her parents' address, makes me promise to at least let her know when we leave town, and we say our goodbyes.

As soon as she leaves with her quintet, I turn to mine.

"Thank gods," Baelfire grumbles, wrapping me in a very warm hug. "They're nice and all, but I've been fucking dying to hold you. I know how much you hate PDA, so I waited. You're welcome. Feel free to praise me."

I fight a smile and relax into his hug for a second. At least his touch doesn't really seem to trigger my haphephobia now.

To my shock, Everett embraces me from behind and kisses me softly on the back of my neck. The sudden contrast of his cool touch gives me goosebumps, and my brain skips back to Kenzie's suggestion to try temperature play with these two. I wasn't entertaining that idea at the time, but now…

No. Nope. I can't let myself even *think* about that right now when Baelfire is far too good at sniffing out the tiniest hint of my arousal. Besides, Silas is lying fevered on the ground nearby, and he's my top priority. There will be no fucking around until I know he's okay.

Crypt catches my eye over Baelfire's shoulder and grins crookedly. "I'd happily join the huddle, but you look as if you're plotting. Care to share?"

I extract myself from the tempting duo and clear my throat. "Yes. We'll stay at a hotel tonight while Silas rests. I also need to buy a phone."

Baelfire's brows go up. "*You* want to buy a phone? You hate phones. Why don't you just use Crypt's enchanted phone that Silas set up?"

"Lost that somewhere," Crypt corrects.

Bael huffs. "You're as bad as Maven. Just use mine, Boo. I brought it just in case."

I shake my head. "It needs to be a burner phone. I don't want the demon to have your number."

Everett rears back. "*Demon?* No. Absolutely not. You are not getting in touch with a godsdamned demon."

I fix him with a look. "Let me refresh your memory. I grew up in the Nether. I've been surrounded by demons my entire life and know how they work. I've killed more than my fair share, paid the price each time, and find them to be useful. So don't fucking question me."

He opens his mouth and closes it twice in a row before sighing heavily. "Okay, Oakley. You're right, and I'm sorry. But can we at least make sure you're bathed, rested, and cared for before diving headfirst into more danger?"

I think about it. "Fine."

Mostly because I want to see Silas open his ruby eyes before we get to deal with more enemies.

Nearly an hour later, we take a back entrance into a hotel where Baelfire made a reservation for their biggest suite using cash Everett provided. They usher me to a metal door that slides open and reveals…a tiny room.

I frown in confusion.

Baelfire bursts into laugher as he reaches up to cover something above the door inside the little room. "It's an elevator. Never seen one, huh?"

I haven't, but I vaguely recall Lillian telling me about them. She told me about many things I still haven't been exposed to in the mortal world. Honestly, most of what I know about the human world comes from Lillian, watching movies with Kenzie, and random tidbits I picked up at Everbound. There are still cavernous gaps in my knowledge about this world, which I dislike.

Although, I guess I'll be exposed to a lot more now that we aren't on lockdown inside an isolated, gothic castle.

We all step inside, but I tip my head when Baelfire continues covering something up with his hand. "What are you doing?"

"It's a camera," he explains. "Humans have them everywhere. Don't want them getting footage of you."

Interesting. I'll have to keep an eye out for those.

Once we reach the *actual* suite, I'm impressed. It has two rooms with king-sized beds connected to a shared space with a TV, couch, mini kitchen, and glass wall with a view of Hastings.

Even though I'm good with this setup, Everett makes a face at it.

"Don't mind him. He's used to being hand-fed caviar and pissing in golden toilets," Bael rolls his eyes as he goes to deposit Silas on one of the king beds.

"It's just kind of small," the elemental argues, pushing open the bathroom door. It seems clean and spacious to me, but Everett frowns.

Baelfire laughs from the other room. "That's what Maven's gonna say when you finally whip out your—"

"Shut the fuck *up*, dragon."

I turn and lay several simple but effective protective wards on the front door. I do the same thing to the windows. Just as I feel myself lagging, Crypt wraps his arms around me from behind, murmuring gently in my ear.

"Time to rest, love."

"I still need to bathe. Silas needs to be cleaned up, too. I need to track down clean clothes and food and get that phone and some means for disguising you four—" I begin listing everything on my to-do list in my head, fighting a yawn.

He hums. "Sounds like *we* have plenty to do while you rest."

Before I can argue, Baelfire appears on my left side and scoops me out of Crypt's arms.

"I call bathing her."

Crypt smiles cruelly. "So long as you give a sponge bath to the fae, too. Fair's fair. Don't miss his tender bits because, against all reason, Maven likes those."

Baelfire shudders and starts to protest, but Everett pipes up as he approaches. "I can get food and clothes for all of us."

"You'll get recognized," I argue, trying to squirm out of Bael's strong arms. Godsdamn it, I'm way more exhausted than I realized because my attempts are pathetically feeble. They all watch in amusement as I give up, sighing and letting my head hang back over his arm.

"Fine. But we're rearranging things. Baelfire will go out to get food, clothes, and a basic burner phone because he's the least likely to get recognized—*or* frighten the hell out of people and spread unnecessary rumors," I add when Crypt opens his mouth.

The incubus laughs. Bael nods in complete agreement.

"Crypt can keep watch until we know whether the coast seems clear."

"Happy to, darling."

I pause, frowning. "You were in pain earlier. Do you have enough *reverium* to help with that?"

He blinks as if he didn't realize I'd noticed. "I have enough for now."

"*For now* will be fleeting when we're on the run, so gather more from Limbo while we're here. Everett, you'll stay here to wash up because all that dirt and blood has been driving your poor neat freak brain crazy for the last few hours," I say knowingly.

His cheeks pinken slightly. "Come on, Oakley. That's not a priority. Let me help somehow."

"Fine. You'll help wash me."

Now, his blush is flaming red. "I—uh, okay. If…if you want."

I don't understand why Baelfire tries to smother a laugh. Crypt mouths something at the elemental I don't catch, and Everett flips him off.

Whatever. I move on. "Good. Then we'll eat, rest, and look for a way to disguise you four later since I doubt we'll be here long. Hopefully, we bought Silas some time coming here, but they'll be after us, so I need all of you to be well rested."

I realize Baelfire is smirking down at me in his arms. "What?"

"It's just hot as fuck when you take charge. You're a damn good keeper, Maven."

Crypt grins. "That she is, dragon."

"Perfect," Everett agrees quietly, still blushing and adjusting his sleeves repeatedly.

Great, now *I* feel like blushing. Not to mention, how does my quintet still look so fucking gorgeous after the shit day we've had? It's not fair when I know I look like a walking smudge of dried innards. Still, I glance between the three of them and clear my throat.

I seldom do this, but…

"Sorry."

"Whatever for?" Crypt asks.

"You'll be in deep shit from now on. The Immortal Quintet and Legacy Council will try to kill you four for going on the run with me.

I wanted to prevent you guys from getting mixed up with everything my being the *telum* entails, but...I could only be tempted so far," I finish lamely.

Baelfire snorts as he takes me to the bathroom, setting me on the counter and tipping my head up so I'm forced to look into his amber-gold gaze.

"Okay, first of all? Fuck anyone who has a problem with you. Sure, you're the scourge, but it's not like that was your choice—and second of all, we know what you're really trying to do. You're a good person. In fact, you're the most aggravatingly selfless, self-sacrificing person in the world, so you're not allowed to apologize for anything. Ever."

He kisses my forehead. "You've been through hell, and maybe you did some shit you didn't like just to survive it, but that doesn't change the fact that you're a fucking hero to all those humans in the Nether. If you ask me, I'm lucky to breathe the same air as you. Got it, Mayflower?"

4

MAVEN

BAELFIRE'S words do something to me. I'm suddenly unable to look him in the eye because I'm dangerously close to getting emotional. It's one thing to do what I think is right, no matter what it takes or who hates me for it. It's another thing for someone else to see me— *really* see me and tell me I'm still a good person.

I didn't feel like a person for years, let alone a good one.

It's strange to hear.

But also...nice, somehow.

Crypt appears abruptly, sitting on the bathroom counter beside me, making Bael startle and swear. He winks like we share a secret, kisses me deeply, and vanishes again. A moment later, I can't sense his presence anywhere nearby.

"Damned incubus," Everett mutters as he also enters the bathroom. He hands Baelfire a wad of cash and then turns on the shower, testing the temperature.

"Can a snowman like you even test temperatures correctly?" Baelfire points out.

"You're one to talk, you walking furnace. Go get clothes so she has something to wear when she gets out."

"Or we could just keep her nice and naked," Bael grins, nipping one of my ears. He whispers so only I'll hear him. "Please tell me I can hold you tonight, baby. I need my mate so fucking bad."

I nod, swallowing hard.

Gods, I like my needy dragon. The rumble of his voice makes me clench my thighs together, trying to hide my body's instinctive surge of want—but he still groans and pulls me flush against him, hugging me tight.

"I'll go get you some food while you get cleaned up, but mostly because I desperately need your scent *not* mixed with blood. You have no idea how much of a dick my dragon has been about it ever since we left Everbound. I fucking hate knowing I haven't been taking good enough care of you."

I wrap my arms around his neck and kiss his jaw. "Tell your dragon that I hardly mind wearing the blood of our enemies. And come back to me quickly."

Once Baelfire leaves, I see Everett waiting by the shower, looking unsure. And still very dressed.

"Aren't you getting in with me?"

He clears his throat. "You're exhausted. Meaning, I should probably keep this all…you know. Strictly methodical."

For a model who's posed in all kinds of outfits, including half-naked on magazine covers that I used to see students and even teachers toting around Everbound, he's being strangely shy. Or is he so awkward about getting close to me because he still thinks his curse is an issue?

Either way, I'm okay with a methodical approach because it feels like my bones weigh ten thousand pounds. I've revived three times today and nearly *actually* died. Not to mention berserking, which always takes a heavy toll. I've been pushing myself hard to get us to safety—but now that we're here, I can't even bother trying to look sexy as I strip out of my ruined clothes and drag myself into the shower.

When the warm spray hits my skin, I sigh in pleasure and shut my eyes. "Thanks."

It's quiet for a moment, and then I hear the rustling of clothes as

Everett removes his. He steps into the shower behind me, which increases the steam significantly, thanks to the chill of his skin.

He hesitates. "My touch isn't exactly pleasant. Are you sure you want me to…?"

I peek open one eye and immediately open the other to get a better view.

Oh, gods. He's so fucking *gorgeous.*

I used to roll my eyes about the girls drooling over him at the university all the time, but I get it now. All that perfect skin, the lean muscles, that angelically handsome face and striking white hair, those ice-blue eyes…

Everett blushes so hard that he tries to cover his face. "Cut it out, Oakley."

"Am I making you uncomfortable?" I grin.

"You're making me way too fucking hard to even think about touching you," he mumbles so quietly I almost miss it.

That takes my gaze downtown quickly, and I once again need to press my thighs together. I've sucked his cock in the dark and loved it, but this is my first time really seeing it.

Flawless, just like the rest of him.

And *very* hard. I lick my lips.

"*Oakley.* Please. You're killing me here," he rasps. "Just tell me if you're comfortable with me touching you to wash you. I don't—we won't do anything else, okay? I want it to be special when it happens, so right now, you really can't let me get…"

"Fucked?"

Because as exhausted as I am, all this tension between us makes me think that's an excellent idea.

Everett covers his face again, muttering a prayer to Arati that I don't catch. "Look. I really, *really* need to take care of you tonight, but this isn't the right time for my first—*our* first…damn it. Maybe I should just leave."

How is he this wildly flustered? It's adorable but confusing.

And then it hits me.

His first. As in, Everett is freaking out because… he's never had sex. Meaning *I'll* be his first, but he doesn't want to do it here and now. He wants it to be special.

A strangely possessive warmth hums through me at the thought of being his first. I pull his hands away from his face and nod.

"Wash me. I like your touch."

His cheeks and ears are an adorable shade of pink. "Even though I'm cold?"

Turning over one of his hands, I place his palm against my face. "More like refreshing."

Everett swallows hard, nods, and gets to work. I mostly said he could wash me earlier so he'd have a way to contribute. Still, the more his skillful hands carefully wash away every lingering trace of filth on me, shampooing my hair and working my tired muscles, the more relaxed I feel.

Gods, I think I needed this. I could melt into a puddle and sleep on the shower floor.

His hands shake as he nears my tits, and then he pulls back. "Are you sure—"

"Everett. I've sucked your dick. That means we're past second base."

He's so taken off guard that an actual smile escapes, showing off his ridiculously photo-worthy dimples. "No offense, but how the hell do you know about bases?"

"Kenzie taught me."

I reach for the soap and lather my hands, reaching for him. He jolts as soon as I touch his chest, closing his eyes. "Shit—I don't know if you should…oh, dear gods, that feels so *good*."

I almost laugh when his head falls back with an expression of rapture. Does he really like me touching him this much, even in a non-sexual way? I wash his arms, chest, and back. But when my hand starts to dip lower, his grip encircles my wrists.

I glance up at him, enjoying the torn desperation on his flawless face. "I'll keep it methodical."

"Way too fucking late for that," he grits before he's suddenly pressing his lips to mine.

Immediately, we're tangled in each other's arms under the rain-like spray of the water, exploring one another as I tease his tongue with mine. It's incredibly satisfying to feel just how sensitive he is to everything. When my fingers skim over his side, he shivers, and when I gently nip his bottom lip, he groans and presses me against the shower wall.

That unintentionally presses his erection against my stomach, and he breaks away to swear, hanging his head.

"Gods help me, you're so fucking *warm*. I can't get enough of you." When he looks back at me, his pale blue eyes are pools of longing again. "Do you have any idea how much I want you? It's been torture since I saw you on that stage. I fucking *ache* to be yours. If we can just circumvent my damn curse so I know I'm not going to hurt you—"

I capture his lips again. "You won't hurt me. Just kiss me."

Everett moans and gets rougher and more daring as we kiss in the steam-filled shower. His lips skate down my jaw, and he peppers kisses along my neck, scooping me tighter against him so he won't have to bend as much while his hands slip to my ass and squeeze hard. I close my eyes, dizzy from the lack of oxygen and the blissful hum of desire in my veins.

For someone with no experience, he is incredible at this. I'm so consumed by him that it takes a moment to hear the slur of words.

I've memorized these…yes, sir, three vials of ogre blood…two pinches of stardust…

I stiffen and pull back from Everett. He's breathing just as heavily as I am as he tries to get himself under control, but lucky me, he can't seem to remove his hands from my ass. He rolls his forehead against mine with a soft, tortured groan.

"Sorry. I didn't mean to get so—"

"It's not anything you did," I say quickly.

A strange emotion floods me as I realize that while I'm in here getting a taste of my ice elemental, my fae is still in terrible shape.

I think they call this emotion…guilt.

"I heard Silas in my head. I should check on him," I explain.

Everett nods as I back out of the glass shower—but the residual hunger on his face leaves me breathless. He licks his lips and drags a hand through his hair, which looks silver when wet. His glacial gaze traces every exposed inch of me, and my mouth parts as I watch his free hand slide down to slowly stroke his wet, straining erection.

Gods. I should be reaching for a towel to cover my wet nakedness, but I can't tear my attention away.

I meet his gaze, determined to get what I want before I go.

"Faster. I want to watch you finish."

Everett's breathing hitches. I expect him to argue, to keep resisting this. Instead, the chillingly beautiful man braces one arm against the glass of the shower and starts stroking himself in earnest as the steam continues to billow around him.

It's so fucking erotic seeing him like this. Dripping, a blush on his cheeks and neck and shoulders as he chases his release, with those crystalline irises pinned on me.

"Maven," he whispers, his gaze still on my body.

"Close?" I murmur, watching his fist fly over his thick cock.

He nods, panting and groaning. Gods, I love seeing him like this. Flushed and overwhelmed, on the brink of pleasure. All that careful, icy composure from when we first met has melted away, leaving this sinfully handsome creature coming undone under my gaze.

"Dear gods, your body," he moans. "And...fuck, I *love* you watching me."

That makes two of us.

I had no idea I liked watching this much—not that it's a shock when he's so ludicrously attractive. But it's clear Everett enjoys an audience.

I wonder what else he likes. When we get to it, I do want to make his first time special.

My own first time was quick, painful, pleasureless, and ended with the slightly less fun version of strangulation. I didn't get to explore what I did or didn't enjoy with a trusted partner—hell, I only had sex with Gideon out of morbid curiosity and to get him to shut up about his imagined feelings.

Now? I want to explore much more with all of my matches.

"You're gorgeous," I whisper, letting my hand steal down to brush through the new wetness between my legs. I can't help moaning slightly at the pulse of pleasure that sends through me.

Everett swears softly. I watch in rapt fascination, my pulse pounding eagerly as his cock jerks and his cum paints the foggy glass shower wall between us. He's shuddering and breathless when our gazes meet again, but his gaze is now so full of emotion that it pins me in place.

"No holds barred, Oakley," he whispers. "I mean it. If we can avoid my curse, nothing is going to stop me from finally fucking belonging to you."

Too late. He's already mine, whether he's prepared to accept it or not.

I finally break out of the incredibly sensual trance I've been stuck in for the last few minutes, wrap myself in a big white towel, and hurry out of the bathroom.

It's hard to steady my breathing, and now *I'm* the flushed one.

But when I slip into the room where Baelfire put Silas, my lingering arousal and building hope fizzle to nothing. He's still unconscious, fighting to breathe with a damp cloth on his forehead.

Silas, I try again.

Seven dried ghost orchids…two vampire fangs, his voice slurs back.

It's nonsense. He's completely out of it.

But at least I can fucking hear him again.

Taking a deep breath, I grab a towel and bowl of water so I can at least make sure he's clean while I wait for however long it will take to get my fae back.

5

SILAS

THE VOICES ARE GONE.

Once the endlessly harrowing, paralyzing agony fades away, I lay marinating in dark silence. It's bizarrely serene. For the first time since childhood, mine is the only voice inside my head. Paranoia is not shredding me to pieces, there are no taunting whispers, and keeping my eyes closed for longer than a blink no longer fills me with that ominous, unspeakable dread.

Is this what being sane feels like?

Thank the gods, I think.

Those idiots are useless. Thank me instead.

My heart stutters.

That was Maven.

Murky memories and realizations slowly piece together as I pull myself out of a dark depth unlike anything I have ever experienced. My debilitating paranoia is absent, I've been hearing my keeper amid the murky hell I just passed through, and...I feel different.

Not bad. Only different.

Perhaps even stronger.

I open my eyes and stare at an unfamiliar ceiling. The bed I'm lying in is also unknown to me. I'm still puzzling out where I could possibly be when Baelfire's face appears above me, breaking the quiet when he slurps loudly on the straw of a milkshake.

"Welcome back, Si. Thought you wouldn't make it for a hot second, but it's nice to see I didn't have to carry your fevered, dead-weight ass around for no reason."

Prick.

But he's nudged aside, Maven's face appears in my field of vision, and everything else in the world promptly disappears except us. There's something different about her, too. It's something I can't put into words, as if her presence has a rich darkness that draws me in.

Her enchantingly dark gaze holds me hostage. When her fingers trail gently over my face, I stop breathing momentarily as it sinks in.

We're bound. Maven is mine.

Mine.

My keeper's lips twitch when she hears that. To my absolute delight, the following words she sends me are in the fae tongue, inside my head.

How do you feel, my handsome lunatic?

I should have a million questions. Perhaps I should also be mourning the fact that I just woke up as a necromancer, one of the most hated creatures of all time who are outlawed from existence in the mortal realm.

But none of that matters because *gods above*, I'm bound to Maven. I can feel it between us—an intimacy of a different kind. A preternatural, irreversible link that settles into my very being.

I feel…elated. So godsdamned euphoric, it's nigh surreal.

I also feel extremely thirsty.

For her.

The need to have her as close to me as possible is so sudden and intense that I don't hesitate before I pull Maven onto me. I know my blood blossom feels the same urge as I do—this craving. I groan into the side of her neck, wrapping her tightly in my arms.

I'm never letting go of you again.

She shivers when I gently nip at her earlobe. Just that tiny reaction has me nearly frothing at the mouth. I've always been attracted to Maven, but it's verging on painful at the moment. I want her in so many ways that I'm simultaneously lost and found.

"Damned newlybounds," Everett grumbles somewhere nearby. "Get a room."

"They're *in* a room, dickwad," Bael points out.

I trail kisses up and down Maven's jaw and neck, relishing how she's wrapped me up in an equally tight hug. I am drowning in relief, exhilaration, and a deepening desire that makes my mouth water.

Or…is it her neck that's making my mouth water?

No, that can't be. I'm no longer a blood fae, so I must stop salivating like this.

I'm so keyed in to Maven that it hits me like an anvil to the head when she tenses ever so slightly. It's only then that I realize how wrapped up she is in me and how any lingering remnants of her haphephobia might be resurfacing.

Immediately, I release her from my arms, but I can't resist keeping her in my lap as I sit up.

Forgive me, sangfluir, I apologize through our bond.

Maven ignores the apology as if her lingering fear isn't worth acknowledgment. Instead, she studies my face. While she looks at me, I glance at our surroundings. I realize we're in a hotel, and Maven and I are the only ones in this room now. The door is open, and Baelfire and Everett are in the central area of what must be a suite. It appears they left to give us space, while Crypt is nowhere to be seen.

That is uncharacteristically thoughtful of them, but I want more of my keeper right now.

I lift my hand and try to focus on closing the door, but my muscles burn instead. It's the same sensation I used to get when trying to cast blood magic when I was utterly spent.

Maven leaves my lap despite my protest to shut the door herself. When she turns back to face me, she smirks and slides off her shirt in one smooth movement. My cock surges with need, but then my gaze settles on her chest.

And my emblem there.

Oh, fuck me. I *love* seeing that.

"Come here, *sangfluir*," I say thickly, burning for more of her touch.

She approaches slowly, discarding articles of clothing piece by piece, so sensual and calculated that I could swear that she's hypnotized me by the time she reaches the bed and fixes me with a look.

"You shouldn't have," she says simply.

I slip off my own shirt, so captivated by her that it takes me a moment to understand what she's talking about. Then I scoff.

"You think I wouldn't sacrifice my magic for you? I would sacrifice *anything* for you. Even had I never woken up, that risk was well worth—"

She's on me in the next moment, her lips colliding with mine, and then we're both hungry, ravenous, *searing* with need. Rolling, I pin her to the bed and take over the kiss, groaning when her hands tangle in my hair. I rock my hips, and heat shoots down my spine when she grinds against me in return with a soft groan.

"Maven," I whisper, trying to shed my pants as fast as fucking possible. "I want to cherish you. I want to spend every day of the rest of our lives worshipping your body, but right now—"

"Sex now. Talk later," she agrees, wrapping her legs around me insistently.

Gods above, I'm in love with her.

I never expected that.

My entire life, being in a quintet was always a given for me. It was how I would break my curse and how I intended to grow even stronger. It was never going to be anything more, not when I suspected I would be too ruthless and intense to be romantically compatible with whoever the gods matched me up with.

But Maven is a force of nature. She's steady, stubborn, and vicious. Mine.

Mine, mine, mine.

Yours, she responds, and then gasps and arches her back when I line myself up and thrust into her in one savage drive.

Fuck.

It feels so godsdamned good. Her pleasure and mine, twisting together, eating me alive in a way I will never recover from—nor would I want to. I thrust into her again, harder. When she moans and digs her nails into my back, I lose it, fucking my keeper with wild abandon as our blazing need drowns every ounce of sanity I just got back.

It's too intensely pleasurable for me to last the way I need to, so I try to slow down as I kiss along her neck, utterly losing all that I am in Maven. In fact, I'm so lost in her that it takes me a moment to realize I'm licking and sucking the skin over her carotid artery.

I pull back, going perfectly still.

"Silas," she huffs, rolling her hips insistently.

"There's something very wrong with me."

"I'm already in the mood. You don't have to try seducing me more."

I shake my head, aching to move but equally confused. "Maven, I…I'm thirsty. Desperate."

Maven gives me a testy look. "So am I, but *someone* is trying to fucking edge me again."

"No, I'm not. I mean that I'm craving…" I stare at her neck, conflicted.

I'm a necromancer now. Aren't I?

So, what the hell is wrong with me? Why does the thought of Maven's blood send mouthwatering desire coursing through me? Why are my teeth aching the way they always used to before my fangs emerged?

Maven registers what I mean and seems thoughtful. "Try it."

"No. It's wrong. If I'm no longer a blood fae, I shouldn't be—"

"Says who?" she challenges. She brushes dark hair off of her beautiful neck, reaching up to tease one of her nipples, so now I'm both aroused out of my mind and salivating again. "Bite me, Silas."

Fangs descend just as I bite her neck.

The intoxicatingly potent flavor of Maven's magic sears across my tongue, and I moan, immediately drawing deeply from her as I begin thrusting again. The euphoric rush of pleasure-feeding and fucking at once sends me into an unbridled frenzy, and soon Maven is trying to muffle her cries as the headboard bangs against the wall.

Sangfluir, I think frantically, unable to control myself as I bite the other side of her neck and twist her hair in my grip. Her addictive blood drips from my chin, the scent of it pushing me into a new brand of madness.

Maven gasps abruptly. Her pussy squeezes me so fucking tight that I can't breathe as her orgasm claims her. Slamming deep and finally releasing her neck, I grit my teeth as I find my own release. The sharp wash of pleasure only cements my eternal need for her.

The newlybound buzz of voracious arousal eases slightly between us. As soon as I catch my breath and begin to think with clarity, I grimace at the sight of Maven's neck.

I lost all control, I lament in my head. *I hurt you again.*

My keeper smiles, her eyes alight with satisfaction. "I like it when you lose control. But if it bothers you, give it a try."

She means...try to heal her.

Licking my lips clean, I pull out and can't help the surge of satisfaction I feel watching my cum begin to leak out of her well-loved pussy. Refocusing takes a moment, but I move my hands over her neck and mutter the necromantic healing spell I memorized from forbidden books long ago.

The words taste acrid. Bitter cold sweeps through my body as my blackened fingertips tingle—but the bite wounds on Maven's neck begin to close until there are only streaks of her delicious blood remaining.

Maven's alluringly dark essence deepens, and I examine her for a moment, again trying in vain to understand what I'm sensing from her. Whatever it is, it compels me.

My keeper nods knowingly. "The necromancers used to say I emanated death. That's what you're sensing. You'll pick up on it more around fresh kills like I do. But now that you've fueled..."

She looks at the door meaningfully. My heart pounds as I raise my hand and try the handle again from this distance. To my astonishment, it slowly swings open through a crimson swirl of red blood magic.

I blink down at Maven.

"You're a hybrid caster like me now," she deduces quietly, frowning.

Clearly, she's right. But *how?* Is it because my keeper is so powerful? Is that what has given me this ability, or was it some other fluke of nature? Is this a flaw that will create problems for us later?

I was more than willing to sacrifice my magic for her. I was prepared to lose it all, never to open my eyes again so long as I knew she remained alive in this world—let my renowned blood magic be damned.

So, is my magic really not affected? How...anticlimactic.

Utterly strange, yet also thrilling.

A buzzing sound from a nearby dresser draws our attention, and my succulent keeper slips out of the bed to pick up an old flip phone. She checks the number.

"It's Kenzie. I tried calling her earlier to make sure her quintet is okay. She probably realized this is my burner."

When she regards me as if debating if she should leave me alone again, I put her mind at ease. "I'm capable of fending for myself, *sangfluir*. Apparently, more so than ever."

I'm still pissed at you for trying to sacrifice yourself for me, she sternly says through our link.

Tell me to atone with apologies between your pretty thighs again, and I will happily do so.

Her eyes flash before she slips her shirt and panties back on and leaves.

6

SILAS

I REDRESS in the same pants I awoke in—from my combat attire which is burned and stained from First Placement. Walking out of the bedroom, I glance over to see three glares of pure hatred pinned on me.

"Jealous?" I smirk.

"Taunt me right now, and I'll snap off every finger you laid on her," Crypt warns from where he appears to be rolling cigarettes at a small table.

"All of them, then," I taunt anyway.

Baelfire flips me off from the couch. "The only reason I didn't break down that door and toss you out to give it to our keeper the *right* way is because Maven deserved a moment alone with you after all the worry and shit you put her through."

That gives me a pause of guilt, knowing my keeper was so worried about me.

"I can't believe you couldn't keep yourself from mauling her immediately when you look and smell like *that*," Everett adds, completely revolted as he turns back to glare out the window that is not-so-mysteriously hazing with a slight frost.

Bael stands and folds his arms, regarding me. "Huh. Thought

you'd look different as a necromancer. Like a skeleton or something. So how the hell can you use both kinds of magic?"

Of course, he overheard. I look down at my hands and my slightly numbed, darkened fingertips. Perhaps I'll need to start wearing gloves as Maven does.

"I'm not sure. More importantly, how long was I out? Where are we?"

Everett crankily grumbles a short explanation—that it's been three days since First Placement, and we've been hiding out in Kenzie's hometown while they waited for me to recover. There has been no sign of us being followed yet. Still, apparently Asher fucking Douglas and countless other bounty hunters were assigned to look for us.

That means it's just a matter of time.

Once he's caught me up, he glances over his shoulder. "So… it's really gone?"

The other two stare hard at me, and I realize we're discussing my curse. How oddly relieving it is that I can now look at these three without seeing inevitable backstabbers out to annihilate me. Not that they're pleasant to look at still, but at least I'm no longer in danger of losing my mind and killing one of Maven's other matches.

Or worse, hurting her yet *again*.

"It's gone," I confirm.

They all look away, and it gets unusually quiet, except for Maven's muffled voice from the suite's other room. I suspect Baelfire can hear every word she's saying on the phone.

"I have a theory," Crypt muses.

Bael begins to pace. "I do, too."

"That makes three of us. Are we sharing these theories, or is it every man for himself as usual?" Everett asks.

Crypt answers by disappearing into Limbo.

Baelfire shrugs. "Let's not make another stupid fucking competition out of it, but Maven will be wearing my emblem next."

Everett rolls his eyes and returns to brooding. I mull everything over in my head as I shower and clean up. If we're being hunted, it will be difficult for Maven to go after the Immortal Quintet. I can't say that bothers me. Knowing that assassinating them would mark the end of her purpose and, therefore, the end of her life fills me with unspeakable anger. Although she plans on leaving one alive in her complex plan to free the humans in the Nether, I'd much prefer to spirit her away, far from anyone who wants to harm her.

But Maven made a blood oath to free those humans. I'll help however I can, so long as it doesn't put her at even more risk.

I'm just stepping out of the bathroom when Maven emerges, her lips pressed together. She looks painfully good in only panties and that shirt, the wide neckline of which shows off the top of my emblem. Seeing it makes my mouth water all over again.

"We're leaving tomorrow," she announces.

Baelfire is immediately at her side, shooting me a glare as he tries to wipe away the remaining dried streaks of blood on her neck.

"Leaving to where, Raincloud?"

"That, I haven't decided. Somewhere more rural than this."

Baelfire kisses her temple. "My family's territory near the Purcell mountain range is nice and remote. Only a fucking moron would try to trespass on Decimus land to get to you. My mom would roast them alive—not to mention, I'm sure she's been dying to meet you."

Maven hesitates. "The eyewitnesses who escaped along with the faculty have probably been running their mouths. She'll know by now that I'm the *telum*. My identity isn't a secret anymore."

Everett swears. "Damn it. You're right."

"My parents won't care," Baelfire confidently insists.

"I'm the Entity's scourge. I'm very literally a heartless, unnatural, death-fueled monster. Does that scream *take her home to meet the parents* to you?" she asks dryly.

Crypt abruptly appears next to us and grins. "It does, actually. I, for one, couldn't wait to introduce you to my parent."

"And now he's dead," our keeper points out.

He leans down to kiss the tip of her nose. "My point exactly, and yet another reason I adore you."

Twisted bastard.

Not that I blame him in this case. Somnus was a literal monster.

"Why do we need to leave tomorrow?" I ask, trying to get back to the topic at hand.

"That was Kenzie telling me that some older legacy knocked on her parents' door asking if they'd seen people matching our descriptions. Her parents didn't reveal Kenzie was there with her quintet and said they hadn't seen us, but it probably means the bounty hunters are getting close. So we'll leave first thing tomorrow morning."

Everett nods and then frowns. "Was that the only update? You were in there a while."

"Kenzie spent fifteen minutes telling me about introducing her matches to her parents and ten more minutes trying to convince me that we should go to her favorite local diner for a date night. She insisted that we need a sense of normalcy as a quintet after everything we just went through, and as the keeper, it falls to me, etcetera, etcetera," Maven shrugs. She hesitates, glancing at us and then away before clearing her throat. "It's probably a bad idea, but would you guys want to...?"

Is she...asking us out?

It's almost amusing how nervous our typically unshakable keeper clearly is, but my blood blossom suggesting a date night sends eagerness racing through me. She fought this quintet so hard, so it's still a novel thing to know that she not only accepts us but *wants* us.

"Yes," all four of us say at the same time.

Crypt groans in disgust at our synchrony and pantomimes shooting himself.

"All right. It's a date."

Baelfire flashes her a bright, excited smile. "Fuck, yes! I've been dying to just do normal quintet shit with you. Can we make it dinner and a movie? It can be a gory slasher. Anything for my Spooky Boo."

"Call me that again, and you're uninvited."

"Fine. You want a new nickname? How about..." Baelfire rubs his face as if in deep thought. "Angel..."

We all burst into laughter at Maven's priceless expression. "You're kidding. Have you met me?"

"I wasn't done," he laughs. "*Of Death.* You're our pretty little Angel of Death."

Crypt winks at Maven. "Admit it, love, it's fitting."

She fights a smile and turns to me. "*Anyway.* If you four are coming with me tonight, we need to ensure you're all less recognizable. Especially Everett. Silas, can you access ingredients for a camouflage spell?"

Summoning blood magic to my fingertips, I reach into the pocket void I set up when I was six years old. It's a surprisingly simple spell, folding space in on itself to create this small storage that can be summoned anytime. It's stocked with all manner of ingredients. I pause when my fingers brush against the colorless plant that Crypt brought back from the Divide.

That elixir didn't work for Maven's last episode because I stupidly created it with blood magic. I'd felt painfully helpless when she faded away.

But now that I can use necromancy...

"Si?" Bael prompts. "You still with us?"

I shake off my thoughts and withdraw a small collection of ingredients we'll need—eye of newt, unicorn horn dust, a handful of dried moly leaves, a mortar and pestle, and so on.

Maven's face lights up at the promising display. It's such a rare expression on her that I can't help staring. Witnessing even the slightest amount of her happiness is like a dose of dopamine straight to my soul.

It makes me...

I can't tell if you're horny, thirsty, or...reverent, she thinks to me, arching a brow.

All of the above.

Baelfire squints between Maven and me. "Are you guys...?"

"They're having a telepathic conversation," Crypt agrees bitterly.

He may be an unhinged maniac, but no one can say he isn't observant.

All three assholes are glaring jealous daggers at me again, but Maven just holds up the moly leaves.

"Mind helping?"

I quickly begin helping her measure out the ingredients we'll need for a camouflage potion that should last for a few hours, but I note there are only four batches.

"Won't you need some?"

Maven studies the unicorn horn dust. "You've all been high-profile legacies your entire lives. I know for a fact you can easily be found on both human and legacy social media sites because Kenzie digitally stalked you four after the Seeking. The only picture ever taken of me is on Baelfire's phone from when I was trying to make you all hate me. He took the picture during class when he thought I wouldn't notice."

Baelfire grins unabashedly. "You saw that, huh?"

"You weren't subtle. Also, it's set as your lock screen."

"What can I say, cutie? You weren't taking it easy on my heart, and I wanted something besides your delicious scent to beat off to constantly."

Everett mutters something under his breath as I roll my eyes.

Crypt nods as if he finds the dragon's antics completely understandable. "You know, you might've shared, Decimus."

"As if you weren't beating your meat to the sight of her all the time from Limbo anyway, Stalker Boy," Baelfire rolls his eyes. "Plus, you didn't have a fucking phone at the time, so how was I supposed to send you anything?"

"That's beside the point. We really must get more photos of our girl."

"In lingerie," Bael nods. "Or literally anything."

"Or in nothing," Crypt counters.

"Hell, yes. I pick Option C."

"My *point*," Maven goes on quickly, ignoring our smirks at her obvious need to change the subject, "is that I'm not recognizable. I don't need to be camouflaged."

I watch her skillfully grind the newt eyeballs and moly leaves together in the mortar. She will obviously have no trouble brewing this potion on her own, and once again, my thoughts return to the colorless plant in my pocket void.

Necromancer or not, never again will I sit helplessly by while my blood blossom is in pain.

When are we leaving on this date? I ask telepathically.

"As soon as these potions take effect," she mutters, not seeming to realize she replied out loud as she grinds more leaves.

The others watch her curiously, but I retreat to one of the rooms to try my hand at perfecting the elixir she may need again soon.

7

MAVEN

OF MY MANY PROBLEMS, two have my full attention as we walk through the blustery, cold December night in downtown Hastings toward the diner Kenzie told me about.

My first problem is that I'm starting to…feel things. For all four of my matches.

Sure, I wanted them before. I decided they were mine and that I would fight for them.

But now?

Every time Silas looks at me or speaks in my head, I feel this rush of *rightness* now that we're bound together. Whenever Everett comes anywhere near me, I get the urge to reach out and pull him closer—though right now, he's trying to keep his distance, grumbling that it's cold enough without him making it worse for me. Baelfire keeps finding tiny excuses to touch me anywhere he possibly can to warm me up, and damn it, I *like* that.

Adding the fact that I can feel Crypt watching my every move from where he walks behind us just as obsessively as he does whenever he's in Limbo…

My entire life has been spent carefully locking away my emotions, so I have no fucking idea how to deal with all of *this*. Can't all of these stupid flutters in my stomach wait until I kill off the rest of the Immortal Quintet and have more time to process them?

Catching feelings is so damn inconvenient.

But my second problem is that we're being followed.

I first noticed it two blocks ago and haven't said anything to the others yet. It's better to play it cool until I have more information on this potential threat, especially since we're doing an excellent job of blending in with the other humans bustling about this small town, blasting holiday music outside every little shop.

Baelfire opens the door to the busy diner. "After you, Boo."

"One of these days, that nickname has to go."

He winks and tries to kiss me as I pass by, but Everett shoves the dragon shifter back, lowering his voice.

"Remember our cover. Humans are typically monogamous, so we're pretending she's with me. If the rest of you idiots get handsy with her, they'll figure out we're a quintet of legacies."

On top of the camouflage spell that should make their exact features and appearances impossible to remember for others for the next few hours—except for me, since I brewed the potion—I decided to take extra precautions with Everett. To try to dull his modelesque appearance, he's wearing a frumpy coat, oversized scarf, and a fur-lined trapper hat that my fashion-conscious match has made no secret of loathing in the extreme.

Bael flips him off. "Thanks for the reminder, Professor Cockblock."

I slip into a corner booth with my quintet, quickly surveying my surroundings. There are seven potential exits. If a fight finds us, I'll get us out of here in no time to keep these innocent humans from being in too much danger.

The person on our tail hasn't come into the diner.

Curious. If it were a bounty hunter, being in a public place wouldn't have stopped them. Is someone else after us? Are they just waiting outside for us to emerge?

What is it, sangfluir? Silas's voice asks softly in my head.

Nothing yet, I reply telepathically, glancing at my bound match across the circular corner booth. The fae is wearing a dark maroon sweater that somehow suits him perfectly.

Yet?

"If you could stop with the telepathy until the rest of us figure out how to join in," Crypt drawls, glaring at Silas, "that would greatly reduce my desire to crush your skull. Wouldn't want you to lose your head so soon after getting your sanity back."

"Oh, that I could lie so easily," Silas fires back, opening a menu.

Crypt is dressed in a black hoodie smattered in fake blood that reads, "I put the laughter in slaughter." I know for a fact that Bael didn't buy that when he went out to get clothes for us, but I was already aware that my Nightmare Prince has sticky fingers.

Baelfire did, however, buy me a nice oversized black sweatshirt and something called jeggings, which are far tighter than anything I typically wear yet somehow comfortable. I can't prove that he bought the tighter pants just so he can check out my legs and ass, but I keep catching all of them doing just that.

No complaints here.

Baelfire throws an arm around the back of the booth and slides closer to me, flipping open the menu on the table in front of me and whispering in my ear.

"Hungry, hellion? I'm dying to feed you."

Everett smacks Bael's arm away to put his arm around me instead —but we all jolt in surprise when an animalistic snarl rips out of Baelfire's throat as he bares his teeth at the elemental. His gaze has shifted to the fiery golden-eyed slits of his dragon.

Shit. He hasn't hunted today.

Immediately, the gorgeous shifter flinches and buries his head under his arms on the table like he's trying to silence his dragon.

"Damn it. Sorry, Boo," he rasps quietly.

Luckily none of the humans nearby seem to have noticed that outburst. Resting my hand on Baelfire's knee under the table, I rub it reassuringly.

At least, I hope it's reassuring. I suck at shit like this.

"Maybe you should go hunt a squirrel or something."

"I'm not leaving your side."

"But—"

"I *can't* leave your side," he grits, voice muffled. "My dragon won't let me. Just keep touching me. It helps keep him in check when nothing else will."

Seeing my charming, cheerful match so tortured irks me deeply. Before I can demand that Baelfire go and kill something to appease his curse, a waitress approaches the table. Even though she's smiling as she greets us and starts filling water glasses, there's an unmistakable eyebrow raise of suspicion as her gaze flicks around the table.

"Happy holidays, and welcome to Bella's Diner. What can I get for you...*five?*"

Yep. She definitely suspects that we're a quintet of legacies.

Except for Crypt, the others place orders while I try to decipher the menu. When my turn comes, I still have no fucking idea what's in most of the dishes listed. I decide to play it safe with something Kenzie ordered for me when we used to go to Halfton.

"I'll have potatoes."

"Mashed or baked?"

Neither sounds right. What are those things called again?

"She means chips," Crypt offers, spinning a butterknife on the table out of boredom.

The waitress frowns. "Like, just a bag of potato chips? We don't have that here."

"Fries," Everett clarifies.

Right, that's what those are called.

My ice elemental goes on with, "Let's make that a large order of parmesan fries, the Southwest salad with absolutely no chicken or bacon, and the vegan specialty black bean burger. What else?" he glances at the others.

"She's never tried hot chocolate. Let's also add the French toast," Silas says. He looks at me and telepathically asks, *Yes or no to whipped cream on that?*

What the fuck is whipped cream?

"Extra whipped cream," he decides aloud.

"And a hot fudge sundae," Baelfire tacks on, sitting up finally. "Or do you want a milkshake instead, Mayflower?"

Hang on. Are they trying to order all of that just for me?

I'm about to remind them that I'm not a bottomless pit like Baelfire, but then I notice the waitress's wary expression. Obviously, witnessing that interaction has only cemented her suspicions. Now she's staring at us like we're sprouting horns and tails before her eyes. If I don't do something, she'll ask to see legal legacy identification from all of us.

The best way to distract someone from suspicion is by making them wildly uncomfortable. Thinking fast, I recall a musical movie Kenzie forced me to sit through weeks ago and give the waitress an exasperated look as if I'd rather not be here.

"Awkward, isn't it? I'm trying to figure out which one is the baby daddy."

Everett chokes on the water he's drinking and Baelfire does a double-take. Silas and Crypt catch on to my act simultaneously. The fae nods solemnly since that's the most he can do to aid the lie. Meanwhile, Crypt heaves a dramatic sigh.

"While I'm certain it's mine, perhaps we should get a paternity test once our adorable little nightmare comes along. Unless you'd rather enlist the help of a legacy to detect the father now?" He fakes a disapproving frown.

I put on an exaggerated grimace. "Legacies? Gross."

"Freaky little fuckers," Bael agrees smoothly, now on the same page. "Here's a thought: let's just assume it's mine."

"Right, because your family is known for their strong swimmers," Everett grumbles.

Baelfire tenses, and I remove my hand from his knee when I feel a sudden surge of heat emanating from him as his temper slips. "Watch your fucking mouth, *professor*. At least my parents aren't overcontrolling nightmares who try to micromanage every part of my life."

Gods. These two just can't get past the whole fire and ice thing, can they?

I don't miss the way Everett's face flashes with anger before he checks out, looking out the window like this isn't a topic he'll touch. The waitress seems just as confused and uncomfortable as I'd hoped when I turn back to her, trying to move on quickly before anyone else loses their temper.

"Unless you want to stay and referee the dick-measuring contest that will inevitably happen between these four, that's everything for our order."

The waitress shakes her head quickly and hurries away with our order, bumping into a table and apologizing profusely in her rush to get away from this pretended awkwardness. Poor thing has no idea how amusing it is for me to watch. I can't hide my dark smirk by the time I turn back to the others.

Crypt's purple eyes are full of mischief as he grins back. "Brava, darling."

"Our clever little sadist," Baelfire agrees, his shifter emotions swinging from anger to laughter in the blink of an eye.

Silas lifts his glass, which I notice is now filled with dark wine that he drains quickly, leaving no evidence for the waitress to see when she returns. If he weren't fae, I'd be mildly worried about his drinking habits.

Dinner goes off without a hitch after that. The waitress has to return several times to bring all the dishes. Although I point out that there's no way I can eat everything they ordered for me, my matches eagerly watch each time I try something new. It's borderline ridiculous how much they want me to enjoy myself.

In their defense, all of the food is fucking amazing.

Still, the sundae is by far my favorite. Whoever invented ice cream deserves a Paradise of their very own.

When I go to try the steaming cup of hot chocolate, I flinch back at how hot it is when it touches my lips. Everett quickly takes the mug from me. Glancing around subtly to ensure no one is watching, he blows on the cup like he's cooling it off. I can see the white frost on his breath, and when he hands the mug back, it's the perfect temperature.

Icy breath. Why is that so hot to me?

I glance over as Baelfire bites into a burger. He's on his second, which isn't surprising. He ordered almost as much food for his shifter metabolism as they collectively ordered for me. When he catches me looking, he holds the burger towards me.

"Want to try?"

"Not if it's meat."

Everett tips his head, picking another olive out of his salad. Evidently, he is not a fan of those. "What made you decide not to eat meat anyway? Does it make you feel sick?"

That particular memory isn't worth sharing. "Something like that."

By the time everyone is done eating—aside from Crypt, who only licked my ice cream spoon once it'd been in my mouth to get a reaction out of me—it really does feel like this is an ordinary human date. The waitress comes to take our payment before scurrying away again, obviously wanting nothing to do with the fake drama I fed her.

Baelfire steals a bite of my remaining ice cream. "So, how is this date gonna end, hellion? I'll give you a hint: the right answer is with you sitting on my face until I pass out."

My neck abruptly feels hot. "You're set on that, I see."

"If I don't die getting smothered by your sweet ass, I'll consider my death a complete failure."

It's dangerously easy to imagine riding his face…and sucking the others off at the same time. I could play with Crypt's piercings and listen to all of them moaning and see that adorably overwhelmed blush on Everett's face as I trace my tongue around his tip…

Gods. I was dicked down just a few hours ago. How am I this horny already?

Their gazes darken on me as they collectively seem to sense the sinful direction my thoughts have taken. One side of Silas's mouth lifts as his crimson gaze flicks over me.

"Do you have any idea how addictive your desire is, Maven?"

Before I can decide what I'll do with them to quench this building need, a shadow moves outside one of the diner's front windows. I snap to attention as I recognize a face just before it slips around a corner.

"We need to go." I nudge Everett to slide out of the booth. "Now."

Baelfire tenses, looking out the same window as we all get up. "What is it?"

"You'll see. Follow what I say exactly."

A moment later, we leave the diner. Baelfire and Silas turn left while Everett and I head right. We pass a tall man dressed in a red suit and fake bushy white beard, carrying a pot and jingling a bell. I don't get this holiday character at all, but Everett tosses a thick wad of cash into the pot without saying a word before we turn down the alley I told him to.

Crypt is with us, unseen in Limbo. The moment we round the corner of the diner into a small back parking lot area that appears to be nothing but a few overfilled dumpsters and broken bottles on asphalt, I can feel it—the sharp hum of a trapping spell.

The world flips as Everett and I are suspended upside down in the magic snare. Cold explodes from beside me as he tries to use his powers to get free, but when I barely tap into the dark, malicious power inside my veins, the spell shatters, and we fall to the asphalt.

A shadow leaps toward me. I instinctively roll out of the way— but not before a sharp pain explodes in my left shoulder, rendering my left arm useless as I take a defensive stance. Silas and Baelfire round the opposite corner into the parking lot, racing toward us. Crypt drops into the mortal realm, tackling the figure from behind.

There's a startled grunt, and another surge of magic explodes from the mage. Silas deflects the spell easily with a blinding burst of red blood magic, and finally, Crypt and Baelfire have the caster pinned.

Crypt rips the hood away from the man's face, and Baelfire snarls.

"*Gibbons?*"

8

MAVEN

EVERBOUND'S interim headmaster squirms under their tight hold, whimpering at the sight of Crypt's glowing markings and the dragon shifter baring his teeth. I approach with every intention of tuning out my bleeding arm—but when Everett sees it, he scowls and pulls back the sleeve of my now-ripped hoodie to reveal what the mage stabbed me with.

A chorus of vicious swears goes up from all four of them when they see the nevermelt embedded in my shoulder. It's the same shard I saw in Everett's office. He must have stolen from there.

The mage was aiming for my heart. Safe to say he knows what I am.

I've never been stabbed with nevermelt before, but my entire left arm is now so cold it burns, the nerves searing from freezing pain. I compartmentalize the sensation and crouch beside the deposed mage, staring him down. The terror and revulsion practically waft off of him in waves, which makes it hard not to smile.

I've never liked this mage. There's something about him I can't put my finger on.

The bulging vein in Gibbons' forehead looks like it's about to pop. "Y—you're a… you're the—"

"Revenant. Scourge. Unnatural, semi-undead bitch. Call me

whatever you want now, because you won't be speaking much longer."

The mage sneers. "You may have corrupted the most promising legacies of this generation, but you will never unleash the Entity on this world, you filthy, cursed *abomination!*"

This time, I can't help the grin that pops up on my face at the thought of "corrupting" my quintet.

Sounds fun.

Crypt looks at the nevermelt stuck in my arm again and promptly snaps one of the mage's upper arms. Gibbons' startled scream is satisfying, but then I watch in twisted fascination as Crypt's fingertips dig into the flesh around one of the mage's eyes.

"What the hell are you doing, you sick fuck?" Everett scowls.

"This bloke's aura is nauseating, and he's watched us with these beady little eyes for far too long."

"Don't like how he keeps glaring at my mate," Baelfire agrees.

Gibbons' screaming grows louder, so I glance at Silas.

"We'll need privacy for what I have in mind."

He nods and pricks his finger to cast a blood magic spell. Runes flare to life in a large circle around us. Although I can still hear the faint echo of holiday music outside the parking lot between the interim headmaster's screams, I'm positive we won't be overheard now.

"Now that we're nice and alone—" I begin.

"Hang on, Oakley. Silas, come here," Everett says, gently pulling me to my feet and trying to pry the shard from my shoulder with his fingertips.

Pain lances out from the injury. I try to brush him off, but he pins me with a glacial glare unlike any expression I've seen on him so far.

My elemental is pissed.

"Hold still. You need to be healed."

"That can wait. Silas needs to conserve his magic for what I have in mind for Gibbons."

Gibbons' delectable screams of pain turn into sobs as Crypt casually tosses one of his eyeballs to the side. Baelfire bares his teeth again.

"I have several things in mind for this kiss-ass for trying to kill you. Why rush?"

"There's the spirit, lizard." Crypt grins in maniacal approval, pressing into the mage's broken arm so Gibbons shouts again. "Let's take it nice and slow so our girl can savor his screams."

Seeing the vengeful, twisted fury on their faces just for me makes my stomach flutter.

Like I said. I'm catching feelings.

"Ready?" Everett checks with Silas, who stands behind me with a necromantic healing spell already prepared. He's removed his winter gloves so his blackened fingertips are visible, which earns a gasp of horror from Gibbons.

"Necromancer!" the old caster croaks, sniveling as he tries again to free himself. "No, no, it can't be! H—how could the brightest student now be one of the damned, soulless—"

"Shut *up*," Baelfire snaps.

Everett finally pries the nevermelt from my shoulder while I try not to show pain. The moment it slips free and the blood begins gushing, Silas's spell sinks into my skin. It's the same prickling, unnatural sensation I've experienced countless times at the hands of the necromancers in the Nether, but somehow…more intimate.

Probably because of our bond.

Better? Silas asks in my head, his focus still on the arm he's healing.

I nod. *Let's hope you have enough magic left over for what comes next.*

Which is what, exactly?

I'm going to corrupt you further. Hope you don't mind.

He smirks and lightly kisses my brow just as he finishes the spell. My arm still aches, and my fingers are ice cold, but the worst of the damage is gone.

I once again crouch beside the interim headmaster. He's a bloody, one-eyed mess who glares like he wants to kill me.

"I have three questions for you."

His lips curl in disgust. "I'm not telling you anything. You are the prophesied doom of the mortal world, the scourge of all mortals! Wretched, nasty little horror—"

Crypt reaches down and breaks the mage's nose with one twist of his hand. "One more word from you that isn't an answer to my keeper's questions, and you'll be fodder for the wisps."

Gibbons makes a strangled sound, puffing air to try to blow off the blood. *"Fine!* Fine, I'll talk. I'll tell you anything you want if you let me go after!"

My nose wrinkles. Ally or foe, there's nothing worse than a person with no loyalty. "First question. How did you know what I am?"

"T—the Immortal Quintet figured it out. They sent out an official alert to legacies in high positions. We're all under orders to keep it from the humans to avoid mass panic."

Wise of them. "Are you still in contact with the Legacy Council?"

His gaze darts to Everett. "Yes. I've been in contact with Alaric Frost since the day his son returned to Everbound. He gave me a scrying brand to report back to him on everything."

Scrying brands are an ancient practice—a temporary magical marking within one's skin, similar to a tattoo, that allows communication no matter the distance. They're painful to acquire and never last longer than a year or two, but they're efficient.

Especially because they're also imbued with tracing spells. Which, in this case, was precisely what I was hoping for.

Everett doesn't look surprised to learn his father was spying on him, but he still glares at the mage. "Thanks for that."

"I promise it wasn't personal, Mr. Frost! He was only concerned for you."

Everett scoffs. "If you believed that, you have shit for brains."

The mage's face reddens. "He said you have exhibited alarming, family-shaming qualities ever since you left home early, and he was worried you would get mixed up in shameful dealings. And clearly, he was right! It is shocking that you, of all people, would *willingly* remain matched to this hellish, Undead corpse—"

Crypt grips Gibbons' broken nose between his knuckles and twists hard. "*Manners.*"

The mage yelps and struggles again. I sense a small pulse of magic from him, but clearly, he's tapped out.

That's fine. I don't need his magic. Just him, since he has that scrying brand on his body.

"Final question. Who did you tell that we're here?"

"Everyone," he says immediately. "The Legacy Council and the bounty hunters. T—they'll be here any moment."

I stare at him, watching his dilated pupils as sweat rolls over his brow. There's a slight twitch in his right eye, and his gaze keeps skipping elsewhere.

"You're lying. You haven't told anyone yet."

He spits more blood out of his mouth before swallowing hard. "No. No, all right? I sent a message to Alaric to let him know I have an emergency update regarding your whereabouts, but he must be preoccupied with the newest surge at the Nether. No one knows that you're here yet, but it's only a matter of time before the finest bounty hunters come to rain down hellfire upon—"

Baelfire's growl cuts him off, his voice more gravelly than usual. "Let me kill him now, my mate."

He doesn't usually refer to me like that. Not to mention, he seems far more bloodthirsty than usual. Either he *really* doesn't like this overly prying caster, or his dragon is once again making himself known.

I peer down at the seething, bloodied mage. "You have two options. Make me a blood oath of complete loyalty, and we'll leave you alive…or else we'll do this the fun way."

"A—a blood oath? I cannot!" Gibbons sputters. "There is no priest or priestess here to bless such a thing on behalf of the gods!"

I lean down to meet his one remaining eye better. "Here's a secret: you don't need them. Even a filthy, cursed abomination like me can make a binding blood oath. So, what'll it be? Will you swear your allegiance to me until your final breath, or does my quintet end you here and now?"

Gibbons shakes his head in terror, struggling hard again. "N—no! I gave you answers for my freedom! I only attacked you for the sake of the future of the mortal realm. H—how could you possibly justify killing me now that I cooperated? It's not right! You *know* it's not right! How could you do that to a respectable, old legacy like me?" He pouts his bloodied lips, trying to appear frail and pitiful.

I roll my eyes. "If you're hoping I'll have a moral conundrum, that's a grave mistake. Emphasis on *grave*. Besides, you'll be more useful to us dead."

Everett frowns. "But...how? He'll just be dead."

"Actually, he'll be a puppet once Silas uses the spell I can teach him."

Reanimation usually takes a few tries, but given how powerful Silas is as a caster in general, I have high hopes.

All four of my matches absorb that, and Everett covers his face. "Oh, dear gods. No. This is *way* too fucking dark, Oakley."

Such a baby. Besides, it's not like I'll make Silas do it if he doesn't want to. When I look at him, the fae's crimson gaze is unfocused far away, as if he's deep in thought.

I want to use him to throw the Legacy Quintet off our trail for a few more days, but not if it makes you uncomfortable, I tell him through our link. *Morally speaking, I know it's a bit—*

He scoffs. "As if that's an issue either one of us has. Give me a moment. I'm just trying to recall the correct spell. I'm certain that I read it somewhere."

Gibbons begins to scream and shout again, terrified of this new fate. The others glare down at him. Before I can decide how to end the problematic interim headmaster, Baelfire reaches down and snaps the mage's neck with an angry snarl.

It's so sudden and unexpected that even Crypt raises his brows. Silas jolts, gawking at the place above Gibbons' body. I've known enough necromancers to know he's staring at Gibbons' ghost.

The moment the body stops twitching, Baelfire grips his head, shaking it as if to clear it before he blinks in surprise at the dead interim headmaster.

"Whoa. Fuck, that's my bad."

"Are you seriously implying that was all your dragon just now?" Everett asks indignantly.

Bael glances at me, his golden gaze both apologetic and relieved, as if now he can think straight. "Honestly? My memory is a little spotty for the last few minutes. I mean, I remember wanting to kill him for hurting Maven, but…I didn't mean to actually *do* it. Feel a lot better, though."

Crypt releases the dead body with a sharp hiss as his markings light up.

"Damn it all," he mutters, standing and glowering in a random direction.

His markings are lighting up far more often. Is his curse getting worse, somehow?

Then it clicks.

Fuck. Of course, it's getting worse. Since two members of the Immortal Quintet are now dead, the Divide is weakening, which creates more turbulence in Limbo, which he has to deal with alone.

What will happen to the Nightmare Prince when only one member of the Immortal Quintet is left?

Unease washes over me. I frown up at Crypt, but when he sees it, he just offers a tight smile. "I'll be swift, darling. Hopefully, by the time I return, we'll have a new puppet to play with if Crane doesn't muck it up."

Silas does not respond as he continues staring at something only necromancers can see.

Crypt shrugs and kisses the top of my head before vanishing.

I grumble like a petulant child about him leaving. Now, on top of carefully enacting the next steps of my plan, I also need to figure out a way to keep Limbo from turning into perpetual warfare, or he'll have to pay the price for my gambit.

Everett brushes soothing, gentle fingers over the skin of my newly healed stab wound as he looks at Silas. "Well? If we're going to dive feet-first into the dark arts, let's just get it over with."

Silas continues to stare pale-faced at the place above Gibbons with wide eyes like he just saw…well, a ghost. I frown. Surely he's not this terrified of a specter? That seems unlike him.

Baelfire sighs. "Great, he's lost it again. Si? Hello, earth to Silas?"

"I…believe I just saw the reaper goddess," the fae finally manages, his voice hoarse.

Everett startles. "You what now?"

"Syntyche. She just reaped Gibbons in front of me. I only caught a glimpse of the cloak and scythe, but…" Silas breathes out, shuddering and rubbing his face. "That was acutely horrifying."

Interesting.

"None of the necromancers in the Nether ever saw Syntyche because, for whatever reason, the spirits there aren't reaped," I muse aloud.

Everett frowns. "If they aren't reaped, what happens to the ghosts?"

"They wander the Nether, looking for a way to pass into the Beyond. When I was young, I used to stay up late at night listening to their whispers. They would gather outside my window to weep and beg for a final resting place. Some of them haunted me for a while."

In fact, they followed me around constantly. It annoyed the necromancers that I could see the spirits until Dagon finally placed a powerful hex on me so that I could no longer perceive ghosts. My ghostly groupies allegedly moved on once they realized I couldn't hear or help them.

My guys stare at me until Baelfire sighs heavily. "We need to get you into therapy, Boo."

Weird take after I just shared one of my most nostalgic memories.

"Did everyone see ghosts in the Nether, or was it just you after you were turned into…you know?" Everett asks, brushing the frost off his fingertips.

I shrug, but the truth is it was just me—and I could always see ghosts, even well before they started experimenting on me. Lillian hadn't seemed surprised whenever I told her about the specters, but she told me not to mention them to anyone else.

Maybe she knew it would bother the necromancers.

Finally, Silas pulls his shoulders back and regards the corpse on the asphalt. Snow is falling lightly now, and the quiet peels of holiday music in the distance lend a somewhat eerie tone to this situation.

"All right. I remember the spell. Don't stand too close."

Everett backs the furthest away. We all watch as Silas begins softly chanting in Nether tongue. I feel the familiar prickling chill skitter over my arms when I hear him start the ritual to raise a corpse. I've heard it so many times that I could recite it in my sleep.

As Silas completes the ritual, his eyes darken entirely until no whites are left. His fingertips blacken where they're extended over Gibbons' dead body, which begins to twitch and spasm. A final wave of unearthly dread sweeps through the cold air before Silas staggers back.

Baelfire steadies him. "You good?"

Blood drips from Silas's nose. I frown at that sign of strain, but he wipes it away quickly and shrugs off the dragon shifter. "Let me go, you big lug."

Everett inhales sharply when Gibbons' body jolts. It twitches and flexes, slowly rising to its feet with its head still hanging at a broken angle. Finally, the bones in its neck pop into place, and we're left staring at a soulless Undead, staring at nothing with one pitch-black eye.

If any other necromancer raised it, it would try to eat us. Fortunately, the Undead are perfect puppets who won't harm the one who raised them or their perceived allies.

"Holy shit," Baelfire grunts. "That's fucking creepy."

Everett mutters a prayer to the god Koa, asking forgiveness for us for using this type of magic. "Yep, there goes my sleep tonight. What now?"

Reaching out, I tip Silas's face to examine it better in the dim light. His nose is still lightly bleeding, but his eyes have returned to normal.

I appreciate your concern for me, sangfluir, *but I'm perfectly fine.*

I arch a brow. *How can I know for sure? Can you lie telepathically?*

His gaze alights with curiosity. *Let's find out. Ask me an obvious question.*

All right. What am I?

The love of my life.

Oh, fuck.

I was not prepared for the intimate intensity in his beautiful ruby irises. And him dropping the L-word like that, completely straight-faced and unflinching?

My face feels warm. *All* of me feels warm.

I quickly drop this topic for another time and turn back to the reanimated corpse, clearing my throat. "It should be simple from here. Since Gibbons told Everett's father he had an update about us, it's only a matter of time before Alaric tries to contact Gibbons back."

Why are you so uncomfortable, blood blossom? Silas asks in fae inside my head, smirking as if he finds my brush-off amusing. *Is it because I mentioned love?*

Let's not use the L-word, I scowl through the bond.

Love? Don't tell me you're philophobic.

I pretend I don't hear him. "As an Undead, Gibbons can't talk now. When communication fails, Alaric will trace Gibbons' where-abouts using the scrying brand to get a new lead. All we need to do is send him on a wild goose chase to buy us more time."

The others nod, but Silas is laughing quietly now as he realizes how badly I want to avoid this particular discussion.

At least we know now that I cannot lie even through our bond, he muses. *You do know this is an inevitable conversation you'll need to have four times, right? Perhaps I should warn the others that you'll try to avoid any admittance of feelings—*

I focus on tuning him out until it feels like a door shuts between us in the bond, cutting off whatever he's saying. He laughs again.

Now that he's not tortured by voices and paranoia, is he going to tease me all the time?

Fucking miscreant.

Baelfire frowns, looking between Silas and me as he realizes he's missing something. "More time for what, Raincloud? We came here to wait for Silas to recover, so what's the plan now?"

Now, I need to get my hands on etherium. "Tomorrow morning, we'll leave to find another place to lay low until I find a way to contact the black market dealer I'm looking for. He's notoriously difficult to trace."

Everett studies me. "I have connections. They may know who you're looking for."

"Big fucking surprise that the *Frost* has shady connections," Bael scoffs. "I bet your family practically owns the black market."

"So what if they do? Connections come in handy."

The elemental turns back to me, trying to adjust my torn sweatshirt to better cover me. When that fails, he slips out of his bulky coat and wraps me in it. It's not warm coming straight from his body, but his soft mint scent clinging to it soothes me.

"Tracking the dealer can wait until tomorrow. Let's finish *this*—" Everett pulls a face at the motionless, one-eyed Undead. "So we can get back to our actual date."

His squeamishness about the Undead is too funny not to tease. "This *is* our actual date. So far, it's the best date I've ever been on. Maybe we should invite our Undead friend to join us."

"Gross. Stop it."

"Taking him home is the least we can do after raising him from the dead."

"*Stop.* You know it's freaking me out, Oakley," he grumbles.

"Is that a no to inviting him into bed? You could all have a fivesome while I watch."

Everett gags and throws his hands in the air, turning to stalk away. "That's it, you two deal with her. I'm going to go puke."

I burst into laughter, and then gasp when I'm immediately hauled up against Baelfire. He cradles me against his toasty-warm chest and nuzzles the side of my neck. I can feel his smile against my skin.

"Holy shit, I love your laugh. Just love everything about you."

Mayday, mayday—that word is being tossed around *way* too

fucking much tonight. It makes my chest tight, and my stomach twists into knots.

Again, I desperately try to ignore it and look over at Silas as I wrap my arms around Baelfire's neck.

"Send Gibbons to wait anywhere near the Divide in Maine."

"Why Maine?"

"That's where I originally entered the mortal realm when I left the Nether. The Legacy Council will piece that together, track Gibbons there, and assume I have a connection or an ally in that area. That should throw off the bounty hunters for a bit longer."

He nods and turns back to the Undead mage, instructing it in the Nether tongue. Although he doesn't speak it as fluently as the necromancers who experimented on me for years, I'm still surprised how much he picked up just from studying.

Meanwhile, Baelfire bundles me closer, kisses my cheek, and heads back toward the hotel. His singed cedar scent wraps around me, cozy and warm.

"All right, hellion. Let's find a scary movie for you to watch while we cuddle."

9

BAELFIRE

"They picked literally the dumbest place possible to hide," Everett huffs, making a face as the monster rips two more humans apart offscreen.

We found this old holiday-themed horror movie while scrolling through the channels. It's complete with cheesy acting, gratuitous amounts of fake gore, and a ridiculously fake monster chasing screaming humans and legacies around an abandoned mansion decked in lights and mistletoe.

It's exactly the kind of movie I'd usually make fun of, especially because of the thinly veiled humans-are-better-than-legacies shtick they have going.

But oh my *gods*, I can't focus on any of it with Maven in my lap like this. She smells insanely good, her subtle midnight scent wrapping around me when she brushes some of her dark hair out of her face. I want to lean down and lick her neck to see if I can taste this scent that drives me fucking nuts.

Or I could lick her pussy.

Damn it, I want to taste her so bad.

The only thing stopping me from carrying her back to one of the rooms and begging her to let me make her come until she passes out is the fact that she's actually enjoying this movie. She's dressed in the comfy pajamas I picked out for her—a tank top and shorts that barely reach her thighs, which means I can't stop staring at all of her exposed skin. She's not wearing a bra, and *fuck*, it's so hard to keep my hands off those gorgeous tits.

She's turned sideways, her feet in Everett's lap. Her dark gaze is pinned on the suite's TV. When a handful of the humans in the movie escape the mansion and race into the woods, she boos.

Everett side-eyes her, fighting a smile. "You're rooting for the monster, aren't you?"

"Of course I am. Everyone else in this movie is too stupid to live."

I bury my nose in the side of her neck again, my heart doing double time when her scent engulfs me. I can't get enough of it. My cock is stiff and has been for the last fifteen minutes, but Maven hasn't noticed since there's also a thick blanket in my lap acting as a buffer.

"You're so fucking cute, Boo," I rasp.

She gives me a stern look that makes my cock twitch, keeping her voice low enough that only I can hear her over the movie.

"If you keep calling me either of those things, I'll *actually* punish you."

Gods, yes. Please.

Holding her is doing wonders for me. It's keeping me in my own fucking head when the asshole living under my skin has been wrenching control from me over and over again today. We've had so much going on—First Placement ending in disaster, her and Silas mysteriously bonding, going on the run—that I've been waiting to find the right time to tell Maven that I've started blacking out for a couple of minutes at a time.

Because my dragon is figuring out how to take control of my *human* body.

This has never happened before. It's freaking me the hell out. So far, the asshole hasn't done anything horrible that I know of, and no one's noticed...at least, not until he killed Gibbons. Ending that annoying-ass mage seems to have quieted my dragon for the moment, but I'm still an anxious fucker as the movie ends and we watch the credits roll.

Maven yawns. "It was good until they killed the monster."

Without looking, I hear Silas wander out of one of the back rooms to store something in the hotel suite's fridge. He's been doing caster shit ever since we got back from dinner. When he moves to stand beside the couch, I catch a whiff of him.

He smells like that colorless herb Crypt found in the Divide. I catch his eye and nod, appreciative that he's still working on something for the next time my mate's shadow heart starts to hurt her.

Maven's gaze slips toward one of the suite windows, and her lips press together. It's a subtle expression since she's still wary of showing her feelings even around us, but it's clear that she's worried about her psychotic incubus.

I pick up the remote and flip through the channels to distract her. "Should we look for something else to watch, or is it finally Sit-On-My-Face-O'Clock?"

That does the trick. Maven starts to say something quippy when the TV settles on a news channel that shuts us all up.

"—anonymous resource, a former employee of the Immortal Quintet, reported that the Legacy Council has now launched a manhunt for a legacy named Maven Oakley," an anchorwoman is reporting, standing outside of Everbound University with the castle as a background in the distance. My pulse jumps at the mention of my mate's name. "While we have no record, photos, or footage of this legacy, here is the physical description we were given of her."

Everett swears, glowering at the screen as she rattles off a description.

I don't know which idiot went to the human media to spill about Maven—but when the anchor's description makes her sound like some plain, unpleasant frump, I decide I'll let my dragon kill the leak if we get to hunt them down.

"It remains unclear exactly why this manhunt has been launched, but the legacies' premier mandatory graduate school, Everbound University, is now completely abandoned as we humans are left to wonder what in the world is going on. Sources in Halfton, the town closest to Everbound, have reported constant comings and going of special teams sent in by the Legacy Council, which has refused to officially comment on this situation or the whereabouts of the Immortal Quintet. Another anonymous source claims that a bloody massacre of epic proportions took place at this legacy hub of learning, leaving no one behind for the Legacy Council's response team to question."

"An exaggerated report, I'm sure," Silas muses.

Maven shakes her head but doesn't explain.

The news anchor goes on. "The lack of response from the legacy government has greatly alarmed the president and the secretary of defense as we reach a crisis level of surges near the Divide. Local governments have ordered multiple evacuations along the East Coast, so unfortunately, many families will spend the holidays in emergency aid stations and hotels this year. In addition, countless frantic reports have been received declaring the emergence of a new kind of shadow fiend. No video or photo evidence has been submitted yet. Still, reports indicate that this faceless new threat causes terrifying hallucinations and induces extreme levels of panic —so much so that it quite literally leaves victims paralyzed from fear. Hospitalizations from this unknown menace are occurring at a rapid rate throughout South Carolina and Tennessee—"

I abruptly notice how still Maven has gone. She's got that same poker face she puts on whenever she's hiding a strong reaction to something.

"Hey. You okay, Boo?" I ask.

She moves out of my lap to stand as the news anchor signs off. Everett takes the remote from me and turns off the TV, standing as he gauges Maven's reaction.

"If you're worried about the humans knowing your name now—"

She shakes her head but is still clammed up.

"Is this about the new threat?" I ask, gently pulling her closer so I can wrap my arms around her hips and look up at her. "I'm guessing you know what it is?"

Maven seems to debate what to say before rubbing her face. "There are a few shadow fiends that could cause that. I have a call to make. I'll be right back."

"Who are you calling?" Everett asks.

"The demon I mentioned. Hopefully, he'll answer this time. If not, I'll still call Kenzie and let her know we're leaving. She threatened to tell me explicit details of her past sex life if she doesn't get regular updates to let her know I'm still alive."

She starts to leave and then pauses, glancing at Silas. "Heal Crypt."

He nods. "When he returns—"

"He's been here for a while," she mutters before slipping into the room on the right.

It's still trippy as fuck that she can sense him in Limbo. For a second, I wonder why he's staying unseen, and then I remember how upset Maven was the last time he came back injured.

On cue, the moment she's out of the room, Crypt appears collapsed on the other couch with a soft wheeze.

Damn, that's a lot of blood. He's covered in so many tiny lacerations, his clothing torn to shreds, that he looks more like Swiss cheese than a powerful incubus. He's missing most of an eye, and one of his arms is seriously fucked up. I'm pretty sure that's a bone sticking out of it.

No wonder he was staying out of sight.

Crypt drops his head back over the armrest, grimacing as his markings light up briefly. His voice is strained but sarcastic.

"While all this staring is overwhelmingly helpful, either listen to our keeper and heal me or fuck off."

"What the hell happened to you?" Everett gawks.

Crypt tries to flip him off but ends up coughing hoarsely, gritting his teeth. Incubi are supposed to heal as fast as shifters, but since his body isn't healing, it must mean he needs to feed ASAP.

I overheard Crypt and Maven talking. I know he's basically in charge of Limbo. The others don't know, but they should—we might not like each other, but we're still a quintet.

I hesitate, not sure if I should spill on his curse. Ever since we were young, I've always hated Crypt DeLune. He was cruel and way too much like a full-blooded monster. He had no empathy, emotions, or any redeeming qualities.

At least, that's what I'd thought.

Now I know he was watching out for me in his own fucked-up way. He's still a creep, but...I owe him. Hell, I can even say I respect him. Partly for the way he had my back before I knew I needed it, but mostly because it's clear he would do anything for Maven.

We all would, and we all know it. Which is why Silas doesn't say a word as he starts patching up the incubus he's spent years hating far more than I ever did.

As expected, Everett doesn't let Crypt off easily. "Where did you go?"

"Caroling."

"Spit it the fuck out, DeLune," the elemental demands.

"You will mind your tone with me."

That prick is going to fight this tooth and nail, but it's time to clear the air.

"He went to deal with shit happening in Limbo. That's his curse. He's the steward of the dream realm, so he has to deal with wisps and shades before they can affect the mortal plane of existence," I explain.

Crypt levels me with a murderous look. At least, he tries. It misses some of its heat because the fucker is missing an eye, and he's in no condition to try picking a fight with me.

"Breathe one more word, Decimus, and—"

"Yeah, yeah, I know. You'll give me bad dreams, snack on my madness, tie my organs into a bow, blah, blah, blah. Threaten me all you fucking want, but they need to know because obviously, your curse is getting shittier just like the rest of ours."

I recap what I learned about Crypt's curse. Silas continues to heal him with blood magic, pricking his fingers periodically as he works. When I'm done, the incubus glowers at nothing in particular, and the others are quiet.

Everett shuffles, rubbing the back of his neck. "If it's getting worse as the Divide weakens…I mean, if there's a way we could help—"

"Offering to let me feed you three to the shades, are you?" Crypt's voice is dark and angry. "I was fantasizing about doing just that anyway."

"At least now we all know one another's curses," Silas mutters, wiping his bloody hands off on Crypt's shredded sweatshirt. "Or rather, your three remaining curses. It's good to know yours doesn't put Maven at risk like Everett's."

Everett glances down the hall. I can faintly overhear Maven in the other room, patiently waiting for her friend to finish a long rant about awkward family dinners.

I consider what Silas said for a long moment before sighing. "You know what? All curses suck ass, but Snowflake's actually could end up taking my mate away from me. Then I'd have to roast him alive, only it would be a million times less enjoyable. So…maybe we should try to get him bonded to her next."

Everett blinks at me in surprise, his pale blue eyes guarded. "Why would you suggest that? What's in it for you?"

"Maven's safety," Crypt mutters, closing his eyes. Which is good because his missing one is finally trying to regenerate at a snail's pace, and it was fucking nauseating to look at. "In other words, the only thing that really matters."

We all nod in agreement.

I sigh. "All right. Theory-sharing time."

No one says shit.

"Stalker Boy, you go first," I suggest.

Crypt peeks his nasty semi-healed eyeball at me. "Personally, I think it's because of something called *gohf.*"

"Gohf?"

"Yes. As in, *gohfuck yourself*, you loose-lipped lizard.*"

I rub my face. "Motherfucker, I swear—"

"Here's my theory," Everett interrupts, rubbing frost off his fingertips. "I think Maven might be a saint."

I burst into laughter. "Yeah, you've obviously never been with our Angel of Death in bed because, let me tell you, there is nothing saintly about the way she takes control. *Gods,* she is so fucking hot when she gets all dominant."

I adjust my semi as I try to push the mouthwatering image of Maven taking my cock for the first time out of my head.

Everett's cheekbones darken a few shades, but he shakes his head. "Will you shut up and focus? What I *meant* is I think she's a literal saint. Someone selected by one of the gods as a baby to work miracles on their behalf. Think about it—only the gods can bind legacy hearts together, so they must have had a hand in this. They blessed Maven and Silas's bond. Not to mention, Maven is…kind of in my personal prophecy. I think she was selected as a saint by Arati."

That's the queen of Paradise and the goddess of a bunch of shit like passion, fire, love, warfare…combat.

And it's true that my mate really fucking loves a good fight.

"It's a valid theory," Silas admits, finally stepping away from Crypt.

Crypt hums. "Or she bonded with Silas because he used a large amount of his power on her. Perhaps there is something in our abilities which links us to her."

I frown. "You chow down on her dreams all the time. Wouldn't you have bonded with her already with that logic?"

"I haven't permanently marked her psyche as that of my muse. Yet," he tacks on softly, flexing his now-healed arm. "The ceremony takes great power, which may trigger the bond. I plan on asking her permission soon."

In a way, his theory also seems reasonable. But it's way too complicated.

"You're all overthinking it," I shrug confidently. "Pretty sure Maven bonded with Silas first because he's the one who technically fucked her first—and he's been the most intimate with her overall."

Silas rolls his eyes. "Your theory centers around sex. No surprise there." He paused, considering. "Although...perhaps it *is* that simple."

"Let's test that theory first," the Nightmare Prince agrees, finally sitting up and arching his brows at Everett.

The ice elemental turns bright red as we all smirk at him expectantly.

"Absolutely fucking not. I'm not having sex with Maven just to try to break my curse. That is not how it's happening."

"It's not about breaking your curse for *you*, dickhead. This isn't about you—it's about keeping her safe since you're clearly already whipped like the rest of us," I point out. "What if your cockblock curse catches up tomorrow, and we lose her just like that?" I snap my fingers to illustrate my point. "None of us know if a metaphysical killing curse would be permanent on her. How the fuck are you going to live with yourself if it is?"

He flinches, shoulders slumping as he looks away. "Believe me, it's all I've been able to think about. Stupid curse is taking its time, though. It's supposed to kill anyone I fall in love with, and... honestly, I'm pretty sure I fell for her the second I saw her on that stage."

I get it. I was ready to burn the world for my mate, even when I only knew her scent.

Crypt tests his recovering eye. "Hearing you get sappy makes me wish the shades finished me off. If we're testing this theory first, don't fuck it up. Maven deserves no less than unparalleled pleasure after all she's been through, so make that your priority."

"I know that," Everett snaps.

"Don't rush things," I add. "And if you're having trouble finding her clit, try—"

"Will you shut up already?" the red-faced professor scowls. "Just because I haven't participated doesn't mean I haven't seen plenty of sex. My first year as a student at Everbound was spent getting invited to every fucking orgy. I did a lot of watching and learning."

"Perv," I joke.

He shoots me a scathing look. "I wonder if Maven knows how many of those you've jumped dick-first into, Fuck Boy."

It's my turn to flinch, remembering Maven mentioning other girls rubbing my past in her face. Gods, I was a full-blown idiot before I met her.

Maybe I still am, but at least I'm a loyal idiot.

"Watching and doing are two separate things, Frost," Crypt drawls. "Try biting her nipples. Our girl likes a bit of pain to temper her pleasure."

Everett again starts to protest this unsolicited coaching, but Silas interrupts him.

"Whatever you do, do *not* edge her. Take it from me, she will loathe it and possibly try to leave."

"I didn't ask for advice," Everett seethes, going to the suite's kitchen to dig a bottle of water out of the fridge. He uncaps it and then pauses, considering. "She really doesn't like edging?"

"Hates it," Silas confirms.

"Unless she's fast asleep," Crypt adds. When we all turn to make various faces at him for dropping that little nugget of too much information, he smirks. "Oh, please. As if you lot have any pearls left to clutch, when Crane and Frost would gladly watch, and Decimus would happily get on his knees to beg our girl for far less."

I mean...he's not wrong. I fucking love being on my knees for Maven.

Everett mutters that he didn't need to know *that* before taking a sip of water and frowning. "She's still struggling with physical touch, even if she won't admit it. What helps with that?"

"She needs to go at her pace," Silas says. "If she needs a moment, she'll tell you. Believe me, Maven will be the one calling the shots."

"And you'll love it. My mate's absolutely fucking perfect like that," I sigh.

"Agreed, dragon," Crypt nods, gently poking at his now-healed eye.

After a few moments of silence, I see that Everett looks stuck in his head as he takes another painfully slow sip from the water bottle.

He used to do this when we were little, too—begin to overthink shit until he freezes up. The poor fucker will be here for the next three to five business days unless someone snaps him out of it.

"You know what? Just shrimp it up because it's not like you'll ever outshine me in the bedroom anyway, Popsicle Prick," I tell him cheerfully. Then I frown, a thought crossing my mind. "Hold up. Is your jizz cold? Like a sperm Icee?"

That does the trick. Everett does a spit take, choking like he's about to die.

Silas stares at me, appalled. "What the fuck is wrong with you?"

"I'm just saying, if it is...ice cream is Maven's favorite. She has a thing for frozen treats, meaning he might have an unfair advantage there. So if he's firing little Frosties—"

"Shut up. Don't talk to me again tonight, you fucking freak," Everett grumbles, throwing the open water bottle at me. "And never bring up my...*that* again. Ever. Ugh."

I call after him as he storms toward the second bedroom. "We're gonna be seeing each other's dicks the rest of our lives. Get over it before you make it weird for everyone."

He slams the door.

Silas rubs his temple. "You've already made it weird for everyone, Bael. So incredibly fucking weird."

He leaves, too, and I glance at Crypt on the couch. He shrugs one shoulder.

"I thought it was a perfectly reasonable question."

Fuck. Seriously? I'm only in agreement with *Crypt* of all people?

Maybe my curse is fucking up my head more than I realized.

10

MAVEN

I SIT CRISSCROSS on the bed in one of the suite bedrooms, observing my quintet argue about who will sleep in the bed with me, who's in the other room, and who's sleeping on the couch. Silas insists that newlybounds deserve closeness and privacy, which earns him a rough shove from Baelfire, who snaps that Silas doesn't need to rub it in. Everett says there isn't enough space for them both without crowding me on one king bed and calls them both dickheads.

I heard the shower come on earlier, but Crypt is in this room now, still unseen in Limbo. Silas said he healed the worst of any injuries, but we all need to sleep so my incubus can feed on my dreams and recuperate faster. I'm not thrilled that I can't see with my own two eyes that he's one piece, but I at least trust Silas's healing abilities.

"You're too damn hot!" Everett snaps back at something Baelfire said.

"Weird time to hit on me, Snowflake, but tell me something I don't know."

"Quit being an idiot. I'm saying our poor keeper is going to swelter to death if you try to squash her all night long, you lumbering space heater. And if we don't watch Silas, he's going to make a snack out of her—"

"How ironic that *you* are insulting *my* control," Silas scoffs, gesturing toward Everett's frost-covered hands. "How is an obviously undisciplined ability like yours lauded so highly, anyway? It's downright bizarre."

Their arguing continues. I usually enjoy listening to a good verbal sparring match, but it's time to wrap this up so we can sleep and Crypt can feed.

"While it's flattering that you three feel so strongly about who gets to lay unconscious next to me for the next six to seven hours," I begin, "I think we should—"

My voice gives out when agony explodes in the center of my chest, so unexpected and brutal that I'm left grasping at my chest as my head spins. Shouts surround me before I'm suddenly cradled in Baelfire's warm arms—an intentional move since my body temperature is plummeting as everything grows blurry.

Keep breathing, sangfluir. *I'll be right back*, Silas's voice echoes hurriedly in my head.

Everett tests my temperature, brushing my hair off my face while Silas disappears from the room. He returns with a vial full of liquid, but I see another goddamned needle in his hand.

"Don't—needle—" I manage to choke out. My chest squeezes painfully as my brain begins to fog.

Don't stick me with that fucking needle, I try again telepathically.

We have to try this, Maven. I promise you won't feel it.

My harsh attempts to breathe echo in my ears as I clench my teeth against the pain while he rushes to get the injection ready. My jaw grinds so hard I think my teeth will break.

Gods, the pain is so much worse than usual. It feels almost as excruciating as the moment Amadeus ripped my heart out five years ago.

Crypt's finger pries apart my teeth, slipping between my molars. I don't know when he appeared, but his violet gaze traps me. "Bite down, love. Use me for the pain."

I do, but I'm embarrassed when a soft sob still escapes. My vision cuts out. For a moment, everything starts fading as the agony overtakes me—but then warmth blooms in my chest. Silas whispers a necromantic charm and bit by bit, my eyesight gradually clears. I can hear my rattling breaths again.

The pain lingers in my chest, but it's like this episode has decided to retreat. The hyperventilating slows as my eyelids grow heavy.

Holy shit. Silas's elixir works.

"Did you really have to inject it there?" Everett asks roughly after a long, quiet moment.

"An intracardiac injection is the fastest solution." Relief is written over Silas's features as he gently removes the needle from my chest so I don't even feel it. "I wasn't certain if it would work with her shadow heart, but…"

Baelfire adjusts me in his arms, trying to warm up exposed skin. "Fuck. Just…fuck. You scared the shit out of us—and damn it, you're *freezing*. Is the pain gone, baby?"

My body feels heavy. I start to speak but end up nodding because I'm half worried another sob will escape if I open my mouth, and I've already been far too fucking weak for one night.

I taste the tang of blood. My tired, post-episode brain can't piece together why until Crypt carefully removes his finger from my mouth. He quirks a small smile down at me.

"There she is. Lay her down, Decimus. Our girl is dead tired."

I snort softly, my voice a scratchy rasp. "Dead tired. Nice one."

They all roll their eyes at my loopy humor, but I can't keep my own eyelids from slipping shut. Baelfire gingerly tucks me into the middle of the king bed while Everett hovers nearby, fussing over me. Silas and Crypt are quietly discussing getting more of the colorless plant—but they also haven't stopped watching me, as if they expect me to give up the ghost any second.

"I'm good now," I insist.

"Unless there's a delayed adverse reaction," Silas frowns. "We need to watch over you just to be sure."

"You need sleep. Crypt doesn't. He can keep watch and feed on my dreams while he heals."

Silas is reticent about the idea but finally slips into bed beside me, curling an arm around my middle and kissing my neck. As soon as we're touching, I realize how badly I needed to be close to my bound match. This casual intimacy that once terrified me now soothes something deep inside me.

It just feels right.

Baelfire slips in on the other side, resting my hand on his chest so I can feel his soothing heartbeat. It's crowded enough in this bed that it might've triggered the remains of my haphephobia if I wasn't so drained. Together, their combined warmth lulls me to sleep.

I'm vaguely aware of Crypt's alluringly dark, ever-watchful presence in my dreams as he ensures I sleep deeply. Peacefully.

Until sleep evaporates completely when my senses sharpen to needle points like they always do whenever a shadow fiend is near.

Except I know this one.

It's *him*.

My eyes snap open. I bolt upright, my pulse pounding. Ignoring Baelfire's sleepy grumble of confusion and Crypt emerging from Limbo with a questioning frown, I bolt out of bed to turn on the lights in the room.

Everett startles awake from where he dozed off in the room's cushioned wingbat chair. He's immediately on his feet. "What's going on?"

"We're leaving. *Now*. Get dressed so I can transport us," I tell my quintet, flipping on the extra bedside lamps just to be safe and the light in the small closet.

"You're still recovering from your almost-episode," Silas protests, his dark curls mussed from sleep as he throws his legs over the side of the bed. "The transportation spell will be too taxing—"

"I know my limits. I'll handle it. *Get moving*."

When shadows linger in one corner of the room, I summon a weak, basic common magic spell to dispel them—but I can't keep using magic when this next transportation spell will burn up so much of the life forces I've taken recently.

I just have to make sure I don't dip into Somnus's life force…but honestly, if that's what it takes to get away from *him*, so fucking be it.

My matches share a shocked look in reaction to my apparent state of panic before they launch into a blind rush to get dressed—except for Crypt, who abruptly appears at my side.

"Darling? Tell me what's—"

He cuts off sharply, whipping around as he steps protectively in front of me, his pale swirling markings lighting up. Outside the window of this fourth-story suite bedroom, I glimpse a dark mass moving in the starless night before it vanishes.

I suppose it's not surprising that the madness-inducing Nightmare Prince can sense a fellow fear-wielding being. My nerves begin to itch as they always have around this fiend.

Damn it.

I'm a fucking idiot. I should have transported us the moment I heard that news report.

Baelfire reaches for the bedroom door handle as if he's going to grab something from another room. I cover the handle quickly to stop him.

"You can't go out there."

"A lot of our shit is in the other room, Boo. Clothes, food, cash—"

I shake my head. "All replaceable."

"What's going on?" he demands.

The lights flicker, and for that small moment, I swear I have a heart attack despite the fact that I don't have an actual fucking heart.

"Silas, cast an illumination spell. Now. One that leaves absolutely no trace of shadows in this room," I instruct quickly.

Why? he asks telepathically, already pulling out his bleeding crystal and pricking his finger.

"He moves through darkness, even the slightest bit. He can't be in any well-lit space," I explain, slipping on the leather gloves I discarded earlier. Grabbing Pierce and the burner phone from the bedside table and stepping into my boots without lacing them up, I turn to shove a chair aside so I'll have enough space for the transportation spell.

"He? He who?" Everett asks, frost crawling past his elbows as the temperature in this room starts to drop in accordance with his emotions.

Something scratches softly at the door, and a chorus of hair-raising whispers rises from somewhere in the hallway.

They all sound like *him* gone wrong.

"Maven, Maven, sweetest raven." The taunt grows angry. *"Remember our game of finder's keepers?"*

That voice sends that too-familiar prickle of apprehension throughout my body. As I always used to, I slow my breathing and repeat my mantra to myself.

I am nothing but deadly calm. I feel nothing.

Sangfluir? Silas's voice demands in reply to my thoughts, concern permeating his tone.

Baelfire's eyes shift to that of a dragon's as he growls, "How the hell does it know your name?"

There's a loud crash elsewhere in the suite, and the lights flicker once more. The moment they go out completely, red light fills the space as Silas's illumination spell takes hold. The metaphorical skeletal hand gripping my throat releases, and I immediately recite the words for the transportation spell.

"Hold on to me," I demand as the scratching outside the door turns into a pounding, and his whispers intensify into shrieks like howling wind.

All four of my matches immediately touch my arm, shoulder, and neck—in Baelfire's case, his arms are wrapped around me like he wants to be a shield.

Somewhere far in the distance of the dark night, a woman's bloodcurdling scream splits the air before cutting off—and then the bedroom's window shatters as a decapitated woman's body is flung through it with brute force.

11

MAVEN

ONE MOMENT, we're being pelted by shards of broken glass, and then the spell kicks in, and the world turns inside out. When the transportation spell ends, we're standing in the falling snow, surrounded by deep snowdrifts, thick, white-frosted pine trees, and gentle moonlight.

Baelfire swears and picks a shard of glass out of his quickly-healing shoulder before tipping my face to look up at him. Those amber eyes scan me for signs of harm before turning hard, unyielding.

"Maven. What the motherfucking hell was that thing?"

"A wraith."

Exhaustion trickles into my veins from that transportation spell, but I glance up at the stars visible overhead through all the pine trees. I'm guessing it's close to one in the morning here in Washington. This is where Lillian lived many years ago, and she talked about it often.

Silas pockets his bleeding crystal, cleaning the blood off his fingers with his tongue, which happens to be *very* fucking distracting.

"We've learned about wraiths. They are faceless, silhouette-like figures that feed on fear and can only be killed with blessed bone weapons. Otherwise, they're known to be harmless compared to other shadow fiends since they are completely intangible. Are you sure that wasn't something else?"

"Nope. It was a fucking wraith. He just has some extra bells and whistles, thanks to the necromancers. And he's very tangible."

Not to mention, far stronger than other wraiths and completely out of control. Amadeus wouldn't have sent him—he must have broken free of the Divide the moment he realized it was weak enough to go after me.

After all, that wraith has developed an addiction to the taste of my fear.

I start moving in the direction I think we need to go, but Everett gently stops me with a hand on my waist.

"You keep saying *he*. You were terrified back there. Who was that, Oakley? Tell us."

All four of my matches are staring me down. They clearly have no intention of letting this go.

I'd rather swallow broken glass than tell them this, but they deserve to know.

"That was Gideon," I admit.

It's comedic how all their mouths drop open at the same time.

"*What?*" Baelfire and Silas roar in sync. All of Crypt's markings light up as unadulterated murder flashes across his handsome features, and Everett swears profusely.

"You said that sick motherfucker was ripped apart," Baelfire says furiously, blue fire flickering under his skin as his temper rises. The snowdrift we're standing in is melting quickly around him. I take a small step back since I am notoriously not fireproof.

"He was. By the king of the Undead, who rarely lets any of his subjects have a truly permanent death." I pause, considering how to explain it. "When I became the *telum*, they didn't stop experimenting on me. The same went for Gideon. Amadeus wanted to know if a human could be brought back as a wraith with its memories intact. He wanted to imbue it with more power. After a year or so, he succeeded, and the wraith who was once Gideon was incorporated into my training."

Silas's jaw clenches, a muscle jumping in his cheek. "Define *incorporated*."

It's impossible to forget the times I was forced to run through the monster-filled forests in Amadeus's kingdom, fear thick as tar pumping painfully hard through my veins as I could sense *him* hunting me. There is no way to kill a wraith without blessed bone, a substance that doesn't exist in the Nether due to its lack of priests, prophets, or anything else to do with the gods.

Amadeus called it fear endurance testing. He said for me to be a worthy *telum*, my pain and fear tolerance levels needed to be impenetrable.

I developed a tolerance for physical pain that surpassed his expectations.

Fear, on the other hand?

There is no such thing as true fear tolerance. Once you learn to function through one phobia, there is another, and another, and another. There is no fucking comparison between physical and psychological agony. I would accept a thousand more tortures before I let Gideon assault my mind again.

I can't let that wraith break my quintet like he did me. I need to make sure he doesn't get anywhere near them again.

Where is your beautiful mind, sangfluir? Silas asks in my head.

I realize I've tuned out, so lost to my dark memories that they seem to have let the subject go, which is an unexpected win. Crypt has vanished, and Baelfire is checking his cell phone, which he must have managed to grab from the room before we left. Everett is doing his best not to come near me since the cold is already making me shiver, but he's still watching me with a soft, sad blue gaze like he can see the pain in my past.

Silas moves to wrap me in his arms, but I step back from him.

"Wait. Let me get myself under control—"

"No." His scarlet irises are unbearably gentle as he steps closer, reaching for me again. "I don't want you under control, Maven. No version of you or your emotions will burden me. *Sanguis a' sruthadh unus gh'a, tha sinn unum mar,"* he murmurs in fae.

It's an old fae adage meaning, *"Our blood flows as one love, so let us be one."*

He wraps me in his strong embrace, saying nothing as I shut my eyes and try to re-compartmentalize shit from my past.

Silas just holds me through it, his slight spiced bourbon fragrance subtle but comforting.

And there it is again. That soft, vulnerable, painfully sweet emotion that makes my stomach flip and my hands feel suddenly sweaty in the gloves. I finally can't take any more and pull away—and thank the fucking universe, that's the exact time that Baelfire turns his phone around to share the map he has pulled up.

"Okay, cutie pie. Crypt went to scout, but we're right here—"

His phone is on silent, but the map on the screen abruptly switches to show that "Mama Dragon" is calling before he swipes something on the screen to get rid of it. He goes on with a sigh.

"We're about six miles from some tiny-ass town called Tall Pine, Washington. Pretty damn rural. Actually, I'm not sure this even counts as a town. More like a municipality with a gas station that doubles as the local market."

"Is there a hotel?" Everett asks.

"There's a place called Auntie Ethel's Finest Motel and Grill. Pretty sure they'll let us use their old outhouse if you say please with sugar on top without turning your snobby-as-fuck Frost nose up at them."

"Outhouse? Tell me you're kidding. There is no way in hell I am ever stepping foot in an outhouse that *you* have access to, you dragon-sized piece of shit."

I sense Crypt just before he appears directly beside me, gently dusting snow off my hair and shoulders and wrapping me in a surprisingly luxurious plaid throw blanket. He stole this, too.

He's thoughtful like that.

"I found an uninhabited cabin at the edge of the little human town. It seems a decent enough place to lay low, so long as

Douglas doesn't track the transportation spell we just used," he murmurs.

Shit. I forgot about Douglas.

Part of me wouldn't mind if the bounty hunters caught up. It's been days since I was in a good fight.

Still, we're short on time. The longer it takes me to find etherium, the longer it will be before I can hunt down and kill the next member of the Immortal Quintet.

Not to mention the ticking clock Amadeus has set for each of my "tasks." If I'm taking out the Immortal Quintet too slow for his liking, he'll begin threatening Lillian and the humans again.

"Even though we won't be here long, we'll need a powerful concealment spell," I say, turning to trek in the direction we need to go. "If I don't reach that demon soon, we'll track down my next lead in Argentina."

Everett sighs as he walks along beside me. It's bitterly cold in these woods, but the blue moonlight lends an uncanny glow to this wintry, barren scene, making it both chilling and beautiful. My ice elemental fits right in, seeming utterly oblivious to how fucking cold it is.

"I know you said demons are useful, but can we please try my connections first?"

"Depends. Are your connections legacies who will turn around and report us to the council?"

"They're black market dealers. Of course, they won't go to the council—that would endanger their business."

"Think, Frost. What need would they have for any more business if they got the bounty on Maven's head?" Crypt drawls. "Your father has clearly pitched in loads for the reward money. Anyone who turns on us will live like the gods."

"You mean like vain, overhyped, apathetic assholes?" I clarify.

Call me bitter. It's true.

Crypt bursts into laughter, but Everett shoots me a disapproving frown. For an ice elemental, he's absurdly hot when he's scolding.

"Don't blaspheme."

"But it's such fun."

"Oakley, I'm being serious. I want to help you get whatever you need from the black market, and the people I know are trustworthy in their own way." He pauses, frowning as the perfectly intact snowflakes on his hair and skin glisten in the moonlight. "By the way, what *are* you trying to get?"

I wrap the blanket tighter around myself, walking around a taller snowdrift. "Etherium."

"Isn't that like…glass from Paradise?" Baelfire asks.

"You've heard of it?"

He shrugs. "My caster dad, Ivan, loves to study rare magical shit. He's mentioned etherium once or twice but said that substance is always confiscated by the Legacy Council as soon as it turns up, so he hasn't gotten to learn much about it."

I nod. "The dealer I need to contact is notoriously elusive. It's said he has a significant stash, but otherwise, everyone is incredibly tight-lipped about him."

I'm going to loosen Melchom's lips, one way or another.

We walk silently for a moment, and then Everett huffs grouchily. "At this rate, our keeper will wind up with frostbite. It's far too fucking cold for her out here."

"If only we had an oversized fire-breathing egomaniac around to keep her warm," Crypt muses, feigning shock when he turns to spot Baelfire. "Oh, wait."

Bael glances down at my snow-covered boots and promptly scoops me up. "On it. I'll keep her nice and toasty."

"Nope, I'm walking," I say firmly. "My feet are fine. Carrying me is overkill."

"But your cute little toes are cold."

"Boo fucking hoo for them. Put me down, Baelfire."

He tips his head from side to side, debating. "Mmm, nah. I'm carrying your sweet ass all the way there. That way, when we go back to acting all monogamous around the humans, they'll figure *I'm* your man, and Snowflake will just have to fucking deal with it."

Gods. This dragon is something else. I fight a smile as Everett looks heavenward like he's supplicating the heavens for patience.

It's not that I mind being in Baelfire's warm, deliciously corded arms—but even with shifter strength and endurance, he'll be pushing himself harder than necessary, carrying me six fucking miles in deep snow, and we're already poorly rested. Not to mention, I don't know if my haphephobia will rear its ugly head out of nowhere.

So I'm going to walk my own ass into Tall Pine.

"Last warning. Put me down."

He flashes a bright, flirtatious smile and dips his head to kiss along my jaw, sending pleasurable tingles over my arms and legs. "Yeah? Or what, hellion?"

"Or I'll make you."

When he ignores me and licks the crook of my neck, where shifters mark their mates, I jolt in surprise and immediately twist his nipple through his athletic shirt as hard as possible. He yelps and loosens his arms, so I slip down easily to escape.

I adjust the blanket again, pretending like my neck doesn't feel warm—but it does. Gods, they all affect me way too fucking much when they get flirtatious.

"So cute, yet so mean," Bael sighs dramatically, but the way he leans down to kiss the top of my head as we start walking tells me his ego is as unharmed as ever.

"You four had plenty of warning on that front," I point out with a smirk.

"Touché."

12

EVERETT

I SLIP inside through the front door of the tiny cabin, adjusting the paper bags in my arms so I can force the door shut against the pressure of the howling wind.

The shit weather outside tonight is a sharp contrast against the cheery holiday music playing from Baelfire's phone in the combined kitchen and living room area. Baelfire is brushing snow off a short blue spruce tree he just brought in. Festive holiday-toned fae lights twinkle around the windows and above the fireplace, which is crackling with blue fire.

I squint. "How the hell did you make the fire blue without shifting into a dragon to light it?"

"Trade secret," Bael grunts, wandering into the little kitchen to check something baking in the ancient-looking oven.

With how hectic things have been since First Placement, we almost lost track of what day tomorrow is. We've been in Tall Pine for nearly two days, and Baelfire wasn't shitting us when he said this town didn't have much.

Which means it was really fucking hard to find decent gifts for Maven for Starfall Eve.

Still, I think I managed.

Since arriving here, we've slowly recovered from recent events under the thick cloaking spell Maven and Silas put up on this little cabin. Our quintet has spent most of the last thirty-odd hours sleeping or fucking.

I mean—I'm not having sex.

Obviously.

But it's been the only thing I've thought about ever since the others gave me unsolicited advice and insisted it may keep Maven safe from my curse.

To make things a hundred times worse, I walked in on Maven sitting on Baelfire's face in bed this morning. She was completely naked, leaning forward to tease his cock while his muffled moaning made him sound like a very happily dying man.

Now, I can't stop fantasizing about being in his place.

Last night, she was with Silas—and Crypt did *something* with her in the shower this morning. I know because I overheard her pretty little gasps as she came.

They all keep wringing those fucking *perfect* sounds out of her.

It's like listening to a heaven just out of reach.

I don't mind listening. Or watching. In fact, I can't seem to get enough of seeing my keeper come undone if I happen to be in the same room—which keeps happening because these assholes are intentional about when and where they pounce on her. They're trying to drive home their point that I should be trying to bond with her.

All day, I've been flushed and distracted.

Gods above, I'm barely holding it together through how much I want her.

What if the others are right, and the best way to protect her is by trying to bond with her as soon as fucking possible?

But wait. What if I finally get to worship Maven, and that finally triggers my curse?

Or—shit, what if there is literally *nothing* I can do to protect my keeper? What if I'm still risking everything I've ever wanted just being here with her?

My head hurts.

"Careful, Frosty. I hear that if snowmen stand by the fireplace too long, they melt," Baelfire snarks, picking another holiday song on his playlist.

I blink, realizing I've been frozen with anxiety for way too long just inside the door of the cabin. My attention drifts to the closed bedroom door. There aren't any sex sounds coming from inside. I'm both relieved and bitterly disappointed.

And still *really* fucking horny.

"What's in the bags?" Bael asks.

"Gifts for Maven," I mutter, rubbing my face.

"Better include a sex toy you plan to use on her to finally fucking test the theory," he says chipperly, mixing something in a baking bowl.

All the shit in this cozy little cabin was either bought by me yesterday in Tall Pine's little marketplace, or it was stolen from gods-know-where by Crypt. It was left empty and lightly furnished when we found it—probably someone's summer cabin.

"This is hard enough without you opening your fat mouth," I grit out.

"Pretty sure you mean *you're* hard enough, Professor Blue Balls."

"Shut up. Is Silas still keeping Maven distracted?"

The plan was to set up a miniature Starfall Eve to surprise her. Even though we're considered public enemies and we're only here until we have a lead on etherium, we decided this was an important first for our keeper. After all, we're all pretty damn sure she never celebrated the holiday in the Nether.

Starfall started as the celebration of the day the gods first cursed monsterkind. It's said that when the humans' prayers were answered, lights like stars rained down from the sky—the wrath of the gods visible to the naked eye. All monsters in the mortal realm suffered vicious curses that humbled and subdued them once they learned they needed to find their quintets. That led to armistices, treaties, intermingling with humans, and eventually legacies.

Hundreds of years later, that day is still the biggest celebration of the year, even if it is too commercialized for most elementals' liking.

Baelfire opens his mouth to answer my question, but Crypt blurs into existence right in front of me, making both of us swear.

"They're having a bath together," he drawls, trying to peek into the paper bags. I hold them away from him. "I offered to join, but an awful lot of that telepathic rubbish was going on. Also, Crane very dramatically insisted that he would rather castrate himself than climb into a bath with me."

"Yet another sign that he's completely sane now." I set the paper bags on the small table and begin tidying up some of the messes Baelfire has left in the kitchen.

He slides a dough-filled bread pan into the oven, his voice becoming oddly strained. "Back the fuck off. This kitchen isn't big enough for two."

"It's not big enough for *you*," I correct.

He shoves me slightly. I shove him back, intent on cleaning some spilled flour—

But I suddenly go airborne before slamming into one of the living room walls. It knocks the breath out of me, and my element slips quickly out of my control.

Ice explodes around me like a shield of spikes, which ends up being good and bad when Baelfire impales himself on one of the massive icicles a second later. The snarl that rips out of him is entirely inhuman. He starts tearing at the ice with his bare hands, his shifted eyes pinned on me with pure, animalistic malice.

Fuck. This isn't Bael.

His dragon is trying to kill me.

Just as bright royal blue fire burns through his skin, and his features begin to transform, Crypt grabs the shifter by the back of his neck and vanishes into Limbo.

Uh oh. Is that incubus going to kill him?

I've often said that I'd like Baelfire dead, but quintets are supposed to protect each other. Losing one of us would hurt Maven more than I like to think about.

The door of the bathroom slams open, and my keeper bolts into the living room. Dark magic crackles at her fingertips as she scours the room, probably expecting bounty hunters or another threat.

She's completely naked and dripping water, which is why I stay flat on my ass, staring at her instead of saying anything useful— because my brain is hyper-fixated on every single curve and dip of her toned, wet body.

Dear gods above. How can she be this sexy? Those hips, those dusky pink nipples, the gentle slope of her neck, the flash of danger in her dark gaze…

Even the bit of blood on her neck from an obvious feeding session with the blood fae is a beautiful splash of macabre color on an immaculate canvas.

"Maven," Silas shouts in alarm, following her into the room.

At least he's wearing a towel wrapped around his waist. He blinks at the damage my impact did to the wall.

"Godsdamn it all, what happened?"

Seeing Maven move too close to one of the wickedly sharp icicles, I immediately melt the ice around me and get to my feet, ignoring the ache in my bones. Nothing feels broken, but my ego isn't the only thing that will be bruised later.

"Sorry, I didn't mean to inter—"

Her hands frame my face as she checks it for injury before moving on to survey the rest of me. When she sees I'm unharmed, she exhales slightly and meets my eye.

I can't say I'm doing the same for her. Her naked body is a sensual weapon, and I also can't stop staring at the House of Arcana emblem on her scarred chest.

I need my mark on her, too. So fucking badly.

"Where are the others?" she asks.

I replay the last couple of minutes in my head. "Baelfire's dragon just took over while he was still in human form. He lost control, and…Crypt took him away through Limbo. Outside, I guess."

She turns to the front door.

"You're not going out into *that* naked," I snap at the same time Silas grasps her hand to keep her from leaving.

I can tell our reactions have irritated her. Luckily, before she can put us in our place, Crypt reappears, brushing snow out of his messy dark hair and off of the distressed leather jacket he picked up at some point.

"Not to worry, darling. Your pet lizard just needed to go hunting. He'll be perfectly well soon enough."

"Except you took him into Limbo."

"Only briefly. I doubt his psyche was in true danger when his dragon was wholly in charge."

Maven absorbs that, nods, and moves on, her dark gaze flicking around this festive space.

"Why the fuck is there a tree inside?"

"It's tradition," Silas supplies. "It will look better decorated for Starfall."

"Decorated with what? Bones?"

"Why the hell would we put bones on it?" I ask, disturbed.

She shrugs. The movement once again draws my attention to her pretty tits and the tempting curve of her hips.

"It's what monsters in the Nether do to mark their dens. They also hang up the skins of their kills and stain tree trunks with blood. They actually make decent decorators whenever they're not using human skin."

Oh, dear gods. "Baelfire was right. We need to put you in therapy."

She seems genuinely confused by the suggestion, but the conversation derails entirely when Crypt leans over to lick a streak of the remaining blood from her neck.

Silas pulls Maven away from the incubus freak immediately, glaring at him.

"What?" Crypt asks innocently, licking his lips as he gazes at Maven, who looks like she's fighting a smile. "It was only a taste. You get both her blood and her thoughts right now. Consider me jealous."

"Still, what the hell? You can't siphon from her blood," I huff, noting that Maven is now eyeing the paper bags on the table. Meanwhile, we're all eyeing her from head to toe.

"What's your point, Frost?"

Never fucking mind. I keep forgetting that logic is useless against this psychopath.

Maven finally notices that we're all practically drooling over her body. She twists her wet hair up out of her face, turning toward the bedroom. I have to physically bite my tongue to keep from groaning at the sight of her round, flawless ass.

"I'll be right back," she says over her shoulder, closing the door behind her.

Silas immediately glares at us, brushing still-dripping black curls off his forehead. "You three need to figure your shit out and bond with her."

"Fuck off," I scowl. "I told you, we're not going to just use Maven to break our curses—"

"It's not about the curses anymore." He checks to make sure the bedroom door is still closed before lowering his voice. "The magic in Maven's blood tastes stronger now that we've bonded. I think completing the quintet bonds will help her be even stronger than she already is—and if that fucking *bastard* is after her, I want our quintet to be as strong as possible to help keep her safe."

My teeth clench at the reminder of the wraith who came for Maven. I'm no empath, and she's good at hiding her feelings—but the hollow, haunted expression she wore after the run-in with the wraith was clear as day.

I can't imagine the horrors in Maven's past, but if I have anything to say about it, her future will be nothing but comfort and pleasure.

So even though I'm nowhere near good enough for her, even though I've hurt her and been a complete asshole…if there's a chance that bonding with her will help us take on whatever comes next, then I'll try anything—any of the theories.

My expression must reflect my new determination because Silas nods, smirking.

"I need to gather some final ingredients for my Starfall Eve gift to Maven out in the woods. Otherwise, I'd stay and watch. Just remember: no edging."

Heat floods my face. This damn blood fae is just as much of a voyeur as I am, but the jackass also seems to have figured out that I happen to like the idea of an audience.

"Don't worry. I'll show our innocent virgin how to treat our keeper right," Crypt drawls, patting my shoulder.

I smack his hand away, my face red. "I'm not innocent, and shut the fuck up, both of you."

"I'll return shortly," Silas goes on, "but if you three are still at it, I'll happily—"

Crypt's markings light up, and he visibly cringes. He mutters something about wisps, and the air warps as he blurs out of existence to take care of Limbo.

"Curses left and right," I sigh.

"Everywhere but right here," Silas brags before going into the bedroom to change.

I roll my eyes and tidy the kitchen, ensuring nothing burns in Baelfire's absence. By the time Silas slips into one of the coats on the coat rack and leaves the cabin, I'm a nervous wreck once again.

Because I'm alone here with Maven. Who I can't stop thinking about.

As if the gods are testing me, my keeper comes out in only an oversized black hoodie—no pants. I'm not sure if she's wearing panties.

I realize I've been staring at her legs far too hard, trying to figure out that little mystery, when she grins and hops up to sit on one of the counters.

"This a better angle for you?" she teases.

I whirl around, pretending to check a steaming casserole dish on the counter to hide the heat on my face.

"Um...no, I was just—sorry."

I hear a soft scraping sound and look over to see her twirling a little dagger on the kitchen counter beside her, her gaze far away. It's not Pierce. Where did she even pull that thing from?

And since I'm weak, I glance down between her legs to see that she's wearing lacy black panties under her hoodie that has ridden up to show off her legs.

When my keeper speaks, I'm still frozen with longing, my gaze locked on those beautiful thighs begging to be touched.

"If you're not too busy staring, what's in the bags?"

I startle so hard that I almost knock the casserole dish off the counter. "Shit, I didn't mean to...um, they're gifts. For you."

Maven blinks. "Why would you get me gifts?"

"First of all, I always want to get you gifts. But second of all, it's a Starfall Eve tradition. Humans have been giving gifts to celebrate the end of the reign of monsters for a long time. The humans even invented some old tale about an old guy with a beard in a garish red suit who passed out gifts to the poor right after the wars."

"Like that guy you gave money to. Seemed generous."

I shrug. "Yeah, well...it's an overly commercialized holiday, but the perk is that there's a lot of charity this time of year. More importantly, I get an excuse to spoil you. Not that this is much, since we're out in the boonies, but...here."

I pull out the first item from one of the bags: an oversized, comfortable, skull-patterned black hoodie. I have no idea if Maven will like it, but—

Her face lights up.

I go weak in the knees.

Holy shit, I love being the reason for that expression on her pretty face. I swear to myself that as soon as we're not on the run, I'm going to buy her the entire fucking world just to see more of that look she's wearing right now.

She accepts the hoodie with a grin when I offer it. "Thank you." Then her brow furrows. "Fuck, I didn't get you anyth—"

"I also got you this," I interrupt because there's no way my keeper gets to feel bad about not following a tradition she knew nothing about.

She tips her head as she reads the label on the bottle. "Sore muscle massage oil?"

I nod, my cheeks warming as I realize she might not like this gift.

"You push yourself hard constantly. I thought you probably get sore, and this might help. If you want. If you don't like it—"

"I do. Will you massage me with it?" Her smirk is teasing and tempting at the same time.

I fumble, swallowing hard as my heart starts to pound. "If...you want."

"I do want."

Maven slides off the counter, grabbing my free hand to still it. Only then do I realize I started fidgeting with the buttons of my wool car jacket.

Her mesmerizing, dark gaze doesn't move from mine, pinning me in place as she studies me.

"Romance doesn't come naturally to me," Maven begins hesitantly. "I'm abysmal at expressing myself unless it's with a blade, but I know that you're terrified of hurting me with your curse."

What an understatement. Even now, anxiety has frost climbing up my arms as I subtly try to move away, just in case my proximity to my keeper will somehow do her harm.

I can't stand the idea of ruining everything we could have together. I shouldn't be alone with this gorgeous, confident, brave enigma, and I shouldn't be aching for her like this.

Massage oil? What the fuck was I thinking? I can't massage her—she won't like my cold hands on all that smooth skin. Gods above, I hate myself for how badly I want her when I could end up hurting her.

When I take another step back, Maven steps forward until I'm backed against one of the counters with nowhere to go. I try to swallow again but fail.

"Maven..." I warn.

"I want to show you there's nothing to be afraid of."

"But what if—"

"Everett." She reaches up to brush her fingers through my hair. "I want you. Do you want me?"

So fucking much it hurts.

But I only manage to nod, my hands itching to land on her hips and close the space between us.

"Good. That's all we need," my keeper insists.

"But—"

"Your curse is supposed to kill anyone you fall for. I know." Her gaze is both astute and careful at once. "So tell me. Why hasn't it hurt me?"

My heart is pounding. She's right. It's the most obvious thing in the world that I've fallen for her, so why hasn't my curse done anything to her yet?

Unless…what if…

A new idea forms, steeling itself in my mind. A realization that should have dawned ages ago—one so unpleasant that it takes me a moment to breathe again once my world stops adjusting on its axis.

If what I suspect is true…

Fuck, I should've known.

I don't say anything because there's no fucking way that I'm going to let *them* ruin this moment when Maven is looking up at me with the beautiful kaleidoscope of dark colors that make up her irises.

Instead of saying something, I finally pull her closer to close the gap between our bodies. Her perfect warmth soothes the cold shards of hurt that started spiraling inside me with my realization.

I feel like I'm in some torturously tempting dream with this gorgeous woman looking up at me with dark, playful eyes. I want this so fucking badly, but what if I say or do the wrong thing and wake up in a cold sweat with a raging hard-on to realize this fantasy was nothing but a dream?

I can't mess this up.

"I don't—I mean, if you…the massage might make me, um…"

Damn it. I'm already messing it up.

Maven fights a laugh, her eyes glittering like she's genuinely enjoying watching my struggle. Knowing her, she probably is.

"You're adorable when you're nervous."

I blow out a breath, covering my face. "I've never been this fucking nervous before. It's just that massaging you will make me even more..." I trail off, realizing how that would sound.

"Horny?"

"I don't expect this to lead to anything," I say quickly, adjusting my collar twice. My brain doesn't want to function with this beautiful woman against me. "I promise that's not why I got the oil. I just think it would be good for—"

"Everett. You're overthinking it. Follow me."

13

EVERETT

MY BRAIN SHUTS off when Maven strips off her sweatshirt, leaving her in nothing but those tantalizing panties.

Arati save me.

On second thought, no. I absolutely do not want to be saved from this.

The fire crackles beside the layers of thick, soft blankets as Maven lays facedown. She set up this spot for me to massage her, and now she's waiting.

For my hands on her.

Holy gods, I'm about to massage my keeper.

Focus. This is about making her feel good. Keep it wholesome, and don't fuck it up, horndog.

I can barely think as I kneel beside her and briefly hold my hands closer to the fire to warm them. She said she found my touch refreshing, but I'm still worried my natural temperature will be unpleasant during a massage.

I pour some of the oil into my hands, rubbing them together. I try to get my head out of the gutter as I gently but firmly begin massaging Maven's shoulders and upper back. At first, her entire body tenses, and I pause.

"I can warm up my hands more—"

"Don't. It's just...I'm not used to touch like this."

Godsdamn me, I didn't even think about her lingering phobia of touch. She's seemed fine—happy, even—with the quintet's casual touching, but this is definitely...touchier.

"Maybe this was a bad idea," I backpedal.

She props up on one elbow, turning on her side to give me an arched brow look. "I didn't say stop. I'm just adjusting. Hello? Everett?"

Shit. I was staring again.

But how the hell am I supposed to stop when she's posed lying on her side like this and looks like every filthy dream I've ever had?

I clear my throat, nodding. "Okay. But if it starts to bug you, let me know immediately."

Maven lays back down, and I get started again. I learned a thing or two about massage during my time as a model, but holy fuck, this is hard to do when all the blood in my body has rushed south so fast that I'm lightheaded.

Her skin is just so warm. The curve of her spine, the globes of her gorgeous ass, those legs...

When I press more firmly to work out what I think is a knot near her shoulder blades, she moans softly in pained pleasure.

Holy gods, it's like she's fucking trying to kill me. I pause to try to get a grip, swallowing hard.

"I want to massage all of you. If that's okay."

Maven nods, exhaling contentedly.

I move on to her legs and arms, unsurprised by all the toned muscles that need to be soothed. After all, she's trained this body to be a fucking weapon. I hate to think about what my keeper has gone through, but it's pure bliss when she moans again as I move back to rub her lower back.

Trying not to overthink again, I let my hands glide over her ass, massaging as methodically as possible. But when Maven's breathing picks up, and she squirms, I know she's as affected as I am.

"Turn over," I whisper hoarsely.

She does, and the luxurious heat in her gaze as she lies ready for me to pamper makes my already-hard dick twitch. It's uncomfortably stiff in my pants, but I'm not about to let the damn thing out. This is about making Maven feel good, and if I start removing clothes, she'll think I expect more.

I add more oil and gently massage Maven's feet, calves, and thighs. My desperate, frayed hunger is starting to get the best of me —so before I get any closer to her panties, I reach for one of her arms again instead.

But before I can do anything, Maven sits up, cups my chin, and kisses me.

I'm immediately on my knees, straddling her as I kiss her back. Her lips are fucking divine. She pulls back to peer at me, her gaze fierce with want, just like mine.

"Strip," she murmurs. "So I can return the favor."

I kiss down her jaw and neck, pressing her shoulder so she lays back again instead of sitting up. "Some other time. I'm enjoying how much you enjoy this way too much."

"*Strip*," she repeats, pulling me down with her to continue teasing and biting my lips.

I quickly get my clothes the fuck off, not disrupting our kiss as I throw it all aside and free my raging erection. She wants me naked? I'll be naked. I'll be whatever the hell she wants as long as she never stops kissing me.

Her body arches against mine, her thigh brushing against my hard cock, making me lightheaded. I break away to let her catch her breath while I kiss lower and lower—her neck, between her tits so I can feel her scar against my lips, down her stomach until I can move aside her panties to finally slip my tongue between her thighs.

Oh, fuck. She's so wet and warm and completely fucking *irresistible*.

I immediately slip a finger into her, reveling in how she feels. When I curl my finger and continue lapping at her pussy, Maven gasps, her fingers tugging at my hair.

I need more of that. The tugging, the sounds she's making—I *need* it. So I continue to lick and pinch and tease, taking my time to learn what exactly makes Maven pant, what makes her moan, and what makes her tug even harder on my hair.

"Everett," she groans, trying to grind up impatiently for more.

I pin her thighs down, giving her a chiding look before I slowly strip down her panties and toss them aside. Then I reposition myself and lick a path up her wetness, blowing softly on it.

Maven gasps sharply as her wetness frosts over, her hands sweeping over my shoulders and her fingers digging into my skin from surprise at the temperature shock. That bite from her grip is so damn good that my cock twitches, desperate for more.

I just as quickly lick the cold away to smile up at her.

"Nice party trick," she laughs breathlessly. "And dimples. So fucking unfair."

Party trick? Okay, if she's going to tease me, she deserves more.

I lick her entrance again, sucking her clit as I slide a second finger into her. She starts trying to grind up against me again, making all those fantastic fucking sounds. This time, when I breathe frost all over this beautiful wetness and Maven tenses, I double down, plunging my fingers deep into her as I devour her pussy.

She swears and grips my shoulders as a sudden surge of heady wetness drenches my face, sending my control out the window as my cock twitches. I moan as pleasure races through my body. Her entrance pulses around my fingers, rhythmic and subtle.

Gods on high. I'm officially addicted to this—to her pleasure.

I smile breathlessly up at her, but Maven's eyes widen as she sits up.

"Fuck. Did I just…?"

"You squirted," I sigh happily, already going down for more.

But she twists her fingers in my hair to keep me in place, her brow furrowing. "Is squirting normal?"

"It's phenomenal, so don't even fucking think about getting self-conscious about it," I warn. "Now, lay back and let me play with you."

"It's time I play with you," she counters.

"I'll need a few minutes." I lower my head, ready for a repeat of one of the best moments of my life.

But then I'm left stunned when her legs lock around my shoulders, and she twists, rolling me over. She moves blindingly fast, so one moment, her thighs are beside my head, and the next, she's straddling me with a smirk.

"You blush so nicely for me," Maven hums.

Then she leans down to kiss my neck—and she bites me.

I swear the tiny spark of pain shoots my soul to Paradise for a second. Just like that, I don't need a few minutes.

When she sits up to study her work, her eyes sparkle. "And your skin is so…markable."

"Mark it, then," I whisper once my tongue starts functioning again. "It's all yours. I'm all yours. Just—"

Maven's mouth skims down my throat before she kisses me again, biting and sucking as I squeeze my eyes shut in pleasure. One of her hands brushes over my abdomen and chest, and when she teasingly pinches one of my nipples, I jolt as something new crashes through me.

Growing up, I felt like a glass object. The mirror image of my father, the unfeeling Frost heir, something perfect to stare at on a pedestal but never to touch.

I need that touch now—her touch. Brutally. Urgently. In the most intense way that I can possibly get it from my keeper.

"Can you…" I swallow, but I'm not sure how to word it.

I just know that I want…

Maven studies me as if trying to understand what I want. Then she arches a brow and gently drags her nails down my chest. I gasp and moan at the sharp sting.

"Hurt me more," I whisper.

Maven's gaze darkens in a way that makes my already-pounding heart try to escape. "You enjoy pain?"

My breathing hitches, my words coming out in a rush.

"Pain from you is just pleasure." Then I realize something

amazing and smile up at her. "And…you enjoy hurting me a little. Right?"

A soft smile crosses her lips, and she leans down, kissing me while her hands slip between us. I can feel her raise slightly and don't know why until she delivers a firm, short slap to my heavy balls.

It's an immediate injection of pain and pleasure. I swear, light-headed with how much I love it.

"More than a little," she confirms in a whisper, kissing my jaw.

"Fuck, yes," I groan.

I want to ask her for even more, but then she rubs her soaked entrance against the tip of my cock, and I suddenly can't breathe. She meets my gaze as if checking to see if I want to keep going.

I'm pretty sure I'll die if I'm not inside her, so I grip her hips and drag her down, my cock plunging into her hot wetness as we both moan and gasp.

I thrust up into her just as she rolls her hips.

Fuck, she feels incredible. So wet and hot and tight.

Dear holy gods above.

Honestly, I shouldn't even be praying to them with how sinfully blasphemous my thoughts are right now.

Because now, I want to relish Maven's body until she's so over-whelmed with pleasure that she prays for me to stop. I want to spend every second inside this perfect pussy—fuck her raw on an altar and revere her the way she deserves. The others can watch until it's their turn. Maven enjoys us all worshipping her—and gods on high, I enjoy seeing her worshipped.

And I especially want more of her ferocity. More of the burning sting paired with mind-numbing bliss.

When she starts to really ride me, one of her hands twisting in my hair for that perfect dose of added pain, I bite one of my fists to contain myself.

"Wait, Maven," I gasp. "*Fuck.* Slow down. I need this to last—"

She slows, leaning down to kiss me. For a moment, we move at a languorous pace as my heart hammers against her chest and my hands brush over her perfect body, exploring. The sheer intimacy of being with her like this is the best godsdamned thing in my life.

Gently rolling until I'm on top, I wrap Maven's arms around my hips and thrust harder, gritting my teeth against the mounting need to come. She moans and tips her head back, eyes shutting and mouth parting slightly, so now I get to watch how utterly fucking gorgeous she is as she comes again, shuddering and swearing softly.

The wind howling outside, the fire crackling beside us, her soft gasps in my ear as I drive home over and over again, delirious over every warm, addictive sensation…

Perfect.

This is perfection. *She* is perfection.

Finally, I can't fight it anymore as the release smashes into me. I gasp and swear, clutching her tightly against me as I finish thrusting hard several more times.

I swear it's like she just fucking took my soul out through my dick.

I have never felt this good.

"Gods," she laughs breathlessly as I gently pull out and turn so she's cuddled against my chest. I rub her back, her arms, her side—I just can't stop touching her.

"That was…" I have no words.

"Special enough?" she checks.

Is that something she was worried about? I tip her head to peer at her so she gets how much I mean this. "Everything with you is special. Every single fucking moment. So yeah, it was. Also…I'm glad you liked the massage oil."

Maven grins. "I loved it."

I just have to get another dopamine hit seeing her open the last gift.

I kiss her temple, giddy and high on everything that is Maven.

"Wait here a moment," I whisper.

I slip into the attached kitchen and quickly return with the remaining paper bag, offering it to her as I sit beside her. I'm heavily aware of how her beautiful eyes trail over every exposed inch of me before trapping my gaze like she's mapping out both my body and mind.

"If you don't stop looking at me like that, your last gift will have to wait for another round," I warn, unable to keep the smile off my face.

She leans forward unexpectedly to kiss my cheek—where one of my dimples is. "More incredible sex? Oh, the horror."

She sits up, bundling one of the blankets around herself up to her shoulders. I'm seriously trying to come up with the best way to politely tell her that I need to bask next to her naked body as long as possible. Now that I know how divine and fucking *warm* her pussy is, my cock can't seem to calm down. My entire body feels both primed and relaxed at once.

I force myself not to fidget nervously as she rubs at her chest through the blanket before pulling out the last gift. She blinks and turns it side to side, admiring the carvings on the handle.

"Is this…a dagger made from bone?"

"It's a Salish deer bone knife," I nod. "The man who made it and sold it to me said it's best used for carving fish or putting on display. It's not really a weapon, but…I thought it looked nice. You don't have to keep it if you don't like it," I tack on, stating the obvious like an idiot.

Besides, the moment we're out of this mess, I'll buy her a dozen of the world's best daggers if she wants. Anything she wants, and even stuff she's never thought of wanting.

Maven studies it closer, a soft smile curving her lips. "Thank you."

Then she squints, turning the blade to show off the *Oakley* engraved on one side.

Maybe it's time I come clean about my fake last name, she muses.

"I know it's fake," I shrug. "To be honest, I've been wondering if your last name is actually Ama—"

I cut off when it sinks in that her mouth didn't move. Her eyes snap to mine as she rubs the center of her chest again, finally dropping the blanket to look down.

A surge of breathless delight makes me go dizzy.

A perfect square is centered on the line and scar on her chest—the emblem of the House of Elements, with the four corners representing each of the elements. It's such a stark new design on my keeper that for a moment, we both stare at it as my entire world seems to *finally* click into place.

At last.

She's mine, and I'm hers, and nothing will ever take her away from me.

Not even a fake curse.

I'm so overwhelmed that I don't think twice before pulling her into my arms, cradling her as powerful emotions swirl through me.

Relief. Excitement. Joy.

All my life, I've been told I would ruin this. I stayed alone and pushed everyone else away for their own good, determined to save them from my curse. I assumed I would die alone after rotting in misery all my days, painfully cold and lonely and so damn empty that I would gladly give up the ghost when Syntyche came to reap my soul.

But now?

I'm bound at last, which means I'm…free. No more curse—falsified or not. I can breathe for the first time since Arati's high priest opened his mouth and ruined any chance at my happiness.

Dear gods, I thank you.

Maven runs a finger over the new emblem on her chest, her gaze heated when it moves back to me. "It worked, but why?"

"Why?" I echo, too busy grinning to puzzle out what she means.

"We just had sex."

"Not nearly enough of it, if you ask me," I reply honestly, my attention trained on her finger drifting over my emblem.

My emblem.

On Maven.

This is the best fucking day of my life. I don't even know how to handle this level of happiness, which is probably why I'm both lovesick and borderline loopy at the same time.

She laughs and shakes her head. "I mean, I haven't exactly been abstaining with the others. If sex is all it takes to make this non-gods-approved bond happen, then why did it only work now?"

It's a fair question, but once again, all I can think about is that I'm hers. I scoot closer to Maven because I can't get enough of her warmth—but I freeze when she subtly scoots away from me.

Maven sees my expression and quickly says, "It's not you. My body is just finally catching up with the massage, but I'm fine. It passes quickly."

It kills me that my keeper is downplaying whatever remains of her haphephobia.

Then she tips her head, frowning. "What did you mean earlier about knowing my surname is fake?"

I hesitate.

Ever since we learned more about Maven's past and her being abducted by shadow fiends when she was young, I've wondered about the human brought into that courthouse years ago. Pietro Amato—that was his name. He said his daughter was alive in the Nether, that he needed to rescue her, that she was special…

What if Maven was his daughter?

And what if he was saying that because she's a saint?

Saints are selected by their patron gods at birth. They're supposed to live pious, celibate lives as representatives of Paradise, able to use holy magic to a certain degree so long as they abide by the rules of the god who selected them. They bless humans, travel the world, heal the sick, and tend to the temples. Many of them have become great humanitarians who have gone down in history.

If my keeper were picked by one of the gods as a baby, it's no wonder her father would be desperate to get her back. And I'm almost positive Amato was her father, but what if I'm wrong?

Before I can confess my thoughts to Maven, she straightens and looks at a nearby corner of the room. I tense, worried that fucking wraith has somehow found us again, but she sounds more relieved than worried.

"You're back."

It's quiet for a second before the air ripples beside the front door and then I'm looking right at a very pissed-off incubus. He's standing with his arms folded, some blood smeared on his hands, and tears in his leather jacket, but at least he doesn't look as shitty as the last time he came back from something in Limbo.

"You're *bonded*," he mutters, looking like he wants to kill me.

Not that it's a surprising look on him. I've seen it plenty of times. It gets old pretty damn fast.

"Take your jealousy somewhere else, asshole. You're ruining our afterglow." I adjust the blankets to cover Maven and me more.

Crypt smiles darkly, without humor. "Enjoy it while you can. You'll have to sleep eventually, and when you do, I'll be there."

What a creep.

Maven laughs at the face I pull. The sound is pure heaven. I move her onto my lap and grin like an idiot when she pecks me on the cheek.

I'm going to spoil the godsdamned soul out of this woman.

I'm all yours, you know that? I tell her telepathically. *Like I said. No holds barred. I know I'll never actually be worthy of you, but I'm sure as hell going to try my best. Now that I finally get to love you the way I've been needing to—*

I'm interrupted and shocked when Maven actually *blushes* and covers my mouth with one of her hands like she's trying to stop the words.

You know this is in our heads, right? I check, laughing.

All of our heads, actually, Silas's voice inserts, making us both blink. He's not back at the cabin, and I suddenly wonder how far the telepathic bond goes. *Not to make it a competition, but my proclamations of love are much better. Aren't they,* sangfluir? *Shall I let Everett know how much you enjoy sweet confessions whispered to your head?*

Quiet or I'll block you out, Maven sends back.

Crypt mutters something under his breath and pulls out a lighter and *reverium* cigarette, igniting it despite my protest as he stalks toward us. "Enough with the telepathy."

He sits and promptly pulls our keeper out of my arms and onto his lap instead, kissing her before taking a drag from his cigarette.

"Don't get that fucking smoke on her. And everyone knows newlybounds need to stay close," I scowl, pulling her back onto my lap.

He resists, wrapping an arm around her waist. Maven smirks up at us when she winds up halfway on his lap and halfway on mine, her newly-marked chest on display right as Baelfire pushes through the front door with a gust of wintry wind. The dragon shifter is stark naked, covered in dirt, melted snow, animal blood, and a surprising amount of ripped-up feathers.

He halts, blinking at the scene in front of him.

"Holy fuck. Snowflake finally got laid? Damn, that's a lot of hickeys."

I flush, but it's not like I have any regrets—especially not when Maven smirks and reaches up to brush one of the marks she left on me.

Baelfire brushes snow off his shoulders. "Okay, Angel of Death, I have a *very* serious question for you. Was his jizz normal, or was it cold like a—"

"Shut the fuck up, dragon," I cut him off with an eye roll.

14

MAVEN

Once Baelfire is in the shower, Silas returns and gifts me a new concoction he's been working on—an elixir I can drink to fend off my next episode.

Which means no more fucking needles.

Thank the universe.

Baelfire's gift is a mouthwatering dinner and several new ice cream flavors to try, which is how I learn that vanilla really is my favorite. Crypt got me a beautiful, scandalous dark red lingerie set that I am one hundred percent sure he stole from a store somewhere in Washington. He also got me a graphic T-shirt with a coffin on it that says, "Get in bitches, we're going to the Beyond."

I found it fitting and hilarious, even though Everett told Crypt his sense of humor was more fucked up than he is.

All the gift-giving was great, but it also made me feel shitty. I had no idea gifts were a thing on Starfall, so I have nothing for them. Silas picked up on my frustration and teasingly insisted that kisses counted as great gifts.

Still, I'm going to get them all something as soon as I get the chance.

Now, the fireplace in the little bedroom is flickering softly with pale blue flames as I listen to Baelfire sleeping softly to my right. He tried curling up around me, which was great until I started to break into a cold sweat and couldn't breathe right after about thirty minutes. He noticed and backed off, instead resting my hand on his chest so I could feel the steady, soothing thrum of his heartbeat as he drifted to sleep.

Apparently, my stupid fucking touch phobia is going to be a bitch to get rid of entirely.

On the other side of Baelfire, Everett looks like a contentedly sleeping angel, the faint blue firelight casting an almost eerie wintry glow to his white-blond hair. I smile when I glimpse some of the hickeys I left behind on his neck, others hidden under his pajama shirt.

Silas is quietly sleeping in the chair in one corner of the room. He fell asleep reading a book he pulled from his pocket void earlier.

Crypt is watching me in Limbo. I'm sure he's waiting for me to fall asleep.

That makes two of us.

I'm not ready to admit out loud to him or the others that sleep eludes me the more I think about Gideon being here in the mortal realm to hunt me down. Not to mention the looming threat of falling behind on my tasks as the *telum*. I haven't even found etherium yet, let alone hunted down another member of the Immortal Quintet. Melchom hasn't answered calls, and while I would gladly track down another demon to wring answers out of, I can't risk getting found by a multitude of enemies who would waste more of my time.

Still...even with the dread hanging over me like a cloud, I can't help tracing the thin, square House of Elementals emblem now decorating the center of my chest like a delicate rune.

I'm officially bound to Everett Frost.

That painfully gorgeous, conflicted, brooding, adorably awkward, perfectionistic snow angel is all mine.

The rightness of it makes me smile, and finally the Nightmare Prince appears. He's sitting on the hardwood floor, arms folded on the edge of the bed beside my pillow as he rests his chin on them to gaze dreamily at me. There is also an undeniable edge of lust in his silver-flecked purple eyes.

"Restless, love? I'm happy to send you off to sleep. The only thing I ask in return is that you let me slowly devour that sweet little cunt of yours while you bask in sinful dreams."

Heat floods my neck and pulses between my thighs.

Gods, he's silver-tongued—and I wouldn't mind indulging my somnophiliac as much as he wants. The last time he played with me while I was unconscious, I had the most fantastic sex dream and woke up to all of my matches delirious with need.

It's one of my favorite memories.

Still, I hesitate. "I was with Everett earlier."

He hums in agreement. "Are you asking me to wake him up to join? If so, I'm for it. I hardly mind sharing when watching you come undone in so many ways is so delectable. Anything you like tonight, my darling, so long as I get to taste you as you dream."

Fucking poetic incubus. Now I'm really flushed.

I try to play it off by rolling my eyes. "I *meant*, he finished inside me."

I showered afterward, but still.

His lips turn up devilishly. "Lucky him. What's your point, love?"

How is he not getting it? "My point is, you don't want to go down on me after he's…"

The Nightmare Prince's grin widens, and he leans to whisper against my ear on the pillow.

"Don't I?"

Oh, gods. That raspy voice, his accent, his sweet leather scent, and the way he slowly kisses down my jaw…

Okay, this incubus can have whatever the hell he wants. The effect he has on me is completely unfair.

Clear my throat twice in a row, I finally nod, trying to ignore the burning heat and excitement trickling through my system. The idea of him between my thighs while I'm unconscious is doing all kinds of things to me.

Crypt leans forward and kisses my forehead. "Use your words."

"I told you already. You have my full permission to use me at night. That has no expiration date."

He groans softly, his voice turning ragged. "Close your eyes. I swear I'll give you nothing but pleasure."

I do, and a moment later, a deep sleep washes over me.

At first, it's exactly what I want—what I *need*. Deep rest laced with wicked dreams, untold desires, and orgasms that flood my subconscious with pleasure again and again, lulling me deeper into a sensual void of perfection.

But then, my chest suddenly goes cold. A hollow darkness creeps into the corners of my mind, overshadowing everything until I can no longer sense Crypt.

Instead, I find myself striding through a stone hallway. Not just any stone hallway—this is the vast entry within the citadel I used to loathe visiting. Is this a memory? I try to place it, but it somehow feels both familiar and unfamiliar.

Finally, I come to a stop in the dream and find myself facing... children. Thirteen children of varying ages, with gray-draped necromancers standing guard around them. Dagon's voice echoes beside me, sending chills down my spine because I've heard his sickly voice far too many times.

"My liege, these are they who survived passing into your great kingdom upon your command. Through the efforts of the liches you sent, these few were able to withstand the Divide...but my everlasting lord, I must still warn you. Mere mortals cannot reasonably survive the things which I shall put these younglings through."

My gaze catches on a very young girl standing at the edge of the little mortals. Her black hair is a tangle around her serious face. The others are crying, trembling, sobbing at the sight of me, but she is utterly still and watchful with large, dark eyes. Fear is thick in the air except for around her.

A strange pride fills me, but it doesn't feel like my own.

"Begin with that one," a rattlingly deep voice booms...from my mouth.

It sends fear coursing through my veins. Pain shoots through my chest, shock sluicing through my system as I jolt awake, shedding the dream in an instant. Immediately, I feel Crypt's hands cradling my face as he leans over me flat on my back. His silver-flecked violet eyes are wide, panicked.

The others are awake, too, gathered around me on the bed. The only sound in the room is my struggle to breathe and the fireplace's crackling. I'm vaguely aware of the fact that I'm completely bare from the waist down and still incredibly wet from whatever Crypt was doing with me.

"What just…" I trail off, disoriented.

"I couldn't get into your subconscious anymore. No—I was pushed *out* of your subconscious," Crypt growls, his face darkening with pure fury as his light swirling markings light up faintly.

"A lot of fucking good you are to her," Baelfire snarls, his eyes shifted into draconic-slitted pupils. "Maybe if you were more focused on protecting Maven's dreams and less on using her for your sleeping fuck doll fantasy—"

"Change your tone before I rip your tongue out, dragon. *Never* has this happened before in all the dreams I've walked," Crypt snaps before turning back to me. "What was that, love?"

I swallow to try steadying my voice, more disoriented when I see sunlight streaming through the small window of this little cabin bedroom. "It was a dream of a memory. But not mine."

"Whose, then?" Silas demands.

"Amadeus's."

They all recoil.

Crypt swears. "I cannot pass through the Divide even in dreams. That must be what ripped me from your subconscious and prevented me from waking you. If you're sharing a dream state with that Undead bastard, it means your psyche is somehow linked to his."

Everett stiffens. "Through the shadow heart in her chest?"

"Perhaps," the Nightmare Prince mutters, tracing the side of my face as he watches me with tender concern.

All four of them look concerned, actually. Far too much.

I sit up, finding my discarded panties and pants to slip into. "We need to go to Argentina."

Baelfire scowls, his shifter temper flaring. "Are you seriously going to brush this off like it's fucking nothing? You just shared a dream with the asshole who put you through hell! Don't act like it didn't freak you out, too. We need to—"

"What?" I interrupt, fixing him with a stern look. "We need to what? Spiral and spew theories about why this is happening? Panic? Crack open my fucked-up head to see what's going on?"

He snarls again, more viciously and far less like Baelfire. His dragon must be fighting hard for control. "Don't even fucking joke about that right now," he warns.

"We have bigger problems to focus on," I point out, looking at each of them as my own emotions spike in the wake of that off-putting dream. "If I don't get etherium soon, my plan goes to shit. I need to keep you four safe, but if I don't end another one of my targets soon, Amadeus is going to start killing off humans, starting with—"

My voice breaks, and I shut my eyes.

"Maven?" Everett asks softly.

"Starting with Lillian," I finish, trying to compose myself. "I can't let that happen. I just…can't. So yes, I'm brushing this off for now."

It's quiet for a moment, and I feel that same uneasy excess of energy that I always do when I wake up. I would love to slip into my regular morning routine to burn off the anxiety—or gods, I could kill for a good fight.

Finally, Silas nods, rubbing his face. "All right, *ima sangfluir.* Let's figure out a way to get to Argentina without using magic. The last thing we need is Douglas tracking us from here to your new lead."

Everett suggests we could charter a selection of private planes to take us there, but Baelfire is still testy and snaps that he isn't flying unless it's with his own two wings. Silas tells the dragon shifter to get over himself as he begins slipping any relevant belongings into his pocket void. Crypt glowers silently, still pissed about getting kicked from my dream.

Baelfire tenses abruptly, his head whipping toward the window.

"What is it?" I ask, slipping my hand under my pillow to find that Pierce is there. They all know I like to sleep with my favorite dagger close at hand. I wonder which one of them put it here.

"Howling," he grits.

Hellhounds.

Immediately, we're all getting dressed for combat as fast as we can. I don't realize I'm smiling until Everett sees me and blinks.

"Dear gods. Please tell me you're not excited for this fight."

I grin. "Why lie?"

Crypt kisses my cheek on the way out of the room, calling over his shoulder, "Let our girl have her fun. But if she's injured, I'll gleefully kill all three of you."

Everett huffs and crouches down to tie my combat boots.

"I can do that," I protest.

"I know you can. Just let me, please," he grumbles, evidently crabby first thing in the morning with an ambush on the way.

Baelfire tips his head, his shifter hearing picking up far more than we can. "They're getting closer."

Maybe if you stay in here… Everett begins telepathically, shooting a pleading look up at me.

And let you four have all the fun? Not a chance.

Silas captures my free hand to kiss my fingertips.

Keep in mind that we're all on a thin ledge right now, sangfluir, he says through the bond. *You want us to work as a team, but with only half of us bound to you and Bael quickly losing control…*

He trails off, but I see his point.

"You four could stay in here while I deal with it," I suggest. "There's just a high chance I'll lose control, which means you'd have to kill me to snap me out of it once I start—"

The angry roar that breaks from Baelfire is entirely inhuman, and then he grips his head, grimacing in pain. "Nope. Hell no. That is not a fucking option."

I study him, noticing the tightness around his eyes and how he grits his teeth. Typically, he fights with his inner dragon on and off, but right now, it's like a continuous battle.

My cheerful, charming dragon shifter is struggling a lot more than he wants me to know.

If only I knew the reason Everett, Silas, and I were bound, I could try to break his curse, too.

Even if it's only temporary.

"Fine. Let me handle Douglas," I tell them, trying to push that aching thought away as I slip on gloves and grab anything we may need in the event of a quick getaway.

Not three minutes later, the howling outside becomes noticeably louder, and then the entire cabin is surrounded by the chilling chorus. Magic flashes outside. I sense their attack on the magic wards a fraction of a second before a hellhound crashes through the living room window.

Everett freezes it immediately, but then they're coming through the front door and the other windows, howling outside as bounty hunters shout and shots fire. Since chaos has broken loose, I spare no time dashing outside and spotting the leader.

He's a large, burly redhead who immediately takes aim with his metallic weapon and fires.

The bullet lodges high in my left shoulder. I jerk back, glancing at the stinging wound. Lillian told me about guns years ago, but this is my first time seeing and feeling them in action. I suppose it would hurt more if I weren't a certifiable monster who trained to tolerate high levels of pain for over a decade.

First impression? Guns seem so inelegant. What's the fun of a fight if you can't watch your enemy's flesh part and their blood ooze around a knife, up close and personal?

A hellhound launches at me from my left, and my instincts send me into action. I duck under the monstrous hound, dodge its slashing claws, and then turn and fling myself over it, straddling it to get my arms around its neck.

Snap.

It drops dead as a fresh buzz floods my veins. I roll to my feet, breaking into a dead run towards Douglas. I expect him to panic, shout for help, or try some other idiotic strategy, but he stands his ground, keeping his sights set on me.

Bang. Bang. Bang.

Three shots, all to my stomach. They hurt, but with the familiar rush of adrenaline that comes with a fight, I tune it out to keep my pace. As soon as I get close enough, I launch forward, grabbing his weapon and sending it back into his face.

Crack.

15

MAVEN

BREAKING Douglas's nose is satisfying—but it's far more satisfying when his new injury doesn't throw him off.

Though he's dropped his gun, he's already withdrawing a dagger made of blessed bone, aiming for where my heart would be. I knock it from his hand, but in an impressive display of agility, his other hand catches the weapon before he tries again to drive it into my chest.

I dodge, but a grin splits my face. Douglas's movements are concise, and his technique is solid. So far, he hasn't started monologuing or screeching like many people do in a fight.

"Nice to meet you," I tell him, genuinely meaning it because a decent combat partner is hard to come by.

"Fuck you," he retorts, trying again.

He stabs, I dodge, and when I test a savage kick to his side, he tries to grab my leg. I let him and then jump, simultaneously wrapping my other leg around his arm to bring him to the snow. He breaks out of the hold quickly, trying to slam the butt of his gun into my head, but I roll aside.

"We found your little one-eyed, rotting distraction in Maine. You're fucking demented," he spits.

"Thanks." I dodge another strike.

"Where's that depraved little incubus shit?"

Screams echo behind us, so shrill that we both glance over in time to see one of the bounty hunters literally clawing a fellow hunter's face off. Another bounty hunter is tearing his own hair out, laughing maniacally, and shooting in every direction as blood dribbles from his nose, ears, and eyes. One moment, he's there, and then Crypt's hand flashes out of nowhere before they both vanish.

How gruesome. I grin.

"Looks like he's playing with your friends."

Douglas is pissed, and his next blow is twice as brutal. For a moment, we're trapped in my favorite dance—the deadly tango of a good old-fashioned knife fight. He slashes, I sidestep. I stab, he swerves. Our movements could be mistaken as coordinated if someone stumbled upon this scene without context.

Gods, I've missed a good fight.

Other bounty hunters and hellhounds cry out, no doubt falling to my formidable matches. I'm not trying my hardest, but Douglas is doing so well that I decide to test him. Slipping Pierce from my sleeve, I butt the end of it into his forehead and take advantage of his momentary surprise to make a move for his chest. I don't actually intend to kill him yet—this fight is too refreshing.

He breaks away to regain his footing, but it's too late. He missed it.

"Disappointing. You missed a golden opportunity," I sigh.

He wipes blood off his face as we circle, and I notice that his green eyes light up momentarily when one of the caster bounty hunters casts a spell nearby.

"Bitch, what the fuck are you talking about?"

"When I went for your chest, mine was wide open. I assume you're not holding that blessed bone dagger for shits and giggles. Try harder."

This time, when I launch toward him, I feign right before crouching to sweep my leg, connecting with the backs of his knees so he falls back into the thick snow on the ground. He shouts, but the moment I'm on top of him, ready to strike, he finally finds a new opening and drives the dagger into the place where my heart would be.

Fuck, that hurts. I didn't expect him to actually land the blow.

Still, the thrill of finally meeting someone worth fighting has me grinning as the agony spreads through my chest and my blood dribbles onto him.

"Much better."

Douglas blinks down at the blessed bone in my chest, then squints at me.

"What the hell kind of freak of nature are you? They said you were a revenant. This should have killed you."

It might, temporarily. I was having too much fun, and now I'm at risk of passing out from blood loss, which would be really fucking inconvenient.

Instead of addressing his confusion, I shrug. "I'd return the favor, but you're surprisingly fun to fight. Between you and me, I miss daily combat. So I'll let your little ambush slide—but the next time you find me, if you target any of my matches, I'll rip your beating heart out and feed it to you. Got it?"

Before my words can fully sink into his ginger head, I slam Pierce's butt into his temple hard enough that he's knocked out cold. Blood steadily trickles from his nose as I stand to check my surroundings. Several bounty hunters lay frozen or dead in the snow alongside hellhounds, but I still hear fighting on the other side of the cabin.

I want to check on my matches, but first, I need to make sure they don't have a synchronized aneurysm seeing me stabbed through the chest yet again.

Yanking the blessed bone blade from my chest, I watch it crumble to ash. That's the kicker to blessed bone weapons—they're only good for one use. Grimacing as my vision wobbles, I use the hellhound's life force for a patchy healing spell to get rid of the worst of the damage inside my chest.

By the time a very blood-spattered Crypt appears and pulls me into his arms, I'm no longer on the verge of fainting from blood loss.

Everett is at my side a moment later. I check them both for injuries, but aside from a hellhound bite that's already nearly completely healed on one of Crypt's arms, they're okay.

Where are you and Baelfire? I send to Silas.

Not far. He was shot with a shifter-specific tranquilizer that prevents him from healing, but I'm fixing it.

My teeth clench at the knowledge that Baelfire is hurt, but Everett gingerly lifts the edge of my sweatshirt and swears.

"There are fucking *bullets* in your stomach," he seethes.

I glance down and pick one out, flicking the bloodied metal away. My head spins since I've lost more blood than I anticipated, but I ignore it like I was trained to, just like I ignore the lingering waves of pain in my stomach and chest.

"They didn't hit anything too important. More importantly, that was far too small a group of bounty hunters for the threat we pose. Others will probably arrive soon."

I need you to transport us away from here, I tell Silas telepathically.

Are you running low on life forces to wield, my vicious revenant? he asks, teasing.

Yes, actually. I don't want to risk dipping into Somnus's life force before we find etherium.

In that case, I can certainly—

He goes suddenly silent.

I tense. *Silas?*

His voice is strained, even telepathically. *Gods above, I will never grow accustomed to seeing souls reaped. I have yet to see the reaper goddess's face, but I dread the day I finally do.*

Meanwhile, Crypt's tempestuous glare drops to Douglas, who is still passed out in the snow. "Shall we take this one's head as a trophy before we go, love? It's the least he can repay for harming you."

I shake my head as Everett carefully pries another bullet from my side. He's so upset by my injuries that he's trembling, but to his credit, there is no frost climbing up his arms. In fact, the only frost here is blooming wherever he gently brushes his fingers, skillfully sealing my wounds with a numbing cold that somehow soothes the pain.

I've never seen his ability so accurate.

Interesting.

"Douglas can live for now," I tell Crypt. "He's a fun opponent. Besides, he now thinks I'm *not* a revenant, which he'll relay to the Legacy Council. The more confused they are, the better for us."

A buzzing from one of my pockets startles me, and I fumble with the phone before finally answering the damn thing. Before I can say anything, a familiar voice crackles over the line.

"Forty-eight motherfucking calls? Are you shitting me? All right, stalker caller. You had better be a really hot bitch with huge tits and a raging demon kink because if I find out you're just some fucking spammer trying to tell me about my car's extended warranty, I'm going to—"

"Let me guess. Rip my head off?" I say coldly.

Melchom goes dead silent. Meanwhile, Everett pulls my phone away from my ear to tap a button. The next time the demon talks, it's much louder, so they can both hear the slight tremble in Melchom's voice.

"Oh! I—it's you. I, um…thought you said you wouldn't need me again, *telum.*" He chuckles nervously. "Look, babe, about that whole changeling thing—I swear on my tail that I had no idea those Remitters were going to send it to Everbound to fuck with your plans. I never would've sold it a single speck of nightshade root powder if I knew—"

"You're a shitty liar, Melchom."

Everett grumbles unhappily about hearing the demon's taboo name. Crypt leans forward to speak more clearly into the phone.

"Melchom, is it?"

The demon hisses. "Who the fuck is that? That's more than enough infernal name-dropping—"

"Oh, hardly." Crypt's tone turns pitch black, his markings lighting up ominously. "Our pretty scourge seems to think you intentionally misled her, which resulted in a rather agonizing memory for me. So you had better pray to hell or hedonism or whatever it is that demons believe in that you have useful information to offer her. If not, I will hunt you down, drive you mad, rip your horns out, and shove them up your flaccid little prick."

I smirk at the menace lacing my match's tone—and because I can't help finding Everett's disturbed expression funny.

Melchom audibly gulps. "Flaming shitballs. Is it...it's you! Never thought I'd talk to *the* Nightmare Prince. You're running with the *telum* now, huh? Listen, I'm a *huge* fan, but you gotta be more specific about what you want from me."

"There's an elusive black market dealer with a stash of etherium," I say smoothly. "Tell me everything you know about him."

Melchom sounds like he's smoking. "Ah, now what's this? The *telum* wants god rocks? Odd. But you know, if my slut of a girlfriend heard this, she'd be tickled pink. See, she bought into all these outlandish rumors that were circling the demon community years ago—"

He's wasting time. When I spot a haunted-looking Silas and exhausted Baelfire walking towards us through the trees, side-stepping corpses and massive shards of ice that must be from Everett, I decide to speed things along.

"*Invoco te Melchom, filium tenebrarum, filium gehennae,*" I recite in the Nether tongue.

It's the very beginning of a demonic ritual I witnessed necromancers perform countless times when I was young. Melchom must not want a piece of my dark soul in exchange for being shackled to me for all eternity because he makes a horrified, inhuman squawking sound.

"No! Stop! Stop it right now. The dealer you want goes by The Scarab, and that's all I fucking know! Okay? That's it!"

Silas and Baelfire finally stop beside us, and I'm relieved to see Bael has healed. But as if the gods want to see how much they can throw at me at once, distant howls sound.

More hellhounds. Fucking great.

"Well?" Melchom demands, still pissy about my nearly invoking his essence. "I told you: The Scarab. All I know is his fucking name, I swear. And if you try to scare the living hells out of me again—"

"Don't threaten my mate," Bael snaps.

Melchom pauses. "Whoa, there. *Mate?* Hang on a motherfucking second. *Telum,* don't tell me you...got *matches?*" He bursts into riotous laughter. "Is that why the Nightmare Prince is with you, too? Hells and bells! Hate 'em or love 'em, the gods do have one wild fucking sense of humor, huh? Hey, you know, you're a scary little fuck, but you're kinda hot, so if you're looking to add to your bouquet of dicks, mine's not half bad—"

I hang up before the four extremely pissed-off matches surrounding me can snap my burner phone in half. More bounty hunters are on their way, and all I got out of Melchom was a stupid name, so it's time we move on.

Except Silas's ruby irises trap mine. "Did that demon say your dealer is called The Scarab?"

I nod.

I can practically see thoughts clicking into place in his head as he mutters to himself. "The symbol of the life cycle. Rebirth. Clever, and if it's true, I always suspected..."

"If you know something, spit it out," Everett snaps, irritable from the call with the demon.

Howling erupts alarmingly close to us this time, but all my ice elemental has to do is look in that direction, and a sharp blast of ice sweeps past us. A loud crack echoes through the woods before the howls become startled barks. Bounty hunters shout in alarm, and then it all cuts off at once, leaving the woods eerily silent again.

We all look at Everett.

"They were crossing over a frozen lake I noticed yesterday. Makes freezing shit easy," he mutters.

Impressive.

And again, far more concise than usual.

Silas looks back at me, his expression intense. "The Scarab is..." His mouth moves, but his voice cuts off, and he huffs. "I know who we're looking for and where to find him. I can do the transportation spell, but I'll need to feed—"

Before he's finished speaking, I sheath Pierce and step forward, pulling my hair away from one side of my neck.

"Take it."

"No," Everett cuts in, stepping in front of me. "She's lost enough blood as it is. Drink from someone else."

I start to argue that he could literally drink *all* of my blood, and I'd still wake up just fine sooner or later, but Crypt holds out his wrist.

"Quicky now, Crane. Before more meddling hounds descend."

Silas pulls a face, but being a pragmatic fae, he bites into the incubus's wrist. Crypt doesn't even flinch.

But the moment Silas swallows, he breaks away, choking on and promptly heaving Crypt's blood back up into the nearest snow drift.

Shit.

What if…

I awkwardly rub Silas's back in the most supportive gesture I can manage. When he's no longer gagging, I offer a reassuring smile and use one of my dark sweater's too-long sleeves to wipe lingering red off his face.

"I think you have to feed from me."

He considers that and nods wearily before casting a disgusted look at Crypt. "Your blood is revolting, by the way. It tastes like carbonated battery acid."

Crypt hums. "Not nearly as nice as Maven's, as I've discovered. Her blood is just as lovely as she is."

He's just saying that to get a rise out of Silas, and it seems like it's working. Actually, it seems like his boat-rocking is beginning to piss off the others, too, since they're still annoyed from that little phone call.

I look over at Douglas and notice he's starting to stir, groaning quietly. With a sigh, I withdraw Pierce and walk back to him as his eyes flutter open.

"Too soon. Back to sleep."

Slamming the dagger's blunt end into his opposite temple, I watch as he blacks out again. He'll wake up with a fucking nasty concussion and a raging headache. Shaking out my hand, I turn back to the others. They're all frowning at me.

"Why leave him alive?" Silas frowns. "That seems uncharacteristic of you."

I shrug. "It is, but I like him."

Baelfire growls. "You *what?* That's it, I'm with Si. Let's kill the guy."

"Slowly and violently," Crypt agrees. "I call dibs."

"Fine by me. I think we'll all *like him* more when he's dead," Everett adds crisply.

Gods. They're all so jealous and over the top, it's damn near toxic. I love it.

"Are we worried about Douglas tracing your magic where we're going?" I ask Silas.

He shakes his head, his pupils dilating when I offer the side of my neck again. He cradles the other side of my neck with his hand, tenderly brushing his lips against the place he's about to bite.

No, my blood blossom, he says telepathically in fae. *No one will be able to breach where we're going.*

Good. Then bite me. It's time we meet The Scarab.

16

BAELFIRE

WHEN SILAS'S red magic fades, we're standing under a dark sky, like it's about to turn twilight. Snow billows around us, sliding across a white landscape spotted with a few spruce trees. I've flown to a lot of remote wildernesses to hunt over the years, and if I were a betting legacy, I'd say we're somewhere in the Arctic Circle.

That would explain the subzero temperature.

Crypt immediately drops into Limbo to scout. A gust of wind sends a waft of Maven's addictive, delicate scent to me, and I glance down to see that she's already shivering. The cold doesn't affect me, but even though my mate is the toughest fucking person I've ever met, she needs a coat ASAP.

"Here, Boo." I wrap my arms around her.

She groans with relief, even though she's still shaking. "Fuck, you're warm."

Pin her. Claim her. Mine, mine, mine—

I grit my teeth against the sharp urge to bite the side of Maven's neck. My inner dragon starts snarling and pitching a fit, aching to hunt and kill if he can't permanently mark our mate right this second.

Even though I killed a couple of hellhounds back there, it hasn't helped much. My dragon's always been an impatient asshole, but it's ten times worse lately. When he pushes at the boundary inside my head again, trying to take control, I squeeze my eyes shut and fight like hell to keep him from attempting to kill Everett or one of the others again.

Maven's gloved hand gently squeezes my arm. I realize she's looking up at me with a question in her eyes, brow furrowed.

"I'm good," I say, not wanting her to worry.

Even though I'm really fucking not good.

Silas has me lift an arm so he can check on Maven's wounds. "Forgive me, *sangfluir*. I should have warned you about the cold, but I promise it won't be for long. We'll be untraceable by the time Douglas awakens and traces my magical signature here."

Everett slides out of his coat, and I help him wrap it around Maven. Obviously the walking Popsicle doesn't need a coat, so I bet he put it on earlier in case she would need one.

Kinda respect that.

She accepts it, her dark gaze sweeping over our surroundings curiously.

"We're in far northern Alaska," Silas explains before whispering more creepy-ass-sounding words as he slowly heals our keeper's stomach and her neck where he bit her.

His nose starts to bleed from whatever magic shit he's doing, but he wipes it quickly away, ignoring Maven's sharp look.

"This is the midst of polar night, hence the darkness. The sun won't rise much above the horizon for weeks."

She's still staring hard at him. He sighs and gives her a placating look. Everett rolls his eyes.

Another silent fucking conversation. I'm starting to understand why it gets under Crypt's skin so much.

Speaking of the stalker, Crypt reappears, tipping his head at Silas. "There is nothing for miles save a barren expanse I cannot enter. Almost as if it's an inhabited dwelling. Care to explain?"

Silas takes Maven's gloved hand and begins walking in the direction we need to go. "If I could, I would have by now. Everyone who comes here is sworn to the utmost secrecy."

I take her other hand, so hopefully, she'll be a bit warmer. I want to pick her up and cradle her little body against the cold wind, but I learned my lesson after the last time—my fierce little keeper doesn't like to be pampered.

Which just makes me want to pamper her sweet ass even more.

After a few minutes of traveling through white nothingness, Maven slows, eyeing the emptiness in front of us.

"Something is about to happen."

Silas nods. "We're about to pass through the first wards once I use the key spell."

"What's on the other side? A fight?" she asks, sounding hopeful.

"Possibly. The security of the exterior ring is constantly being changed out, so it may be a dangerous terrain, guards, monsters, shadow fiends...still, to gain entry into the next layer of—" He cuts off, like his voice has just stopped working, and sighs. "It's a blind risk we must take."

Maven's cute nose wrinkles. "I don't do blind risks. Hang on."

We watch as Maven steps away from us, removes her gloves, and makes the same weird symbol with her hands as she did when we were hunting the changeling—which feels like fucking forever ago. Darkness swirls around her, climbing up her legs and waist as she whispers magic words I don't understand.

And then, just like when we were hunting the changeling, she falls into some kind of trance.

"What the fuck is she doing?" Everett whispers like he doesn't want to interrupt.

"She's about to sacrifice you to dark spirits," I offer. "Probably because she was wildly disappointed by your first time with her, but hey. Don't feel too bad, Professor. I'm a tough act to follow."

He glowers at me. "You're a damn idiot."

"Yeah, but I'm her favorite idiot."

Crypt snorts, brushing snow off the shoulder of his leather jacket. "Not even in your dreams. Everyone knows I'm the favorite."

"And yet you're still not bound to her," Silas smirks.

Dick. He doesn't have to keep rubbing it in our faces.

But on that note…

"So, what'd you do?" I ask, turning to the ice elemental.

"Excuse you?"

I wave him on, impatient. "When you popped your frozen cherry with Maven. What exactly did you do to make the bond snap into place? And did you listen to the stuff we told you about?"

Everett's face turns red. "It's not your business, so fuck off."

"Bonding with Maven *is* our quintet's business, actually," Crypt drawls. "So is her pleasure. If you didn't treat her right, we'll leave your body buried in the snow just here."

"I treated her right," the Frost grumbles.

Silas arches a brow. "Really? Tell me, did you last long enough to get her to finish, or did she have to do that part all by herself?"

Everett's glacial eyes flash with insult, and he lifts his chin. "Not all of us fuck and tell like you and the dragon, so if you're looking for a play-by-play, you can go fuck yourselves. And it was really obvious that Maven had never squirted before with any of *you* assholes, so you can all shut your fucking mouths."

Crypt's brows go up, and Silas blinks in surprise. They're not the only ones.

"What?" I blurt in excitement. "You're kidding. My mate is a squirter? Fuck, yes. Okay, but how the hell did *you* get her to squirt? Was it some trick with ice, or—actually, scratch that. Instead of telling me, you're going to show me as soon as we find privacy and a bed for her. Gods, I can't fucking wait to see Maven squirt."

Too late, I realize the others have all started miming *cut-it-out* motions and shaking their heads because…Maven's done with her trance, and now she's staring at me with one dark eyebrow arched.

I grin. "Hey there, my pretty little Angel of Death. Don't mind us. That was just guy talk."

She rolls her eyes, but there's a definite flush to her cheeks before withdrawing her favorite dagger.

"All right. Let's do this. Leave the fight to me because I know what to expect."

"What? How?" Everett asks, baffled.

Maven ties her black hair up in a ponytail as she speaks, which tells me shit is about to go down.

"When it comes to death, battles, or misery, Amadeus can sense the future and change his tactics accordingly. It makes him incredibly difficult to outmaneuver. When I'm close to death, I can tap into that ability. I assume it's a side effect of the heart he crafted for me."

Hang on a fucking second.

"That spell was for you to grow close to death?" Silas grits, equally upset as he puts it together.

"Calm your tits. I'm fine, and this fight will last less than five minutes. Ready?" she checks, her dark eyes sparkling as she twirls her dagger skillfully.

I love that my mate enjoys combat, but *fucking gods*, this fearless woman is going to be the death of me.

Silas sighs but turns and whispers a spell, motioning with one hand.

It's like a door to nowhere opens up right in the middle of the cold Alaskan wilderness, and we all blink at the lush green field and massive maple trees in the distance. The sky is still dark from the polar night, but we may as well be looking at a scenic summer.

"Fuck," I manage, peeking into the door.

But as soon as I do, I see them. Three figures in black clothing standing several yards away. They immediately send a flurry of spells hurtling toward us, and my hair stands on end as my inner dragon snarls in warning.

I'm no magic expert, but even I can sense that these three are powerful casters.

Maven lurches forward into the green area, lifting one ungloved hand. Dark tendrils erupt from her palm, shattering the incoming attack spells. Ominously dark, crackling energy buzzes around us as more magic flares to life around her bare hands.

The grass dies beneath her feet, blanching to an unnatural white.

Huh. I guess our keeper can draw from plant life in a pinch. Good to know.

One of the attackers starts to make another move, but Maven is already on him, snapping his neck and immediately sending a far stronger blast of dark magic towards the other two.

Each move they make, she clearly knows in advance. For a moment we all stand transfixed as she gracefully dodges a physical attack before taking down the caster with a few expert slashes of her dagger. The last one drops dead a moment later, his magic fizzling to nothing as his slit neck gurgles disturbingly.

Three powerful casters, and it was a fucking cakewalk for her to rip down their spells. She was right—that took less than five minutes.

When Maven turns back to face us, she's smiling. Gods, I *love* her smile. It's still my official goal in life to see it more often. Seeing Maven smattered in blood, her eyes sparkling from fresh kills, looking like a dark fucking queen...

Gods, I'll be her throne any day. She's my fucking queen.

"Impressive," an accented voice says.

We all glance over to see a middle-aged man with dark skin amble onto the field with a shining gold walking stick. He's dressed in brightly colored clothes that look like they were fashionable two hundred years ago, complete with a burgundy waistcoat tucked into weird pants, a cravat, and even a top hat.

I instinctively step in front of Maven to keep her out of sight, but his attention is all on Silas as he walks closer. The man notices the fae's blackened fingertips and scoffs.

"To think my very brightest would turn to necromancy, of all things. As if your magic was not strong enough. If it were for more raw power, one might understand, but to sacrifice such an unparalleled gift for no apparent rea—"

Maven steps out from behind me to get a look at the stranger, who cuts off as he looks her up and down. He glances down at the dead grass, looks questioning at the sky for some reason, and then barks out a laugh.

"I take it back—I certainly see why you made such a career change. Now, moving on. You ought to have written, you know," he turns back to Silas. "You do know what I do to unannounced guests."

"As if you haven't been melodramatically requesting that I pay you one final visit for months," Silas says dryly before taking Maven's hand. "*Ima sangfluir,* this is my mentor, the Garnet Wizard. Evidently also known as The Scarab."

Oh, shit. *This* is the Garnet Wizard?

My mom's always said that even though he can be useful and she agrees with him on some politics, he's also a dangerous eccentric who can't fully be trusted. The fucker's too much of a mercenary at heart, according to her.

The Garnet Wizard throws his head back in a laugh. "Aha! I see you have finally learned of my hand in the black market. Quite a fitting moniker, is it not?"

Silas seems amused. "It is, sir."

The wizard nods and turns to examine the rest of us like he's on a safari and we're wild animals.

"Well, of course, I remember *you,*" he says to Everett. "The only Frost who has ever dared to haggle with me. Pray, what were you then—a mere eighteen? Quite the brass neck."

Everett ignores our curious frowns at him as the wizard leans a little too close to examine my eyes. "Hmm. Brigid Decimus's son... every bit as scaly and proud as she is, I can see." He tips his head at Crypt, who's smoking without a care in the world. "Ah, and the current steward of Limbo—evident, of course, by those eyes. That's always a clear marker."

I frown. "I thought his ink marked him as the steward."

"I am not tattooed," Crypt says on an exhale of smoke, but the wizard talks over him.

"Yes, indeed, those as well. However, each steward throughout history has had exceedingly different markings, so much so that one cannot determine by the markings alone whether they have been gods-given. The eyes, however, are always unmistakable. After all, purple is the chosen color of the gods. And last but assuredly not least..."

The Garnet Wizard leans down to meet Maven's gaze better. She stares back at him with that ironclad poker face she's perfected.

I don't like this legacy studying my mate like she's some fascinating rare creature, so I pull her closer to me.

"My keeper," Silas says with a cutting edge to his tone like he's also wary of how the powerful caster will react.

The wizard smiles, not looking away from her. I randomly note that his hair has a lot more gray than I noticed earlier.

"Your true name, *telum?*" he asks.

"Maven."

"Maven, what?"

"Just Maven."

I frown. Wait, is Oakley not her last name?

He *tsks* like that wasn't the correct answer. "Your parents. Go on and tell me their names. Surely you know by now. Or don't you?"

She pins him with a look, her tone even and firm.

"Cut the shit. Based on that little smirk, you believe you already know who my parents were. But if you think I'm interested in pandering to you for that useless information, you're wrong. We're only here for etherium. If you're open to striking a deal, we'll stay. If not, don't waste my time."

I fucking love how blunt she is, but I'm a bit worried this highly revered legacy is about to try killing her for her boldness. Instead, a smile scrawls over his face, stretching wider until he starts to laugh.

"Etherium, you say?"

"Yes."

"You," he gestures meaningfully at Maven as he keeps laughing. None of us get why, but he's clearly enjoying the hell out of his own inside joke. "*You* want etherium? Great gods, this is just too interesting."

He circles us, tapping his walking stick thoughtfully. "You know, despite my fondness for Silas, I still had my mind set on having you all skinned alive and doused in liquid copper or silver or what have you until it hardened just below your neck. Then I'd have watched you all slowly devoured by a clan of golems for trespassing in my Sanctuary."

"Creative," my mate acknowledges.

"I certainly thought so. But now…well, how can I resist? Of course, we shall discuss a deal, *Maven*. Let us get you five settled in for now, as I can see you've just left a fight. Come."

The wizard turns and strides away, whistling cheerfully as he steps over one of the corpses Maven left behind. I shoot Silas a look.

"I don't trust your crazy-ass mentor."

"Neither do I."

"He's always been bright like that," the Garnet Wizard calls over his shoulder. He's rubbing his lower back like it's suddenly giving him trouble. And his hair is *definitely* lighter than it was before.

We follow the wizard as he leads us through the green field, all of us keeping close to Maven in case more trouble fucking pops up out of nowhere. It's like walking through a warm park at night, except hints of the Northern Lights are beginning to snake very slowly into the dark sky overhead.

Finally, the wizard stops and opens another invisible door, motioning us onward with his walking stick. "Welcome to the inner ring of the Sanctuary. Do mind your step on the bridge."

We all stare at the lush green landscape. It looks like someone took a slice of some peaceful English countryside and plopped it down in the middle of nowhere. Old windmills turn lazily under the twilight sky, a creek babbles under the stone bridge we're about to cross, and past that are several thatched cottage-style houses gathered together in clusters with lit windows casting a slight warm glow. Other old buildings dot the area. A thick forest sprawls in the distance next to what appears to be an old farm.

Two guys dressed in dark clothing wait just past the bridge, watching us with deep frowns. One is scrawny with dark hair, while the other has curly blond hair and an overbite.

When Overbite spots Silas, he scowls deeply. It's pretty clear that he knows the blood fae and hates him.

Relatable.

We walk through the magical doorway, except Crypt slams into an invisible barrier. He's walking ahead of Maven, and I can't help laughing at his irritated expression.

"Sucks to be a siphon," I grin.

"Ah, right," the wizard muses. "One must invite him in."

"Don't!" the dark-haired caster says quickly, eyeing Crypt. "I've heard of him—we all have. That is the fucking Nightmare Prince. He'll infiltrate our minds if we're not careful."

The Garnet Wizard stares down the acolyte. "Then be careful. You know the first rule of my Sanctuary."

"Let the idiots die," Silas supplies.

"Precisely. Anyone who fails to arm a dreamcatcher and lets this subconscious leech into their minds deserves whatever madness he bestows upon them. You may enter, Mr. DeLune."

Crypt flicks the butt of his dead cigarette into the nearby creek, smirking at the outraged reaction that earns from the two casters. He steps through the magical doorway, but when Maven walks in last, Overbite gets pissy.

"Her too?"

"Got a problem with my mate?" I demand.

He rolls his eyes. "*Mate?* How primitive you shifters are. Of course, I take issue with her—not only is she obviously the *thing* that the Legacy Council is hunting down, but she is also a *she*. Females are not permitted within the Sanctuary except in extreme situations."

I gawk at the absolute stupidity of the words that just left his ugly face before turning to Silas.

"So you grew up in a hidden compound of nerdy, sexist virgins who call women *females*? Talk about fucking primitive."

Silas shrugs as if he agrees, but now the two casters are really pissed off. The dark-haired one turns back to the Garnet Wizard.

"Sir, we've all heard the rumors of the *telum*. You cannot possibly mean to allow *that* to take shelter here?" he says, gesturing at Maven with disgust.

Did he just call my mate a '*that?*' My dragon snarls, ready to rip his throat out.

Maven doesn't react to any of this. She's busy surveying our surroundings like she's charting a map of potential future exits. The Garnet Wizard adjusts his walking stick as he regards his acolyte. I swear he's slowly growing wrinkles by the minute.

"Alas, your cynicism and prejudice blind you, Ross. Use your rare gift on her, and you will see what I have already determined. Go on."

The idiot, Ross, grumbles but turns back to Maven. I almost shit myself when a third eye appears smack in the middle of his forehead, blinking open with a glowing blue pupil. Everett jumps, too, swearing about how damn creepy it is.

Meanwhile, the acolyte becomes incredibly pale, as if he sees Maven in an entirely new light. His third eye vanishes, and he drops to his knees.

"By the heavens," he whispers. "I—I had no idea. Please, forgive me, for I swear that if I had known—"

The wizard interrupts, whispering a string of words before a red rune appears on the acolyte's throat. Ross grimaces.

"There. That shall keep this game silent for my own amusement," the wizard smiles.

Wait…what the hell is he talking about? Is it the fact that Maven is a revenant? Did this guy get a glimpse into her past and see how noble she really is, or was this something else?

I'm so fucking confused.

When I steal a glance at the rest of my quintet, they seem to be in the same confused-ass boat—except for Maven, who remains carefully composed as she watches the caster. If she's unsure what just happened, she doesn't show even a hint of it.

The Garnet Wizard breezily tells the two acolytes where to take us for our stay. Overbite still seems pissed, but we follow him and Ross over the bridge and down a long cobblestone path toward a cottage in the distance beside a seemingly endless stretch of green fields.

As we walk, my phone buzzes loudly in my pocket. I blink. "How the hell do you guys get reception here?"

Overbite throws a glare over his shoulder. "How else? Magic. However, unexamined, unsecured cell phones are not permitted. Give it here."

"Make me, Teeth," I dare him, allowing my eyes to shift momentarily.

He whips around immediately, muttering under his breath as we reach the cottage. Ross walks behind us but darts ahead to open the door, dipping his head low to show respect to Maven.

"Please let us know if these quarters aren't to your liking. Only the best for you, my lady."

My lady?

"Okay, what the fuck did you see back there?" I demand at the same time Overbite hisses, "What is wrong with you? She is the scourge!"

Ross ignores both of us. As Maven passes by, he catches her ungloved hand like he's about to kiss the back of it. When she loses her composure and visibly flinches at the surprise, unwanted physical contact, I see red—

And so does Crypt because he promptly pulls out his enchanted sword and cuts off the caster's hand that dared touch our keeper.

17

MAVEN

"HANDS OFF," Crypt seethes.

Ha. Nice.

I wonder if that was an intentional pun or if he's too pissed to realize it. Guessing from his murderous expression that matches the others', I'm guessing the latter.

Ross cries out, cupping his bleeding stump of a wrist. The blond caster whirls on us with magic glowing at his fingertips, ready for a fight, but Everett freezes him solid so quickly that I almost miss it in a blink.

As much as I like seeing these gorgeous legacies get feisty on my behalf, we're only here because the Garnet Wizard seemed to find something about me amusing. If we make enemies or kill acolytes left and right, we may be booted before I talk to the wizard about etherium.

Ross's touch was as revoltingly unwelcome and torturous as touch used to always be for me, but I quickly compose myself and bend to pick up the dismembered hand, offering it to him as a macabre peace offering.

"I assume you acolytes know the more advanced healing spells."

He nods, biting back pain as he accepts his hand.

"Good. Go get patched up right away. Dismembered limbs hurt like a bitch, but it only gets worse if you wait to get it reattached."

He thanks me in a strained voice before rushing away from the cottage.

You say that as if you've experienced it firsthand, Silas growls in my head. *Tell me that's not the case,* sangfluir.

Yeah, right. If they react like this to someone just touching me, there's no fucking way I will ever fill them in on the more morbid aspects of my past.

I glance at the frozen acolyte, decide he can wait until my guys are a bit less testy, and slip through the front door.

It's a studio-style living space, simple but tasteful. The large bedroom blends into a seating area beside the dining room, and the kitchen seems nice from what little I know about kitchens. The Sanctuary looked extremely old-fashioned when we arrived, but there's a fridge, modern oven, and even a small TV mounted on the wall beside the door to the small attached bathroom.

Baelfire was right about the reception because my burner phone starts to buzz. I check to make sure it's not Melchom calling back, but I answer when I recognize Kenzie's number.

"Oh my fucking gods! You're still alive!" she squeals on the other end.

Silas begins laying additional magical wards, Crypt cleans his sword on the hand towel in the kitchen, which pisses off Everett, and Baelfire flops onto the big bed, watching me curiously.

"I'm still alive-ish," I confirm.

"Go ahead," she sniffs. "You better have a phenomenal apology for not texting me back and dropping off the face of the planet for the last couple of days. Do you even know how worried I've been? I was so sure that you were hunted down that I couldn't eat or sleep or fuck or *anything.*"

"You, not fucking? I really must be an omen of the end of times," I joke, sitting on the bed beside Baelfire.

He kisses my thigh, gazing up at me with molten gold eyes like...

Well, like he has the same overwhelmingly sweet, stomach-flip-ping feelings I've been trying like hell to ignore.

Kenzie is legitimately irritated. "You haven't texted me in two fucking days, there have been record surges at the Divide, the human world is in total uproar, and all I know is that my best friend is getting hunted down by some of the most powerful legacies and monsters in the entire fucking world. Put yourself in my shoes, May. Wouldn't you be freaking out?"

I shuffle, absentmindedly playing with Baelfire's hair, which makes him smile contentedly. Thank the fucking universe that at least my matches' touch doesn't bother me much anymore.

"You're right. I should have responded sooner, but we're really fine."

The lioness shifter sighs. "You're forgiven, but only because you're my favorite endearing, gloomy little not-human. Where are you, anyway? No, wait—don't answer that. I probably shouldn't know, just in case a bounty hunter shows up and tries to get the info out of me, right? Okay, instead, how about…how's your quintet? How are things going with them? Are you finally ready to admit just how crazy head over heels you are for them?"

She's teasing, but Crypt appears on my other side with a devious smile.

"Do share how smitten you are, darling," he whispers, twisting strands of my dark ponytail between his fingers and kissing my chin.

Baelfire gently bites my leg as his fingers skim up and down my stomach, brushing aside my shirt as my breathing stutters. Everett and Silas are gazing at me from where they stand, their eyes sharp contrasts of blood red and soft blue.

"I, um—"

Damn it, I need to change the subject. It feels way too warm in this room, and I would rather be strapped back down in Dagon's laboratory than sit around on my ass talking about *feelings.*

"How's Vivienne doing now?"

"Aww, come on!" Kenzie laughs. "She's great, but you're so obvi-ously dodging the question."

You are, Silas agrees telepathically, smirking. *Look how flustered you are. You're blushing.*

"Shut up," I mutter, meaning to respond to him, but it makes everyone laugh, including Kenzie.

"Girl, seriously. My quintet has been dropping *I love you's* all the fucking time because hello? We just went through some majorly traumatizing stuff, and it's better to say it now before the next wave of shit hits the fan and it's too late, am I right? I mean—it's obvious you're all obsessed with each other, and I'd bet my gorgeous new manicure that you've *finally* fucked all of them by now. Right?"

Oh, my gods. "Kenzie—"

"She sure has," Baelfire pipes up, snickering when I grab a pillow to hit him in the head.

Kenzie pauses. "Wait, am I on speakerphone?"

"No," I assure her.

All my guys crack up. I don't get why until Crypt kisses my cheek.

"You are, love. Can't you hear the difference? It's this button here. See?"

Damn it. I fucking hate phones.

Kenzie bursts into laughter, too. "This was supposed to be girl talk! No wonder getting you to fess up about your feelings is like trying to pull teeth."

"To be clear, it's always like this with her," Silas supplies. "She's scared of the so-called *L*-word."

I grab another pillow to throw at him. "Silas fucking Crane. I said *shut up.*"

"Wait, really?" Everett tips his head, smiling so those completely unfair dimples are displayed. "Why, though? You should already know how we feel by now, so why would it—"

"Let's talk about literally anything else," I interrupt, grabbing Baelfire's wrist to keep his hand from creeping under my shirt. He just smiles and winks without shame.

Someone knocks on the door of the cottage.

Thank the universe—an interruption.

"Shit. Kenzie, I need to go," I sigh.

"Fine, fine," she says petulantly. "But wait—can you guys please make sure that your way-too-practical mate keeps up with her bestie? Girl time is *mandatory*. She can't just be surrounded by testosterone-fueled, obsessive, wildly horny matches all the time, or she'll start to get dickmatized."

That doesn't sound like a real thing, especially because they all burst into laughter again. Kenzie calls them some choice words and then makes me promise to text or call her back soon. I agree and hang up, glowering at my amused matches as I walk to answer the door.

"Gods. You're all idiots," I grumble, still annoyingly flushed.

"Who are really fucking in love with you," Baelfire inserts, suddenly serious.

I die inside, especially because the others don't argue. That unspeakable emotion tries to well up, and even without a heart, something in my chest aches.

I quickly turn away, opening the door for a distraction from these damned feelings.

It's Ross. His hand is reattached, wrapped in bandages, and he dips his head far too low, almost like a bow.

"My lady."

"Call me Maven."

"M—Maven," he corrects, glancing at the frozen blondie beside him. "The Garnet Wizard has formally invited you for a business discussion, after which your entire quintet is invited to dine in the Great Hall for our grand Starfall Day dinner. Also…would you, um…mind unfreezing Parker?"

I look over my shoulder at Everett.

He sighs and moves to stand beside me in the doorway. All at once, the ice around the blond acolyte melts away. Parker chokes and gasps for air, falling to the porch in a shivering mess. Ross helps him stand, but the toothy caster sneers at me, brimming with contempt.

"You fucking—"

"Stop there if you want to live," I advise.

He huffs, still shivering with blue lips. He glares at Everett, who has his bored-arrogant-professor face on.

"Your boy toys may be formidable, yet I am one of the strongest third-grade acolytes ever to come to the Sanctuary. I can take them."

"First of all, I don't know or care what that rank means. Second of all, stop fucking talking."

He starts to say something else to me, but Ross covers his mouth with a sigh. "I'm so sorry. He has no idea that you're, you know…"

Just like earlier, I have no fucking idea what he's talking about. I can only guess, and that seems like a waste of time I could be using to barter with the Garnet Wizard.

"All right. Let's go," Everett says, stepping outside.

Ross shuffles uncomfortably, finally letting Parker go. "Only your keeper will be allowed to speak privately with my mentor. You were only invited to dinner."

The Nightmare Prince materializes in front of Ross, who yelps and leaps back.

Crypt's voice is pure warning. "She will go nowhere alone."

"Oh, *she* won't?" I challenge, arching a brow at him. "I'm going, and I'll be fine."

His purple gaze is tumultuous as he turns his back on the casters, an insult in the world of legacies that indicates he doesn't see them as a real threat. He cradles the side of my face and speaks quietly.

"You being *fine* and you being properly treated and watched over are two entirely different things, darling. Having you out of my sight is not an option. Besides, if you leave me alone with these buffoons, I'm liable to rip all three of them apart out of boredom while I wait."

I smirk. "Bullshit. If you really didn't like them, you would have driven them insane years ago. Instead, you've watched their backs. Most people would call that touching."

He studies me, his lips curling up. "And what do you call it?"

"Convenient. It means I don't have to *actually* worry about you killing them or vice versa."

"As if he even fucking could," Baelfire calls from inside the cottage.

Silas moves to the threshold, too, pressing a gentle kiss against the side of my neck. He ignores that Parker is glaring daggers at him like he has a personal vendetta against the blood fae.

"You will not *truly* be alone," Silas murmurs in my ear, softly enough that I doubt Baelfire can even hear him.

He goes on telepathically. *Everett and I are a mere thought away. And although my mentor has his idiosyncrasies, his obsession with knowledge drives him. You're a curiosity to him, and as such, he will not allow harm to come to you. If anyone else tries—*

I'll kill them, I reassure him before leaving to talk to the wizard.

18

MAVEN

THOUGH MY QUINTET isn't happy about this situation, twenty minutes later, Ross opens the door to an expansive study room within one of the many other buildings in the Sanctuary.

It's something between a library, alchemist lab, and indoor garden, with books lining every wall and a small sitting area beside thriving plants. Ross again dips his head and continues acting far too fucking formal with me before closing the door, leaving me alone with the Garnet Wizard.

Who has aged considerably within the last hour and a half.

When we first met him, I would have guessed he was in his late forties. Now he's definitely in his fifties, and his hair has grayed into his eyebrows. He's sitting in one of the cushioned settees sipping tea and smiles when he sees me analyzing him.

"Silas did not warn you of my curse beforehand because he has been sworn to the utmost secrecy, as is everyone who enters my Sanctuary."

He nods at the teapot and cup waiting for me on the small coffee table beside a small stack of ancient-looking books. I briefly skim the titles on their old, cracked spines.

A Complete History of Paradise

Divine Compendium: All We Know of Gods and the Saints Who Walk Among Us

Sancti, Semidei et Prophetae

I'm still translating the last title in my head when he motions again at the teapot.

"Tea?"

I don't trust eating or drinking anything offered freely, but I take the opposite seat and study him, putting the pieces together.

"It's your curse. You age quickly."

"Four years per hour, to be precise. My life cycle resets each midnight—or rather, it used to. For centuries, ever since I lost my keeper and quintet, it has always been the same, but recently, the aging cycle has become quite unstable. I might wake old in the morning and age backward, for example. Extremely tedious and something I have taken as a sign of my probably-impending death."

I see now how Silas matched this curse with The Scarab nickname. This is one of the most severe curses I've heard of, so it's also no surprise that Silas wants Baelfire's scales to try to treat his mentor's condition.

Still. It's fucking weird that he's openly telling me about such a taboo subject.

The wizard sees my expectant look and shrugs, setting down his teacup. "That was my way of offering you transparency, for I am not one to beat ineffectively around the bush."

"Me neither."

"Excellent. Then, let us be frank with one another. I have long stopped caring about keeping the Nether out of this world. Indeed, my untraceable Sanctuary is my own world. It is safeguarded from any monster, human, or shadow fiend that I do not wish to admit. Only my deeply loyal acolytes and I know how to leave and enter through two rare spells, which I can change anytime. If the prophecies are true and you are to bring about the end of balance between the five planes and wreak havoc on this world, I and my collection of knowledge shall be quite safe here."

I absorb that. At least now I know Gideon can't get into the Sanctuary, even if he does track us here. It also means Douglas and any others after us won't reach us for now.

"All this to say, we are not enemies," the wizard clarifies.

"We're not allies, either."

"Agreed. We simply both exist and can benefit from one another if the option arises. If you need etherium or my assistance, I only require one thing in return."

I glance down at my hands, which feel odd without gloves. "Knowledge. Silas says it's what drives you."

He smiles. "How very true. He's always been quite bright—my only official apprentice for the last two hundred years, and I daresay someone I could almost consider a friend. And to think, I nearly refused to take him in. Those damned immortals would have raised him if that elemental of yours hadn't stepped in."

I blink. "What?"

The Garnet Wizard peruses the little teacakes on the table.

"Indeed. I charge a rather exorbitant fee for tutelage, let alone raising and apprenticing someone for many years. The Crane estate and fortune ought to have passed to that young prodigy when his parents killed one another—but their will was suspiciously altered, and his distant Crane relatives descended like wolves. He would never have survived on what little they left him with, and he knew it. He sent an application to me, but I overlooked the boy because of his severe lack of funding."

He huffs with disdain. "Not to mention, I knew how much the Immortal Quintet wanted to make a Crane into one of their obedient, brainwashed pets. You see, I like to avoid them entirely, so I was resolved to ignore the so-called prodigy and continue as I have."

"But...Everett stepped in?" I press, still stuck on that. "How?"

"He had contacted me and paid quite handsomely a few years prior for a very special trinket—intended for an empath, I believe. He contacted me again after the death of the Cranes, but instead of money, he offered nevermelt. At the time, it was worth far more than a fortune would have meant to me. After quite a lot of haggling, wherein I realized he seems to have inherited his annoyingly keen business sense from that prat father of his, I agreed to take in Silas as my apprentice." He laughs. "Looking back, it is one of the finer decisions I've made in my very long life. Quite a lad, your blood fae."

Oh, my gods.

Knowing Silas's life could have been so drastically different at the hands of the Immortal Quintet and that Everett stepped in like that…

"Silas doesn't know about this," I realize.

"No, to be sure. Secrecy was part of the arrangement. I assumed the elemental would tell him eventually."

I try to tame my smile, but it's surprisingly tricky.

Those fucking legacies. They're all secretly a bunch of softies, aren't they? They can gripe about each other and fight all they want, but the sense of brotherhood they deny having any trace of has clearly played a part in all their lives.

You're getting a blowjob tonight, I send just to Everett.

There's a shocked silence, followed by a very flustered, *I…you… um, what?*

Just say yes and thank you.

Yes. Thank you. But only if I get to return the favor. Also, please *tell me you're safe.*

I reassure him that I'm good as I finally pour myself tea. If the Garnet Wizard was going to try hurting me, he would have done it by now.

Thank the gods. But keep talking. We're kind of dying over here without updates, Snowdrop, Everett's soft voice says in my head.

Whoa. Hang on. Snowdrop?

Not you, too. You cannot nickname me, I protest telepathically. *Just call me Maven or Oakley like usual.*

As we discussed, your last name isn't Oakley.

For the last time, I will not be named after a motherfucking flower.

But it's symbolic. I put a lot of thought into it, unlike Baelfire with his ridiculous string of nicknames. If he gets to call you everything under the sun, at least let me call you 'Snowdrop' and 'mine.'

Gods. What the hell am I supposed to do with all these fucking nicknames? It's ridiculous.

"Back to the subject at hand," I mutter, realizing I've zoned out while the Garnet Wizard sips his tea. "What knowledge do you want in exchange for etherium? And more importantly, what will you do with anything you learn from *me*?"

The Garnet Wizard smiles. "I see you've learned to ask the right questions, Maven. You are from the Nether, are you not?"

"I am."

"Do you have any idea of the confusing theories permeating the secular world about the Nether? It has long tormented me with its mystique. I want to know the truth about it."

"Meaning, you want to know about the Entity."

He snorts. "Not unless you deem it interesting information. No, no, I'd much rather know about *you*, actually, and what you think you are. You strike me as one having a plan of her own, not to mention quite the story to share. Tell me everything simply to satisfy my curiosity, and I promise you may have all the etherium you like."

It seems too easy and too good to be true. What if he wants all this information to turn around and tell the Immortal Quintet and Legacy Council? Not that he seems fond of those groups, but still.

My suspicion must be evident because the wizard nods and stands, gripping his walking cane and gesturing that I should follow.

"Not one to be taken in easily, I see. I applaud your reluctance to trust, for it is the best mode of survival. Come, then. Let me show you something as a show of good faith."

We leave the study through a set of double doors, and the Garnet Wizard chatters casually as we walk down a long cobblestone path toward a colossal wall of hedges with a gate in the center.

Blood blossom, Silas reaches out telepathically, just to me so Everett won't hear. *Tell me you're still breathing. Now, please.*

So bossy. I thought your paranoia was gone, I tease.

I will never feel sane in your absence, not to mention your very existence drives me mad with need. Where are you now?

We pause in front of the gate, and the Garnet Wizard mutters about his lousy back before giving me a look.

"You seem the action type. I warn you not to react rashly."

"Noted."

We're just walking into a garden. No big deal, I report to Silas.

When the gate to the garden opens, I stare at the couple sitting together on a bench in front of an enchanted koi pond.

One of them is a vampire, judging by the trickle of blood dried on his chin as he rests his head against the woman's shoulder. He's handsome, with a shock of red hair and an abundance of freckles. He brings the woman's hand to his lips to kiss the back of it.

When he looks over and makes eye contact with me, I don't look away despite the disconcerting chill that washes over me. It reminds me of the feeling I get when I sense death nearby—or when I'm tapping into Amadeus's abilities to see the future.

But my interest in the vampire and that feeling shifts quickly.

Because the woman is Engela Zuma.

She's dressed in an old-fashioned-looking dress. When she sees me, she remains still, as if she doesn't know who I am and what I'm meant to do to her.

What the fuck?

What is it? What's wrong? Silas asks immediately.

Are you hurt? Everett demands.

Oops. I didn't mean to send that through the bond.

I'm fine, I say quickly before blocking them out because all this telepathic communication gets distracting.

This wizard knows I'm the *telum,* and therefore that I'm supposed to kill this immortal…yet he's introducing us?

"A moment of your time, Engela?" he calls.

The earth elemental monster leaves the garden, stopping in front of me. Her neck has noticeable recent puncture marks. Whenever I ran into her at Everbound University, she gave off an odd, unsettling feeling—but it's gone now. She seems more present somehow, more focused as she looks me over without hostility.

"Who is this?"

I frown at her. "We've met."

Her gaze turns distant as if she's trying to remember. "We have, haven't we? I believe...you may be the one they are hiding from. Natalya and Iker, I mean."

"And you're not hiding with them?"

Engela shakes her head, her expression sad and wise at once. "No. I only escaped once I saw my chance. If I return to them, Natalya will only meddle with my mind until I feel and think nothing, just as I have for the last few centuries. I would much rather spend my last days with the one I truly care for before I finally am taken to the Beyond. If you are who I believe...I accept my fate. I only ask a few more days with my Bertram before you do what you must."

Well, then.

This is really fucking unexpected.

I glance at the vampire who waits on the bench patiently. If he knows I'm supposed to kill his girlfriend, he doesn't react. He just watches, giving off that same off-kilter energy that I can't figure out.

"So, you're fine with dying?" I reiterate, looking back at Engela. "You expect me to believe you were being mind-controlled by your keeper when you stabbed my dragon shifter with a fucking mountain?"

She studies the twilight sky, which is streaked with even more hints of the aurora borealis. "I apologize if I did injure him, though I do not recall it. But whether you believe it or not, truth is truth. I have not been within my own untarnished mind in so long that I can barely remember when the tarnishing began. I know it was after I met Bertram, at least," she adds, looking over her shoulder with a small smile. "I thank Arati that he returned to me after losing him for so long."

She looks back at me. There is still a slight inhuman stilt to the way she speaks, evidence that she is no standard elemental but one from the Nether.

"I have lived hundreds of mortal lifetimes with monsters who made me feel nothing. I have seen atrocities that they made me forget and been forced to do things that I wish they *would* make me forget. In all the nothingness of my existence, finally experiencing mortal love is the only thing that has brought me…this. Serenity. I don't need lifetimes of it, *telum*. Mere days would be enough, for it is more than I have hoped for in far too long. And when you deem it time, I shall gladly depart this life."

I examine her at length. She doesn't seem to be lying, but just to be safe…

"Prove it. You know what I'll need."

Engela's smile is soft before she pulls something out of one of her dress pockets.

At first glance, it looks like an expensive diamond-encrusted bracelet. But then I sense that one of the decorative beads is made of the glass-like substance I'm looking for.

I was right, then. They all have an etherium anchor.

For a long moment, I stare at the bracelet as I consider everything. Finally, I hand it back to Engela, meeting her dark gaze.

"Tell me where the other two are, and I won't need this."

She's surprised, as is the Garnet Wizard. But when I don't take it back, Engela pockets the etherium bracelet and thinks.

"As I said, my mind has been meddled with for quite a long time. My quintet has many safehouses and may have found new hiding places. I will make you a list of their likeliest whereabouts, as well as their etherium life links, but I warn you that they will be trying to have you killed long before you can find them."

More fun for me. Let them try.

Engela turns to return to her lover but pauses, looking over her shoulder at me with an almost sad expression. "Your incubus. Somnus's son."

"His name is *Crypt*," I say pointedly, guarded.

My Nightmare Prince says little about his past, but I've deduced that the Immortal Quintet was brutal to him growing up. Still, Engela did deliver those messages from him to us. Maybe that counts for something.

"I ask that you offer Crypt my apologies for any part I may have played in his past," she says quietly. "I gave up fighting them long before he came to be, or else he would have had someone watching over him. Instead, I'm afraid he abandoned all feeling and became quite twisted just to survive."

She returns to her lover in the garden, and for a moment, I stare at the koi in the pond.

I became twisted to survive, too. So did the others.

Now, I just need to make sure they keep surviving once this is all over.

I turn back to the Garnet Wizard. "Etherium for knowledge. I accept your deal with one other condition."

"Which is?"

"Engela Zuma must be safe here. She needs to remain this well-protected until I can re-stabilize the Divide."

His brows go up. "Re-stabilizing the Divide is a part of your plan?"

"Agree to the condition and find out."

The Garnet Wizard smiles. "It's a deal, *telum.*"

19

SILAS

She isn't letting me in.

I pace impatiently outside the guest cottage, examining the layout of the other buildings. The Sanctuary hasn't changed since I left months ago.

I can't fathom my mentor being dangerous to Maven, not with all the questions he will have about her—but the other acolytes could pose a threat. They know that if they can best someone here and get away with it, they will not be punished, even if it is a guest of the wizard.

The Garnet Wizard was an excellent mentor but also taught me how brutal the world is for legacies. There was no safety here outside of what I afforded myself.

I hardly think of this place as home. Apart from anywhere Maven is, I have no home.

"Hey, Crane," a hostile voice calls.

I sigh when I see the trio of acolytes approaching quickly in the dimness. Speak of the devils. I expected something like this to happen upon my return, but it is still irritating when I'd rather keep my attention on whether Maven is all right.

"Turn around now, gentlemen," I drawl.

One of the acolytes lifts his hands, calling forth a glowing amber spell that highlights the disgust on his face.

"So it's true? You're a fucking *necromancer* now?"

"You shouldn't have turned to death magic, and our mentor should never have let your putrescence in here," another adds, preparing his own spell.

They never learn, do they?

As if my paranoia hadn't been severe enough, over the years growing up here, I learned that the only way to survive was to show no mercy. Many acolytes, even those I once thought were friends, made it clear that they wanted to be the top student and would happily kill me to have that honor. Sparing them for sentiment led to worse attempts on my life, so I chose to be ruthless instead.

These casters would happily kill me to rid the world of the necromancer I have become. Unfortunately for them, they have failed to strike first. As our mentor would say, all bark and no bite makes for a fresh grave.

I need to feed from Maven again before I can use more blood magic.

Necromancy it is, then.

Calling the chilling, unnatural power to my fingertips, I level two of the acolytes with necromantic bone rot spells that quickly bring them to the ground, twitching and screaming as their insides fall apart. The first acolyte who spoke finally hurls his magic at me, but I deflect it with a flick of my wrist.

For a moment, we're locked into a hair-raising magic duel, his amber flashes of light eclipsed by the darkness I now wield.

Finally, one of my attacks cuts through his center. He drops, choking and gasping until he goes still just before the murky, semi-translucent, humanoid shape of a ghost rises from his fallen corpse.

The evening returns to silence as I look down and rub my fingers together, studying the blackened skin. It's as if there was frostbite or a severe burn, though my ability to feel is only slightly numbed. I feel relatively normal.

Until once again, my head begins to spin, my heart racing unnaturally as blood drips from my nose. I sigh and wipe it away. I suppose it would have been too much to hope I could wield both types of magic without some toll being demanded.

Thanks to becoming a necromancer, I can sense the three spirits hovering nearby. The rich, tantalizing feeling of death hangs in the air, but although the ghosts fascinate me, I keep my eyes averted when I sense *her* arrive.

Syntyche. The reaper goddess.

My hair stands on end, and I can't breathe because of this proximity to the goddess of death herself. A hollow, chilling whistle cuts through the air—once, twice, three times. I've learned that sound accompanies each swing of her scythe as she reaps souls.

Hardly a blink later, I can sense she's gone. I finally inhale, clearing my throat as I try to stop my hands from shaking.

There is a very short list of things that frighten me in this world. Though I've yet to see her face, the goddess of death is quickly becoming the top item on that list.

Crypt emerges from Limbo, leaning against the outside of the cottage as he cracks his neck. His markings lit up nearly an hour ago, and he promptly vanished, yet they still glow faintly as he watches me start to pace. It makes me wonder if he went to tend to Limbo or if he was, in truth, waiting outside whatever dreamcatcher-protected room our keeper is in.

"Update," he demands, ignoring the fresh corpses nearby.

I rub my face. "Maven stopped giving me any. It's beyond aggravating."

He smirks. "Dislike not having access to her pretty mind? Welcome to the club, Crane."

"Shut up and make yourself useful." I motion at the bodies. "They'll be devoured in Limbo, won't they? Maven shouldn't have to see them when she returns."

"We both know she would enjoy such a welcoming party," Crypt muses, but he grabs hold of two of the corpses and vanishes with them. A moment later, the third disappears, and then the Nightmare Prince returns to stretch languidly and lean back against the cottage.

Baelfire wanders outside. He clearly just showered. "Thought I heard a fight out here."

"It wasn't much of a fight, I assure you," I mutter.

The dragon shifter grunts and squints into the distance. "Which one is the Great Hall? I'm fucking starving. Do they do an actual Starfall dinner here, or is it all like…weird shit?"

"Why wouldn't they have a normal Starfall dinner?"

"I don't know, why the hell would women not be allowed in?" he counters. "This place is backward-ass enough that a holiday dinner made entirely of literal shit wouldn't surprise me."

"Women aren't allowed in because the Garnet Wizard thinks romance is too much of a distraction to his acolytes."

"What, he thinks gay romance just doesn't fucking exist?"

I snort. "It's not a rule I agree with, but he's several centuries old and has cherry-picked which modern values to adopt. He respects women well enough, but the thought of a coeducational environment sends him into fits."

"Weird fucker," Baelfire mutters.

I've often thought so myself. Still, I respect my mentor. There is no more powerful caster in the world.

A moment later, Everett also walks out and frowns at us. "What are you three doing out here?"

Crypt lights another of his cigarettes. He's going through them at a rate that would be alarming—or would be if I cared two fucks about him.

"Drugs," he says cheerfully, taking a puff and offering it to Everett.

The ice elemental rolls his eyes but joins us outside, watching the slight colors in the dark sky until Baelfire turns to him, folding his oversized arms.

"So, what did the wizard mean about remembering you? You know him?"

I've been wondering about that, too. We all look at the Frost, who feigns disinterest as he picks invisible lint off his sleeve.

"Must've gotten me confused with my dad or something."

I scoff. "We all know that's a lie. He talked about you at eighteen. What did you—"

"Just drop it," he snaps. "My business is my business, so unless you three shits want to stand around a fire holding hands and singing kumbaya, leave me the hell alone."

Always so godsdamned moody.

But then I tip my head, curious. "Show me your hands."

"What?"

"You're upset. Show me your hands."

Everett mutters about me being an asshole but pulls his hands out of his pockets, showing us.

"No frost," Crypt muses. "Does this mean what I think?"

It means your curse isn't what you thought, I tell Everett telepathically, shocked enough that I forget to speak out loud.

The ice elemental shoots me another glare before looking away.

"Yeah. I've noticed it since Maven and I—since she broke my curse, I mean. I have so much more control, it's fucking laughable. I'm not unleashing ice with every tiny thought and emotion. I don't…I don't really know how I didn't figure this out a lot sooner. Honestly, I feel like a damn idiot for not realizing the truth."

We all absorb it until Baelfire finally seems to piece things together.

"Hold up. Is it just because you've gotten that much more powerful, or…" His eyes widen. "Holy shit! What if your curse isn't what you thought it was? What if it was actually being shit at controlling your abilities?"

"Way to catch up, Lizard Brain," Everett mutters.

"But then why the fuck would Arati's prophet lie to you?"

Everett glowers into the distance. "I can think of five reasons, and they raised me just right so that I would never think to question a prophecy. I've seen my parents bribe others plenty of times. Just never fucking thought they would bribe a high prophet to translate a prophecy the way they wanted him to."

We're all silent for a long moment until Baelfire whistles.

"Damn. So...your cockblock curse was a big, fat lie. They were just trying to control you."

"Yep."

"To keep you lonely and miserable."

"They do prefer me that way," he says dryly. "They've always said lonely people are the easiest to make useful."

Bael shakes his head. "Your parents are fucked up."

"You have no idea," Everett mutters, rubbing his face. "At least now I know the truth. That all the sickening panic I felt about putting my keeper at risk every time I was around her was just good old-fashioned psychological torture from my gold star parents."

He's bitterly sarcastic, but the truth is that when we were young, I thought he *did* have perfect parents. A perfect life. Far more perfect than mine ever could be.

Now, I also feel like an idiot for thinking that.

"I'll kill them if you like," Crypt offers like he's just offering a stick of gum, blowing out more smoke.

I glare at him. "You *are* the expert at killing families. At least this time, there will be a reason for it."

Baelfire makes a sound I don't get as he gives Crypt a look. "Yeah, about that..."

"Keep your fucking snout shut, or I'll drag you into Limbo again," Crypt warns, flicking his still-lit cigarette at Baelfire. "Only this time, I'll leave you in there."

Of course, the heat does nothing to the dragon, who looks back at me. "He had a reason."

Crypt's eyes flash. "Don't test me, Decimus."

I look between them, uncertain, but Baelfire seems to decide to drop it for now as he rolls his eyes and mutters something under his breath. For several long moments, we're all quiet again. The tension remains between Crypt and me, though he ignores the glares I'm sending his way.

"So…back at that diner," Bael breaks the silence, rubbing his neck.

"In Nebraska?" Everett frowns. "What about it?"

"With Maven acting like she was…you know. Pregnant." The dragon shifter clears his throat. "I can't stop thinking about it. It's just that—with all this bonding, do you guys think that could actually…"

When he trails off again, I give him a droll look. "What? Spit it out."

"Some of our curses are broken," he mumbles.

It takes a second for me to realize what he's saying, and then I'm floored. Maven has no curse to lift, so she isn't affected by the same inability to procreate that we legacies have.

Or that we *did* have. When we were cursed. But now that Everett and I have been with her, unprotected, uncursed…

Gods above. I wasn't even thinking about that.

Everett drags a hand through his hair, and he must not be paying attention to filtering his thoughts through the bond because I catch a hint of his inner prayers to both Arati and Koa.

What are you gods-aboving and praying about? Maven asks telepathically, making both myself and the ice elemental jump nearly out of our skin.

Just…nothing, Everett sends back, pulling at the neckline of his shirt like he's flushed.

"Nothing?" I huff, glaring at him. "We need to bring this up with her."

Crypt's purple gaze darts between us and he scowls impatiently. "Are you two asses talking just to each other now, or is our girl finally done with the man behind the curtain?"

Everett ignores him, glaring at me. "No shit. We'll talk to her when the time is right."

You guys are weirdly quiet, she notes. *Did something happen? Who do I need to kill?*

So eager, I tease. *Everything is fine. Are you nearly here?*

About that. Let's meet at the Great Hall, Maven suggests. *My visit with the wizard is nearly done.*

We'll be there waiting for you, I reply, already striding in the direction we need to go.

"This way," I tell the others. "I don't want her arriving at dinner alone. You may call me cutthroat, but the other acolytes here quite literally cut each other's throats when they can. It's only a matter of time before someone here tries something with our keeper."

20

SILAS

I'ᴛ's ʜᴜsʜᴇᴅ between the four of us, bordering on awkward, as I lead them to the Great Hall.

We slow as we approach the massive open-air dining room lit by a cacophony of holiday-colored mage lights drifting around the Grecian pillars surrounding the dining area. Holly, mistletoe, and other festive plants deck the hall while classy holiday music plays courtesy of someone's spell. Three or four dozen acolytes are already here, discussing holidays back home, philosophy, religion, holiday foods, and so on. Many glare as we pass, and I'm not surprised when one of them throws a slice of baked ham at me.

It bounces off an easy spell, but I keep my hands in my pockets to draw less controversial attention to my blackened fingertips as we head toward the grandiose main dining table. I'm sure the Garnet Wizard will want us seated near him so he can talk to Maven.

"Is it just me, or do these other nerds hate your guts?" Baelfire asks as we sit. "Especially Overbite."

"Parker," I nod. "He tried outranking me a year or two ago. I humiliated him, and he isn't over it. The others have similar stories."

"You, friendless? I'm shocked," Crypt drawls, tapping the empty plate in front of him. "Where's the food?"

"You don't eat," Everett reminds him.

"My thanks for informing me of the fucking obvious, Frost, but I meant for Maven. I want a feast ready for her."

I tap his plate, activating the prepared charm on it. Popular holiday foods appear: prime rib, turkey, baked ham, scalloped potatoes, roasted Brussels sprouts, minced pies, stuffing, and gravy.

"Only casters can use these plates," I explain.

"If you make me ask you nicely for dinner, I'll let my dragon eat you instead," Baelfire warns testily.

I smirk and activate their plates, adding an additional protection charm to each of them out of habit.

Just as I transfigure their water glasses into festive fae wine, a hush falls over the Great Hall. My quintet turns to see Maven walking in with the Garnet Wizard.

The expressions on the other acolytes' faces are priceless. They range from appalled to furious to outright fascination as they watch her join us at the head of the main table set apart from the rest.

I note that one of the gawking acolytes' attention quickly moves from Maven to Everett, and he gets that same obnoxiously starstruck expression on his face as the former model received at Everbound all the time.

Baelfire frowns deeply as he watches the Garnet Wizard take a seat at the head of the table. My mentor is far more wrinkled and grayed than earlier. I've seen him at every phase of his curse—having been around it for nine years, I forget to find it odd.

Dinner proceeds. Now that we're more or less alone where the other acolytes aren't likely to hear, I address my old mentor.

"What do you know of hybrid casters? Those able to use multiple types of magic?"

"I know your keeper became one through years of torturous experimentation," he muses, sampling the potatoes. "Otherwise, it is highly uncommon."

Baelfire cuts straight through his plate with his dinner knife, his expression stormy as his eyes shift to dragon slits. He covers his face, trying to calm down.

"Boo," he says roughly, clearly wanting answers.

"He's making it sound worse than it is."

She's lying. I'm getting better at reading her, but when she pointedly ignores our stares and pretends like the Brussels sprouts are fascinating, I sigh and turn back to my mentor.

"I can still use my blood magic. It wasn't burned away in the fever transitioning into a necromancer."

His face lights up with fascination. "Truly? Show me."

"I can't until I feed on her."

The wizard rubs his graying facial hair. "Only from her, eh? How very unprecedented. Perhaps it's all to do with who you are bound to, as she is *also* quite unprecedented. After all, the most powerful keepers result in the most powerful quintets and have been known to influence the range of their quintets' abilities. Or perhaps this has something to do with you being bound to her shadow heart."

I frown, telepathically reaching out to Maven. *You told him we're bound? And about your heart?*

I told him a lot of things. The good news is we'll get etherium as soon as it arrives from where he's been storing it outside the country.

What's the bad news? I press. *The price?*

She stabs a sprout. *He wanted knowledge. I've had to tell him about shit I've tried hard to forget.*

"Pity, though, that you had to become a necromancer," the wizard tuts, interrupting us.

I look at my own plate. "I regret nothing."

"Besides, it's the best of both worlds," Baelfire pipes up, his shifter emotions swinging back to cheerful as he finishes his ham. "Now you can heal our keeper *and* see dead people. I see it as a win."

"Except for the part where he's now a feared pariah of society," Everett points out.

Crypt isn't eating, of course. He's trying to balance forks in a tower as he smirks. "Aren't we all, though?"

Very true.

"E—excuse me?" the starstruck acolyte says, approaching our table nervously. He dips his head respectfully at the wizard but turns quickly to Everett, eyes wide. "You're *the* Everett Frost! I'm—gods, I'm a huge fan. I'm an atypical caster," he adds almost sheepishly. "Grew up in New York, and my mom and I are both fashion enthusiasts. She's actually an editor for Vogue, so I've been to lots of shows and…again, I'm just a big fan."

Everett slips into a pleasant, practiced persona I'm sure he perfected for his career, thanking the fan despite Baelfire snorting derisively and Crypt tossing scalloped potatoes across the table at them.

"Sorry to bother you, but…" The acolyte holds up a permanent marker hopefully.

Everett autographs the caster's arm, politely answering a couple of questions to say he isn't going to be at Paris Fashion Week next year, and, yes, he is friends with some famous human singer I've never heard of.

When the acolyte finally thanks him and hurries away, Maven tips her head.

"Kenzie told me about autographing, but I still don't understand. Does that happen often?"

"Much more often among human fans." Everett turns back to his food.

Baelfire scoffs. "Okay, it's so fucking bizarre to think that *you* have fans. Clearly, they don't know what an asshole you are, outside of whatever the fuck models do."

"I'm not an asshole to everyone. Just you three because you fucking deserve it," Everett corrects in a grumble. "I happen to be really good with humans. Believe it or not, there's a reason the Everbound staff assigned me to teach Advanced Human Relations."

So *that's* what he supposedly taught.

Baelfire continues to rib him about it as I refill Maven's cup of wine. Dinner continues for a while with light conversation until, as has happened with every holiday dinner since the beginning of time, politics arise.

Baelfire makes an offhand comment about Everbound's recent

anti-legacies troubles, and my mentor launches into a tirade about his political views.

"...of course, those immortals relish their influence in the mortal world, but at least the Reformists are not nearly so thickheaded as those blasted Remitters," the Garnet Wizard says, finally taking a moment to sip his wine.

"The Reformists are the other faction of anti-legacy activists?" Maven clarifies.

He hums. "The Legacy Council labeled them as anti-legacies, and so everyone believes it—but that is utter horseshit. The Reformists lobby for legacies and humans to have equal footing in the mortal world, and they question the current system as a whole. They insist we are far more civilized than monsters and thus should be allowed to mingle with humans freely, choose other careers, and even inter-marry."

He scoffs at that.

"You disagree with them," she surmises.

"They're idealists. Dreamers. If the world could work the way they want, it would take such a major upheaval that it would create far more problems than it could solve. Their intentions are in the right place, but it hardly helps their cause that they were founded by a human who openly fraternized with demons. I disagreed with the council's decision to execute Amato, but he certainly contributed to the current unrest between humans and legacies."

Everett chokes on his wine, cursing as he spills it on himself. I raise a brow at him questioningly, but he shakes his head, glancing at Maven quickly before frowning down at his food.

Our keeper is thoughtful as she slides the steak and ham from her plate to Baelfire's. The dragon shifter pantomimes swooning and kisses her cheek.

"The Reformists sound less insane than the Remitters. After all, the system *is* archaic," Maven mutters. Then she pushed her plate away, clearly done as she regards the wizard. "Do you have a training area?"

Shit. I know what this line of question is leading to. So do the others because we all groan in synchrony.

"Indeed, I do. Looking to train more, *telum?* From all you've told me, I would rather think you lack very little in that department."

My gorgeous, vicious keeper smiles too sweetly as she looks at the four of us.

"It's not for me."

"Hey, we survived First Placement," Baelfire protests.

"Barely."

"That was a skewed result," I argue. "We fought some of the Immortal fucking Quintet, not to mention their band of followers. Take that into account, at least."

Maven sips her wine. "You four are not getting out of this. Suck it up."

Everett sighs and telepathically says, *That's okay. I love even the sadistic, merciless side of you, so I accept the hell that tomorrow will bring.*

She downs the rest of her wine, shooting him a look. *Stop using that word.*

Admit it, sangfluir. *You* love *that we can't get enough of you.* I grin when she flips me off.

"All this telepathy shit is getting so fucking old. You don't happen to know what made those two pricks bond when I haven't, do you?" Bael grumbles to the wizard.

My mentor smirks. "You are asking the wrong question."

"What the hell is that supposed to—"

Fuck, Everett swears, standing to pull Maven's chair back.

It takes me a moment to realize he's freaking out because even though she's keeping her face free of pain, one of her hands is clutching at her chest.

Do not make a fucking scene, her strained voice echoes in my head.

Damn it all.

I stand, glancing at Crypt. He nods once and vanishes, not needing to be told what to do.

Meanwhile, Baelfire surprises me by not blowing up with shifter emotions in reaction to our keeper's episode. Instead, he turns to the

Garnet Wizard to politely excuse us as Everett walks hand in hand with Maven away from the table.

She's stopped clutching her chest, but I can see the sweat breaking out on the back of her neck as we walk under the holiday mage lights and pass the other acolyte tables full of stares and glares.

"Leaving so soon, *your ladyship?*" that bastard, Parker, mocks from somewhere.

I'll hex him with some horrible disfiguration later. Right now, I take Maven's other hand as she keeps pretending everything is fine. I know she doesn't want to appear weak in front of the acolytes here, which is wise, but knowing she's in pain is fucking awful.

"Breathe. You're doing great, Snowdrop," Everett murmurs gently.

It's bizarre how soft he is with her when he's always been such an icy prick.

As soon as we're out of sight of the Great Hall, Maven sways, choking and clutching harder at her chest.

"Fuck," she grits, voice breaking. "Something's wrong. Different. I—"

Her legs give out, but Baelfire is abruptly there to scoop her up. He hurries toward the guest cottage, cradling her like the precious cargo she is as we follow.

"Crypt will have the medicine ready," I promise, opening the door and then locking it behind us. Earlier, I gave the incubus a draft of my new batch, the kind she can hopefully take orally, in case we were caught by surprise precisely like this.

Maven's face is twisted in agony, shaking her head as Baelfire gently lowers her to the bed.

"S—something feels fucking *wrong*," she chokes again.

Crypt appears and brings the vial to her lips, looking as tormented as the rest of us to see our powerful keeper like this.

"Here, love. Open up for me—"

Maven suddenly goes slack as her eyes slip shut. At the same time, something tugs so godsdamned painfully in my chest that I cry out. Everett does, too, staggering against the wall as he grapples over his heart, grimacing.

My vision blurs as pain blossoms through my center, and then a chillingly deep voice rumbles in my mind through the bond.

What game do you play, my daughter? You begin to test my patience. I sense a change in the shadows within you. You wax stronger, but how?

"Silas? Snowflake? Shit!" Baelfire swears, trying to shake me out of this trance.

A horrible sensation fills me as I hear flesh-crawling screams from somewhere far away. A chorus of people in agony, and one woman in particular sobbing out Maven's name.

I give you five days until your next mark must fall. Fail me, and they shall perish and be devoured.

I can finally draw in a breath as the tugging feeling fades, though the terror and pain lingers in my chest, wrapped around my pounding heart like a vice.

I realize I'm propped up against the wall, coated in a sheen of cold sweat. Everett is just as shell-shocked as I feel.

Maven is still out. Gone.

Crypt and Baelfire are nowhere to be seen. If I had to take a wild guess, I would venture to say the dragon shifter lost his shit again, seeing his mate like this.

At this point, I don't fucking blame him.

I swear and rub my face, moving to Maven's side to feel her arm. She's freezing and pale, her hair a dark mess around her face, and she remains unbreathing.

Everett mutters a quiet prayer to Galene, the goddess of life and healing. When he speaks to me, his voice is hollow.

"That was the Entity."

I gently check Maven's pulse. It's still missing.

"As she anticipated, he's threatening her," I mutter, anger slowly replacing the lingering fear.

A dragon roar from somewhere far outside the cottage briefly draws our attention before Crypt reappears with a groan, slumping into one of the dining room chairs. He's covered in burns that are quickly healing as his clothing smokes slightly.

"How is she?" he rasps, gaze on Maven.

"Expired." I rub my face.

He swears. "I fucking hate this."

"We all do," Everett mutters. Then he pins us with a look. "Maven has her plans. She's driven and does whatever it takes to get shit done, but right now, she's doing it on her own. What have we done for her besides tag along and try not to get killed?"

"Very little," I agree, glowering out the window. "She's no longer fighting us, yet she does everything necessary for her plan entirely on her own. If we could just contribute something, *anything...*"

We all consider it until Crypt tips his head.

"Suppose Maven succeeds, and the humans in the Nether manage to make it into this plane of existence. I assume our clever keeper has a thorough plan to help them out of hell, but what then?"

Everett frowns. "So many humans arriving out of nowhere will cause mass hysteria, especially because it was thought impossible. The media will run rampant, the human government will be scrambling...and you know what? There may be more than just humans slipping into this world. The weaker the Divide gets, the more surges of shadow fiends will escape."

"The Nether humans will need somewhere to go, not to mention supplies and healing. Knowing what little we do of their lives there, it's safe to assume they will be in dire condition," I muse, casting the Frost a long look. "If only we knew someone with deep pockets and shady connections who could fund suitable aid in preparation for their arrival."

He nods slowly, thinking. "Although, it will be a pain in the ass to keep my connections from stirring up rumors."

"Leave that to me," Crypt smiles darkly. "It's amazing how tight-lipped people become when their sanity is on the line."

We're all quiet again for a moment, considering this new pursuit.

"When it's all over—when the humans are safe and Maven has

fulfilled her blood oath…" Everett sighs. "What happens if she doesn't fulfill her purpose as a revenant?"

That question has been weighing on my mind, too. Guessing by Crypt's unusually somber expression and the way Everett can't stop rolling and unrolling one of his sleeves, we're all equally dreading the answer she hasn't given us.

We're such a morose trio that I startle when Maven speaks.

"Gods. You guys look like someone died or something," she jokes.

Crypt immediately moves to the bed, pulling her into his arms. She peers over his shoulder at me, appearing exhausted.

"How long was I out?"

"Not long. But, *ima sangfluir*…we need to talk."

21

MAVEN

"SOMETHING TROUBLES YOU," the Garnet Wizard notes.

That's a fucking understatement.

I set down my cup of morning tea, studying the wizard sitting across from me. A small breakfast has also been laid out, but I have no appetite, so I ignore it. I came to his study early in the morning, so he's currently in his mid-twenties. Not that it *feels* like morning since the sky has remained a beautifully forlorn twilight cycle since we arrived here in Alaska.

We've been in the Sanctuary for two days now. Most of my time has been spent training my matches, answering the Garnet Wizard's seemingly endless questions, and thinking.

Lots of thinking.

And now I've developed a plan.

"I told you about my episodes," I begin.

"Yes. The way you 'expire,' as you call it."

I nod. "Last time it happened, my bonded matches were affected. They heard Amadeus's message to me through our bond, which makes me further believe they're bound to my shadow heart, which links back to him. So…"

When I trail off, the wizard arches a brow. He's handsome as a younger man, with closely cut black hair, a clean-shaven face, thick brows, and cunning brown eyes.

"So?" he prompts.

Better to just fucking spit it out.

"You know all about my gambit, but I haven't told you how my story will end," I say, smoothing my gloves before meeting his eye. I force my voice to stay steady. "If I don't fulfill my purpose as a revenant, one of two things will happen. I will either slowly decompose until I fade to nothing and pass into the next life, or my shadow heart will give out. It was never intended to give me life for years, just long enough to fulfill my purpose."

He considers that. "In that case, your bound matches' curses are not truly broken. When you pass on, those blights shall return—and take it from me: curses come back with a vengeance when a keeper is gone."

"You mean when the keeper's *heart* is gone. After all, that's what they're bound to—this spell in my chest. What if you could remove my shadow heart before then? Keep it intact somehow so their curses remain unbroken?"

The Garnet Wizard's brows go up, and he leans forward with interest.

"An intriguing theory. One I would be very curious to put to the test."

"Then test it. Once I've bonded with all of them and accomplished my mission…I'll return so you can try to remove my shadow heart. If you preserve it after I pass on, it may prevent their curses from returning."

He's quiet for a long moment, staring off into space thoughtfully.

"All this, you are sacrificing for the humans in the Nether," he finally muses quietly. "Why?"

What kind of question is that?

"I told you about their living conditions, if it can even be called living. I'm the only one who can help them escape. It's hardly a sacrifice when I'm doomed anyway, so why wouldn't I?"

"They're only humans."

If he starts spouting off about how much better legacies are than humans, I will throw this fucking teacup at his face.

"So was I, once upon a time," I point out with a warning edge in my voice.

He throws his head back in a laugh before checking the nearby grandfather clock, which is wreathed in thriving vines.

"I shall consider your theory, Maven. I'm afraid I have another engagement that will take up much of the day, but the etherium withdrawn from my storehouses will arrive later today."

Thank the fucking universe.

As I leave the study, I go over my plan.

I only have three days left to kill off another member of the Immortal Quintet. With etherium, I can now store Somnus's potent life force, which has sat heavily in my veins for days as I've resisted the temptation to tap into it.

Once I copy the spell Felix and I perfected to store life forces in the etherium, I can take it to a temple for the blessing it will need from a priest or prophet to continue sustaining the Divide.

But that will come after the human exodus out of the Nether.

The moment I kill four of the Immortal Quintet, the Divide will become thin enough for humans to pass through. Felix will slip into the mortal world to mark their exit point with the etherium I stole from Amadeus's crown before he starts to guide the humans out of the Nether. Right now, Lillian, Felix, and the other humans are watching for the signs that it's time to flee, just as we planned. They have a simple system for relaying information to the various compounds.

As soon as they can escape, it will be a race for their survival. The humans kept as pets in the citadel will be told the plan, too. Whether they choose to stay or escape is up to them.

It's a complex plan, and so many things can go wrong. But as long as I don't fuck up, we'll be able to get the humans out of the Nether and refortify the Divide with the etherium containing the life forces of the Immortal Quintet.

They'll be free. My blood oath will be fulfilled. And before I fade to nothing, I'll give up the shadow heart in my chest so my quintet's curses can remain broken.

Baelfire's voice breaks me out of my deep thoughts, making me realize I'm standing at the edge of the vast green field we've used for training over the last couple of days.

"There's my pretty little Angel of Death." He's on me an instant later, wrapping his arms around me and nuzzling my neck. He sighs. "Fuck, I missed your scent."

My face goes hot because A, he's gloriously shirtless, and all his warm golden muscles are wrapped around me, and B, the others are also not wearing shirts.

Four ludicrously attractive, shirtless legacies wait beside me with heated gazes, ready to pin me down.

How are they all so handsome? Everett with his lean muscles and flawlessness, Silas's corded forearms and dark smirk, Crypt's mesmerizing eyes and those light and dark swirls curling over his shoulders, arms, and abs...

Fucking gods.

Maybe I should call off training today so we can do some naked cardio back at the cottage.

Bael groans, picking up on my arousal. "Godsdamn. Baby, I'll give you any fucking thing you want if you sit on my face again."

I swallow hard, squirming breathlessly as I try to get a grip. "I should really train you guys."

"In bed? We accept," Crypt winks. His markings are glowing slightly, but he's not reacting to them like they hurt.

Baelfire begins kissing down my neck. I *really* want to abandon practice to fuck the living hell out of him—out of *all* of them.

But no. Because I'm training them for a damn good reason.

I guess it's time to share that reason.

Baelfire essentially has my arms pinned, so I drop like a ragdoll. When he catches my upper half, I hook my legs around his body, kicking into the back of his legs to throw him off balance. Rolling when we hit the ground, I quickly have him pinned in the grass with his wrists over his head as I smirk down.

Until I see the pure pleasure on his face and feel the huge, hard bulge just behind where I'm sitting on his stomach. His breath is ragged, golden eyes twinkling with eagerness.

"*Fuck*, Raincloud. I love it when you're on top."

I lean down to teasingly nip at his jaw, which earns a breathy laugh from him.

"Are you going to be a good boy for me and actually train?" I whisper quietly enough so only his sensitive ears will pick up on it.

He shudders, swallows hard, and nods.

"Good."

I release him and stand up, fighting a smile when I see all three of my more voyeuristic matches enjoying the scene in front of them.

"You can all save the bedroom eyes for later. Your training is important."

I start to strip off my baggy top shirt since it's warm in this magical sub-realm, and we're about to work out. But Everett immediately stops me, casting a frown toward the nearby buildings where acolytes are studying indoors.

"Don't. They'll see you."

"It's dark. Also, I doubt they care that we're out here."

He huffs. "Over the last two days, I've caught them staring at you constantly. They know we're out here. Of course, they'll want to see you training without a fucking shirt on."

"So?"

His glacial gaze is chillingly possessive. "So, they aren't worthy to enjoy the sight of you. I won't have them watching you."

Silas laughs. "Ironic, since we all know how much you enjoy being watched."

He's obviously talking about last night when Everett again came just from eating me out and making me squirt as the others watched and groaned and occasionally lent a wicked hand.

Which led to me bouncing between Crypt and Baelfire. Right before I sucked Silas off in the shower, followed by a fingering-and-feeding session.

Those memories have my face nearly as red as Everett's as he mutters, "Shut up. It's different when it's anyone outside of the quintet. They don't get to gawk at her."

"Not unless they want their eyeballs plucked out like our dear Undead puppet," Crypt agrees, stretching languidly so I get a delicious view of all those muscles.

Damn these men for being so distracting.

"Fine, I'll keep my shirt on."

Silas sighs. "Such a tragedy."

He's gotten more playful now that voices aren't plaguing him. I'm glad. But now that I have their attention, I lift my chin.

"I'll be candid. I'm not just training you four to take out shadow fiends or bounty hunters. I'm training you to take me down whenever I lose control."

They all stare at me for a beat.

Then Everett rubs his face. "Yeah, no. That's not happening."

"Yes, it is—"

"Not. Happening," he grits.

The others nod, all folding their arms.

Oh, *now* they start agreeing with each other? Fucking legacies.

"It's going to happen. In a real fight of any decent size, I lose control and berserk. And if you four let me spill innocent blood because you're too afraid to take me out, I'm not going to forgive that," I say, folding my arms, too.

"This is asking too much," Baelfire growls, shaking his head as his temper mounts. "I can't hurt my mate. Don't ask me to do something I'm literally fucking incapable of doing."

I glance at Crypt. "You've seen the aftermath. You know I'm not myself. When I lose it, I become a literal monster."

"A very pretty monster," he grins. "I hardly minded the mess, love."

"That's because those weren't innocents. What are you going to do if I'm berserking near humans? Families? Helpless *children?*"

His smile dies. He looks away.

"That's what I thought." I look at the rest of them, trying to drive the point home even if sharing this fucking hurts. "Of all the times I woke up covered in blood after losing control in the Nether, the worst was the time I realized Amadeus sent a human into the arena when I was already berserking. He was eleven."

My voice is dangerously close to catching, so I clear it. "I don't remember slaughtering him, but waking up to see what little was left..." I take a deep breath and try to push the memory back to the dark recesses of my mind, looking at them in turn. "Don't let me become that again. I *need* this. Please."

They exchange glances, wavering. Finally, Silas moves to the side and takes a ready stance.

"We will do this for you," he mutters.

All four of them are unhappy and remain uncharacteristically quiet as we run drill after drill, but at least they aren't fighting me on this anymore.

And for once, Crypt takes it seriously. Instead of dipping in and out of Limbo, poking fun at the others, and whispering things in my ear to try to get a reaction, he falls into a focused, deadly calm that I have to admit does something to me.

This time, when I finally spar with him one-on-one, I'm shocked to realize he's actually...good.

Really good.

In fact, during a blindingly fast combat sequence, when I dig an elbow into his side and try to maneuver around him, he sweeps my legs out from under me, knocks my arms when I try to catch myself, blocks my instinctive attack, and pins me in a brutal hold.

We're both trying to catch our breaths as I study him. Baelfire whistles low nearby because this is the first time any of them have managed to actually pin me without cheating.

The Nightmare Prince's galaxy gaze is consuming and intense before he leans down to whisper against my ear. Although he's not wearing his shirt or jacket, his sweet leather scent mixed with sunlight and clean sweat is tantalizing.

"Anything you ask for, darling, I will become for you. If you want a weapon, use me. If you need air, breathe me. I will shield you from the pain in your past. All I ask in return is that you fucking *tell me* when these memories are haunting you."

I close my eyes, focusing on his heartbeat against my chest.

I've memorized all of their heartbeats. Four unique, steady lullabies I can't get enough of.

"You can't protect me from memories, Crypt."

He nips my ear. "No? Watch me."

Someone clears their voice nearby. When I realize it's not one of my quintet members, I crane my neck to see Ross, who is averting his gaze as he waits to talk to me.

In his defense, the way Crypt has me pinned is almost inappropriately possessive.

"Instead of merely cutting off his hand, I should have run him through," the Nightmare Prince mutters.

His brutality gives me butterflies.

"Your mistake," I grin before raising my voice to a normal level. "Need something, Ross?"

"You and your quintet missed breakfast, my lady—Maven," he corrects. "I saved some prepared enchanted plates so that you all may still eat. You deserve a far greater meal, of course, and I apologize that it's not worthy of—"

He's starting to babble. If I don't say something soon, he's going to end up pissing off one or all of my matches. They're testy each time he shows up, which is almost annoyingly often. I'm pretty sure the only reason they aren't telling him to fuck off right now is because they hope this will get them out of more training.

"Thanks. We'll be at the Great Hall soon," I interrupt Ross.

He scurries away from the glares of my matches as Crypt finally releases me. Once I'm on my feet brushing grass off, I notice Everett's thoughtful frown.

What is it? I ask telepathically.

Do you think he acts like that around you because his third eye saw that you're a saint?

I make a face. He's sold on this whole sainthood thing, and I'm starting to think the others might believe him. But from everything

I've heard of saints—namely, that they're kind, selfless, nomadic humanitarians who travel the world doing great deeds, praising the gods, staying celibate, and leading boring-ass lives—

No.

I'm not a saint. Even if I was selected to become one as a baby, which I doubt, I'm a fucking revenant now. If I met a saint, I'm sure they would try and fail to exorcise me.

We head to the Great Hall, with Silas on my left and Crypt on my right, each holding one of my hands. They all keep finding little ways to touch me, and I'm really fucking glad that whatever creeping unease remains of my haphephobia is barely noticeable around them.

No one else is at the Great Hall as we sit around one of the tables. Not even Ross, though he seems to have left all of this food steaming on platters. I don't recognize much beyond fruit, scrambled eggs, and some bread, but Baelfire lights up when he takes in the display.

"Fuck, yes. I'm starving. Here, try this, Boo."

He picks up a piece of bread slathered in green stuff and offers it to me.

"Hell, no. The last time you fed me weird green shit, it was revolting. I'm nauseous just thinking about it."

"I promise I will never make you eat Jell-O again," he laughs. "This is avocado toast. You'll like it."

Everett is busy rearranging my plate to substitute the meats with other foods. "He's right, try it."

With a sigh, I eat the stupid avocado toast. Surprisingly, it's not horrible, despite the way it looks. I also like the 'mixed berry medley parfait' he makes me try next. Finally, Baelfire seems satisfied that I'm enjoying the meal and digs into his own food, as do the others— aside from Crypt. He isn't sitting at the table anymore, instead leaning against one of the distant pillars to smoke.

I wonder again if his curse is hurting him.

But my thoughts take a sharp turn when my stomach begins to churn. The nausea is so sudden that I freeze, confused. I don't get nauseous—not unless I'm having an episode. But my shadow heart isn't hurting me.

Instead, my stomach seizes painfully as dizziness sweeps over me. My mouth goes dry while the rest of my body flushes, fingers and toes tingling. My head starts to pound.

This doesn't feel like an episode. It feels more like...

Fuck.

My matches shout in alarm when I leap up and lurch away from the table, barely managing to make it to the edge of the open-air dining area before falling to my knees to puke my fucking guts out.

22

MAVEN

I HEAR Crypt swear before he's holding my hair back. Someone else rubs soothing circles over my back.

Three rounds of heaving later, and I'm ready to repeatedly stab the prick who caused this. When my stomach *finally* stops trying to escape through my throat, I wipe my face with a shaky arm and straighten to see four pairs of eyes pinned on me.

Everett is beside me, his hand still rubbing soothing circles on my back. Baelfire and Silas are close, standing guard, and Crypt hasn't let my hair go as he stares at me with a…tender smile?

What the fuck?

I'm confused by their strangely intense, happy expressions until I hear Everett whisper a quiet prayer of thanks to Koa, the god of fertility.

Yikes.

Talk about jumping to conclusions.

"You'll feel bad for smiling in a moment," I inform my overly pleased, very mistaken matches.

Baelfire beams, his golden eyes misty. "My mate is pregnant. How could I not smile?"

Oh, gods. I guess we'll have to talk about that.

I sigh. "Calm down. It's not pregnancy. It's just poison."

Nightshade, to be precise. It's not nearly as potent as its root powder, but those were unmistakable symptoms from a potent batch. It's a good thing that I was forced to build up a tolerance to a wide variety of poisons, including nightshade, or I would be dead and reviving right now.

My quintet stares at me for a moment as they absorb my words. Then all hell breaks loose.

"*What?*" Baelfire booms, going from emotional and thrilled to murderous in an instant.

Silas swears furiously as he storms over to examine my plate for the culprit. Crypt goes deceptively still as Everett scoops me up like he thinks the ground might try to hurt me next.

Being swept off my feet doesn't help with the dizziness my body is trying to combat. I pat his chest, swallowing down more bile.

"Set me down. Now."

"Who the fuck is trying to poison you?" Baelfire snaps, blue fire flickering under his skin. "Ross? I'm going to fucking *kill* that guy."

"Right after we make him beg for mercy that he will never get a fucking ounce of," Crypt agrees, vanishing in the next moment.

"It's not Ross," I protest before the incubus can slip away unseen. "He thinks I'm important somehow. It was probably—"

Before I finish speaking, a massive, glowing, wolfish form appears in the Great Hall out of literally fucking nowhere. It leaps toward Baelfire with claws extended. I shout, but Silas is already whirling to hit it with a bright blast of blood magic.

The wolf makes no sound, gnashing its teeth as it recovers. No sooner does it turn toward Everett and me than a thick, deadly spike of ice erupts from the ground, skewering the strange beast high in the air. It twitches and evaporates.

"What the fuck was that?" Bael snaps.

"My familiar," Parker's voice says from nearby, and we all turn to see him glowing with blue magic as he glares at all of us from the end of the Great Hall. "And there's far more where that came from."

He raises his hands, and spells cascade from his fingertips. Bright blue lights shift into vague animal shapes that immediately begin to attack. Silas quickly fires back with his own magical attacks. Baelfire snaps a familiar's neck before charging toward the acolyte. He's blasted into one of the nearby pillars hard enough that I hear a *crack*.

I scramble out of Everett's arms, ignoring the lingering nausea and weakness as I withdraw Pierce from a hidden arm strap. It's a full-on battle with magical beasts all around. Everett sends a wave of ice to knock many aside so I can dash toward Parker.

His attention is on me until Crypt emerges in the mortal realm and tries to snap the acolyte's neck. But Parker has so many defensive charms glowing around him that Crypt is electrocuted immediately, dropping and spasming as blue light sizzles across his skin.

Silas cries out somewhere behind me. When I risk a glance toward him, my gaze latches on Baelfire, who is trying to fend off another familiar despite his broken back, which isn't healing fast enough. Silas is bleeding heavily from a bite to his arm. Everett freezes another familiar and is immediately tackled by a glowing blue jaguar.

How dare he harm my matches?

Anger floods me along with the life forces of the guards I killed days ago, and I run faster. As soon as I near Parker, he fires off a spell that would be agonizing if I didn't rip through it immediately. A paralysis spell, a death spell, madness maledictions, hexes—I tear through each of his attacks as darkness crackles around me.

I was made to destroy anything. To be nothing but deadly calm.

Parker shouts in horror as I reach out, ignoring the pain that lashes through my system momentarily before my magic shatters the remaining charms protecting him. He falls back on his ass. I immediately plant a foot on his chest, forcing him to his back so his head smacks with a resounding sound against the Great Hall's mosaic floor.

When he tries lifting his hand to defend himself with another spell, I fling Pierce down so it stabs him through the wrist, pinning it against the floor. He screams, thrashing as the rest of his summoned familiars dissipate.

My head is still pounding, and now the adrenaline is mixing with the nightshade in my system. It's not a good mix, as evidenced by the nausea that barrels through me again as the world tilts.

Hands and arms marked with intricate swirling patterns reach around to steady me from behind.

"All right, darling?"

I nod, trying to focus on the acolyte, who I realize is bleeding heavily from his head. Pierce's adamantine begins to taint his veins, blackening his skin as he curses at us.

"Fucking *monsters!*" Parker spits as Silas stalks over. Everett isn't far behind, allowing Baelfire to lean on him as my poor, grimacing dragon shifter still hasn't healed. "Your patchy excuse for a quintet deserves every misery it gets—starting with this fucking bastard biting the dust," he adds, glaring at Crypt.

Is he really trying to threaten Crypt when the adamantine is sucking his life away?

I roll my eyes. "And yet he will far outlive you."

He sneers mockingly at the incubus, showing off his unfortunate overbite. *"Far?* Ha! No. Maybe for another couple of years, until he burns out early like the rest of the fucking stewards. Didn't know I knew that about you, did you, Nightmare Prince? You fucking deserve it. It's an insult that the gods ever chose Somnus DeLune's monster spawn to tend to the—"

Crypt releases me and kicks the acolyte's head in.

Blood splatters everywhere. The others react with scowls and disgust, but I'm still registering what Parker just said.

The other stewards of Limbo…burned out early.

As in, they died.

"How long?" I whisper.

The DeLune picks up on the fury in my voice as the others go quiet. "Darling—"

"Don't *darling* me right now. How long do you have left?"

He hesitates. "I'm not certain."

"But you've known about this."

"Yes. It's an inevitable side effect of my—"

"Were you ever going to tell me?" I demand roughly, crouching to yank Pierce out of the corpse. I angrily clean it on one of Parker's sleeves, trying to ignore the sting in my eyes.

Crypt is dying, and he wasn't going to fucking say anything.

He told me his curse differs from other curses because it can't be broken. That means bonding with him won't change this. Even if the Garnet Wizard manages to preserve my heart to keep all their other curses at bay, Crypt's will still eat him alive.

I fucking hate the gods right now.

He crouches beside me, gently tipping my chin so I'll have to look at him. Which is annoying because he's gorgeous and mine and *dying*, and there is not one godsdamned thing I can do about it.

I despise feeling helpless, but especially when it comes to them.

"It is what it is, love," he whispers, smiling wistfully. "I didn't want to sully the precious time we have together. Besides, with all the world against us, there are far better things to spend such lovely tears on."

"I'm not crying."

Crypt reaches out to brush away a traitorous teardrop, pressing it to his lips for a taste. "All right. You're not crying."

"I'm mad at you."

"I accept."

Someone shouts in the distance. It's Ross, and he's running toward us. I look over my shoulder at my other matches. Silas is finishing healing his arm, Baelfire is frowning deeply at the ground, and Everett watches me with a soft sorrow in his pale blue gaze.

Ross grinds to a halt when he sees Parker's dead body. "Oh, heavens. What happened?"

"We killed him," I mutter, looking away in case he can tell I was just fighting tears.

"Yeah, but I mean, why..." He trails off, shaking himself. "Forgive me. You don't answer to me—and besides, I believe I know why. Parker told me he would offer you up on a silver platter to the Legacy Council. When I tried to alert the Garnet Wizard, Parker got me with a paralysis hex, and...*please* forgive me for not preventing this."

The caster seems genuinely upset about this. Meanwhile, all four of my matches give him the evil eye. I have no idea why he's so respectful to me, but I stand, sheathing my dagger on my arm strap again.

It's good that he showed up right now. If I have to linger on Crypt's predicament or the fact that I can't think of a single fucking thing to do about it...

Something inside me cracks.

I lift my chin, forcing composure onto myself like a shield.

"Is that why you ran over here?"

"Oh—no, actually. I had no idea Parker was here. My mentor sent me to let you know he has something for you."

The etherium must finally be here.

Good. More to focus on instead of the anger and helplessness.

I step around Ross to march toward the Garnet Wizard's favorite study, not surprised when my matches follow. Given what just happened, it's no surprise they refuse to let me go alone this time.

And honestly? I don't want to go alone. I want them beside me.

Our quintet has always been on borrowed time, but I feel that truth like an anvil on my shoulders as we walk down one of the cobbled paths, the sky overhead the deep royal blue of a polar night.

As we walk, the final symptoms of the poisoning fade, ultimately useless against the tolerance I built up over the years. When we turn down a path near the brook, I decide it's time to address that little incident back there.

"I can't get pregnant," I inform them quietly.

Everett gently takes one of my hands to slow my pace a bit. "You're right, it would be the worst possible timing. So we'll take all the right precautions—"

I stop to look up at all four of them, shaking my head. "No, I mean that I *can't*. It's physically impossible. Think about it. The Undead can't reproduce because they're dead."

"You're not dead," Baelfire interjects angrily at the thought.

"I'm also not alive. As a semi-existing *thing*, I'm...sterile."

I hesitate, picking at the hem of my black shirt. This isn't something I've ever lingered on. It just became fact after my heart was taken from me. I never considered how this might bother my matches—but everyone knows that legacies prize having heirs.

"If that's a dealbreaker for you guys—" I begin with a frown.

Everett interrupts. "Do you want children?"

"We just went over this. They're not an option."

"But if they were. If there was a way, would you want that, *sangfluir?*" Silas presses.

I've never given it thought before. Daydreaming about a future family isn't a luxury I've had, not when survival alone seemed unlikely. Not to mention, trying to picture me in a maternal lighting is laughable.

But if miracles did exist, my life continued, and my matches wanted to be fathers…

I shrug. Curiosity aside, it's a moot point.

"The only thing I want right now is every possible moment I can get with all of you."

For a moment, I worry that's not the answer they want, especially Baelfire. After all, he's a shifter, and his family has been struggling to continue their lineage.

Instead, he beams. "Hang on a second. That kinda sounded like a confession of love to me."

"It certainly did," Crypt grins when I scowl.

They all tease me as we continue to the Garnet Wizard's study. Part of me is profoundly relieved that they don't seem disappointed, but they're also clearly trying to lighten my mood from everything that just happened.

It's sweet, but I want to kick their asses for teasing me so much about this. Talking about feelings is one of the purest forms of torture. How do they not get that?

Silas opens the study door for me, and I see that the Garnet Wizard is now middle-aged and jotting down notes of some kind with a quill and ink pot at a desk in one corner of the study. He glances up and motions at a briefcase on the coffee table beside the same stack of books I noticed before—although now they're filled with bookmarks.

"Please do help yourself, *telum*. I have something for you once you are done."

We walk into the room, but I realize Crypt is stuck outside the threshold. A dreamcatcher hanging beside the desk keeps him from getting any closer, even in Limbo.

"I'm not inviting that one in here," the wizard says without looking up from his writing. "Though truthfully, I'm surprised I'm allowing *any* of you shirtless, dirty, gore-smattered barbarians indoors. One would think you were raised in a barn, Silas."

"Barnyard animals might've taught me more manners than you ever did," Silas retorts.

The wizard laughs good-naturedly as I unlatch the sides of the briefcase and open the top, studying the velvet-wrapped pieces of smooth, glass-like etherium. The pieces are in various shapes and sizes. Just like the first time I saw this element in Amadeus's crown, something about it draws me in.

I pick up a piece and unwrap it for a better examination. It gleams in the overhead mage lights, completely transparent but full of promise.

Thank the fucking universe. Now, my plan can go on.

"How have you gathered so much etherium?" I ask.

"Despite the Legacy Council trying to horde it all to themselves, you mean? Why, collecting oddities has long been a hobby of mine. I have always had a fascination with Paradise."

"Clearly," I say pointedly, looking at the well-read books on his coffee table.

Everett picks up one of the said tomes, skimming curiously through it as the wizard replies.

"Old favorites of mine. I merely desired a refresher. Now then, is the etherium to your liking?"

I nod.

He smiles and selects an envelope and a small, empty vial from his desk before approaching with his walking stick.

"Excellent. On to more business, then. Engela Zuma wrote this missive for you. It contains exact descriptions of those immortals' *life links*, as she calls them, along with many of their safehouses and anything else she believes you may find useful. I only ask for two ounces of your blood in return."

Silas's gaze snaps to his mentor. "Absolutely fucking not. Her blood is mine."

"And mine," Crypt calls from the threshold in a sing-song voice.

That earns a sharp glare from Everett. "Shut up, freak."

"Why the fuck do you want my mate's blood?" Baelfire demands, lounging in one of the settees. It's an antique piece of furniture clearly made for smaller people, so he looks comedically burly in it.

The Garnet Wizard looks at me. "They're terribly possessive. And clingy."

I smirk in agreement. "Like a bad rash. I'm a lucky revenant."

Just admit you love us already, Everett's voice teases in my head.

I roll my eyes and set down the etherium, getting back to the wizard's request. "You all need to relax. It's just two ounces of blood."

Silas grumbles unhappily about it and goes to browse through books on one wall under a section labeled *"Restricted for Fools."*

What are you looking for? I ask him telepathically.

Anything he has on necromancy that I can borrow. I must adapt and learn new spells to complement what I am now.

The Garnet Wizard isn't aware of our internal conversation as he offers me the vial and a large needle.

"Keep the needle," I grumble, pulling out one of my other daggers to slice through my palm.

I hold my hand over the tiny glass, watching it fill up. Baelfire grunts unhappily about it while Everett quickly stands at the ready with a clean rag he picked up somewhere in this wannabe alchemist lab.

"Why do you want my blood, anyway? Revenant blood is exactly like Undead blood."

The Garnet Wizard throws his head back in a boisterous laugh, again giving me the impression that I'm missing something. "My dear Maven, that is certainly not the case, for Silas loathes the taste of Undead blood."

Silas frowns, looking up from an old grimoire. "That's true, actually. The magic in your blood tastes nothing at all like the Undead."

It must be because of all the experimentation. Or perhaps the gods made me tasty just for you for the sake of sticking us in a quintet together, I shrug, keeping it telepathic.

Perhaps, he echoes, now lost in thought.

When the vial is full, Everett quickly wraps my hand, his touch as gentle as silk. I clean and restash the dagger. As I do, my sleeve moves, and the Garnet Wizard tips his head when he sees Pierce sheathed to my forearm.

"By the gods. Adamantine. I've studied weapons formed in the Nether extensively, and I must say that one appears to be of excellent workmanship. Did you make it?"

I shake my head. "It was gifted to me by one of the humans in Amadeus's citadel."

I met Olivia when I was twelve. We were the same age, and she was considered a pet of one of the blacksmiths in the citadel. She was fascinated that I came from the mortal world and would sneak to see me between my trainings and laboratory sessions. Though I never spoke more than ten or so words to her in all the time we spent together, she declared us friends and stole Pierce from her lich master to give to me as a gift. I thought it was harmless to acquiesce to her attachment to me.

Until Amadeus found out.

She's the ghost who haunted me the most until Dagon hexed me.

The wizard hums and hands me the letter from Engela, drawing me from my dark memories.

"You should be aware that one of my acolytes recently used a powerful communication spell to speak with someone outside the Sanctuary. The council likely knows your whereabouts if they did not already."

"Parker paid with his life for that," Silas mutters.

"Poor chap wasn't clever enough to live, then," his mentor shrugs easily, returning to his desk. He peers up at me one more time as he caps the vial. "If you're in earnest about leaving Engela safe here, I suggest you leave promptly. I've thoroughly enjoyed your answers, and I shall greatly like to see how the rest of this plays out —but as you know, I prefer avoiding those immortal simpletons."

I nod and then pause. "Have you considered whether you will test my other theory?"

"I have. Should you succeed, we shall talk again."

I nod and give the briefcase to Silas to stash in his void pocket for safekeeping before we leave the room. I'm trailed by my quintet, who all give me curious looks about what I meant.

"We'll leave in the morning," I tell them instead.

After all, now that I have etherium, there's no more reason to hide.

It's time to hunt.

23

CRYPT

The pain is becoming unbearable.

I clench my teeth as my damned markings light up yet again, brighter as Limbo calls urgently to me from outside of this Sanctuary. But since I cannot leave the wards of the Sanctuary without permission, and I refuse to leave my obsession's side anyway, there's no help for it.

My limbs burn. Each breath scrapes. Even my skin seems to ache.

I'm searing from the inside out, pulled thin by this unbreakable curse—and now, my keeper knows it is slowly but surely destroying me.

I wonder if Crane would mind resurrecting that damned acolyte so I can have the pleasure of killing him all over again. Of course, it being just after midnight, I don't suppose he would appreciate it if I were to wake him to ask such a favor.

Especially not when he's lucky enough to hold Maven in his arms tonight.

I stand at the edge of the room, observing them all from Limbo. The cottage's bed is not nearly big enough, so our oversized Decimus dozes on a simple makeshift bed of blankets on the floor. Frost is on Maven's other side opposite Crane. The whole lot of them are peaceful, their subconsciouses wafting in this space as they pass through vague dreams—most of them centered around Maven.

Lucky bastards. I long to dream of her, too.

And I fully intend to, once I take her as my muse.

My darling has had trouble sleeping tonight, just as she has ever since that godsdamned wraith appeared in Nebraska. But just as I notice her dream finally start to take root, pain lances through me yet again. I'm left trying to breathe through it as I fight the temptation to simply stop feeling altogether.

It's a little-known fact that powerful siphons are capable of almost wholly numbing themselves to pain and emotions. Call it a predator's self-defense mechanism—when feeding on blood, emotions, arousal, or dreams, it's rather pesky to deal with trivial feelings like fear, sorrow, or guilt. We can dull ourselves to physical pain to better focus on the hunt, losing ourselves in our more monstrous heritage.

I distinctly recall the night I first chose to exist in that numbed state.

I was eight years old and so badly beaten that I frightened the other children when I snuck into the orphanage late at night. Saint Eileen's Private Home for Little Angels was located six miles down the road from one of the Immortal Quintet's residences near Sutton. It was my favorite of their ever-changing mansions because when-ever Melvolin or Somnus lost their tempers and took it out on me, I had somewhere to escape and pretend I was gloriously parentless.

But that time was different.

It was my first time visiting these children at night rather than during the day. When I first ventured into their dreams, I witnessed the horrors that haunted some of those defenseless young souls. Their stomach-turning nightmares were filled with true terror and agony at the hands of adults whom they had hoped would be their protectors.

Their psychological pain was excruciating.

After experiencing their dreams—their *memories*—I emerged

from Limbo as numb as a corpse. Turning off my emotions and any ability to sense pain allowed me to hunt down their abusers and anyone else who was taking advantage of the innocent in all the savagely insanity-inducing ways they deserved, and I never looked back.

Not giving a fuck about anything but revenge was freeing. Empty years passed by, and I cared and wanted for nothing.

Until I saw her on that stage.

That's when I decided to feel again—feel *everything*, including agony, hunger, and every other dreadful thing I had numbed myself to. Painful memories. The suffering of innocents whose dreams I experienced. Even the terror of those I took revenge on.

But so long as I can experience the remainder of my existence at my dark obsession's side, I will never numb myself again.

Once the wave of pain eases slightly, I move beside Maven in Limbo. My mouth waters as I watch her dream slowly curl through this plane of existence, saturated with her aura—as if even in her sleep, she beckons to me.

How could I resist when I crave her so desperately?

I reach out for Maven's dream and groan in satisfaction when the flavor of her subconscious floods my mouth. The taste of her dreams haunts me.

The pain in my body lessens slightly, and I find myself in a vague dream set in our quintet apartment back at Everbound. Maven is in the theater room, curled up between Frost and Crane on the sofa as Decimus scrolls through films.

"Oh! This one's a classic," Decimus insists. "I mean, the main girl in it is human, so she gets her panties in a twist trying to pick between two guys when the way I see it, she could've just picked them both and added her hot best friend while she's at it. *But* it has a great sex scene in the rain. We could reenact it." He bounces his eyebrows flirtatiously.

She makes a face. "They're smiling on the cover. It looks cheesy."

"You agreed to watch a romcom, did you not? They're all cheesy," Crane clarifies.

"I only agreed because they're Lillian's favorite," she mumbles, lazily reaching up to tease her fingers through Frost's white hair.

The scene continues, shifting and flitting to other casual instances. It's so rare that my keeper's dreams are so normal or peaceful. For a while, I'm pleased as I bask in her dream space, feeding to my content.

But then I feel it.

The same cold, dark presence that kicked me from her subconscious the last time.

I grit my teeth against the pressure and fight to remain in Maven's dream, ignoring how my markings flare in warning. It's a gut-wrenching sensation as her dream melds with something else entirely—an external memory, cold and brutal as it twists into her dream space. Everything shakes around me as I cling to Maven's psyche.

I won't have it unprotected as it was the last time.

When the melding stops, I drift for a moment in a dark, sinister place. It's disturbingly unfamiliar as I try to get my bearings, still clinging tightly to Maven's aura.

Finally, a memory-spun dream begins to play out. It feels nothing like one of Maven's, yet I can still sense her nearby, present as she, too, experiences this.

I watch as a vague, towering figure stands waiting in a large stone room. Two thinly clad elderly humans with iron collars around their necks are shivering and silent on the floor beside him. Faceless guards line the perimeter of the room. Everything is dark and bland as if color is too afraid to exist in this dim plane of existence.

Finally, double doors swing open, and a bloke in long dark robes enters the room with a sweeping bow. Judging from the blackness at the tips of his spindly fingers, he must be a necromancer.

"My liege. Another of thine chosen mortals has succumbed to a most glorious death."

The Entity shows no emotion. "And my daughter?"

"She awaits just outside."

"Send her in."

My pulse pounds in my ears as the necromancer brings in a younger version of Maven, perhaps fourteen years old. I choke at the sight of my keeper at this age—bruised and dirty, with her hair tied back from her gaunt face so her haunting eyes are even more prominent. She's dressed all in black with gloves as she glances down at the terrified humans, but she makes no expression.

"One may live. Choose who will die and deal the blow," Amadeus's deep voice rumbles.

The younger Maven remains blank-faced. "I choose?"

"Yes, daughter."

In a blindingly fast move, Maven whips a dagger from a sheath at her hip and sends it into the throat of one of the guards standing behind Amadeus and the humans. The guard vanishes from the dream, but the Entity appears unsurprised.

"There. That monster's hands will wander no longer," Maven mutters, turning as if to leave.

The doors slam closed before she can exit. Although the Entity's voice remains strangely emotionless, it is like a coo.

"My murderous, moral maniac. You displease me."

Shadows move in the dream, wrapping around the humans and lifting them from the ground. The remaining guards are strangled by the darkness, falling to the floor with heavy thuds just as Amadeus's hands plunge into the chests of the two shackled humans. He drops their hearts to the ground, and the shadows release the corpses.

It all happened within the blink of an eye. Young Maven struggles to cover her shock, trying to compose her face despite the moisture gathering in her eyes.

The Entity leans to whisper to her, and I can barely make out the words. "You are weak. If you had obeyed, they would all yet be alive."

"I don't kill innocents," she says, voice breaking.

"There is no such thing as a true innocent. Every being has a dark side—and you must become *only* your dark side. Then, you will be my telum."

He straightens, moving to the doors. "You failed this test. Dagon will take you to the dungeons for your punishment."

When the doors close behind him, I feel a change in the dream. It's Maven's memory now as her face crumbles. She drops to her knees beside the two dead humans, biting back a sob as she scrambles to grab one of their hearts. My throat tightens as I watch her whisper dark words, some ritual as she tries to return the hearts to their owners.

Again and again, she tries.

They remain dead. Her sobs wrack my body with aching sorrow.

I need to take this dream away so it will stop hurting her, but when I try to reach out with my own subconscious, a shock of alarm and fury rocks this dream space. Pain cripples me, bringing me to my knees as the true owner of this dream—the Entity himself—realizes his mind is not alone tonight.

All at once, I'm removed. I stumble out of Limbo, catching myself against the wall of the dark cottage as I try to catch my breath. The slumbering scene before me is as serene as I left it, except now Maven rouses, her eyes seeking me in the dark.

She cannot see as well as I do, but I move closer to brush my fingers against her cheek.

"I'm here, love."

Her voice is hoarse. "What just happened?"

"We lost your dream to that bastard again."

She's disoriented as she gently disengages from Crane. He's out cold, sleeping extremely soundly as he has ever since his curse was broken. I suppose he must catch up for all the sleep he lost as a paranoid madman, though it is a shame I don't see his eye twitch nearly as often.

I grasp Maven's hands in the dark to steady her as she leaves the bed.

"Gods," she breathes, shuddering slightly. "I need to get rid of this awful energy."

I nod. "Shall we, then?"

We leave the cottage, but we only make it a few steps before I realize she's only in an oversized black T-shirt and the deliciously scandalous pair of dark red panties that came with the lingerie I gifted her for Starfall Eve.

She looks edible. Though she may not be cold in this temperate Sanctuary, my attention drops to her bare feet.

"I'll get your boots," I offer.

"Don't bother. The grass is nice."

Maven takes a deep breath, tucking her hair out of her face and taking in the midnight blue sky. Tiny streaks of the aurora borealis have begun to wind their way through the heavens, creating an ethereal scene as we walk away from the guest cottage out into a seemingly endless, surprisingly well-maintained field of grass.

My keeper is quiet for a long time as she walks off her restlessness, but the silence is companionable. Finally, when the cottage is nearly out of sight, she stops and turns to study me curiously.

"Food is optional for you, but is it possible for you to sleep?" she asks.

"Only after I take my muse." I tip my head. "When shall we schedule the ceremony, by the way?"

"Ceremony?"

"When an incubus takes a muse, they can only do so through a ceremony in one of Syntyche's temples."

After all, the goddess of reaping is also the goddess of fate, dreams, and time itself.

Maven considers that. "What would it mean for me to be your muse?"

Everything.

To me, at least.

"We would share dreams while asleep and sense one another more keenly," I murmur, brushing my fingertips through the dark hair framing her face. "I would be incapable of feeding on anyone's dreams except yours, but that is already my preference. And...my psyche would be open to you, just as yours is open to me in Limbo.

It's said to be an extremely vulnerable, intimate connection unlike any other."

Precisely what I crave when it comes to Maven.

She studies me thoughtfully before winding her arms around my neck. The press of her lithe body against mine sends excitement coursing through me as her lips brush over my jaw.

"How many muses can an incubus take?"

"One." For eternity.

Again, precisely what I'm craving with her.

She pulls back slightly to examine me. "And if your muse dies?"

Dark anger flickers inside my chest. I give her my most warning look. "You won't."

"I expire all the time."

Is that all she means? It had better be. "That's not a true death."

"But if it were?"

I sigh, ready to move on quickly from even the notion of losing her. "Incubi die when their chosen muse does. It doesn't go both ways, so if Crane, Frost, or Decimus ever tried to do me in, you'd be perfectly safe."

Maven snorts. "That won't happen. You're all softies for each other."

What a horribly disturbing sentence that was. Decimus is all right, but I'll need to rough those other wankstains up more often if she thinks we've gotten so chummy.

Then her expression falls, and she peers up at me. "Would me becoming your muse help your curse in any way?"

It's a beautiful kind of agony, knowing that she also hurts over the idea of losing me. I wish I could reassure her and promise a lifetime of this sordid obsession, but all I can do is shake my head, kiss her temple, and let go of the topic that is causing my keeper pain.

"What's your answer?" I whisper, my hands skimming over her sides. I curl my fingers in the sides of her panties, grinning when it makes her shiver.

Maven's gaze is trained on my mouth now. "My answer?"

"Will you be my muse, darling?"

When she meets my eyes, there is a depth and emotion I can't decipher.

"You're mine, you know," she whispers. "Bound or not, your muse or not, whether I get you for years or only days...you are fucking *mine*. If I ever speak to the assholes in Paradise again, I'll have to thank them for finding other souls just as twisted as mine. Your broken edges match mine perfectly."

24

CRYPT

My heart races at Maven's words. I press my forehead to hers, pulling her tighter to me.

"You still haven't answered my question, love."

"If we survive the next few days, I'll give you an answer," she promises, pressing her lips against mine.

That's all it takes before we're kissing frantically. Her tongue slides along my lower lip, teasing as my fingers tangle and twist in all her glorious hair, tipping her head so that I can deepen our exchange.

Finally, my keeper breaks away, fighting for air. "Why are you still wearing clothes?"

That is an excellent question. I quickly remedy this newfound problem, stripping and tossing my clothes off to the side. Before I can pull her back to me, Maven gracefully gets to her knees, tracing one hand over my chest as she goes so she can teasingly tweak the piercing in my left nipple. I exhale harshly at the delicious sensation before she wraps one hand around my hard erection and pumps it slowly.

Her touch is both relief and torment, yet something about her on her knees doesn't sit well with me. My darling is a powerful, dark, dominant force of nature—sovereign of my entire existence.

She should kneel for no one.

Maven smirks up at me as if she knows just what has me frowning. "I'm doing this because I want to. Next time, you'll be on your knees for me."

I smile, tracing her lovely face. "The perfect position to enjoy every moment of your pleasure."

She returns the smile before leaning forward, her soft lips sliding over the head of my cock to wet it. It feels divine, and then I jolt, gasping when she uses her teeth to gently tug on one of my piercings. The sensation sends raw need dancing along my spine while Maven looks up with that glimmering, mischievous gaze I can't get enough of.

She licks slowly around the tip, exploring further and further until I can no longer hold back my groans of bliss. Then she pulls back to murmur, "I want to feel you in my throat."

Fuck me.

I nod and tangle one hand in her hair, desperately trying to keep my wits about me so I don't snap and become too rough with her.

"Open wider for me," I whisper raggedly before she sinks lower on my cock.

When she hums in acknowledgment, I swear and bite my free knuckle for something else to focus on besides the consuming pleasure of her deliciously warm mouth sucking my cock so perfectly. Maven sinks further, taking almost all of me as she reaches up to cup my aching balls curiously.

I moan and tip my head back, panting. Gods fucking save me, this lovely mouth of hers.

"Darling...go slower, or I'll—"

She hums and swallows around my head, and my vision nearly whites out.

"*Fuck*," I curse, pulling out of her heavenly mouth as fast as possible to try to stop the intense, telling tingle low in the base of my spine.

Such a naughty tease. As if I'd fucking come before her.

My attention drops to Maven's hand, which is in her panties, circling as she licks her lips and gazes at my wet, aching erection.

"On your back," I rasp.

She arches a brow and moves so fast that I go breathless when I'm suddenly lying in the grass. She straddles my chest, so I have a mouthwatering view of the wetness between her thighs when she slips her panties down enough that I can see her pretty cunt.

"No. You get on your back," she whispers.

So sensually devious. She drives me insane with such sweet cruelties.

I adore the teasing and can do nothing but watch, burning alive as my obsession strips atop me ever so slowly. When she shucks her oversized shirt, her fingers brush softly along her exposed skin, tracing her bare sides. She's not wearing a bra, thank the gods.

I groan with need when she begins toying with her perfect nipples, shutting her eyes before she ever so slowly glides one hand down to slip her fingers through her wet, beautiful little cunt. Her head tips back in a soft moan.

I'm a madman.

I have been for quite some time.

But even though I'm thoroughly enjoying every moment of her teasing, when Maven withdraws her wet fingers and brushes them against my lips, I snap. I can't fucking take any more and reach up, ripping the panties from her thighs to toss them onto my nearby jacket.

I'm keeping those as a godsdamned souvenir.

Then I scoot her forward, cup her ass, and drag my tongue through all the delicious nectar she's dripping just for me.

Maven gasps and arches, grinding against my face as I suck and lick her greedy pussy, my head spinning as my cock weeps and pulses, desperate for her.

"Maven," I whisper against her entrance, rubbing my face there to coat myself in the proof of her arousal.

She groans and pushes me back down, kissing me just as ravenously as I kiss her in return. The taste of her mixing on our lips is a heady addiction.

I want to be consumed by her. Utterly lost. There is nothing but Maven and me under the eerie dark sky streaked with green and purple as my mad obsession sinks deeper into my very bones, taking my thoughts and very breath until finally, I flip over, bringing her with me.

"Take me." I bite her lips, dragging the pierced head of my aching cock through her wet, hungry cunt.

"Yes," she groans, arching against me.

"All of me," I demand. "Always."

"Yes."

I plunge into her, and we both gasp and moan at the feeling. Gods above, I would live buried in her perfection if I could.

I press deeper into her, setting the pace through the pure pleasure. She winds her arms around me, clutching me closer as I fuck my keeper harder, deeper in the dark midnight of this distant field.

Here, we are the only things in existence. Nothing fills this world but our ragged breathing, the way her body takes mine just the way the gods intended—and the way her eyes lock onto mine, capturing me as if she's gripping my black heart in her lovely hands.

She can fucking keep it, no matter what it does to me.

Obsession is fascinating, but it is also agony.

Aching need.

A dangerously endless craving for her that I know can never truly be satisfied.

"Crypt," Maven whispers, gasping when the breathless sound of her voice sends me spiraling, and I pound harder into her. "Fuck— harder. *Gods.*"

She's close.

I'm closer. That will have to be fixed quickly.

I groan and slip one hand beneath her upper back, lifting so she arches her spine. Her perfect breasts are close enough that I can lick and nip at them, giving my gorgeous obsession the extra stimulus she needs.

The rougher I get, the more desperate she becomes for that release—and finally, she gets it, clenching tight around me as her entire body tenses and her breathing catches. Seeing her face and hearing the little sounds that escape as she comes undone pushes me over the edge.

Insanity takes hold as my cock spasms inside her tight wetness, and I lose track of what plane of existence we are in. Space and time cease—it's only us. I bury my face in Maven's neck as I moan and shake with the end of my release.

We're both panting. Her hands smooth over my back as I try to come back to myself, and when I can't stop kissing her, she tries to block my lips.

"Let me catch my breath."

"Let me *be* your breath," I counter, capturing her lips again.

She laughs and pushes at me again playfully before murmuring, "We're in Limbo."

Damn. I didn't mean to do that.

Still, when I look down and see my keeper's dark hair drifting around her face as if we are underwater, those hauntingly beautiful eyes and the way her lips curl up in satisfaction…

Fuck me, she is some mythical creature I wholly belong to. What a divine fate it would be to lose myself in her.

"As irrevocably as I am yours, you are mine," I warn her. "If you ever forget that, I'll be forced to do something drastically violent."

She grins, clearly liking that thought. "Gods forbid."

"The gods hold no power over me anymore. Only you do."

Maven kisses me. I wrap her close and turn again, pulling us out of Limbo so that we roll sideways into the mortal world. She relaxes on top of me, her head on my naked chest so she can listen to my heartbeat as we both come down from the high.

I shut my eyes in utter contentment, memorizing the way her perfect body presses into mine.

Long, blissful minutes pass like this. I would wonder if she fell asleep, except then she starts to slowly trace my markings along my neck, up to my scalp, and back down over my shoulder.

Finally, she yawns and sits up, straddling me and brushing hair out of her face. My attention immediately catches on her chest.

Ecstasy floods me.

There it is—the triangle of my House upon her lovely skin. It nearly lines up with the Elemental square, with the Arcana line straight through the middle on top of her scar.

It's beautiful. *She's* beautiful.

"We're bound," I rasp, relief washing over me.

Maven glances down and breaks into a smile, tracing her new emblem.

So we are, she murmurs...inside my head.

And just like that, I'm ready for her all over again.

Darling.

Yes?

I pull her back down for a kiss, allowing my hands to explore everywhere as she inhales sharply and begins to rock against me. Her deliciously devious fingers again brush up my chest to pinch and tease my piercing.

Gods above.

Allow me to worship you again, I groan telepathically, rolling once more to kiss down her neck and lick the place my emblem now sits proudly on her pretty skin.

Gods. "Yes," she whispers, delving her hands into my hair as we begin again.

Every whisper of her voice in my head, every touch, is excruciatingly perfect. But I need more. I groan and position myself at her entrance, sliding the tip of my cock through the wetness seeping out of her from my last orgasm.

Maven moans, arching her back to add to the friction as I continue to tease her, a desperate madness beginning to buzz through my veins.

"Fuck—those piercings," she gasps.

I thrust hard into her, gritting my teeth against the onslaught of pleasure.

Fuck.

Yes. Fuck. Now, she replies, only heightening the frenzy building between us.

I swear and press her legs back until her knees are beside her head. Her mouth drops open at the stretch before I slam deep into her. Pleasure sparks down my spine, tightening my balls and sending me into a mindless haze of lust as I fuck Maven with abandon, giving us what we both need once more.

Her nails dig into my back, scraping. The slight bite of pain makes me hiss through my teeth. I grow rougher, losing any remaining control.

"So tight," I grit. "So wet. So—fucking—*mine.*"

I slam deep between each word, making her cry out.

"Crypt," she whispers, chanting. "Crypt, Crypt…fuck, I need—"

I will always know what she needs. Cursing as I further unravel, I brace one arm beside her and reach between us to pinch her clit ruthlessly.

Maven swears as she comes, squeezing her eyes shut as the most beautiful, decadent bliss sweeps over her face. Feeling her perfection tighten and gush around me proves too much, and I moan as I bury my face against her neck. My cock pulses once again with release.

Gods. I fucking love your cock, Maven thinks in a daze.

I smile against her skin, kissing it. "My dark little darling, did you just confess your love for me?"

"I distinctly said your cock."

"Last I checked, that's part of me. I'll have to tell the others that you officially professed your undying love to me first. Hopefully, it leads to a gloriously violent altercation."

She rolls her eyes, but I sense the satisfied sleepiness that is slowly weighing her down. My pretty newlybound keeper is going to need more rest before we leave tomorrow to hunt her prey.

I kiss the tip of her nose and gently pull out of her, trying not to groan at the sensation. I scoop her up and begin walking back to the cottage.

"I can walk," she protests through a yawn.

"I much prefer holding you."

She hums and slips into tranquil unconsciousness. A few minutes later, just as I'm nearing the cottage, Frost's panicked voice floods the bond.

Maven? Where are you?

Crane is right behind him. *Are you all right, sangfluir? What happened? Where did you —*

I scowl when Maven begins to rouse from sleep due to their stupidity. Sending the softest ripple of my power through her, I lull her back into a deep rest.

She's exquisite as always, so don't get your knickers in a twist, I tell them telepathically just as I open the door of the cottage.

Their shocked expressions are priceless, made even better because they both squint like idiots, unable to see me well in the dark.

Decimus sits up groggily. "What the fuck's going on?"

I hush him and lay Maven gently beside Crane once more. "Shut your mouths. She needs sleep."

"Were you just fucking her *outside?*" Frost growls quietly. "Out in the dirt where anyone could have seen? She deserves the comfort of a bed at least, you—"

I roll my eyes and touch his leg to send a much less gentle pulse of sleepiness through him, quickly giving Crane the same treatment. But when I turn to Decimus, he's not making a fuss like the others. He's longingly watching Maven sleep.

"So what's it like? Being bound to her?"

"Like beautifully fucked-up puzzle pieces falling into place," I murmur and then sigh. "Don't pout. You'll be bound to her soon enough."

He lays back down, staring at the ceiling. "Yeah, I really fucking hope so."

I slip back into Limbo, leave the cottage to gather our clothes, redress myself, and quickly return to wait for Maven to begin dreaming again.

But Decimus isn't falling asleep. Just as I'm debating putting him out, too, he sits up.

"Hey. Crypt?"

I emerge from Limbo to show I'm here, but the dragon shifter hesitates, rubbing his neck.

"Just spit it out, Decimus."

He clears his throat. "Thanks for looking out for me. Back then, I mean."

Idiot. I thought we had an unspoken agreement not to talk about any part I played in his past, so I roll my eyes again.

"Never mistake us for being friends. If you lose control of that fucking dragon again and come anywhere close to hurting Maven, I'll kill you without blinking," I warn.

"I'd deserve it," Decimus nods. Then he frowns in the darkness. "Was Overbite telling the truth about you burning out from your curse?"

"Piss off."

"Get over yourself and spill, Stalker Boy. Because if you die, it affects the quintet—and it's going to *really* affect my mate, so I have the right to ask, and you're going to fucking answer. How old were the past stewards when they burned out?"

Cocksure prick.

But he's correct that my inevitable demise will affect the quintet, so I sigh. "On average, thirty years old."

"Shit."

"Well-put."

He's quiet for a long moment before glancing at the bed. "She didn't shower."

"Don't you dare wake her for that."

"No shit, creep. I *meant*, she didn't have that delayed reaction where she starts to get uncomfortable about all the touching and scrubs her poor skin raw in the shower when she thinks we aren't looking. If you're still helping her with that fucking phobia of hers whenever she's asleep, it's helping."

I have been, but I shrug. "She still can't stand touch from anyone outside the quintet. Perhaps she's just growing accustomed to knowing we're hers."

"I like the idea of that."

As do I.

He lays back down with a dramatic sigh. "Anyway, no hard feelings about tonight. You were obviously just doing Maven a favor and saving the best for last. Like a dick appetizer."

It's incredible, the things this shifter chooses to let leave his mouth.

His ego is far too fucking loud, so I kick his leg to send a jolt of my power through him, too, sending him into a deep sleep.

25

MAVEN

FEW THINGS in my not-life are as thrilling as the moments before a battle.

As we walk toward the outer ring of the Sanctuary, all of us dressed warmly, I check all the daggers on my person and try to tame my smile.

It's no use.

Meanwhile, my quintet is not as thrilled.

"I understand this is exciting for you, but your eagerness to fling yourself into danger isn't helping our nerves, *ima sangfluir*," Silas sighs.

It's early in the morning as we stop in front of the second invisible magic door, but the endless deep twilight overhead remains just as it has since our arrival three days ago. The unsettling dimness reminds me of the Nether.

Outside the Sanctuary, enemies will be waiting for us. It's inevitable because Parker let them know we're here, and Douglas also probably tracked Silas's transportation spell to Alaska. Since our enemies can't get into the unbroachable, invisible Sanctuary, they'll simply wait for us to emerge.

And since transportation spells, coming or going, don't work within the Sanctuary, here we are. Ready to emerge.

For a fight.

I can't fucking wait. I used to dread the death matches in Amadeus's arena, but now I miss regular combat.

The Sanctuary acolytes were happy to see us go. Meanwhile, the Garnet Wizard couldn't get out of bed because his curse was acting up, and he was somewhere in his early hundreds—but he sent Ross to see us off.

The caster is behind us, fidgeting nervously. "I could help fight if you would like. I would be useful, as I'm nearly a fourth-level acolyte."

"Or you could fuck off, and Maven can stay in here while we take care of things," Everett mutters.

He's been broody this morning, but honestly? He's got nothing on Baelfire, who has been worryingly quiet and downcast. He knows Crypt bound with me last night, leaving him the odd man out. Once we get away from here, I'll give my poor, praise-loving dragon shifter some much-needed attention.

Then, we'll track down my next target.

I snort, replying to my testy elemental. "Nice try. I'm not staying."

"It'll be brutal out there—a bloody massacre," Ross warns, dread written all over his face.

"I already said I'm going. Don't try to sell me on it."

Crypt laughs at that. He's in a phenomenal mood this morning, and I've noticed his markings have been lighting up far less. I'll ask my Nightmare Prince what that means later.

In the meantime, I'm enjoying how right it feels to be bound to him.

"Fine," Everett grumbles. "Let's just get this over with."

"Unless you four want to stay in here," I offer. "That way, if I lose control—"

"Shut the fuck up. We're sticking with you, and that's *final*," Baelfire snarls savagely, not sounding like himself. Then he squeezes his eyes shut, rubbing his temples. "Holy shit. I'm so, *so* sorry, Mayflower. Mr. Alphahole Supreme is really on one today."

"Keep your distance from Maven during the fight," Silas advises.

"And mind your fucking tone with our girl before you become a lizard-flavored kebab." Crypt pulls out his lighter, which morphs into a sword faster than I can keep up with.

I expect Baelfire to snap back, but he grumbles in agreement, not meeting my gaze.

Once again, he must be struggling more than he lets on.

Silas rolls his shoulders, his bleeding crystal in one hand as he approaches the door. He fed from me earlier this morning to fuel his magic for this fight. I may enjoy him feeding from me almost as much as he does, partly because it feels good but especially because of how worked up and out of control he gets.

"Are we ready?" the blood fae checks.

"Wait," Ross says, facing me. "Do you have a phone? Because if there is ever a time you need assistance with anything at all, it would be the greatest honor of my life to assist—"

He yelps when Baelfire drags him up by his collar to glare at him with searing amber eyes. "Are you seriously asking my mate for her fucking number right in front of me?"

"No, not at all! It's nothing like that, I promise. I was only trying to—"

"Scram before I roast your ass."

He drops the gifted acolyte, who rubs his chest and grimaces at me. "Right. I'll go. Please be safe, my lady—Maven, I mean."

He hurries back to the inner circle of the Sanctuary as I turn to face the invisible door.

"Okay, let's do this."

With a collective breath to brace ourselves, we watch Silas magically unlock the outer ring. The moment we all step out of the temperate green sub-realm and into the bitter cold, chaos unleashes.

Hellhounds howl. Magic crackles to life in the hands of dozens of caster bounty hunters and hirelings who surround us. Others shift or take aim with their weapons, the clicking sound of guns rising as a chorus in the wintry wild filled with dozens of tents, proof they were camping here in wait. Dozens of red laser dots appear on me like tiny dancing lights from the guns.

Douglas is at the forefront and aims at the center of Crypt's forehead.

The moment his finger moves on the trigger, a thick shield of ice slams up into place in front of us. Deafening gunshots fill the air, their thunderous echoes reverberating over the stark wilderness around us–but the bullets imbed in the thick ice in front of us.

As soon as the first barrage ends, Everett drops the wall of ice and lifts his arm to send a wave of icy spikes toward the massive group of hunters. At the same time, Baelfire races forward to slam into a lion shifter charging toward us, Silas releases a blood magic spell that neutralizes several magic attacks flashing to life, and Crypt drops into Limbo to wreak total havoc.

They're working much more like a team now. I let myself feel proud for half a second before I roll out of the way of another gunshot and dart towards Douglas. He's probably the most capable opponent here, so it's best to take him out quickly this time.

Whipping Pierce out of his hiding spot, I feign a blow before going for his gut. He sidesteps, but instead of returning the attack, he rolls away and dashes toward an area of the now-raging fight where other bounty hunters are starting to tear into one another, courtesy of the Nightmare Prince.

Apparently, Douglas has a bone to pick with my incubus.

My senses prickle, and I jump aside just before a wave of fire sears a path in the spot where I was just standing. The fire elemental tries again, but a wave of snow, like a sideways avalanche, crashes into the fire to smother it and the elemental.

Thanks, I tell Everett through the bond as I throw myself into the fray. *Does everyone remember the plan?*

Leave no soul alive, Crypt supplies chipperly, still somewhere in Limbo.

No, you fucking sociopath, Silas retorts as he goes toe to toe with three casters at once. *The plan is to escape quickly, even if we must leave the fight behind.*

Meanwhile, you *are supposed to avoid killing so you don't go all revenant on us,* Everett adds.

And Crypt? I prompt meaningfully.

He sighs through the bond. *Yes, yes. I'm also babysitting our dragon.*

I can't see Baelfire in the raucous fight anymore, but the fact that he hasn't shifted into a dragon to rain fire down tells me he's fighting to maintain control. As helpful as a dragon could be in a fight, I don't want to lose him to his curse when we need to make a getaway.

I dodge one of the wolf shifters, vaguely aware of a stray bullet grazing my thigh. Rolling to one side, I slice through a fae bounty hunter's Achilles tendons to cut off her brutal magical attack aimed at Baelfire. She falls with a cry before I finish her off quickly, purely out of habit.

I guess you can take the bitch out of the arena, but you can't take the arena out of the bitch.

A delicious, intoxicating buzz starts to pump through my system.

Crypt laughs from wherever he is in Limbo. *I saw that.*

Oops.

As the fight intensifies, so does the twisted urge that always over-shadows me as I make my way deeper into a battle. Though I'm supposed to be looking for a way to leave all of this behind, I kill another opponent in self-defense.

Then another.

And another.

Dark magic pulses through me, and that exhilarating nothingness starts to gain a foothold as I kick away another shifter. Death hangs thick in the air all around me, a tantalizing cadence of endings and screams that sinks into my very being as a smile grows on my face.

I've been fighting my entire life. Through all the broken bones, blood loss, and agony, the thrill of dancing with death became an integral part of me. I wipe someone else's blood off my face as the killing urge starts to pound through my muscles and head.

This is what I was made for.

And I want more.

More blood. More buzz. More.

Maven, Silas's voice warns.

Where is she? Everett demands.

I'm fine, I insist. *I was just—*

I cut off when, all at once, my senses go haywire, honing in on something nearby. A shadow fiend is quickly approaching.

No, not just some shadow fiend...one that makes my nerves itch. Him. He found us.

I'm so distracted by the approaching terror that I don't see the attack in time. Douglas lands a brutal blow to the back of my head with the butt of his gun. The world goes topsy-turvy as I fall to the snow, hot moisture already dripping from somewhere on my throbbing head.

He takes aim to shoot my chest, but I snap back to my senses, roll sideways, and leap from the ground to take him down. Knocking the gun from his hands, I pin him.

Damn it—why does the wind carry the scent of your blood? Silas demands through the bond, sounding strained. Far away in the battle, I see crimson flashes of his unmistakable magic.

We have a bigger problem, I tell him and the others. My stomach clenches with dread as I feel wraith nearing by the second. *Gideon is coming.*

Their chorus of swears in my head is drowned out by Douglas's shout when I quickly break his arms. I stand and land a savage kick to precisely the right spot on his thigh, snapping his femur for good measure.

He swears so creatively that I'm almost impressed.

"Stay down, or he'll target you," I instruct.

"Who? And why the hell aren't you finishing me off?" he demands, gritting his teeth in pain. "You did this last time, too. What are you, some kind of fucking sadist?"

I ignore him, scrambling to find all my matches in the ongoing bloodbath surrounding me. We need to transport out of here as fast as fucking possible before—

Dark shadows slither across the snow, flinging fresh corpses to the side. Some tendrils wrap around bounty hunters who shout in alarm just before they go pale and drop like flies, paralyzed with horror, their eyes stuck open wide. Douglas inhales sharply when one of his nearby friends is abruptly beheaded by a blade of darkness. The disembodied head is flung hard to crack against the skull of another terrified hunter.

A shadowy figure rises out of the gathering snakelike shadows like a cold, dripping oil—a faceless, looming, all-too-familiar presence wreathed in unnatural darkness.

"Finders keepers, losers Reaper's," Gideon whispers with glee.

"What the…" Asher Douglas trails off, going pale as death.

"Maven!"

Everett's voice comes from somewhere nearby. Fear clogs my throat, so I can only reach them through the bond.

Run. RUN.

And then, even though I feel like a fucking coward, I do the same.

Screams ascend behind me, cutting off abruptly as the wraith's ability to wield fear either leaves them frozen in terror or altogether dead. Shadows snake after me as that chilling laugh dances on the wind—the same laugh I've heard every time he's broken me in the past.

I push myself hard, my boots digging into the snow. Cold stings my face and lungs, but the hot moisture from my head injury continues to drip, my vision swaying.

I barely leave the outskirts of the dying battle when Crypt appears, running beside me.

"No, stay in Limbo!" I shout at him. "It's safer there!"

"If it is, then—"

He reaches for me to pull me into his plane of dreams. But before we make contact, shadows explode between us, flinging me down into the snow.

I can't see Crypt, but his hoarse scream cuts through the polar night.

Baelfire and Everett are shouting nearby. I want to tell them to *run the fuck away*, but before I can speak or even move, a massive centipede-like shadow curls over my body. Its dozens of tiny legs leave needle-like punctures in my skin wherever it roams, but when I try to shove it off, it's like my hands pass through smoke. As it nears my head, I panic and struggle.

I can't let him fuck with my head again. I can't.

But it's useless as his essence coalesces around me like a putrid, inky syrup. The dark shadow circles around my head, lengthening to smother my mouth, pricking my lips and jaw. The other end slides down to crawl into my ear, slinking into my head.

My vision whites out for a moment, and then I'm naked, covered in pale, wriggling maggots. A scream lodges in my burning throat as I try to brush them off—but they're not just on my skin.

They're inside it.

Hatching. Feasting. Multiplying.

They start to crawl out of my nose and mouth—burrowing out of my rotting flesh. I'm nothing but a withering corpse riddled with death and worms.

"Dead yet so afraid of what death brings," Gideon's voice mocks. *"But a corpse needs a grave."*

Oxygen whooshes from my lungs as unbearable weight presses on every side, burying me alive. Dirt fills my mouth, nose, eyes—it crushes my chest until my eyes feel like they'll pop out.

"Let's continue our game of finder's keepers."

I can't move as the wraith's shadowy hand slides into my chest, rooting around for the heart he won't find. What he does find are my crushed lungs, which he begins to tear out slowly.

But just as the internal pain and horror begin to eclipse my every thought, I hear it.

My matches. Screaming.

No.

Gideon's demented laugh scrapes inside my head as if he's trying to gut my thoughts from the inside out. *"They were never yours, broken raven. Now they're mine."*

"No," I rasp, desperate to get to them.

They're *mine.*

I'm not letting this twisted echo of my past hurt them more.

They. Are. Mine.

All the adrenaline, fear, and darkness crashing through my veins reaches a fever pitch when my anger crests. But it feels different, somehow—less the heady buzz of death and more like…something powerful I've never experienced before.

Whatever it is, the next time my psyche lashes out against Gideon's control, I break free from the horrors he's forcing into my head. My vision clears as I roll to my feet, instinctively withdrawing the only knife I have left on me without getting a chance to look at it.

Silas is writhing in the snow beside Baelfire, both of them tangled in shadows that are sliding into their ears, mouths, and noses and warping their minds as they cry out. Crypt is motionless in the blood-stained snow surrounding him. He's missing an arm and leg like he was being ripped apart slowly before Gideon decided to focus on—

Everett. Who is in silent agony as the wraith delves into his mind. One of the blade-like shadows lifts in the air, an onyx-like guillotine poised above my elemental's neck.

My vision goes red.

"No!" I scream, launching forward and driving the knife into the shadow fiend.

It shouldn't work.

But it does.

The wraith shrieks in pain as I stab it again and again, rage rushing through my system. That strange new power burns me alive as I bury the blade deep in the wraith's center.

Gideon screeches loud enough that my ears ring before wrenching away from the knife and dissipating, his shadows slithering into the distant darkness of the polar night.

I drop to my knees, shaking in the aftermath as the adrenaline and strange new strength slowly calm. A dark liquid coats me, and I realize it must be wraith blood.

But how?

The blade in my hand starts to crumble. I blink down just in time to see the bone knife Everett gifted me crumble away to ash.

Just like a blessed bone weapon.

What the hell?

Maybe...shit, maybe I'm a saint after all.

I don't understand, but right now, I don't fucking care. I crawl through the snow to Everett, who lays utterly still with ashen-gray skin. My hands tremble as I check his pulse.

He's alive.

So are Silas and Baelfire, when I check them. Only Silas is vaguely conscious, but he can't seem to focus on me with those beautiful crimson irises. And when I hurry to my Nightmare Prince, hot liquid dripping from my chin, I nearly choke at the amount of blood he's lost. His beautifully marked, dismembered arm and leg are beside his body.

When I check his pulse, his head lolls to one side. He blinks several times before his eyes slip shut as he exhales raggedly.

"You're bleeding," he slurs.

"Shh."

Talking isn't good for him right now. I wipe at the stupid fucking moisture uselessly escaping my face and carefully move his arm and leg closer to his body.

"Hurts, love," he whispers, face contorting in such agony that my chest aches. "Wantto numbit but...I'd feelless ofyou...if I makeit stop..."

His words blend together and make no sense. I gently hush him again before getting the others to bring them closer. In my semi-hysterical state, I think that it's convenient I was given unnatural strength, or else dragging my matches around would be a hell of a lot harder.

The battlefield formerly filled with gunshots and the exhilarating sounds of battle has fallen eerily silent. Anyone left alive is either unable to move and likely falling to hypothermia, or they're heavily injured and will bleed out before the cold kills them.

Except Asher Douglas.

As I finish struggling to move Baelfire next to the other three, my gaze connects with the bounty hunter in the far distance. He's managed to sit up and is healing his broken arms with soft green magic while he watches me, his gun in his lap.

He could shoot me right now. Take me to the Legacy Council and leave my matches here to rot.

Instead, he looks away, taking in the massacre around him.

As soon as my quintet members are all touching, I call on the life forces still pulsing in my veins. Dark magic flares around me, and after a brief, blinding flash, we're abruptly in the same hotel room suite we previously got in Nebraska.

It's the first place I could think of. The universe is merciful for once and no humans currently occupy this room. Lifting my hand, I double-lock the front door using common magic.

Then I sit and stare at my matches as blood drips from me.

Crypt is bleeding out on the carpet, now as unconscious as the rest of them. Baelfire has silver bullets embedded in one of his arms, and Everett is bleeding from a wolf shifter bite to his shoulder. Silas is only bleeding from his nose, a sign of magical strain on the brain, and he looks awful. They all do.

This is why I have to fight like hell to keep them safe

No—it's why they should have accepted my fucking rejection in the first place. If they had, they might've been perfectly safe and matched to some other legacy by now if they had just appealed to the fucking gods like I told them to.

"I warned you guys," I whisper angrily, voice breaking.

But my anger is short-lived.

These legacies were always going to be mine. Right now isn't the time to linger in shock or feel sorry for our situation. I need to help them recover, keep them as safe as possible, and get the fuck on with my plan.

I read Engela's letter earlier. She doubts the other two members remaining in her quintet will be hiding in the same place. I'm almost certain of where Iker Del Mar may be, thanks to Engela's detailed accounts, but I'm sure as hell not bringing my quintet with me for this hit.

They'll need time to heal, but I have to take out another member of the Immortal Quintet before Amadeus harms Lillian or the humans.

Yet the idea of leaving them behind...

Gods. This is going to fucking suck.

Newlybound legacies need time with their matches, basking in the afterglow of bonding and growing closer as the bond strengthens. I'm not a legacy—but damn it, if only we had time for all of that.

Oh, well. Life is a bitch, and so is death.

As I plot out my next move, I work. I'm not a gifted healer with common magic, but right now, there is so much power from the battle pumping through my veins that I harness to stitch Crypt's arm and leg back to his body. His incubus healing can take care of the severeness of the injuries slowly. I carefully remove the silver bullets from Baelfire before cleaning and bandaging Everett's shoulder.

Snowdrop...

I pause to study Everett's face, but he doesn't rouse from the stupor that Gideon left them in. With a grimace, I reach behind my head and breathe the necromantic words for healing the worst of the injury there. It's far less potent without spell ingredients, but the bleeding stops.

Next, I bundle Silas and Crypt in blankets from the two bedrooms to help them recover from the lingering Alaskan cold, place heavy protective wards on the entire suite, and leave all the lights on. I add a few light spells for good measure and slowly back away from them, studying all four of their handsome, blood and dirt-streaked faces.

If I had to guess, they might shake this in a couple of hours. Possibly sooner—especially Crypt, who must have a serious tolerance for true horror, considering his history.

But that still gives me time to get shit done without putting my quintet in more danger.

"I'll be back soon," I quietly tell my unconscious quintet as I prepare a transportation spell, unnatural magic humming to life around my blood-darkened gloves. "Get better because I…"

I can't survive losing any of you.

The words catch in my mouth, and I instead mutter, "Because I'll be pissed if you don't. And when I get back, we're going to Canada."

26

MAVEN

I STEP out of the cuchillería, scanning the streets as I discreetly slip the small knives I just bought into concealed locations on my person. One in my boot opposite Pierce, two up my sleeves, one at the waist of my pants.

It's taken two hours to prepare, and now the sun is low on the horizon in this part of the globe. As much as I would love to draw this out and enjoy the kill, I need to wrap it up quickly and return to my quintet.

Gods, I can't stop thinking about them. I know they're not awake yet, or I would have heard them in my head by now.

Humans are out and about, enjoying the sunset as they stroll the walkways or buy steaming food from street vendors. They mind their own business as I walk toward the coast, where the street I'm looking for will run parallel to the ocean.

Iker Del Mar is here in northern Spain, in this little town.

I'm going to kill him, even though I am fucking exhausted.

After transporting to Madrid and then here, I'm running tragically low on fuel for my magic. The fight in Alaska, the run-in with Gideon, and being unable to picture anything except my matches bleeding out in the snowy wilderness have left my eyelids and bones feeling heavy.

At least I now have everything necessary to take down the immortal hydra shifter efficiently.

I magically mixed the tiniest amount of my nightshade root powder with a tranquilizer I stole from the American embassy security room in Madrid. I had to knock out lots of humans, magic wards, and a few security cameras to get to it, but I managed.

It's a standard but powerful emergency tranquilizer that authorities are mandated to keep on hand in the event of a feral shifter. It prevents a target from shifting, regardless of size, and will force a shift back to human form.

Laced with nightshade root powder, it should weaken Del Mar so much that killing him off will be a breeze.

Ignoring the exhaustion weighing on me, I slip onto the street described in Engela's letter, adjusting my sunglasses. I'm also wearing a big black sun hat in the interest of disguise since humans have heard my description on the news.

Beautiful pastel houses rise up the side of the mountain to my right, vibrant in the golden sunset. The street ends abruptly to my left with a road and a small fence before dropping off into the dark blue ocean.

I've never seen the ocean before. It's immense—a beautifully brutal, undefeatable facet of nature.

If we make it through all this, I'd like to visit a private beach somewhere with my quintet, like Kenzie once talked about doing. I can easily see Everett lathering himself and me up in sunscreen while Baelfire cracks jokes about nude beaches. Silas would probably read aloud to me under an umbrella to stay out of the sun. Crypt would go swimming with me and steal my bikini top.

Damn it. I need to get back to them.

I want every possible fucking second I can have with my quintet because I know there's a limit to what we can experience together before I fade to nothing.

If I could just find a way to exist after seeing my mission through…

I stop a few houses down from a mansion where two men chat

outside the front door. They have their parts down perfectly, dressed like human tourists, but I note how they scan the area.

They're security. Most likely strong legacies.

It's good that this coastal street is empty except for the three of us.

One of them notices me lingering. As soon as his eyes narrow suspiciously, I rush toward them, waving and shouting because one of the best ways to throw an opponent off is by being as loud and conspicuous as possible.

"Hello! I'm so sorry, but do either of you guys speak English?"

The legacies are still blinking in surprise by the time I arrive at the little gate in front of Del Mar's hideout. I get near enough that I could slip through the front bars if they were wider apart.

"What the hell are you—" one of them begins, reaching for me.

The moment his hand is on me, I break his wrist and twist his arm, turning so he's in front of me when the other legacy reacts by firing off a shredding hex. It kills the one I'm holding as a shield immediately. I drop him, dodge an attempted blow, and drive Pierce into the other guard's chest.

He collapses, clawing at his bulging, blackening torso. He tries to scream, but I can't have attention drawn from the house, so I smother his mouth and nose as I search his pockets for a security amulet. I find it just as he stops twitching, the buzz of a fresh kill sweeping through me.

I check to see if I've raised any alarm. A couple is just walking around the corner, but one stops to take a picture of one of the charming houses, and the other checks something on their phone. While they're distracted, I quickly haul both legacies to the edge of the street and toss them over the fence into the ocean.

The human couple walks past several moments later, completely oblivious. Once I'm alone again, I use the lifted security amulet to slip through Del Mar's front gate as silently as possible.

Most of these houses run together with little to no space between them, but Del Mar's monstrosity of a safehouse is surrounded by gardens. When I notice a curtain move in one of the windows, I slip behind a large stone fountain.

I can sense the magical hum of powerful wards nearby. The amulet will get me through those. Thank fuck, because even though I have fresh life forces dancing in my veins, I want to conserve my strength for the heart of the fight.

Plus, I'm too fucking tired to do more than necessary right now.

Darling?

Crypt's raspy, weary voice trickles to me through the bond, taking me by surprise. It's very faint—I assume because of our physical distance.

I'm safe, I promise, cleaning Pierce on my sleeve out of habit as I wait to ensure I won't be spotted.

Why can't I trace your aura?

Probably because I transported. Have you healed?

I wait several moments for his reply, but there is none. That worries me slightly, but this is the wrong time to get distracted by telepathy, so I push down my worries and peek around the fountain to plan the best route into the house. Before I can move, the front door opens. I hide again as voices pass by on the way toward the gate.

"They were *just* out here. What, did they go to take a piss together or something?"

"Who fucking knows. Garrett just said to look for them out there because Del Mar will start killing people again if he gets his moody hydra ass out of that fucking indoor pool and realizes they've gone to buy more *conchitas*."

So, Del Mar is currently in hydra form inside.

Good to know.

Once their backs are to me, I round the fountain and slip through the front door, the security amulet granting me access through the suffocatingly heavy wards. I pause, scanning the entry hallway. It must lead back to the indoor pool since I can hear the soft sloshing of water up ahead. I step in that direction, but someone darts down the steep staircase to my left and tackles me with a snarl.

The vampire sinks her teeth into my throat, but before she can tear into me, I rip her heart out. She slumps to the tiled ground, her head smacking audibly.

More security members shout upstairs. The water sloshing gets louder, and a deep rumbling sound precedes several reptilian hisses from up ahead.

All right, fuck sneaking. Let's do this.

I bolt down the hall, analyzing my surroundings as I skid into the massive, vaulted indoor pool room that takes up this entire level of the house. Two large legacy security guards in gas masks are posted here and shout when they see me.

But my priority is Iker fucking Del Mar.

Amadeus briefed me on the Immortal Quintet's weaknesses many times. He taught me about the hydra.

Its many heads spew forth poisonous fumes and grow back twice over when cut off. Its great teeth and claws maim, yet forget not the water-abiding beast's true deadliness: noxious blood. The scent of it alone is lethal to the living.

As much as I enjoy bloodshed, I don't want to waste more time away from my quintet suffering an agonizing death because I caught a whiff of Del Mar's hydras' blood. His blood in human form won't pose any risk, hence why the tranquilizer in my pocket is really fucking necessary.

The hydra's nine heads screech in harmony. The sound is hideous, just like the rest of him. He's not nearly as large as Baelfire's dragon, though he is big, scaly, and serpentine.

Just as those nine heads open their mouths and begin to spew a greenish gas into the air, I launch myself into the incredibly large indoor pool where Del Mar's beast is half submerged.

The water turns tumultuous as the hydra whirls, trying to crush me with its draconic legs. Its serpentine tail whips through the pool in search of me, but I latch onto it. Struggling to keep my grip on the scaly appendage underwater, I uncap the tranquilizer from my pocket and drive the long needle deeply between the scales of the beast.

Del Mar shrieks and finally shakes me off, sending me spinning underwater. My forehead smacks against the pool's edge, and then dagger-like claws slice across my back. Searing pain explodes through my spine, and water floods my mouth when my body's reflex is to scream.

Pivoting underwater, I kick up to finally break the surface, coughing up water and gasping for air. By now, the hydra's fumes have dissipated enough, but Del Mar's nine heads are still screaming, hissing, and gnashing their teeth. He staggers, less focused on me and more focused on what I just did to him.

One of the legacy guards standing just outside the pool aims at me with a spell. Ignoring the burning pain in my back, I grip the edge of the pool to launch out of the water and roll away from the attack. Whipping wet hair out of my face, I withdraw Pierce again and drive it through the sorcerer's neck.

A pulse of elemental air slams into me, sending me smashing into one of the house's walls. I hear the distinctive *crack* of my ribs breaking, but I can't waste time processing more pain. Instead, I launch several dark magic attacks in quick succession.

One hits the air elemental. He screams and falls into the pool, drowning while the hydra continues to thrash and screech, fighting the effects of a forced shift.

My vision blurs from pain and exhaustion, but another buzz fills me.

Two of the security members from upstairs race into the room. I hear the now-familiar sound of a gun cocking and dive aside just as the woman opens fire. Using my unnatural revenant speed, I dash around the pool to get to her, but not before one of the bullets lodges in my thigh.

Ouch.

I snap her neck. She drops like a ragdoll.

I wanted to keep this swift and professional—but between the rush of fresh kills and the pounding of a fight inside my veins, I can't stop the unhinged grin that spreads across my face when the other security guard turns and tries to flee. Pulling out one of my new knives, I hurl it at his back. It sinks deep where his heart is, and he falls forward, lifeless a moment later.

Another wave of dark, delicious force floods through my system. My vision dips again, but this time, it's because my berserker side wants to break free.

If I weren't so determined to get back to my quintet as soon as fucking possible, I would let it.

Instead, to stay in control, I recite the list of mantras that Amadeus and the necromancers drilled into me as I approach the pool where the hydra shifter is now shrinking to his human form.

"I feel nothing. I'm on my own. I need no one." Wiping blood from my neck, I take a deep breath and check my broken ribs, which aren't as bad as they could be. "I am but a weapon who is one with death. I am nothing but deadly calm."

Repeating these old mantras staves off the berserker as I crouch beside the pool. Iker Del Mar finally bursts from the surface with a ragged gasp, left naked from the shift.

He lurches forward in the water to bare sharp teeth at me, ready to attack. I beat him to it, sending a silver dagger into his right shoulder. He screams, struggling to tread water through the pain and the effects of the nightshade root powder.

Gripping him by the arm, I yank him onto the pool's edge. The immortal hisses and tries to bite me, but I have a smaller knife already ready that I slice through his mouth, straight across his cheeks.

He hisses in agony.

"*Telum.*" He sprays blood when he speaks, his forked tongue flicking in and out as he grimaces in pain. "This does nothing. You cannot kill—"

"Oh, right. Your life link. Slipped my mind, but give me a moment."

I slit his neck. He gurgles and twitches before going still.

The buzz doesn't fill my veins, of course. I need to destroy his etherium anchor first. With a grimace, I pick the bullet out of my leg and do a basic necromantic healing spell on my leg and back, ignoring the throbbing in my head as I go to look for Iker's life link.

It's a ring. Engela described it in detail, along with all the ways he tends to hide it.

Searching the entire house takes twenty minutes. During that time, five more security team members either return or show up for their shift, only to join the heady buzz coursing through my system —which is convenient since it takes a hell of a lot of destructive magic to break into the enchanted safe Del Mar had hiding under one of the guest beds upstairs.

I grab the little etherium ring, yawning as I drag myself back down the stairs to the pool room littered with corpses. I crouch beside Del Mar and wait.

And wait.

Really, I should just kill the son of a bitch right now. I could destroy the etherium ring before he wakes up and then return to my guys.

But I want a few words with this monster first.

Del Mar's eyes flutter, his gaze whited out for a moment as his neck wound begins to seal itself. Before it heals completely, I stick my gloved index finger through the remaining hole so when he comes to, he chokes and struggles, hissing at the pain.

I wait until his gaze returns to normal, and he glares at me. Once I know he's paying attention, I poise Pierce above the etherium ring, driving it down hard to shatter the gods-given life link.

The monster screams.

Gods. Such a wonderful sound.

Now that he's unable to link back to life using the etherium, I smile at the seething immortal.

"Tell me where the psychic bitch is."

Del Mar's growl rumbles through my finger as he tries to fight, but he's still too weakened from the lingering effects of the night-shade root powder.

"Sent by good old Amadeus, were you?" He spits, choking

slightly when I wiggle my finger to see him wince. "I will not tell you where my keeper—"

"Don't, then," I shrug nonchalantly. "Engela already told me where she is, anyway."

He bares sharp teeth. "Engela would not know, that damned traitor. We entrusted her with nothing—she was far too weak and easy to manipulate. Wherever she says Natalya is, it's entirely wrong."

"So she's not in Baltimore?"

I see the grimace slip through his attempted composure.

I nod. "Thanks for confirming that. Now, I have a question for you because as evil as you are, you're also clever. You know exactly what I am, and you know mine is the last face you'll see in this lifetime. Unless you want me to draw this out, answer me. How can a revenant outlive a failed purpose?"

In other words…how the hell can I stay with them?

He laughs harshly, but it comes out strangled. "You're pathetic."

"You know, I've always wanted to dissect an eye still attached to a functioning brain," I say in a chatty tone, withdrawing the silver knife from his shoulder and poising it beside his eye as a warning.

Del Mar hisses. "For a revenant like you to draw out your failed, inferior existence, you would need the direct blessing of Galene, the goddess of life herself. Or perhaps if some other deity took pity on a creature like you—"

He cuts off abruptly as he inhales, nostrils flaring. Then a hideously wet-sounding laugh rasps up his damaged throat, and his cloudy yellow eyes grow distant.

"I might've known. What an elegant reckoning."

"What the fuck are you talking about?" I demand.

Del Mar's sneer is ugly. "This game the gods play, and your orchestrated existence. I've had enough of this. End me, *telum*."

"I'm not done asking questions."

"You are, for you shall get nothing more from me. And when your time comes soon enough, Sachar will judge you not by what you are but by what you have become. You shall rot for your crimes in the Beyond—"

"*My* crimes?"

I hook my finger further into the hydra shifter's neck, twisting until he screams. Then I lean down to meet his pale, inhuman gaze so he misses none of this.

"We're both monsters, so spare me the holier-than-thou bullshit. I know what *your* crimes are. Natalya may be the keeper, but you're the brains. It was your fucking idea to send that troop of humans into the Nether—which means when you die in a few seconds, Sachar will judge *you* based on every death of those innocents for generations. They say some punishments in the Beyond are brutal—far more brutal than I could do here and now."

I smile again, slowly, savoring the pain and fear in his eyes.

"Still. A bitch can try. This is for any part you had in my Nightmare Prince's torment over the years."

I cut out his forked tongue as he screams.

"And this is for putting a fucking collar on *my mate*."

My anger builds as I shove his wriggling tongue down his throat, forcing him to choke on it. He starts to panic, coughing up more blood as he struggles to get air. I glare at him, pulling my finger from his neck as the rest of my long-pent-up vengeful fury roars in my ears.

"And this is for all the suffering, innocent humans in the Nether, you cowardly motherfucking son of a bitch."

I add an extra twist as I rip his heart out, just to add to his final agony.

For a moment, vengeance is sweet.

But when an unrivaled buzz of power floods through my system with searing potency, I drop his heart, clutching at my own chest. I take a deep breath, trying to steady myself despite the two powerful immortal life forces barely contained inside me.

Just when I think I've reached my limit, I hear them as if they're far in the distance.

Maven, Everett calls, panic saturating his telepathic voice.

Silas is close behind him. *Where the hell are you? Answer us. Now.*

Relief at hearing their voices dulls the blistering power in my veins. I breathe out slowly, getting to my feet.

I'll be back soon, I promise.

But where the fuck did you g—

The front door of Del Mar's safehouse slams open. I block my quintet out immediately, turning to face the next threat as a handful of bounty hunters rush into the room.

Hellhounds howl and snarl as they leap inside, but to my surprise, their masters order them to heel. When the hunters see the dead member of the Immortal Quintet, they shout and swear in alarm while they aim at me, moving as a well-oiled team to surround me. Their red lasers dance over my skin, centered on my head and chest.

One of the hunters snaps a picture of me on a cell phone. Great. I'm guessing that will be all over the news soon.

Oh, well. At least he captured me in my element, coated in blood with Pierce at the ready.

"Don't move," a dark-skinned fae woman orders. "Come quietly, and we won't have to hurt you."

I yawn again, the exhaustion starting to really set in as I squint at these bounty hunters. Gods help them, they just have no idea how not frightening they are. They could all shoot me at once right now, and I would still revive with plenty of time to slaughter them before they could possibly deliver me to the Legacy Council.

"If you're going to threaten me with a fight, at least bring someone who knows what he's doing. Where's Douglas?"

"Still cleaning up the mess you left in Alaska," another one of the hunters growls. The fearful disgust on his face makes me think his trigger finger is getting itchy. "He wants you brought in alive for questioning—but if you resist, we get to kill you finally. Except I say we just fucking take you out here and now."

"Stand down, Radley," the fae girl snaps.

"Look around! She just fucking assassinated everyone here!" he shouts. "Did you forget your cousin was just murdered in Alaska by this bitch? I don't care what Douglas says. We don't need answers—we need the *telum* dead!"

That makes all of them start shouting. The girl in charge is pissed as she glances over her shoulder at them, snapping that Douglas has a plan and they need to shut up.

Their poor unity is the perfect opening. I send a surge of dark magic through the air, sending them all flying backward with shouts of pain and alarm. Hellhounds bark and whine, caught in the entangled mess of agony that my unique magic causes.

I use the fastest transportation spell I can muster to send me back to an alleyway in Madrid. I stumble, bracing myself against the brick wall beside me as I try to catch my breath.

I can heal more of my injuries before returning to Nebraska. That way, my guys won't lose their shit when they see me.

And then we'll have to get the fuck away from any trace of my magic before we're hunted down again—because killing Del Mar just bought me more time, and I intend to use it.

27

EVERETT

It's been nearly three horrible hours since I woke up from what I thought was death.

The first hour was spent in an agonized panic, struggling to form words after whatever the hell that wraith did to me. Silas was the same way, Crypt was nowhere to be found, and Baelfire was still unconscious.

When we tried to reach Maven through the bond, all we got was, *I'll be back soon.*

And then she fucking blocked us out.

In the second hour, Baelfire finally woke up. Except it wasn't actually *him*, just the beast living inside him. If I ever thought his inner dragon was a pain in the ass before, it had nothing on this. Silas had to stun the big oaf with magic twice in a row to keep him from shifting in a blind, snarling rage.

Whatever that fucking wraith did to him, it took a while before Baelfire was able to come to the phone, metaphorically speaking. Then we were a healing, cussing, pissed-off trio on the verge of killing each other—especially because we still couldn't reach Maven. Or Crypt, for that matter.

Until finally, I drew the damn line.

So, Maven decided to leave us here to go do shit by herself? I don't blame her. How useless are we to her that we get in a fight of *that* proportion, followed by a visit from my new definition of hell personified, and yet she had to patch us up all alone and shoulder on? She's probably exhausted, pushing herself too hard to meet the deadline the Entity gave her so she can save people she cares about.

And here we are, whining like a bunch of fucking toddlers.

But not anymore—there is no way I'm sitting around on my ass while she is out there doing gods-know-what. We're going to be useful to our keeper if it's the last godsdamned thing we do.

When I went off on Silas and Baelfire to say all of that, it shut their squabbling right up.

The last thirty minutes have been spent far more productively. By all three of us.

Working and planning together.

Dear gods, it really must be the end of times.

I lean back from the small suite dining table, babying my injured shoulder from the wolf shifter who bit me back in Alaska. Silas can't use more blood magic for healing until he feeds from Maven, not to mention he's in shitty shape himself. We all are.

"All right," I mutter. "I'll make the call. I'll need to use your phone, Dragon Breath."

Baelfire practically throws it at my face before he stalks to the bathroom to shower off the remaining blood he's coated in. Just because we've been productive doesn't mean we aren't still pissed the fuck off about everything that happened today.

I wander into one of the suite's bedrooms as the cell phone rings. I'm almost sure he won't pick up when there is a click and a long sigh.

"Can't you let me fake my death in peace, Evie?"

"I've told you a million times not to call me that," I point out, staring out the window at the sunlit little Nebraska town. Snow is piled up on the sides of the street, and humans chatter happily as they stroll here or there. Such normal lives, taking it easy during the holidays.

I envy them. I'd give fucking anything to spend the holidays with Maven just spoiling her and not on the run.

My contact huffs over the phone. "Yeah? Well, I've told you a million times not to call me, period. Yet somehow I know that when some unknown number calls my fresh start number at an absolutely ungodly hour—"

"It's ten in the morning where you are," I point out.

"You know what? It's always an ungodly time for you to call me because, like I said, I'm pretending to be *dead*. So who's the asshole here?"

"Probably me," I admit.

"Damn straight."

"I need your expertise, Ian."

The vampire grumbles, and I hear something knocked around on the other end like he's rummaging in a fridge. "This is supposed to be my retirement, you know."

"Twenty-five is a little young for retirement."

"Not with a bank account as big as mine," Ian crows, laughing. Then he sighs. "Damn it, that really doesn't land with you, huh? It's like comparing a hill to a fucking diamond mine. By the way, I noticed that all the real estate you bought a few years ago keeps increasing in value, despite what everyone said—including me. You're annoyingly good at business, you know that? Shrewd as your old man."

I grimace. I've gotten that so-called compliment plenty of times. As if it's not enough to look like the councilman, I also have to naturally take after him in so many ways that people can't help comparing me to him. Even Ian, who knows how much I dislike my parents.

Especially now that I know they've been bullshitting me about my curse for my entire fucking life.

Anger wells up again at the thought of that fake prophecy translation and how much it has screwed with me. I pinch the bridge of my nose.

"This is important, Ian. Really fucking important. The *only* reason

I'm calling you is because we grew up together, and I know with absolute certainty that you take secrets to your grave."

"Hence why you entrusted me with taking care of your dogs and discreetly keeping an eye on your sister from a distance. She's safe, by the way," Ian adds, his voice softening.

Shit. Heidi.

Amid all this political upheaval between humans and legacies, she should have been my first thought. There's just been so much going on that I didn't stop to wonder how she's faring in the rural human town where she's grown up.

"She just dumped another human boyfriend," Ian adds. "Might need someone to cheer her up. Like, say, I don't know…a hot, very available vampire who already knows everything about her and would be the perfect rebound, if nothing else. Just say the word—"

"For the last fucking time, no."

"Oh, come on. Why not? We've known each other forever, and you know I'd take good care of her, Evie."

I scowl, lowering my voice enough that I know Baelfire won't overhear from the other room. None of my quintet except Maven knows that Heidi exists, and I'd like to keep it that way.

"What I *know* is that my sister is not up for discussion. She wants a peaceful, human-like life, and that's what she's going to fucking get. She's gone through too much shit to get tangled up with you, of all people. Keep an eye on her and make sure she's safe and has funds for anything she needs. Otherwise, leave her the hell alone, or I will drive an icicle so far up your ass, you'll be coughing up snowflakes. Got it?"

Ian sighs again, muttering under his breath. "Look, just tell me what you need. And to be clear, I will overcharge you for my services."

"I'd expect nothing less."

Fifteen minutes later, I rejoin the others and blink when I see that Crypt is back. He's covered in blood, lounging on the couch completely naked, smoking *reverium* with his sword stabbed into the carpet.

I get that he just returned from tending to Limbo, but seriously? This asshole has no respect for hotel room maintenance.

I scowl. "What the hell is wrong with you?"

"How much time do you have?"

"This is a non-smoking room. And if you're going to be naked, at least take a damn shower."

Crypt ignores me, exhaling a long breath of smoke as he swings one arm in a circle like he's testing where it connects to his body. When I look at Silas and Baelfire to see if they're going to be any help with the naked psychopath bleeding all over this suite, Bael shrugs. Of course, our resident shifter isn't bothered by the nudity.

"He's coping. We're all trying to until she gets back. Leave him alone."

I'm floored. "You're defending him? I thought you hated him."

"Him, hate me? Not at all. We're best mates now," Crypt drawls.

Baelfire rolls his eyes. Before I can say anything about it, Maven's voice *finally* drifts through the bond.

Silas? Can you have the etherium ready for me?

He's already moving, withdrawing the briefcase from his pocket void and laying the smooth pieces of the clear, paradisical substance on the table.

Are you hurt? Is everything okay? I demand. *Where are you?*

Her voice is slightly strained. *No, yes, and Spain, but not for long.*

On cue, a bright flash of light floods the room. Then it's like the weight of the world drops away from my chest, and I can finally fucking breathe again as I wrap Maven in my arms, pulling her tightly to my chest.

She's covered in blood, but at least she seems uninjured—except for a nasty bruise on her forehead. As soon as I notice it, I let one of my hands cool with frost and gently press it to her head to help with the swelling.

"Etherium?" she yawns, rubbing her face.

Shit. She looks dead on her feet.

I let her go, and we all watch as our keeper grabs a shard of etherium and whispers in a language I don't know. But then again,

Silas doesn't seem to get all of it either, judging by the frown on his face.

The shard darkens from a glassy nothingness to something more like a black opal, as if it's now containing something dark. Maven exhales like the life force was weighing on her. She picks up another piece, wiping her brow and tossing a weak smile at us.

"You can all stop quietly freaking out. I just didn't realize how taxing it would be to have the life forces of immortals inside me."

She repeats the action with another piece of etherium. Then she turns to examine us like she's worried *we're* the ones who are about to topple over when it's clear that she's extremely exhausted.

Although, I guess she did leave us looking pretty damn bad.

"We're okay, baby," Baelfire assures her, pulling her into a big hug.

Crypt pulls her away from the dragon next and kisses her deeply, resting his forehead against hers as she shakes her head. I don't hear what they're saying, so they must only be talking to each other telepathically.

Finally, Maven peeks over at me, zeroing in on my shoulder.

"I'm fine," I promise quickly.

"Tell us everything, *sangfluir*," Silas murmurs.

Maven glances at the etherium on the table. "I killed Del Mar."

We all stare at her in shock before I speak.

"You *what?*"

"I said I—"

"I heard what you said," I clarify, frustrated. "How the hell did you know where he was? Why the fuck didn't you tell us that you were going to do this?"

She stares at me like I'm missing the obvious. "You were unconscious."

"I meant *before* we were unconscious. Damn it, Maven." I rub my face.

"Now, now. Don't hold back the details. I hope it was incredibly gory," Crypt pipes up, a sick smile of excitement twisting his face.

"Not nearly as much as I would have liked," she sighs. "To be honest, the fight was disappointing. I thought he would present more of a challenge," she grumbles, rubbing her bruised forehead. "Douglas is much more fun to fight—although the last time we fought, he took a cheap blow to my head. He loses some brownie points for that."

Silas examines her forehead, using necromancy to heal it. It's still weird as hell to think of him as a necromancer since I was taught they were worse than demons.

But hey—at least he can heal our keeper. No complaints about that.

Then I frown. "Wait. How do you know what brownie points are if you grew up in the Nether?"

"Lillian used that term a lot. I don't really know what it means," she shrugs before glancing between us. "I was surprised you four didn't try to follow me."

Bael folds his arms, lifting his chin. "We were busy."

"Doing?"

"Wouldn't you like to know?" I fold my arms, too.

"I would, actually."

"Too fucking bad. Take not knowing as your punishment for running off and leaving us here like useless sacks of potatoes," I grunt, my irritation returning.

Maven's eyes flash. For a half second, as our keeper turns to me with a deathly glare, I regret all my life choices.

"Punishment? I must've misheard you."

Nope. Stay strong. It doesn't matter how scary she can be—I'm digging my heels in with this one. It scared the hell out of me to wake up with her gone yet again, so I lean down to give her my most chilling look.

"You're the keeper of this quintet, but we're still a fucking part of it. If you're going to do shit without telling us and leave us all bleeding and panicked for hours on end, then we don't owe you a single godsdamned explanation about what we were up to while we were forced to wait around for you."

Silas's brows go up. Baelfire whistles low and takes a measured step back from us, shaking his head like he thinks this is it for me. Meanwhile, Crypt is enjoying the show like he can't wait for Maven to hand me my ass.

Maven goes toe to toe with me, her dark glare caustic. "The reason I left you four here was to protect you while I took care of things—"

"That you didn't tell us shit about. I had no idea Del Mar was in Spain or that he was your next target. Did any of you know?" I wave at the others.

"Leave me out of this," Bael says, raising his hands as if to show he's unarmed.

Silas shakes his head in answer. Crypt shrugs, absentmindedly spinning one of the life-force-containing etherium pieces on the table like it's a fancy top.

"No, they didn't." I turn back to her. "And you know why? It's because you don't fucking tell us *anything*. You're so adamant that we're yours now, and that's more true than you even realize. But if we're your quintet, then treat us like a damn quintet and tell us about your plans *before* they happen. Don't just run off and let us wonder if you're ever fucking coming back."

My voice breaks slightly at the end as my emotions get the best of me. Maven still seems pissed, but she looks away.

"Put yourself in our shoes," I press. "How would you handle it if the roles were reversed here?"

She exhales slowly, uncomfortable. "I'd hate it. I didn't mean to upset you by leaving. It's just…you four needed time to recover, and I don't have any time to spare."

"Then *we* don't have time to spare," Silas corrects gently. "There is not us four and you. As I told you before, *ima sangfluir, tha sinn unum mar.*"

Whatever the hell that means, Maven softens further and finally sighs.

"You're right. I should have told you guys sooner about our next target. I'm just not used to sharing plans or…talking. To be candid, I didn't talk at all except sparingly to Lillian and Felix for the last few years. I'm still adjusting." She meets my gaze, hers full of promise. "I'll be better about it."

Baelfire's eyes narrow. "Hold up. Who the fuck is Felix? Is he cute? Did he try to flirt with you? Is he still alive, and more importantly, why?"

"Oh, my gods," Maven rolls her eyes, cracking a slight smile at his possessiveness that lessens the tension in the room. "Felix is an atypical caster in the Nether. He thinks of himself as an older brother to me. I think he's a book-horny nuisance, but he's also gifted. He helped me experiment on etherium in the Nether and figured out some obscure, ancient fae spell to make this work," she nods at the dark shards on the table. "Once I weaken the Divide enough, he'll be the first through it to coordinate with me and lead the exodus into the mortal realm."

We all absorb that, nodding until Baelfire huffs. "You still didn't answer about whether you think he's cute, Boo."

She arches a brow. "Why, are you interested? I'm not sure if he's into shifters, but you two might hit it off. He is pretty damn frail from his upbringing, so careful not to crush him in bed."

Baelfire grins. "Raincloud, if he tries to come anywhere near a bed with me in it, he's toast. You're the only one I'll be careful with in bed. Or better yet, let's ditch *careful* and go for rough and kinky."

"I'm with the lizard on this," Crypt announces.

"Seems like you're back to your usual selves." Maven's smirk falls again as she checks each of us in turn. "Although…are you guys really feeling okay? Gideon is…"

Horrific.

I meet Silas's glance, then Baelfire's. Even Crypt isn't open to talking about this.

I don't know what they experienced, but I'm sure as fuck not talking about what that wraith made me go through, even if it was just inside my head. Knowing that he's been in Maven's mind—that he was tormenting her for years…

Bile threatens to rise in my throat, but I take a steadying breath. "How did you get us out of there, anyway?"

Maven fidgets with her bloodied gloves. "I just…transported us away."

"Lie," Silas says gently, his red irises as sharp as ever. "Tell the truth, *sangfluir*."

"Fine. I stabbed him with the bone knife Everett gave me."

Crypt frowns, tipping his head. He's still naked and covered in drying blood, and I'm alarmed to realize that I started to completely tune it out until this moment.

Does that mean I'm getting used to these three freaks being indecent all the damn time? Ugh.

"Only blessed bone weapons can harm wraiths, love," he points out.

She nods, glancing furtively at me.

Oh, shit. She thinks my theory about her being selected as a saint at birth might be right.

"Anyway. The important thing is, he's gone. Maybe not dead, but let's take what we can get for now. So," she brushes herself off and looks at Baelfire, moving on. "Is your family's place still a safe option?"

He blinks, trying to catch up. "My family?"

"Killing Iker bought more time before I need to hunt Natalya. We should find a safe place to lay low before the bounty hunters track us down again. Not to mention, I want some time with you guys. In general, but also in bed."

I almost choke as the blunt topic change throws us all for a major loop. I fucking adore how assertive my keeper is—but now all I can picture is Maven in bed.

Naked and ready to be worshipped, I think with a quiet groan.

Please tell me you're picturing her and not me, Silas snarks back through the bond.

I flush as I realize that thought wasn't kept to myself. I'm still not used to this telepathy thing. Crypt laughs out loud at my pure embarrassment.

Baelfire is grinning hugely at Maven, ignorant of the telepathic back-and-forth. "Fuck, yes! My family's place will be perfect."

Silas arches a brow. "Are you certain? When was the last time you checked in with them? These are contentious times, and the Decimuses have been known to have big mouths regarding politics. They might have enemies at their doors already."

"First of all, fuck you because our mouths are perfect," Baelfire fires back. "And I haven't talked to my family recently, but that's only because we've been, you know. Busy. On the run. Shit like that."

"Sounds like an excuse." I fold my arms. "Maybe you're just not sure your oh-so-loyal, proud family is *actually* going to accept Maven as your mate."

"It's okay if they don't," Maven adds. "I've been told I'm an acquired taste."

Bael snarls at me, his eyes gleaming a darker shade of amber as if his pissy dragon is just under the surface. "They'll accept her. Not every family is a shitty nightmare like yours."

"Your family has its own glaring set of fuck-ups," I snap.

"Yeah? At least mine didn't lie to me about my curse just to keep me a miserable fucking loner all my life."

I flinch.

Maven tenses.

Baelfire immediately clamps his mouth shut, gripping the side of his head. "Fuck. Yeah, I felt it as I was saying it. Too soon. Sorry, Snowflake."

I try to change the topic quickly. "If we're going to his family's territory in Canada, we should—"

Everett, Maven reaches out through the bond, pinning me with a fierce look.

It's really not important, Snowdrop. I'm bound to you, and nothing else matters to me anymore.

Her lips press together. *That's why your abilities have been so much stronger and sharper. The prophecy was a hoax. Your true curse had something to do with your control. Didn't it?*

So she already suspected it, too.

I nod and try to move on again, grateful when Maven stews

silently and doesn't make me say anything else about this extremely unpleasant new information.

"As I was saying, we should use human means, like a rental car. Transportation magic is tracked too easily, and it would be less than a day's drive from here to the Purcell mountain range."

No one argues. It's quiet for a moment.

Then Crypt grins. "So long as we let our girl drive. I want to sit back and watch other cars on the road panic."

Baelfire laughs, but Maven arches a brow.

"You're an ass. But actually...I wouldn't mind sleeping while someone else drives."

My chest melts as I realize just how fucking tired she must be. Crypt immediately pulls her in for a soft kiss.

"Of course, love. They'll handle everything."

"*They?*" Silas scowls. "And just what will you be doing?"

The incubus grins and guides Maven toward the bathroom. "Cleaning up our girl."

Lucky fucking bastard.

28

MAVEN

"MAVEN WHATEVER-YOUR-MIDDLE-NAME-IS OAKLEY," Kenzie's voice crackles from my phone.

It seems loud. I'm pretty sure that means it's on speakerphone again, but since I have no idea how to fix the damn thing, I adjust on Baelfire's lap so it won't be so loud in his ear.

"Kenzie Something Baird," I reply, unsure why we're doing fake full names.

We're in the spacious middle row of a vehicle Everett painstakingly picked out from some rental place in Kenzie's hometown. It's the nicest car I've ever been in. Silas is driving while Everett is in the passenger seat, frowning at messages on a phone he bought before we left Nebraska.

I'd insisted on Silas feeding on me to heal my ice elemental's shoulder before we left. He only took the barest amount, but at least the worst of the wolf bite is gone.

Crypt is sprawled out, lounging in the back row that he has all to himself, watching the wilderness pass by outside as he plays with his lighter. I've kept note of how often his markings light up. It's far less than it was before we bonded, which makes no sense. Del Mar's death should have caused more surges at the Divide, which should be affecting Limbo like crazy.

Unless…maybe being bonded to me is somehow helping.

I check out the window at the endless green pine trees powdered with snow. I don't know where we are now, but I do know I'm starting to get hungry after the long nap I took earlier.

"Girl, *updates*," Kenzie demands, drawing my attention again. "Now. Or else I'll be forced to start stalking you."

"Nope. Position's already taken," Crypt calls from the back.

The lioness shifter sighs. "Speakerphone again, huh, monk?"

"I hate technology."

"You know, somehow, I think it hates you more. But anyway, congrats on taking out that hydra weirdo. I never liked him—that forked tongue licking his eyeball sometimes? *Major* ick."

I frown, glancing at Baelfire to see if he knows how Kenzie knows about my recent kill. He shrugs and returns to contentedly nuzzling the side of my neck.

Being engulfed in his big, warm arms like this makes me feel strangely dainty and pampered. Even though Everett fussed about us not wearing seatbelts, I've thoroughly enjoyed this car ride so far.

Especially because I can feel how thick and hard my shifter's erection is in his pants. I'm tempted to grind against it but restrain myself so as not to derail our trip—because I'm positive Silas will pull over if I initiate anything.

I could move to my own seat to avoid any sexy distractions…but anytime we go over a big bump, he groans softly, and that's just too fucking delicious to give up.

"How did you know?" I ask Kenzie, getting back to the topic at hand.

"Well…it's kind of all over the news. Along with a *very* hardcore picture of you at the scene of the crime. They didn't really censor much."

I expected as much. Whichever bounty hunter leaked the photo, I'm sure the Legacy Council is pissed.

"The world is losing its fucking mind about one of the Immortal Quintet members dying, and the Legacy Council is still telling legacies to keep a lid on everything because they don't know the full situation themselves, and…ugh, it's a mess," Kenzie groans. "Not to mention, the Divide saw a huge spike in surges several hours ago. They say it's starting to spread inland, so there've been even more evacuation orders along the East Coast."

"Shit," I grimace.

"Don't feel bad!" Kenzie protests. "I mean, maybe feel a teeny bit bad because this is terrifying for the humans, and more shadow fiends are getting into the mortal world and shit—but that aside, you're doing it for a good cause. A *great* cause. Those poor humans in the Nether deserve to live actual lives free in the mortal realm, so I support you all the way."

"At this point, I'm beginning to wonder what I would have to do to get you to stop supporting me so unconditionally," I joke.

She giggles. "I mean, I guess if you went all berserker and killed someone in my quintet or family, I'd get pretty damn pissy."

Oh.

Shit. I still haven't told her about killing Luka's brother.

Baelfire senses my tension and pulls away with a frown. "You okay, Mayflower?"

I nod quickly, changing the subject. "Anyway…how are you?"

Kenzie gushes for a while about how the holidays were perfect with her family and how her quintet is incredible.

"I mean—we're all still really hoping that we find our caster at the next seeking," she sighs. "I know it's almost a year away, but it feels like we're just…"

"Incomplete?"

"Yeah. I don't know how to explain it. I can't get enough of my quintet, and we're all crazy about each other, but the dynamic just isn't perfectly right, somehow. Deep down, we all know it's because someone isn't here with us."

Looking back at the Seeking now, I am so fucking glad that all my matches were there. What lucky timing—especially considering the slight differences in our ages.

I frown. Come to think of it, all of us being there simultaneously was suspiciously serendipitous.

Unbidden, Del Mar's comments about the gods playing a game with my "orchestrated life" replay in my mind. Between the Seeking and now my quintet being bound to me against all odds…

What game are the gods playing, exactly?

"You'll find your caster," I comfort Kenzie, focusing again on the conversation.

"Gods, I hope so," she huffs petulantly.

Meanwhile, Silas turns off the main road and stops at a run-down gas station, which seems to double as a small, chicken-themed restaurant.

Everett makes a face. "Here?"

"Unfortunately for your fine sensibilities, the nearest country club is well over a hundred miles away," Silas replies dryly. "Deal with it because we need gasoline."

"Fine, but we're not getting food here. I am not letting them serve Maven deep-fried roadkill scraped off the fucking freeway."

Kenzie overhears Silas and Everett bickering. "Oh—do you need to go?"

"Possibly."

My stomach growls loudly. Baelfire promptly scoops me up, leaving the car to walk me toward the gas station. Seriously, this gorgeous shifter needs to learn that I have two highly functional legs.

"I'll call you again soon. Or better yet, call me," Kenzie says brightly. "I really do worry about you, May."

"I worry about you, too," I admit. "And I will."

We say goodbye before I pat Bael's shoulder. "Down, boy."

He smirks. "What will my reward be?"

Feeling impish, I lean up to whisper in his ear. "Be a good pet and put me down, and I'll have you crawling for me later. Behave yourself extra well, and I'll let you come wherever you want."

He halts, groaning hoarsely and dropping his head back. "Godsdamn it. I really can't walk around in public with this erection, Boo."

When he lowers me, I make sure to slide against his thick bulge on the way down, grinning when he shudders.

"That's my good boy," I murmur just for him.

Baelfire braces himself on his knees like he's trying to contain himself. "*Fuck.* You're so mean. Please don't ever stop."

I laugh and fall into step beside Crypt, who wraps his leather-clad arm around my shoulders and kisses my temple. Silas and Everett are already waiting by the gas station's entrance.

Everett opens the door for me, grimacing at the handle. "Ugh. I probably just picked up some incurable disease for you. You're welcome and please don't touch anything unless it's necessary."

"What about you? Because it's starting to feel necessary to touch you guys," I inform him honestly.

Silas smirks as he follows me and Crypt through the door. "Thank gods for that."

Once again, thank me instead. They're useless, I send through the bond.

Everett sighs. *You know, they really do smite people for blasphemy, Snowdrop.*

"In that case, I hereby dare the gods to strike me dow—" I start to say, raising my voice dramatically.

Everett clamps his non-door-holding, cool hand over my mouth, shooting me a warning look. I hold his gaze and lick his palm sensually, making him jump and flush all over.

"You are such a menace," he grumbles when I grin.

We all follow as he goes to find the cleanest-looking mini table in the attached semi-restaurant. The place is empty except for a bored-looking employee on her phone behind the counter next to a glowing display of various rotating meats.

Baelfire finally joins us inside and scowls when he glances at the menu behind the counter. "Not many vegetarian options."

"That's fine. I'll eat potatoes again."

He sighs. "My sexy mate, Angel of Death, love of my life—they are called *fries.*"

Again, with the *L*-word. I try not to make a face because I know it will just inspire more of their neverending teasing about this topic. So, instead, I shrug.

"I admit. That's not a terrible nickname."

"None of my nicknames are terrible," he grins.

"Well, we all know *that* is a fucking lie," Silas rolls his eyes.

Everett's cell phone rings as the others examine the menu. He makes a face, rejecting the call to send a text instead. He's squinting a bit, which reminds me that I want to see him in his reading glasses someday.

When the elemental catches me looking, he gives me a frosty look and tilts his phone away so I can't try to read it.

Meaning, it's about whatever the fuck they were doing while I was ending Del Mar.

"Just tell me what you four are up to," I insist.

"Nope."

"You're being petty."

Everett tucks his phone away, adjusting his jacket. "Yeah, I am. But like I said, this is what you get for leaving us out of the loop and scaring the shit out of us."

How is it both aggravating and attractive that he's being so fucking stubborn about this?

I sigh. "I already promised to be better, so cut the shit and…"

I trail off as an unusual chill runs down my spine, alertness washing over me. It's not the same as when shadow fiends are near, but I still know what kind of Nether spawn to expect when I glance at the arriving newcomers.

I just don't expect to make eye contact with Melchom, who sweeps through the door first.

He's in the middle of saying something to the demon beside him, but when he sees me, he freezes, going ashen-faced.

"Fuck me seven ways to hell," he grimaces and tries to back out the door. "Ah, now, maybe we should just—"

"Shut the fuck up. This was the place I saw, so quit being a pussy about it. In you go," a demoness says, shoving him inside.

She's tall and stunning for a demoness, with dark hair in dread-locks, a skull-patterned bandana obscuring her horns, electric blue lipstick, and piercing black eyes that immediately swing to me.

She breaks into a bright grin, showing off pointed teeth. "There she is! The *telum* herself. All the humans on the news are calling you Mav—"

I'm in front of her in an instant, pressing one of my new knives against the flesh of her throat.

"Don't sully my name with your mouth," I warn evenly.

The demoness's eyes widen before she tosses her head back in a booming laugh. I sense my matches behind me, tensed in case these demons mean trouble, but they don't try to intervene or stop me.

There are four demons present—Melchom, this one who is still laughing like I invented comedy, and twin male demons who look like they're on a mission to discover how much of their tattooed skin they can cover in piercings.

The demoness arches her brow at Melchom. "You didn't describe her nearly well enough, dick-for-brains."

"More like you just didn't hear me over all the wailing your little fuck pet does whenever you're pegging the hell out of him, you slut-faced bitch," he scowls.

I look between them, deducting. "You're Melchom's girlfriend."

The twin demons hiss in disgust at me using their pal's name so freely, but she only grins.

"Tell you what, *telum.* I came here looking for a word with you. So, to show I mean you no harm, how's this? The name's Eisha."

Melchom sputters, scandalized. The twin demons hiss again, and Everett sighs and mutters a prayer to ward off the gods' punishment for demonology.

I study Eisha. I can't think of a single fucking reason she could want to have a word with me. It's much more likely that she's competitive like most demons and wants to try her hand at taking out Amadeus's scourge.

"Do I get to make good on my threat now, love?" Crypt asks in a deceptively calm tone, his murderous glare pinned on Melchom.

My other three matches look fully on board with that idea.

Melchom gulps loudly. "W—whoa! Hang on here, studs. Look,

my airhead girlfriend just got really fucking excited when she saw the *telum* on the news. Claims she was one of Amato's allies back in the day, which is complete unicorn shit if you ask me—"

Eisha rolls her eyes. "How would you even know, micro-dick? You fucked up, lost your horns in '97, and didn't respawn for over a decade. Missed all the fun."

"Hang on," Everett frowns. "Amato? As in, Pietro Amato?"

"Oh yeah. Bet you know all about him, don't you, Gorgeous?" Eisha purrs, checking out my increasingly uncomfortable, fidgeting elemental in a way that makes my teeth grit. "Your dad helped make the decision to execute him, after all. Fucking devils, I see now why all the humans drool over you so much. You're pretty enough to stick on a Popsicle and lick right—"

I flip the knife smoothly to slice across the side of Eisha's face, leaving a long cut that begins oozing black blood immediately. She rears back with a snarl, cupping the new injury that will definitely leave a haggard scar.

"Don't look at him again," I warn her, letting my voice drop to deadly levels. "And if you make one more passing remark about any of my men, I will cut those horns off of your fucking head and strangle you with your own spine."

"Aww," Bael coos behind me. "Did you guys hear that? *Her men.* I love when she gets all murderous and sappy." A searing glare quickly replaces his happy grin as he looks back at Eisha. "But to be clear, my mate will absolutely fuck you up, so keep your beady little eyes off the merchandise."

Do I finally get to mutilate Melchom for slighting you, darling? Crypt checks through the bond, his purple gaze imploring as he looks at me. *I'll ensure you get to savor his screaming as long as you like.*

So thoughtful.

Silas smirks. *Why is it unsurprising that you aren't being sarcastic, sangfluir?*

I glance at Everett, getting back to the topic at hand. "What the fuck does the founder of the Reformists have to do with me?"

Eisha laughs as she recovers, wiping dark blood off her hand onto her leather pants. "You mean you don't know? You're Amato's kid."

29

MAVEN

I STARE AT THE DEMONESS.

"You're the whole reason he started the movement in the first place—and now I fucking get why! Quite the scent on her, huh? Told you so, shitface," Eisha adds as Melchom and the twins sniff the air around us.

Melchom looks baffled. "Devils and dicks! I swear on your cheating little sluthole that she didn't smell like *this* the last time I was around her."

He inhales deeply again.

"Stop sniffing my mate," Baelfire snaps, baring his teeth.

I ignore their weird tangent about my smell, still focused on Eisha's words. "You're mistaken. My parents were killed slowly and brutally in the surge before the liches took me away."

The demoness snorts and motions for us to follow them to the tables, scooting them around until we can sit. At least, some of us sit. There aren't enough chairs in this little restaurant, so Bael and Crypt stand behind us, and Everett and Silas sit on either side of me. Eisha takes the seat opposite the table. The other demons go to order food from the very distracted employee who apparently hasn't noticed anything odd going on here.

Eisha examines me, shaking her head. "Infernal hells, I can't believe that man was telling the truth. Told him he was a horny fucking dreamer, but here you are."

"Your vague answers test my patience. Once again, both my parents died."

She smirks. "Nah. Sure as sin, you're Pietro Amato's daughter, kid. You would've been only two years old when they dragged you away, so you can't remember your parents—let alone them dying. Meaning all you know is what the chumps in the Nether told you, isn't that right?"

That's…true.

I frown, considering the possibility that my parents somehow survived the surge Dagon told me about. "What makes you so sure that I'm his kid?"

The other demons return to the table with multiple heaping plates of chicken, some kind of meat wrapped in bread, other steaming dishes, and sodas.

Eisha pushes a plate toward me.

I push it back.

"It's not from your personality, I can tell you that much! Bet you got that shit from your mother." She laughs and shakes her head, taking a whopping bite of chicken and nodding at my quintet, careful not to look at them again. "Do they want some?"

"I mean, if you're offering—" Bael starts.

Crypt elbows him hard.

"No. We buy our own roadkill," Everett says, watching with obvious disgust as the twins chow down like they've been starved for decades.

Eisha shrugs and smiles at me. "Listen, *telum*. Your dad was one hell of a guy."

Hang on a second. "If you're about to tell me you fucked him, I'll vomit on your food."

She bursts into riotous laughter, as do the other three demons.

"Oh, fuck, no," Eisha wipes away a tear finally, shaking her head. "Amato was pussy-whipped by your mom like none other. If you ask me, that's partly why he was so obsessed with getting you back from the Nether—he said you were the spitting image of her. Poor guy was determined to be the best dad in the whole damned world. Wanted to bring you up like a fucking princess all on his own."

That answers that question.

No mother. Dead, or left us before I was taken.

"And somehow, he got along with your type?" I check, glancing at the demons. I'm not sure the twins can speak. Some demons don't get the hang of human tongues very well.

"He was much more open-minded than most humans," Eisha nods.

She offers me chicken again, more insistently, like it's bugging her that I'm not eating. This time, Silas takes it from her and tosses it over his shoulder to drive the point home.

The demoness snorts. "You know, at first, we demons thought Amato was a damned idiot. Fucking soft, that guy. Used to be some hotshot doctor, and he cared about everyone and everything—would give a stranger the shirt off his back if he thought it would help 'em. Always down for a chat about feelings, morals, life's purpose, bettering the world—"

"He sounds exhausting."

"Yes, thank you!" she cackles. "That's exactly what I told the fucker. Honestly, he drove us batty, but he wasn't nearly as bad as most mortals. Even better, he was down to try any kind of shady shit to get you back. Blood tracing, necromantic rituals, soul-scrying—you name it, he tried it all for seven fucking years. That guy was so hells-bent on getting you back that I finally strong-armed him into telling me why. And you know what he said to me?"

I arch a brow expectantly.

"'*My daughter is my whole world. Without her, this one holds no meaning,*'" Eisha recites dramatically, following it with a harsh laugh and sipping her soda loudly. "And then he went on to spin what I thought was the most ridiculous fucking tall tale I'd ever heard, going on about how oh-so-special you were. 'Course, now I get that he wasn't pulling my tail."

I wonder if she's talking about me being a saint. That's still not a can of worms I'm ready to open, so I tip my head.

"But you never met my mother?"

"Nah, I never had the displeasure. From what I hear, she didn't run in the same circles as your father for what little time she was around. A real career woman—and not nearly as open-minded as Amato was about most shit, let alone about demons."

I speak telepathically only to Everett.

So, your father helped vote to execute my supposed father. The more I learn about your parents, the more I'm not looking forward to meeting them.

Dear gods, no. They don't deserve to meet you. Not to mention, they have some psychotic urge to win the telum *over to be manipulated however they see fit. Baelfire wasn't kidding about them being a nightmare.* Then he pauses. *I should probably tell you that I was there. When they executed Amato, I mean. Natalya did it.*

I stare at the plates of food in front of us as the demons continue to devour their meal.

How strange to think that during those isolated, brutal first years of trying to survive in the Nether as a little girl, someone was here fighting like hell to get me back. Some idealistic, kind father who might've even loved me.

When it comes to father figures in my life, my experience has been strange—because, in an extremely inhuman, bizarre way, Amadeus genuinely cares about me. I wasn't lying to Baelfire when I told him my adopted father wanted children. Whatever mysteries lay in Amadeus's past, I'm positive he was once human, and some forlorn echo of his long-ago humanity led to him singling me out as someone he wanted to pretend was his own.

That's why he doted on me—even if his method of doting meant extreme training methods, showing me off in gory battles to his Undead subjects, teaching me to be heartless, and eventually ripping my heart out to make me what he wanted.

Still, for being what he is, Amadeus tried to build an inhuman, paternal relationship with me.

Obviously I don't see him like that.

If this Pietro Amato had somehow rescued me and taken me back to the mortal world to be a real father to me—gods, I can't even imagine what that would have been like. It's too foreign and strange.

But a part of me is almost...*sad* that I never met the man they say fought so hard for me.

He would probably be disappointed to see what I've become now.

I don't realize I've completely tuned out of another conversation until Silas leans forward with a frown.

"What do you mean, you know someone in the Sanctuary? I know the Sanctuary well, and everyone there shuns demonology. You must be lying."

To my surprise, it's one of the twins who snorts. His voice is rough and accented. "Come off it, I'm not lying. Thanks to the weakening Divide, my brother and I fled the Nether recently. First, we took an offer of a deal to escape the citadel, and all we had to do was get a tricky legacy here in the mortal world to accept a big, secret mission straight from—"

The other pierced demon elbows his brother. "Shut the fuck up! What've I told you about keeping your ugly mouth shut? You'll spoil things."

"What things?" I ask, arching a brow.

The pierced twins fumble and announce they're done eating before they hurry out of the gas station.

Melchom rolls his eyes. "Demons fresh out of the Nether are a fucking pain in the ass. They're just bumbling motherfuckers who can't tell their tails from their dicks—but there's family for ya, am I right?" he grins at me.

"I wouldn't know. But if they're related to you, it tracks."

He laughs and elbows his girlfriend. "Ready to go, you infernal whore?"

Eisha rolls her eyes and shoves him so he nearly falls out of his chair. "Go on, and stop yapping at me. I'll follow."

Melchom starts to protest, but when he sees the way Crypt is still looking at him as if he's envisioning the most painful method to peel the demon's flesh off, he quickly leaves. I watch out the gas station window as he gets on a gleaming motorcycle in the parking lot beside the twins on their own motorcycles. The fourth empty bike must be Eisha's.

Kenzie told me about motorcycles weeks ago, but it's my first time seeing them in real life.

Those look fun.

Everett, Silas, and Crypt follow where I'm looking. Everett scoffs, speaking telepathically.

I'd offer to buy you one, but those things are death traps.

You seem to think that's not a selling point. I watch one of the twins start his bike and rev the engine.

Driving an unwieldy, clunky car doesn't come naturally to me.

But one of those? Yes, please.

Baelfire glances between us and scowls. "Damn it, what the fuck am I missing?"

That snaps me out of it, and I look back at Eisha.

"All you did was talk about Amato. You haven't explained why you wanted a word with me, so spit it out."

One corner of her lips draws up. She seems almost wistful, which is fucking weird for a demon.

"This was it, *telum*. Just wanted to meet you for myself."

"Bullshit."

She laughs. "Think whatever the fuck you want, but I just had to see what my old pal's daughter was like. Gotta say, I'm not disappointed. You seem like a hell of a lot more fun than Amato was—but I'd still like to rip that immortal cunt's head off myself for killing him. Speaking of which, I hope you know you've got our backing. Most of us demons in this realm stan you hard, kid."

"You mean a bunch of disloyal, cheating, conniving, innocence-devouring Nether spawn are somehow on my side?" I clarify.

"Sure as fucking sin, we are."

I don't trust demons, but it's a nice thought.

"One last question. How did you find me here?" I demand.

Eisha smirks. "Tracked the phone you used to call Mel a few days ago. Wasn't easy, but did the trick."

Damn it. I should have known. With a sigh, I pull the flip phone from my pocket, snap it in half, and drop it in the demon's soda.

Eisha laughs uproariously as she stands to leave, nodding her chin at me. "Really, though. If you're looking for help shredding the Legacy Council and bringing anarchy to the world, hit me up, *telum*."

She finally leaves. I watch the four demons peel out of the parking lot on those pretty motorcycles.

Crypt drops into Limbo without a word as Baelfire grunts, "You know what? For demons, they weren't as bad as I expected."

"Are you serious? Did you see the way they ate?" Everett grimaces. "Fucking unhinged their jaws."

Bael snorts and then leans down to kiss the top of my head. "All right. Game plan. We'll get fries and shit here, but since we'll be driving through the night, let's also buy you some snacks to try from the gas station—"

Crypt blurs back into existence, holding an armful of candy, chips, and bottled drinks.

"But buying is so overrated," he grins.

"Hey, you. Tattoo Guy," the girl behind the counter says, frowning as she pays attention for the first time since we walked in. "Are you going to pay for all of..."

She trails off, her mouth dropping open as her eyes widen. At first, I wonder if I got some of Eisha's blood on my face or something, but then she points at me and shrieks.

"Wait! You're—you're the maniac on the news assassinating immortals! Oh my gods, oh my gods, oh my *gods*—"

She scrambles for her phone like she's about to call human authorities.

"That's our cue," Everett announces, taking my hand as we run from the gas station.

30

BAELFIRE

I HAVEN'T BEEN HOME in months, but I'm not surprised to hear the distant roar of a dragon as soon as the rental car crosses into Decimus territory.

That was definitely Declan. He must be home for the holidays.

"I just sensed some serious magic wards," Silas mutters from the passenger seat since Everett is now driving. "Should we be concerned, or do they know we're coming?"

"My caster dad, Ivan, set those up forever ago so no one with hostile intentions can pass into our territory. It alerts him, too, so he's probably telling the others about our arrival right now," I mutter, glancing into the back of the car.

Maven is catching up on more sleep, leaning against Crypt as he gently traces one of her hands. She looks so fucking peaceful when she's resting near him.

Gotta admit, I'm grateful for that.

It's still weird as fuck to see the incubus look anything besides apathetic or murderous. That's all any of us saw from him until Maven arrived.

But now? He's not as hateable as I used to think. Not that we are or ever will be "best mates," as he puts it.

When Crypt sees me looking, his eyes narrow. "If they're at all impolite to our girl—"

"They won't be."

The other three remain tense, thinking my family will have a problem with who and what Maven is.

But I know my family. They're loud, proud, and fucking ridiculous but never judgmental or blindly prejudiced. If anything, I'm worried they'll be a little *too* happy to meet Maven and tease the hell out of me about having a mate while they're at it.

Come to think of it, out of the entire quintet, I definitely had the luckiest upbringing. Silas was raised by an eccentric sexist who made him fend for himself, Crypt was a literal monster's son brought up by the Immortal Quintet even though they hated him, and Everett's family is a swarm of emotionally abusive manipulators dressed in designer clothes that cost more than most people's cars.

Meanwhile, Maven grew up in a fucking brutal environment. The little my mate has told us about her past makes me physically sick to my stomach if I think about it.

I'm pretty sure this is going to be her first glimpse of what an *actual* family is like.

Gods, I hope she likes them.

Finally, we round the base of a massive mountain and turn down the long road leading into the valley where my family's huge house, the barn, and several other buildings sit proudly in the vibrant morning light. Snow coats the ground and trees as we pull into the big circular driveway.

I've missed these mountains. Being back here makes me want to go flying with my mom and Declan.

And I would *love* it if Maven rode on my back. I bet my mate would love flying.

Except maybe not yet—not when shifting risks me being lost for gods know how long to my inner dragon.

He's such an unmanageable dickhead. He's been quiet during the ride, but I can feel him stirring. The scaly fucker will be causing more problems for me soon.

I scent the pine trees and something cooking in the kitchen, and I'm not surprised to see one of the curtains move in my family's massive living room. About six or seven familiar faces peer out at us, a couple of them waving.

Yep. They're going to swarm us the second we get out.

Everett parks, his pale blue gaze sweeping over the house mistrustfully.

"Relax. You've been here plenty of times, Ice Prick," I remind him.

All three of these legacies were here all the time when I was little —that, or I was being taken to their houses. Until I was about nine years old, our parents constantly made us hang out. Mostly because my mom is very social, despite how catty Silas's moms were and how snobby the Frosts always acted.

And for some weird reason, my mom has always liked Crypt. She invited him here at every chance. Looking back now, I wonder if she knew how shitty his home life was and wanted him to have somewhere to go to get away from the Immortal Quintet.

It sounds like something she'd do.

Maven's eyelashes flutter open. She sits up, stretching as she checks out the window. "Fuck. We're here."

I pick up on the edge in her voice. "Nervous, Boo? Don't be— they'll love you."

"Though not nearly as much as we love you," Everett tacks on with a sly smirk.

"Cut it out," my mate grumbles. "Just say you'll burn the world for me or some shit like that."

"We absolutely will, *sangfluir*," Silas agrees, turning in the passenger seat to level her with a heated crimson look. "But if you would like to know the reason why, then it's truly because—"

"Stop," Maven huffs crankily, unbuckling like she wants to get out of here as soon as fucking possible. "You're just going to drop the stupid *L-word* again to watch me squirm."

Gods, my mate is so fucking adorable.

We all laugh at how flustered our keeper is as we get out and approach the wrap-around front porch. Just as I expected, the front door flies open, and my lion shifter birth father, Oscar, beams at us.

"You made it!"

He's followed by Declan, who clearly just shifted back and hasn't grabbed a shirt yet. He's grinning ear to ear as he walks up and smacks me on the shoulder. He's my oldest sibling, in his mid-thirties, but he's always worked hard to build a relationship with me despite our fourteen-year age gap.

It helps that he's the only one of my four brothers who is also a dragon shifter.

"Holy shit! Look at you, all grown up and matched and running from the law." He spots Maven behind me and grins. "Here she is! Hi there, sis. Welcome to chaos, also known as our family."

As if to underline his point, two of my other brothers, Cace and Aidan, also come outside with big smiles. A couple of legacies from each of their quintets follow suit. My seven-year-old niece, Quinn, and three-year-old nephew, Bran, skip outside to shout hellos.

It's a barrage of bright smiles and greetings, and I almost want to laugh at how round Maven's eyes have gotten. She's not used to big, warm welcomes, but that's just the Decimus way.

"*Baelfire Finbar Decimus.* Tell me it's not true."

My mother's raised voice makes everyone quiet. They part for her as she marches toward us with her head held high, her one golden eye blazing angrily.

She lost her other eye years before I was born while leading a defensive strike against a surge at the Divide. I've never not seen her with a brown leather eye patch firmly in place. I've been told I look like a mix of her and Oscar—her draconic amber eyes and smile, his dirty blond hair and tall, brawny stature.

I mean, clearly I didn't get my stature from *her.* My intimidatingly strong, confident, outspoken commander of a mother is all of five feet tall if she gets on her tiptoes.

Still, I feel like a tiny kid again when she folds her arms, pissed off as she looks up at me expectantly. I look at Declan to nonverbally ask what she's upset about. He shrugs and glances at Maven as if he thinks she might be the reason.

Oh, fuck. No way.

"If this is about my mate—" I start to warn in a growl.

My mother sputters and waves my words away like that's the stupidest possible suggestion.

"Is what I heard from Keith Erikson's mother about what happened at Everbound true? Did that scaly-assed Del Mar actually put a *collar* on you? On a godsdamned *dragon?*"

I grimace. That had been beyond humiliating, but I'd almost forgotten by now. Honestly, Maven made it so that when we were alone, I ended up loving wearing the collar—just for her.

In public, I still loathed the damn thing.

"Thanks a fucking lot for bringing *that* up right off the bat," I grumble. "I'm glad I'm home, too. Doing peachy, thanks for asking."

My mother snorts. "Please. You know I'm glad my baby is home," she says, wrapping me in a warm hug that feels like my childhood. Then she pulls back and beams. "And anyway, I don't have to worry about wringing that hydra's many necks, according to the news. Speaking of which, move—it's well past time that I meet my new daughter-in-law."

I step aside, not surprised to see that Maven carefully maintains a poker face as she examines my mother. She's good at pretending to be relaxed, but I notice her hands flex slightly in her gloves.

My keeper is nervous. I want to reassure her, but my mom studies Maven just as intently before a huge smile breaks over her face.

"My gods, do you have any idea how excited I am that I get to have you as a daughter? I've wanted to meet you for so long."

What now?

Maven seems equally taken aback by the odd comment, but then my mother wraps her in a tight hug. Pure panic streaks across Maven's face before she can stop it.

Fuck.

I shove my mom away, unable to help the growl that rises from my throat as I pull Maven into my arms. My mom and the rest of my family look shocked by my reaction.

But I can't fucking help it. Maven is tensed in my arms, taking measured, quiet breaths. When I try to peer at her face, she shakes her head subtly at me. She doesn't want a scene.

Too bad I've already created one.

It's solved quickly when Crypt snorts. "Were you so ridiculously territorial when you were a newly matched dragon, Commander?"

Good. Yes. That's a good excuse.

My siren dad, Nico, grins. "That she was."

"She damn near burned down the eating hall at Everbound when a girl hit on me a few weeks after the Seeking," Oscar adds with a booming laugh. "Don't worry, Bael, we won't get in your mate's bubble again. It's very nice to meet you, Maven," he adds.

My family all start introducing themselves. I shoot Crypt a grateful look. He rolls his eyes.

Pretty sure this means we *are* pals now, which is fucking weird.

My mate quietly greets everyone one by one before looking back at my mom. I still haven't let my mate go.

"I take it you aren't considering turning me in to the Legacy Council for a fat paycheck?" Maven checks.

My mom laughs. "Not even remotely. Those pampered bureaucrats can keep their blood money. You five will be perfectly safe here for however long you choose to stay."

"Thank you, Brigid," Silas says sincerely.

My mom turns to the rest of my quintet, putting a hand on her hip.

"Don't you *Brigid* me, Silas Crane. Don't forget I used to change your diapers back when your mothers thought I was a respectable legacy. I still have no idea why they ever thought that," she whispers with a conspiratorial grin at Maven.

My mate's lips twitch. "Respectable is a synonym for boring."

"I couldn't have said it better myself. Now, I'm sure you five have been very busy ever since Everbound went to hell, but *Baelfire* here —" My mother shoots me a reproachful look. "Has been dodging my calls since long before then, so I haven't gotten to hear much about you."

"The school was on lockdown," I protest. "Give me a break."

She turns back to my keeper. "We all want to get to know you, Maven. But first of all, please tell me my son has been acting like a proper match to you all along. I taught him that mates and quintets are more important than anything in the world, but if he was ever a dick about you being the *telum*—"

"Fucking gods, Mom," I cut in, scowling at her. "Way to just throw it out there."

"I just want to make sure he has been a good mate to you despite everything," my mom continues, ignoring me.

Maven is surprised but tips her head back, examining me. I see it in her eyes the exact moment her devious little mind decides to torture me.

"Angel, no. Don't you dare give me a boner in front of my mom," I whisper in her ear, quiet enough that no other shifter nearby will overhear.

She appears totally innocent as she looks back at my mother. "Baelfire has been very good for me. The perfect mate."

Gods, I love my sadistic little keeper. She absolutely knows she's driving me crazy with her praise—and calling me mate? That's below the belt.

Literally. My dick is starting to get hard down there, damn it.

"Good," my mother grins, motioning at the rest of us to head inside. "Come on—as always, you're still officially invited in, Crypt. Breakfast is ready, and we added a second mother-in-law suite to the house a few months ago. You five can stay in there for now."

Everyone starts to head inside, but I stay still for a moment, using Maven as a shield to hide my slowly softening erection. She smirks over her shoulder.

I shake my head, booping her nose with mine. "Hellion."

"You like it."

"I *love* it. Just like I love y—"

"I will twist your nipple again," she warns fiercely.

I laugh.

Quinn prances up to us, bouncing on her toes. She's my brother Grady's daughter through two of his quintet members. Technically, none of my brothers has managed to have a kid. My niece and nephew are both a result of other members of their quintet, but still —my family couldn't be more grateful to finally have kids in the family.

I didn't see Grady here, so he must still be stationed at the Divide. His family stays here in Decimus territory whenever he's deployed.

"Will you guys stay for New Year's? Please?" Quinn chirps.

She's a water elemental. When I was here a few months ago, she liked to splash people's laps and loudly announce that they'd peed themselves.

Maven regards the little troublemaker. "I hope so."

"Me too!" Then Quinn blinks up at Everett. "Hey, why's his hair white? Old people have white hair, but he doesn't got any wrinkles."

"He doesn't *look* wrinkly," Crypt agrees, crouching and cupping his hand beside his mouth like he's sharing a secret with her. "But I promise that on the inside, he's far more boring and wrinkly than any old geezer you've ever met."

"His name is Snowflake," I add helpfully.

"Oh! I like your hair, Snowflake!" she says before hurrying into the house.

Everett sighs. "I fucking hate you guys."

I laugh and take Maven's hand, leading her inside.

My family's house is just as busy and cozy as it's always been: spacious, rustic, and still heavily decorated for Starfall festivities with bows, holly, fake snow, and all kinds of other shit. The tree glitters in the living room right beside their massive TV, which is currently muted.

But I stop in my tracks when I see what's on the screen. So do Crypt, Silas, and Everett.

Because holy fuck.

A newsreel shows a slightly blurred image of a massive room

296 | TWISTED SOUL

with an Olympic-sized pool. Its water is a suspicious red color. Blurred-out lumps in the background can only be bodies, but front and center is a slightly censored, naked, bloodied corpse.

Del Mar.

And standing in front of him is Maven, poised for a fight with her favorite dagger. She's covered in blood, her throat marked with a vampire bite, and her dangerous dark gaze is pinned on the camera, so it's like she's glaring through the screen right into my soul. My mate looks powerful, terrifying, fierce, and—

"Holy shit, you're sexy as fuck," I sigh, squeezing Maven's hand. "How do you make violence look so damn good?"

Silas squints at the screen. "Am I mistaken, or is that a gaping hole in the hydra's chest? You took his heart?"

"He deserved worse for putting a collar on Baelfire," she mutters angrily.

I nearly fucking swoon. She was all vengeful for me?

Gods, I am one lucky dragon.

"All things considered, it's actually a really flattering picture," Everett muses.

Crypt agrees with a smile. "I'll hunt down the uncensored original so we can frame it right next to any other pictures we can get of our girl. How's that going, Decimus?"

"Say *cheese*, Mayflower," I say, pulling out my phone to snap a selfie with her.

She's rolling her eyes and fighting a grin in it, which makes me smile wider.

Quinn skips up and points at the screen, looking at Maven with wide blue eyes.

"Hey! That's you in all the blood!"

Maven's attention flicks to the rest of my family dishing up breakfast like she thinks they might dislike what's on the screen. My lion-shifter brother, Aiden, glances over and grins.

"Hey, I'm just happy I finally got a badass sister-in-law."

"What do you mean, *finally?*" one of Declan's mates scoffs. She throws a tater tot at him and gives us an apologetic look. "We're running out of bacon. Dig in before Cace eats it all."

Cace protests that he would never as he tries to scoot the last pile of bacon onto his plate. My caster father, Ivan, slaps his hand away while my mom warns my brothers that she'll make them run laps if they don't sit their asses down and behave in front of their new sister-in-law.

Home sweet home.

We all dish up—except Crypt, who vanishes—and sit at the ridiculously oversized dining table that is still somehow crowded. Cace is chatting with one of his quintet members, Quinn is showing off how she can balance her fork on her nose, and one of Aidan's mates, Megan, is trying to keep Bran from dumping out his orange juice.

Oscar notices Maven's plate. "Uh oh, did we run out of sausage and bacon? We probably have some ham leftover from Starfall Eve—"

"Nah, she's vegetarian," I say, sliding eggs off my plate onto hers since she's sitting to my left. I like to make sure she's eating enough, and all she grabbed was a muffin and sliced fruit.

Cace opens his mouth across the table. I'm positive he's about to make some smart-ass comment about Maven's food choices, so I throw a hard-boiled egg at him. He catches it and throws it at Declan, who swats it aside.

"That's enough with everyone throwing food at the table," Nico sighs. "You're not children."

My mom is sitting to my right, at the head of the dining table, and she grins at me, leaning over to whisper, "*But* we're about to have some more children joining our family very soon."

Oh, fuck. Is she hinting about my quintet?

Maven must have the same thought. She's surprised enough that she drops her fork, which bounces off the table. Crypt appears, catches the fork before it can touch the ground, and hands it back to her. Quinn claps and cheers like that was the greatest show, and Crypt bows dramatically at the giggling girl before vanishing again.

Everett is sitting on the other side of Maven and gives my mother a meaningful look. "Look, that's really not your bus—"

"Are you over there spoiling the news?" Aidan calls from the other end of the table, giving our mom an exasperated look.

She laughs. "Well, Baelfire's been out of the loop! He should know he'll be an uncle to three now."

"We're expecting again," Megan announces, smiling at my quintet.

A grin breaks over my face at the good news. "Holy shit!"

"Congratulations," Silas offers, offering Maven a sip of what I'm pretty sure has become fae wine.

Someone needs to tell the fucker he's going to get high blood pressure or some shit from drinking so much. That someone is Maven because she gives her day drinker match a dry look as she swaps her water for his wine. It just makes him smirk. I'm pretty sure they're having another one of their telepathic conversations.

Godsdamn, I want to be able to talk to my mate like that. Just thinking of all the shameless innuendos and cheesy pickup lines I'm missing out on showering her with makes me sigh.

"I'm gonna be an uncle, too," Quinn announces excitedly.

My family laughs, and I catch Maven's small smile from the corner of my eye as she watches the madness that makes up my family.

"No, you'll be a cousin," Ivan corrects. "A very responsible older cousin who doesn't splash water on this baby like you did to poor Bran. Right?"

"Okay," Quinn pouts and turns to Everett. "Hey, Snowflake, wanna see how I can balance my fork? See, look!"

She does her trick while Everett looks at me like he wants to punch me.

"You know, I've heard humans have an easier time conceiving than legacies," one of Cace's mates starts from the other side of the table, glancing at Maven.

Damn it. This is exactly what I wanted to avoid.

I open my mouth to tell her to fuck off about this topic

completely, but my mom leans forward to smile at Maven, acting like she didn't hear Cace's mate.

"Just so you know, it's not usually such a huge group here. It's just the holidays, and I wanted us all to be here in the midst of everything going on recently. Most of these hellraisers will fly the coop as soon as the holidays are over—and I'll be returning to my post in Mexico just after New Year's to keep an eye on the Divide."

Maven nods before my brother Cace catches her attention.

"So hang on, did you *really* grow up in the Nether? I heard a rumor about it, but how the hell did you survive?"

"I technically didn't."

The way my spooky little mate shuts him right the hell up has me bursting into laughter.

It's good to be home.

31

CRYPT

THE ROOM'S quiet is interrupted only by the dim light of dawn and soft, restful breathing as I struggle to hold back a moan. I lift my obsession's pretty thigh higher around my waist to press myself deeper into her wet, divine cunt.

All the while, my gaze is locked on her exquisite face.

Maven's eyes remain closed in blissful sleep, lashes resting on her cheeks. Her lips part ever so slightly in dreamy pleasure, thanks to the erotic fantasy I spun for her in Limbo. Her dark hair has half-unraveled from its braid, leaving her deliciously undone.

My attention sweeps down to where I have pushed up her loose T-shirt, and I admire the love bites I left all around those dusky, peaked nipples.

Sating Maven as she sleeps is sending me into a state of intoxicated bliss.

And knowing that I am bound to her now—that she carries my emblem and I am hers...

Your existence ruins me in such glorious ways, my love, I whisper to her through our bond, knowing it will not wake her since I've lulled her into uninterrupted rest.

But deep in her delectable subconscious, I ensured she knows precisely what I'm doing. She knows that I've been taking my time adoring her body, kissing and teasing and losing myself in this twisted obsession that fuels my existence.

When I thrust again, slowly, the breathy whimper that escapes my resting darling sends heated madness down my spine. I'm forced to bury my face in her neck as I try for the seventh time to fend off the acute pressure and need to fill her.

But when Maven moans ever so softly in her sleep, her intimate muscles fluttering and clenching tightly around my throbbing erection, the boundless euphoria breaks free and rushes through me. I edged and refused myself so long throughout the night that the nearly violent release leaves me breathless.

The other members of my quintet are still fast asleep in this ridiculously oversized bed, secure in their dream states thanks to the additional incubi power I dosed them with so I could worship Maven to my heart's content tonight.

I roll over, carefully adjusting my obsession until she lies comfortably half on top of me. I can sense her contentment in Limbo, and I'm tempted to go there to savor more of her dreams.

But if I do, I'll lose this moment to hold her.

So I stay.

Besides, her dreams will soon taper off as the morning quickly approaches. It won't be long before they all start to wake.

At long last, when the morning is waxing strong outside the window, Crane is the first to rouse from the deep sleep I put them in. He immediately sits up to check on Maven, and I don't miss the stark desire that floods his expression when he sees the well-fucked state she's in.

I wholly expect him to get pissed off and accuse me of taking liberties with our keeper, but the previously insane fae surprises me when he gets up to shower without a word.

Oh, dear. Does this mean we've reached a new level of trust? Is our quintet going to have fewer hearty spats now that we're all growing…gods forbid, *closer?*

What a horrible concept. I'll have to think of more ways to stir the pot before they all get too comfortable with me.

Decimus grumbles sleepily, rolling over to blindly reach for Maven. I smack his hand away before he can touch my leg. He peeks an eye open before closing it again, smiling.

"No wonder I'm hard as godsdamned steel. Smells so fucking good in here. Gods, I love her pussy."

I could have sworn Maven was still asleep, but she must have caught that last part because she slides her arms more securely around me.

"No more *L*-word," she mumbles.

Frost laughs quietly, slowly waking up to this exchange. "So damn stubborn."

Maven starts to say something else but then opens her eyes in surprise to peek between us.

"I'm leaking."

I kiss her forehead, speaking through the bond. *That would be our combined pleasure between your thighs, darling. You come as beautifully in your sleep as you do in the waking world.*

That earns a deliciously sinful smile from her. *Do I? Interesting. One day, if you sleep while I'm your muse, I'll return the favor.*

My heart forgets to beat for a moment.

I had no idea I wanted this taboo desire reciprocated until now, but *Scyntyche's scythe,* I need that from her.

But I didn't miss her use of "if."

Maven sits up, adjusting her T-shirt and undoing her dark, tangled braid as she yawns. It's astonishing how captivating she can be with such a simple act as waking up. I watch her at my leisure, ignoring when my pale markings light up insistently.

Frost checks his phone, probably for any updates about our little side mission. Meanwhile, Maven glances at the ground and frowns.

"Weird."

"What's weird?" Decimus mumbles, still half-asleep.

"I don't feel like exercising my ass off," she mutters.

"Good. I like your ass right where it is."

"Perhaps your morning restlessness was curbed," I suggest with a smile. "Sleeping cardio, and all that."

She grins, speaking only to me through the bond. *What a useful kink you have.*

I will never tire of hearing her voice in my head.

"Hungry?" Decimus asks, checking on our keeper through half-mast golden eyes. "My family's a bunch of busybodies. They've probably already eaten, but we could have breakfast in here."

Maven nods absentmindedly, too busy curiously watching Frost as he finishes sending out some messages. Clearly, it still bothers her that we haven't fessed up about our plans.

He slips into the bathroom just as Crane emerges to search for a shirt. This grandmother's suite, as Brigid called it, is a small, cozy apartment built off one side of their house. It doesn't have a kitchen, but it's otherwise outfitted with any necessities—and finally, a bed size fit for a quintet.

The Decimus home has always been a novelty to me. Being back here is strangely…pleasant. I suppose I somehow built up a fondness for this place despite being utterly numb for my entire childhood.

My visits here had been strikingly different from the endless, secret-riddled mansions of the Immortal Quintet. My life consisted of bouncing about from continent to continent, overhearing endless screaming matches, witnessing servants being killed off and disposed of, the constant beatings for speaking out of turn or running away to hunt down predators, and countless other unpleasantries.

In contrast, I was left in peace whenever I was brought to the Decimuses.

If any of the other Decimus family members were wary around me, Brigid scolded them and insisted I was always welcome. I once even watched from Limbo as a young Baelfire lost his temper and got in a fistfight with one of his visiting cousins for calling me a leech.

"Are they hurting?" Maven asks quietly.

I blink, drawn out of my thoughts and into her orbit once again. "Pardon, love?"

She traces some of my markings, and I realize they've lit up. But as it has been ever since we bonded, I barely feel the same painful tugging and aching of my curse calling me to action. I can sense that Limbo is in disarray in distant places, but the agony is so dulled that I can tune it out far easier.

I take Maven's hand, kissing her fingertips.

How could I feel anything but pleasure after enjoying your delectable body all night? I ask telepathically, ensuring only she can hear me.

She smirks. *Those were some wild dreams you spun for me.*

Say the word, and they'll become reality. Between the four of us, I'm sure we can give you anything you desire. And if the other three muck it up, I'll enjoy watching you punish them.

Maven laughs out loud and slips away to enter the bathroom once Frost steps out.

I'm sorely tempted to follow her, but there's a chance she's tending to her business. So instead, out of boredom, I step into Limbo and follow Decimus as he gets dressed and leaves to find breakfast for our keeper.

The Decimus family is ridiculously large, what with all the siblings and their quintets, most of whom appear to be here for the holidays or to avoid the contention arising elsewhere. I don't have an opinion on large families other than how fascinating it is that they make such huge portions of meals.

As someone who doesn't consume food, I must say it's baffling.

At first, it's empty in the kitchen as Decimus dishes up a few heaping plates of leftover breakfast his family made earlier. But then Brigid strolls into the kitchen, smiling brightly at her youngest as she pours herself a large glass of orange juice.

"If you five want breakfast in bed, I can help carry plates," she offers.

He hesitates. "Um—"

"Unless you're not all decent," she adds teasingly. "The last thing I want is to see a bunch of naked asses running for cover—or anything else that will make me want to stab my remaining eye out."

Decimus snorts. "I think I get my lack of filter from you."

"You're welcome." Brigid watches him browse the selection of fruits. Her voice becomes uncharacteristically gentle. "I like her, you know. Maven. She seems tough. Like a strong mate."

"You have no idea. She blows my mind all the fucking time."

"She also seems haunted," his mother adds.

Decimus is surprisingly fierce as he turns to face her, eyes blazing. "My mate's life has been hell. Of course, she's haunted. Now, are you going to keep beating around the bush, or are you going to tell me what the fuck you meant yesterday about wanting to meet her for a long time?"

Brigid grins. "That temper. Just like mine. If you really want to know, I was invited to sit in on a hearing with the Legacy Council about thirteen years ago. They wanted my help in determining the fate of a human—"

"Amato?" he guesses, frowning.

She nods. "At the time, the council was facing backlash for rumors of arresting a human. They wanted strong supporters for public image and even tried to bribe me into voting in favor of the execution. I refused to have any part in it, but it made me curious. I looked into Pietro Amato and learned about the Reformist movement he started. And I learned he claimed to be trying to rescue his daughter back from the Nether. People called him crazy, including me...but I learned the truth too late."

Brigid sips her orange juice. "Remitters show up at the Divide sometimes. Cause trouble with troops, kick up a shitstorm, whine. They want us to go back into the Nether. Pain in the ass, those humans. But the Reformists...they are a much smaller group, but they show up at the Divide sometimes, too. Most of them believe in Amato's cause so much that they ask for my help to create change in the legacy government. They leave peacefully when asked, but others insist they had children taken through the Divide years ago and beg to be let into the Nether. You know why?"

"Why?" Decimus asks warily.

"Because they believe humans are living in the Nether. For years, I thought that was crazy talk. But not anymore." She sets down her glass and regards him with all the severe intensity of a woman who has been through countless battles. "So, tell me. Was Maven the only human in the Nether?"

He tenses, protective of Maven's secrets. "Mom—"

"Baelfire, I haven't been able to stop thinking about Amato's execution for years," Brigid snaps, getting worked up as she shakes her head angrily. "Call it intuition or a guilty conscience or whatever you will, but when the dust settled, I just *knew* that little girl I read about could still be in that damned hellhole. There's no passing through the Divide, not if you want to come back out, so I was forced to live with that horrible thought. But then all these rumors started about the *telum* arriving after a surge in Maine, and you were so tight-lipped about your match—and damn it, I don't believe the bullshit about her being the end of times. Maven is here for a reason. I just want to know if it's for the reason I think it is."

Decimus looks away, clearly conflicted about saying anything without talking to Maven first. But if anyone will be on our keeper's side, it's his mother. She has my respect, which means she's worlds past anyone else we could confide in.

So I slip out of Limbo to sit on the counter beside them, ignoring the flash of pain throughout my limbs from plane-walking.

"You're spot on," I inform her.

They both startle and swear, but then Brigid considers me. "You mean, there are humans in the Nether?"

"Thousands." According to Maven.

"Gods. And Maven is going to free them?" She looks at Decimus.

He sighs, deciding to go along with my judgment call. "Yeah, she is. Really fucking soon, actually."

Brigid nods slowly as if absorbing all of that. Then she smiles at me.

"At least getting *you* to talk to me isn't like pulling fangs. Although I guess I'm glad my son is so protective of his mate. From what little I've gathered of her, she seems worth protecting."

"She is."

"Have you eaten, Crypt?"

"All night." Between Maven's thighs, in fact.

Decimus catches my real meaning and gives me a wide-eyed look as if he thinks I'm insane for implying that in front of his mother. But Brigid smacks her forehead, drawing the expected assumption.

"Oh, right—incubi and dreams. I always forget." She begins preparing herself a plate of food. "I heard about your father. Frankly, I hope you don't want condolences."

"Not at all."

"Thank gods. He was horrible."

I couldn't agree more.

But as Brigid brings up flying later with Decimus and they begin another conversation, I can't help feeling that it's been an excessive amount of time since I last saw Maven. Sliding back into Limbo, I return to the bedroom and immediately relax when I see her perched on the bed, frowning as Frost sits behind her to comb through her damp hair.

"I can brush my own fucking hair."

"But you'll let me do it for you," he says, kissing her cheek. He smiles at her, an expression I've rarely seen on the brooding elemental. "Right?"

Maven melts a little, apparently done arguing. She mutters something about powerful dimples as he gently tends to her hair.

But her attention quickly slips to where I am in Limbo. *There you are.*

I emerge in the mortal realm, winking. "Miss me?"

"Never in a million fucking years," Crane drawls from where he's studying one of the old grimoires on necromancy that he borrowed from the Garnet Wizard's library.

Decimus shows up a moment later with plenty of food for everyone stacked in a nearly perilous fashion. As they take plates and prepare to eat, he glances at me, then Maven. He clears his throat.

"So...my mom kind of knows."

"Knows what?" Frost asks, glancing up.

"About humans in the Nether," I clarify.

Maven goes still.

"She already suspected as much. I merely confirmed it." I hesitate. "I understand if you're angry with me, love—"

"I'm not."

She sets down her fork and examines the four of us. I wonder if our keeper is running out of comfortably loose clothing stashed in Crane's invisible pocket because she's wearing a simple black tank top and dark leggings with Pierce strapped to one thigh.

Her expression is serious. "I cannot fuck this up. This is bigger than me or some oath. And as much as I've trained and planned, I know I'm not enough. Not on my own. I'm providing the humans with a way out, and I'll fight like hell for them, but there's only so much a semi-undead bitch can do."

"Don't call yourself that," Frost cuts in, irritated.

"What I'm trying to say is, if you four have people you completely trust, and you tell them about this, it may be a good thing. If people are willing to help them, I'll be grateful. But if you tell anyone who puts the humans in danger or tries to stop the exodus, I'll kill that person without hesitating," she adds.

"We'd expect nothing less," Crane nods sagely.

They eat for a moment, and then Maven takes a deep breath, giving Frost a pointed look.

"Okay. In the interest of treating you guys like a quintet the way you deserve, you should know that I believe Natalya is in Baltimore. Engela says her etherium life link is inside a choker necklace."

I smile, excited at the idea of bringing down the temperamental spoiled bitch who I've loathed for so long. "When shall we go after her, darling?"

Maven pushes around the eggs on her plate. "Let's wait a couple more days. After New Year's, maybe." She peeks up at us. "Is it silly that I want to spend more time as a quintet before all hell breaks loose?"

Decimus visibly melts, pulling her into his arms with a bright smile. "Fuck, no. That's the best idea I've heard in a while."

"Because it's mine."

Crane cracks a smile at her endearing confidence. "Is there a particular feeling that makes you want to spend time with us?"

"Maybe that dreaded *L*-word," I hint, grinning as I catch on.

Maven scowls, breaking out of Decimus's arms to confront us. "Oh, my gods. You know what? Fine. Let's get this over with. Yes, okay?"

"Yes, what?" Frost arches a brow.

"I obviously caught feelings. Happy?"

Crane tuts. "*Sangluir,* our declarations have been far more romantic. Try expressing how you feel again."

Maven throws a grape at him. "The way I *feel* about you four is like…" She pauses, finding the right words. "It's like death."

Frost coughs. "Ouch. Death? Really?"

She nods, dark eyes solemn. "It's dark, consuming, inevitable, and…frightening, if I'm being honest."

I smile. What an apt description. I understand the sentiment completely.

Decimus laughs. "Of course, you would make something so cute sound so macabre. Are you saying we scare you, Boo?"

"No. The things I would do to keep you four scare me."

I think we all melt this time.

Gods above, what an enchanting keeper I have. She returns to eating like that's the last thing she will ever say on this matter, and the others happily return to their food.

Except, strangely, Decimus.

He goes from looking pleased to looking at me in pained panic, gripping the side of his head. I barely have time to register the blue flames licking at the inside of his skin and how his eyes have shifted before I leap forward, pulling him into Limbo just in time.

Heat explodes around me. I grit my teeth as my skin catches fire. The dragon's roar is warped, echoing in Limbo as the beast completes its shift and writhes, unable to withstand this plane of existence.

I finish patting out the flames on my arms and stomach before drifting up to grab the shrieking dragon by one of his horns. Thank the gods that the laws of physics in my domain are so different from the mortal realm because, just as the last time he lost control, I'm able to guide the agonized beast through the walls and far out into the mountainous woods.

I only release him once I know we're far enough that he won't be a threat to the others.

But when we emerge from Limbo, the beast flops onto its massive, scaly side. It's breathing heavily, smoke rising from its nostrils.

"Fucking dragon," I mutter.

It's good I fed on Maven's dreams before getting to the fun part last night. It means my skin heals from the burns as I wait, watching the idiot dragon to make sure he recovers.

Minutes pass.

He doesn't get up.

Godsdamn it. If I just destroyed Decimus's mind by mistake, I'm not sure Maven will ever forgive me.

32

MAVEN

"*Don't eat the meat, Gideon.*"

Eyes are on us. Slick, inhuman, carnivorous leers fill the colorless stone dining hall, which is littered with bones.

I can feel *him* watching us.

He's here, in this foggy, horrible recollection—I can feel the coldness spreading in my chest. His presence draws me deeper, clinging to my soul like oil, twisting and smothering what little remains of me.

"*Why not? I'm so hungry. They never feed us enough.*"

Young Gideon reaches for the heaping platter just as the other remaining contenders have. They're lifting their knives and forks, licking their lips.

Why is Gideon reaching for it? Doesn't he see what's going on?

I can't move. Shadows flood my chest, suffocating me as I fight for clarity. I *know* what they're doing to us, just like I know now why Olivia didn't meet me after training yesterday, as she's done for months.

She got caught.

"*Stop,*" I try to warn again, sickness crawling up my throat as I watch his fingers close around a thick cut. "*You can't. It's not an animal, it's—*"

A cool hand brushes against my face. My eyes fly open as I jolt, gasping for air.

Blinking away the lingering nightmare takes a moment, and my stomach is still churning when I realize Silas, Everett, and Crypt are all gathered around me on the bed. In the dimness of the room, I can make out that they all look horrified and angry.

Possibly because moisture is trickling over my cheeks.

Damn it. Now I'm even more sick to my stomach. I fucking *hate* crying in front of anyone.

I sit up, quickly swiping at my face.

Crypt swears, his voice a frustrated rasp. "I was forcefully removed from your subconscious again, love. Forgive me, I couldn't—"

"It's fine. I'm good." I breathe out slowly to dispel the lingering nausea.

"You were whispering *don't eat the meat* over and over," Everett says quietly, his soothingly cold hands brushing hair out of my face. "What were you dreaming about?"

I mean to tell them it's nothing, but words pour out before I can stop them. "When I was twelve, Amadeus learned one of the human girls in the citadel was trying to befriend me. She's the one who stole Pierce and gifted it to me. As punishment, he…"

Nope. Turns out, I still can't talk about that incident.

Instead, I take another deep breath, clearing my throat. "The Undead feel a limited spectrum of emotions, but one of their greatest amusements is seeing the living unwittingly eat their own. I could never be sure where meat came from. That's why I still can't stomach it."

Everett looks as sick as I feel. "Oh. Oh, holy gods, that's…"

Silas pulls me onto his lap. He holds me for long moments until he quietly speaks, changing the topic—thank the universe.

"The Entity has sensed changes to your shadow heart because of us, but does he know you are sharing dreams with him?"

I shrug. If Amadeus does know, it doesn't seem like he's been utilizing this strengthened link.

But if he does figure it out—if he gets a sense of my gambit through my dreams...

I glance out the window, letting my worry shift to something more present. After all, my missing match feels like a gaping hole left in this room.

"I'm going to check on Baelfire again."

I can see that Silas and Everett want to protest since they think he may be a danger to me right now. We spent half the day watching the golden beast prowl through the woods, flying, hunting, and generally not behaving like Baelfire. The beast tried to take a bite out of his brother, Declan, when he shifted and tried to speak with him.

Meanwhile, Crypt nods in agreement. I wonder if his support stems from guilt because none of us know if Bael's current condition is from his curse worsening or passing through Limbo while conscious.

Or maybe Crypt is just more fond of Baelfire than he will ever admit.

Not changing out of my pajamas, I slip into my boots and leave the mother-in-law's suite, followed closely by the others. Since it's past one in the morning, it's dark and quiet in the Decimus family home.

But when we step out onto their massive back deck overlooking the woods, Everett swears in surprised alarm.

Baelfire's dragon is staring at me through the snow and trees. The beast's piercing, possessive golden gaze follows my every movement. Its tail slowly curls left and right behind it as it remains perched on the mountainside, its crown of magnificent horns gleaming in the moonlight along with all those golden scales.

"Baelfire?" I check, hopeful.

The beast tips its head to a comedic angle, long neck craning. Smoke rises from its nostrils as it unfolds and refolds those beautifully expansive wings.

"It's just his dragon right now," Brigid Decimus says, joining us on the back porch.

She's still dressed in day clothes, her brown hair tucked into a loose bun. Baelfire's mother stands at the edge of the deck to watch her son, her hands clasped behind her back in a militant posture. She glances at me with her one golden eye, smiling softly.

"You know, this dragon isn't nearly as bad as Baelfire likes to think. Poor thing is just cursed."

I nod, watching my dragon as it stalks through more trees to watch us better. Something about the smooth, sleek movements paired with the massive body and serpentine tail is mesmerizing. Those slitted dragon eyes never budge from me.

"His dragon saved my life once," Brigid adds.

"I heard there was a coup against you." I frown, recalling what Silas and Everett mentioned before. "Five years ago. That would have made Baelfire just sixteen."

She nods, checking a watch with a little screen on it before assuming the same straight-backed stance.

"Yes. It was on his sixteenth birthday, actually. I got permission to let him come for a brief visit to where I was stationed near the Divide so we could celebrate together. I knew some of my new troops were troublemakers, and I already had people I trusted looking into things. What I didn't know was that those troublemakers planned on killing me that day. They found me alone, tranquilized me, and began carving out my scales while I was unconscious. Baelfire's dragon sensed the danger in time and killed them off."

The dragon has now stalked so close that when it lifts its long neck to peer at us, my other matches take an almost synchronized step back.

Brigid and I stay where we are. I stare into the beast's animalistic amber gaze.

It's such a terrifying beast. I love that.

"You're saying we can trust it," I surmise quietly.

Brigid shrugs a shoulder. "Maybe not entirely, with how cursed he is. Not until you five are bound by the gods and your curses broken," she adds.

She has no idea my quintet's curses are already mysteriously being broken—most likely because the gods are messing with us. We've kept that to ourselves.

"I only wish Baelfire was less at war with his inner beast. Even cursed, it looks out for him and those he cares about, whether he'll admit it or not. He's a fierce dragon, and I couldn't be prouder. I'll be even more proud when he's finally in harmony with the damn thing," Brigid adds, laughing.

Baelfire's dragon chuffs, sending hot, dry air at us as it narrows its gaze on me.

I arch a brow. "Are you going to give me my mate back anytime soon?"

It makes a whining, growling sound that definitely means *no*.

"Brat," I mumble.

Brigid laughs and turns to smile at me and my quintet. "I would like to show you all something tomorrow. If you're up for it."

Silas frowns. "Please tell me it isn't another gods-awful fourteen-mile hike through the mountains. I recall you tricking us into that when I was eight."

"Oh yes, the hike from hell," Crypt nods. "It was quite fun to watch from Limbo."

"I had blisters for days," Everett grimaces.

Brigid snorts. "It was character-building for you spoiled little legacies, but this is better than a hike. I think it will be beneficial."

She gives me a meaningful look, which tells me it has something to do with me freeing the humans. I nod, unsure how she could help with a complex plan she knows nothing about.

Brigid says good night and leaves me to admire my dragon. The rest of my quintet talks quietly, occasionally arguing, as usual. Meanwhile, the dragon rests its great chin on the edge of the deck, turning it so it can watch me better out of one eye.

"I like looking at you, too," I grin, stroking the warm scales on its snout. "Such a handsome dragon."

It rumbles happily low in its throat.

"Is it growling at you?" Everett asks, glaring at the beast.

"That's called purring."

Except now, my dragon has turned its attention on the others and bares long teeth, hissing in warning.

"You guys should go inside. My dragon is territorial and fussy right now." I pet it again, loving the warmth of these sleek, gleaming scales. "Aren't you? Yes, you are."

Silas gives me an exasperated look. "It is not a puppy, *ima sangfluir*."

I look over my shoulder at him. "You're right. It's a twenty-five-ton, fire-breathing monster with razor blades for teeth that might fry all three of you. I want to get Baelfire back, and your presence isn't helping."

I can tell they aren't happy about it, but Silas and Everett return to the house while Crypt slips into Limbo. I can still feel him nearby as I continue to pet and soothe the beast. Its undivided, intense attention is entirely on me again.

I lean forward to press a light kiss to the top of its snout. "Listen. I like every part of Baelfire. Since you are one of those parts, that means I'll always like you. I mean, you are a mythically terrifying paragon of deadly beauty. What's not to like about that?"

The dragon rumbles louder, nuzzling me now.

"But Baelfire is *mine*. You aren't going to take him away from me," I warn seriously, still stroking his scales. "Ever. Got it?"

The massive beast huffs.

"Don't test me. I want him back."

To my surprise, Baelfire's dragon shudders and begins to morph, shrinking and unshifting so quickly that I almost stumble when Baelfire staggers against me. He's smeared in dirt and very disoriented, judging by the way he blinks at his surroundings.

He focuses on me and seems relieved, but I'm preoccupied with checking out the gorgeous naked legacy in front of me.

Damn. Muscles on muscles. He's like a wall of golden strength.

And that cock. I want to lick it.

Baelfire huffs a laugh, still getting oriented. "Should I pose so you get a better view? You're more than welcome to take pictures, Rain-cloud—as long as I get to take some of you, too. Also naked."

I grin up at him, relieved to see that he's himself. But he doesn't miss how I'm starting to shiver in the cold of the night. He quickly scoops me into his arms, heading inside.

"Welcome back," I murmur, brushing dirt off one of his broad, golden shoulders. "Did you hunt?"

"Actually, I don't remember what I—"

Baelfire cuts off with a loud snarl, whirling to face Silas and Everett, who are waiting in the hall that leads to the mother-in-law's suite.

"Relax, dragon," Everett begins with an eye roll.

But Baelfire is getting hot. Literally hot. His skin is almost uncomfortable to touch, and when I peer into his face, I see how on the brink he is, a feral gleam in his eyes as he bares his teeth.

He's extremely on edge.

I pat Bael's shoulder as comfortingly as I can. "How can I help?"

He frowns, backing up from the hall and taking a deep breath. "I don't know. My territorial side is going fucking crazy. I just...I need a second alone with you." As usual, his shifter emotions swing drastically, and he beams down at me excitedly. "Hey, wanna see my old room?"

I nod. Maybe this will help his beast calm down more, but I'm also interested to see what his old room looks like. I look at the others over his shoulder as he turns to stride away.

"We'll come back to bed soon," I assure them.

Tell your pet to mind himself. If he loses control again and hurts you... Silas warns telepathically.

He won't, I assure him.

Baelfire turns down a dark hallway I haven't seen yet.

Don't stay up too late. You need a lot more rest, Everett grumbles.

I grin to myself. My perfectionistic ice elemental doesn't like having our beauty sleep getting interrupted.

"Poor fuckers are going to awkwardly lay on opposite sides of the bed in total silence while they wait for you to get back," Bael laughs, opening a door to the right.

He slips inside, still carrying me. I should probably remind him that I like to walk on my own, but fuck it. He's warm, and I'm enjoying his slight singed cedar scent. When Baelfire flips on the light, my brows bounce up.

"Wow."

"Yeah, I used to be into photography. Hey, I'm gonna shower off this shit really fast, if you don't mind."

I nod, distracted by his old bedroom as he sets me down.

It's simple—a big bed, a dresser, a desk, and a small bookshelf. The bookshelf displays a few books beside mementos like sand in a bottle, souvenir shot glasses, magnets, and so on.

There's also a dreamcatcher by the door, which explains why I can no longer sense Crypt's presence in Limbo nearby—he can't get into this room.

But my attention quickly returns to the walls of Bael's room.

They're covered in breathtaking photos of remote landscapes. Awe-inspiring mountains, a tempestuous ocean, a desert glowing in rich sunlight, dazzling lightning storms, towering red rock formations, and countless others. Most of them are taken from staggering heights, which I guess is an option when you have wings to get to the very tops of mountains.

I'm so caught up in admiring scenes unlike anything I've ever experienced that I nearly bump into Baelfire's desk. On it is a camera case, a brochure for Everbound University, a pile of old homework, and a small jar full of…

"Are those your scales?" I ask, knowing the dragon shifter will hear me just fine from the small attached bathroom where he's just stepping out of the shower.

"Yeah," he says, toweling off as he walks up behind me. "Weird fact, dragon shifters treat their first shed scales kind of like humans treat…" He scratches his neck. "Shit, I don't know enough about humans. It's like baby teeth, I guess? They're sentimental, so my siren dad stuck them in that jar."

I examine them, remembering my conversation with Silas about why he wants Baelfire's scales.

But when I turn to broach the subject, I again get *very* fucking distracted. Mostly because Baelfire is studying me with a startling intensity, and he is clean, naked, and completely erect.

It should be a sin how fuckable all of my matches are.

"Small talk seems to do it for you," I note teasingly.

"*You* do it for me. Fuck, I just…"

His breathing is growing rapid. I frown when I notice he's shaking slightly.

"Bael?"

"Can I please hold you for a bit?" he whispers hoarsely.

Again, with the please. It's like he knows just how weak I am for it.

I step into his embrace, going breathless when he drops back and rolls so I'm beneath him on the big bed. He buries his face against my neck.

"I fucking *hate* losing myself like that," he admits quietly, squeezing me against his deliciously hard chest. "I had no idea if I'd hurt you, but I couldn't get a grip to find out. I was just trapped in a dark corner somewhere in my head with no control and no fucking idea when I'd get myself back."

I toy with his damp hair. He's still trembling slightly. Did something happen to him while he was shifted that's causing this? Or was he just that worried?

"You don't remember anything after your dragon took over?" I check.

"Nope. He's a fucking hog like that."

When I trail my fingers down the side of his face, Bael groans, pulling back to peer at me. His molten gaze trails all over me, and the sharp hunger on his handsome face quickly fills me with a matching heat.

He grits his teeth, dropping his face against my neck again. "Fuck. What's going on with your scent, Mayflower? It's so much stronger than usual, and gods, it's driving me fucking *insane*."

He nips playfully at my neck, sending goosebumps rippling all over. Cocooned in this sensual heat, I can't resist dragging my hands down his smooth back, around, and up over his chest and shoulders.

Baelfire shivers, panting like my touch is too much for him.

And then he bites me.

Full-on *bites* me—drawing blood in the spot where shifters mark their mates.

33

MAVEN

THE SUDDEN STING makes me jolt. I push on his chest, blinking up at him in shock.

What the fuck?

"Did you just…claim me?"

His pupils are shifted into vertical draconic slits, traces of my blood around his lips that he licks with an animal growl. But half a second later, he snaps out of it. His eyes return to normal—then widen in complete horror when he realizes what just happened.

"Oh, my gods. *Gods*—I didn't mean to…*fuck*," he swears, sitting up and covering his face.

It takes me a fraction of a second to adjust and become more than okay with this.

So what if he marked me? I'm his mate. Honestly, it was about damn time, even if it was his dragon who forced it.

"Baelfire."

He's spiraling, his shifter emotions taking hold as he panics, speaking quickly. "I am so fucking sorry. I swear I didn't mean to do that, and—gods*damn* it, I wasn't paying attention when we were on the run. I didn't even fucking think to take any with me when we left the university—"

Any what? What is he talking about?

"Bael, it's okay."

I sit up, too, moving his hands away to frame his face between my fingers. Even that tiny amount of touch has him shuddering again. I realize he's covered in a thin sheen of sweat, his pupils blown wide as he nuzzles my hand like he can't help himself.

Oh, shit.

Suppressants. He was talking about not taking any suppressants.

"You're going into a rut," I realize.

Baelfire grimaces and nods, moving off the bed. Dragging his hands through his damp hair, he paces back and forth in the room like a pent-up animal, still breathing raggedly.

I knew little about heat and rut cycles until I met Kenzie, who told me more about what shifters go through. Human women undergo a monthly estrous cycle, but all shifters undergo a more extreme version of that cycle. Certain types of shifters experience it more frequently than others—but with modern magic and medicine, most can get away with taking suppressants to calm down their primal needs.

Kenzie described it as ovulation on "mega steroids." She said if she ever missed taking suppressants, it left her in a brutal, all-consuming heat that always led to bad decisions because she literally couldn't think like herself.

It doesn't seem like Baelfire has reached that point yet, but I assume it's coming.

Bael interrupts my thoughts when he braces his hands at the end of the bed and hangs his head.

"Fuck. Gods, I can't—Maven, you need to get out of this room. Have Silas spell it shut to lock me inside so I can't get to you, okay?"

"I'm not going anywhere," I decide.

"Raincloud," he rasps, looking up at me pleadingly.

Gods. His gaze dragging over me as he grows overheated and desperate makes me squirm with building excitement, which just makes him curse more.

"Why should I go?"

"Baby, I'm going to lose my fucking mind. I'll be insatiable—

already, literally the only thing I can think about is claiming and fucking the living hell out of you. Gods, I just want to covet and mark and fill you until you can't fucking *move*," he grits out, palming his erection roughly with a wince.

It's difficult to breathe, but I shrug. "I fail to see a downside to any of that. If you're trying to convince me to leave, you're doing a terrible job of it."

Bael's gaze is searing as he gets back on the bed and prowls toward me.

"Ruts can sometimes take days. It's said they burn faster with mates, but I've never gone through a rut with *anyone*—I've always just taken suppressants, so I have no fucking idea what to expect. Meaning, I have no fucking idea if you'd be safe in here with me."

He's never gone through a rut with someone?

Knowing I get one of his firsts makes me smile.

"I'm your mate. This was always going to happen. Unless you don't ever want to experience a rut with me?"

"You have no idea how much I want you in here," he whispers, kissing slowly up one of my bare legs and sending more tingling excitement fluttering in my stomach. I'm glad I wore such short shorts to bed earlier. "I'm just so fucking worried—"

"I can handle this."

"Can you?" Baelfire pins me with a half-miserable, half-starved expression, shaking his head. "Maven, what if you get overstimulated and need a second to breathe? What if I'm getting too aggressive and your touch phobia comes up and...damn it, what if I can't stop? I won't be in control. I refuse to do that to you, so *please* just—"

I lean down, capturing his lips in a kiss. He immediately crawls forward to press me against the bed, shuddering as he grinds roughly against me.

Holy fuck, he's hard. And huge.

He's also trying to protect me from my own sensitivities, but that's not fucking happening. Not when Kenzie told me that going through a heat or rut completely alone can be agonizing for shifters.

I break away for air, meeting his gaze. "I want this. Let me help my mate through his rut, okay?"

Bael moans, grinding harder against me. "You really can't keep calling me your mate, or I swear I'm going to fucking lose it."

"Lose it, then."

He shakes his head, grimacing. "But if it's touch overload for you—"

"How about this? I'll use a stasis spell on you if it becomes too much for me. Then, once I calm down, I'll just undo it. It'll be like you blinked, and we'll go back to fucking the hell out of each other."

He swallows hard, nodding. When I caress his strong shoulders, he groans again. "*Gods.* Every single touch is so fucking intense. Pretty sure I'm not going to be able to think clearly soon, so..."

"So?"

I'm surprised when he pulls back again. But this time, he gets on his knees beside the bed, panting as he looks up at me with blazing desire written all over his body, his hard cock jutting out with need.

"You said you'd make me crawl if I was good," he whispers, stroking himself like he's desperate for relief. "Was I good enough for my reward, baby?"

Gods.

He looks so fucking good on his knees.

I scoot to the end of the bed until he's between my thighs and tilt his chin up, arching a brow.

"You were until you started touching yourself without my permission."

Baelfire's hand immediately drops from his erection as he bites back a grunt.

"Fuck, baby. Anything you want. Just please fucking use me until I can't control myself anymore."

I study him, twisting my fingers into his damp, dirty blond hair so I can guide him to look up at me. His eyes are hooded, and he's still shivering slightly as his rut builds—but knowing how badly he wants me in charge is...really fucking hot.

"Stand up."

He obeys, and I'm glad he's so tall because sitting on the edge of this bed gives me a good enough height to begin slowly stroking his already-leaking erection. Baelfire tenses, his hands balled into white fists at his sides as he struggles not to move without my permission.

Leaning forward, I lick the heady, hot wetness from his tip.

"My mate tastes so good," I sigh.

"Fuck. Fuck," he pants, shutting his eyes.

I slowly lick around the head of his cock, enjoying each tremor and swear as I take his incredible thickness into my mouth and begin to lavish it. I really fucking enjoy this—teasing and sucking as his desperation grows. I try to take more and more of him into my mouth and down my throat, enjoying the sensual sensation of his slick hard erection gliding deeper until I nearly fucking choke while he moans.

It's so good that I start to squirm, becoming aware of the greedy throbbing between my legs.

Finally, he can't stop the instinctive little thrusts of his hips.

"*Maven*," he gasps. "Gods, baby, please—"

I pop off of his dick, licking my lips and looking up at my needy shifter. "Crawl to the other side of the bed and lay down for me."

He swallows hard, holding my gaze as he lowers to his hands and knees. I watch the gorgeous muscles on his body work in tandem, smooth and tantalizing, as he obediently crawls to get on the bed and lies down on the other side of me.

His golden gaze is deliciously pleading as he waits to see what I'll do next.

I slowly straddle his stomach, tracing the powerful contours of his chest as I admire my mate. Then I slide back until I can feel his hot erection against my ass.

Gods, he's so hard that my stomach flips with anticipation.

"Such a good pet for me," I murmur, leaning down to kiss his warm lips.

Baelfire moans into my mouth, kissing me back ravenously as I cup his jaw. He's trying to rub himself against my ass, panting in gloriously frustrated desperation.

When I feel the slight trickle of blood on the crook of my neck from him biting me on accident, I break away from the kiss, an idea crossing my mind.

"Bite me again," I order gently.

He's so far gone to the lust clouding around us that it takes a moment before he can focus on the bite wound. He shakes his head, fisting the sheets beside us to keep his hands to himself like a good boy.

"You're already bleeding. I don't like that."

"I want your claiming of me to be intentional. If you don't bite me again on purpose, we'll always remember it as an accident." I kiss his chin and turn my head so he has better access. "Make it real, Baelfire."

He's gentle at first, dragging his lips against the injury on the left side of my neck until he finally bites me again—hard.

Claiming me.

It's a sharp pain and pleasure at once, but nothing like when Silas bites me. This isn't feeding—it's marking. It's meant to leave a beautifully savage scar I'll carry to show I'm his mate.

"Just like that," I praise.

Baelfire's hands go to my hips as he laps the sting away from my neck, his breathing growing more uneven. His cock glides against my ass through my pajama shorts again, more insistently.

"You're mine," he growls. "All fucking mine. *My mate.*"

I nod and try to kiss him, but suddenly, we've flipped. Baelfire pins my wrists over my head, his expression ferocious and lust-filled before he begins licking and kissing his way down my throat.

Sensual adrenaline spikes inside my veins when his teeth close around my jugular for a moment. He doesn't draw blood, but the primal gesture is startling enough that I gasp.

"Bael," I whisper.

"Why the fuck are you still in clothes?" he demands hungrily, dragging his face against my chest before sitting up and literally ripping my loose pajama shirt off of me.

Before I can try to wriggle out of my shorts to speed this process, he rips those off, too—along with my panties.

Then his tongue drags roughly against my dripping pussy, making me arch and cry out in surprise. He holds my hips in place as he devours me, his fingers pressing almost painfully hard into my hips.

He's losing control.

I'm fucking loving it.

"Bite me again," I demand, twisting his hair hard in my hands as I grind against his face.

Bael growls and turns to sink his teeth into my inner thigh. My mouth drops open at how brutally delicious it is. And when I look down to meet my mate's gaze, I see it—golden pools of violent, animalistic need as he's lost to the rut.

Baelfire might like me in charge, but right now, his beastly instincts are calling all the shots—and those instincts drive him to flip me over before he thrusts so deep and hard into me that I scream into the mattress. His cock pounds into me without mercy as he swears and snarls, spreading my legs wider.

He places a big hand against my upper back, pressing me further into the mattress but keeping my ass high as he savagely takes what he needs from my body, rutting like an animal. I moan and swear into the blankets, so awash with sharp, relentless pleasure that I'm not surprised when an orgasm sweeps over me out of nowhere.

"Fuck me," I gasp, pushing back into him as my insides clench and my toes curl. "Yes, gods, *fuck*—"

Baelfire snarls and pushes deep one more time, coming hard. I startle at the sensation of his warmth filling me, but I barely have a second to catch my breath before he flips me over again, kissing a path up my stomach.

Then he slides into me again. He pins my hands to the bed, moaning as he thrusts slow and really fucking deep, setting a pace that is both languid and demanding.

"Bael," I rasp, my pulse still humming as I still haven't come down from my release.

He bites my lip, licking away the pain as he grows rougher—pressing one of my legs up until my knee is next to my head. I groan at the new angle while he growls savagely and fucks me harder, clearly unable to stop ravishing me even for a moment.

Oh, gods.

This rut is going to be brutal.

I smile.

34

BAELFIRE

I THINK I just woke up in Paradise.

Gods, Maven is just so fucking pretty. And she smells like heaven.

In fact, my entire room is perfumed with her sweet, dark midnight scent mixed with the mouthwatering fragrance of her arousal, which makes sense because we've been in this room for…

Shit. How long have we been in here?

I have no idea and can only recall fleeting, foggy moments of the most intense pleasure I could possibly imagine—but I can tell the burning, mind-melting desperation of my rut is finally calming down.

Still, I can't stop staring at Maven as she breathes softly, curled up on her side facing away from me. My attention moves to the new mark on the left side of her neck.

My mark.

My heart does a happy dance—because holy shit, I marked my mate.

I'm obsessed with the hickeys I left all over her. Her messy tangle of dark hair, the slight bruises on her hips from where I couldn't control my strength, the fact that she's still dripping between her incredibly biteable thighs from the last time I fucked her rough and raw...

Godsdamn, I just can't get enough of seeing my keeper looks so ravaged.

Unable to think through the final waves of frantic heat, I kiss my way up her bare spine. Maven hums contentedly, rolling over and stretching so I get a torturously dick-hardening view of her entire fuckable body—

And the new emblem on her chest.

The circle of the House of Shifting laid right over the top of the others, framing the triangle and square.

Holy fuck.

Elation floods me, so now I'm both horny out of my mind and ready to shout from the rooftops.

I'm bound to Maven. To my mate.

Maven peeks open her eyes, her lips curling as she speaks into my head. *About damn time.*

"Tell me about it," I laugh breathlessly, a smile breaking over my face before I lean down to kiss all over that mark and her chest, lapping at her nipples.

Soon I'm sucking on her tits, my hands slipping down to spread her thighs so I can finally thrust back into my mate's warm, greedy, fucking *fantastic* pussy.

"Gods," I grit, trying to take it slow. "Fuck, you feel so damn good."

She moans.

Nope, that's it. Can't do slow. I'm way too keyed up knowing I'm bound to her.

I look into Maven's eyes, loving the way she watches me as I lift one hand to tease her clit and start to fuck her harder. My keeper wraps her arms around me, gasping.

"So tight," I pant, kissing her neck.

I accidentally kiss right where her unhealed mark is, and her breathing catches. I slow immediately, trying to combat the burning need pumping through me.

"Sorry. Damn, I bit you a lot, huh?" I grimace.

She laughs. "That's fine. I bite back."

Then she bites *my* neck.

I immediately see stars, slamming into her as I come so hard I can't fucking breathe. As soon as my cock stops jerking and the relief washes over me, I wrap myself around her, her ass to my lap.

Holy shit, I groan through the bond.

Maven is breathless, smiling over her shoulder at me—and gods, that *smile.*

Still my favorite thing.

"You like it when I bite you."

"*Like* is a fucking understatement," I laugh.

Gods, I feel good. Better than I ever have, actually. My head isn't splitting, there is no growling and snarling interrupting my thoughts, and I'm not so on edge that I want to spit fire.

Instead, my inner dragon is just as ridiculously happy as I am. He feels…different, somehow. I don't want to get my hopes up, but maybe he's not the asshole he was before…now that my curse might be broken.

I realize Maven is studying me thoughtfully. I trace her jaw, unable to stop touching her. Which reminds me…

"So, how many times did you have to freeze my ass with magic so you could take a beat without me mauling you?" I check, anxious at the idea of making my mate uncomfortable.

"Thrice, but one of those times was to keep you from killing the others."

I blink. "They were in here?"

She shakes her head, amused. "In between fucking, you got fussy about taking care of me and went to get food and water in the middle of the first night. They were waiting outside plotting your death for holding me hostage—their words, not mine. I explained this was my idea and that I'd blocked them out on purpose. Then you carried me back in here over your shoulder, caveman-style."

I blink and sit up, noticing the small collection of protein bars, water bottles, and other random snacks on my desk.

"Oh, fuck. I don't remember any of that." Then I pause, her words sinking in. "Wait, *first* night?"

"It's been two and a half days." She studies me. "How do you feel?"

To be completely honest, for the first time in my life, I feel disappointed that my shifter system heals so damn fast. I reach out to gently feel where Maven's mark is scabbed over on her neck.

I frown, thinking. Then I grin when I realize the simple solution.

It's my first time doing this, but I try to push the thought to the right person.

Can you bring liquid silver to me?

Why the fuck would I have liquid silver? Everett demands telepathically. *And if I find out you've been fucking our keeper for two days straight without giving her a rest, I'm going to—*

Nah, wrong one. I block out Snowflake and try again.

Si?

"What are you doing?" Maven asks, arching a brow. "Are you blocking me out on purpose?"

"Not on purpose, I just don't get how this telepathy shit is supposed to—"

Silas's reply cuts me off. Somehow, I can tell he's speaking only to me and Maven.

Look who finally decided to join us. Sangfluir, *are you all right in there? Why would you need liquid silver?*

Maven frowns before understanding crosses her face. She grins at me. *For help marking my mate.*

Her mate. Gods, I will never get tired of hearing her call me that.

Silas is cranky about it, probably because I've kept Maven to myself for two days. But a few minutes later, I open the door and he hands me a vial of silvery liquid. He also hands me a pile of Maven's clothes, and not for the first time, I'm glad someone in our quintet thinks ahead.

The blood fae tries to step past me into the room, but the surge of violently protective panic I feel comes from both myself and my inner dragon. I hold out an arm to stop him, shaking my head.

"You can't be serious," he scoffs.

"You try going through a rut sometime and tell me how serious I am," I challenge. "I'm still coming out of it, and I might accidentally rip your head off if my territorial side comes back."

"Tell your asshole dragon to deal with it," he gripes, trying to get past me again.

I shove him away from the door, growling, "We're in harmony now, dick, so back the hell away."

If Silas's own curse hadn't been broken, he probably would've just gone all paranoid magic madman on me. So it's odd when he just glares at me, obviously weighing the threat before rolling his eyes.

"A *thank you* is in order."

"Thanks. Now fuck off." I shut the door in his face and turn to Maven, beaming as I hold up the vial.

She's fighting a smile. "Your charm and manners have taken a nosedive since we met."

"That's because I care a lot less about pleasing random fuckers and a lot more about pleasing *you*. Speaking of which…" I crawl back onto the bed, surrounding myself in our scents again as I hand her the vial. "How do you want me? On my knees?"

Maven smirks and shakes her head. "Stay where you are."

My heart is pounding again as she leans forward, her lips skimming over my neck before she licks the place she bit earlier. That alone has me fucking weak. The idea of wearing Maven's bite mark on my neck for all to see for the rest of my life has me damn near feral as warm arousal starts to pulse through me once again.

Then she bites me again. Way harder than the first time.

"*Fuck,*" I hiss, gritting my teeth as Maven pulls away and spills some of the liquid silver over the fresh mark before it can start to heal.

Shit. Ouch. Arousal officially cooled.

"Holy *hell*, that burns," I grimace as she recaps the vial. I frown. "Did it hurt that bad when I bit you? Because I wouldn't blame you for kicking me right in the dragon eggs for that."

Maven laughs, shaking her head. "It didn't hurt much."

Yeah, maybe for her. After seeing her brush off getting stabbed with fucking nevermelt, I've decided my mate has one hell of a pain tolerance.

I'd be jealous, but I'm mostly just pissed she had to develop that.

After a moment, Maven leads me to the bathroom to clean up the painful substance. I gawk at us in the mirror. We're both marked, and *damn*, she looks good naked and covered in love bites.

I grin down at her. "Do I have your permission to use the *L*-word?"

"Never."

"Fine. Then I really, *really* liked all that...canoodling."

She swats my shoulder playfully as we both step into the shower to clean up. I genuinely enjoy washing my mate when she peers up at me.

"Can I ask you for something?"

"Literally anything. Tell me to cut off my wings or tail or whatever, and it's all yours."

"What about scales?" Maven asks, tipping her cascade of dark hair back under the spray of the water.

"Sure."

"That easily? You were fighting Silas on this tooth and claw."

"That's because it was *Silas* asking," I snort. "Of course, I'm not going to give him shit." Then I pause, curious. "Are you asking for the scales for him? Why?"

Maven makes me promise I won't say a word to Silas about any of this and quietly explains what the blood fae is trying to develop for my family. He also needs scales for the Garnet Wizard, but by the time she starts explaining that, I still haven't processed that first part.

Silas is trying to help my family with the dragon shifter infertility? I mean, the prick probably just wants to make sure rare dragon scales don't disappear completely when we're killed off...but still.

What a fucking softie.

I nod slowly when Maven finishes. "Okay. How about this? You can have all the scales your pointy-eared nerd needs if you agree to go flying with me sometime. Deal?"

Her eyes light up. "Riding on your back?"

"Definitely my back since the only time you can ride my front is while I'm human, Boo."

She laughs as we finish showering and start to get dressed to emerge from the deliciously sex-scented lair I've been blissfully happy in for the last couple of days.

As I slip into a shirt, I notice Maven studying the photos all over my walls again. "What made you stop?"

"Huh?"

"You said you *used* to be into photography," she points out.

Oh, that. I shrug, watching as she finishes dressing in the clothes Silas brought for her. "It was just a hobby. Legacies don't have career options doing shit like taking pictures—and besides, all dragons are mandated to fight in the front lines at the Divide."

"I didn't know that," she frowns. "That seems…"

"Unfair? That's what I always used to think—but then, it makes sense that they want the biggest, strongest, best legacies there all the time," I grin cockily, brushing my old dreams under the rug and attempting to cheer up my mate.

I don't think she buys my acting. She's sharp like that.

As soon as we're both dressed, I reach for the door handle. Then I freeze.

Oh, shit.

What is it? she asks back telepathically.

I grimace. "There are a lot of shifters in this house with sensitive hearing. I mean, I normally don't give a fuck who hears, but when it's my family—"

"I soundproofed the room with magic."

"Oh, thank the fucking gods," I breathe out.

"Or just thank me. Still, your family isn't stupid. They know what we were up to in here."

She smirks at my groan and slips out of the room.

35

BAELFIRE

THE SECOND we step into the hall, Maven is encircled by Everett's arms. He exhales in relief before jerking back and scowling at the still-healing mating mark visible on her neck, not to mention the other love bites I left.

He lifts the hem of her shirt, ignoring the way Maven rolls her eyes as he checks her body.

The glare he turns on me is chilling. "I know deep down you're a beast, but did you have to bite her so damn much?"

"As if *you* mind biting," Maven teases.

Everett blushes profusely as I raise my brows. "Hold the fucking phone—is Snowflake kinky?"

"Shut up, lizard. Silas, heal the damn bite on her neck."

Maven holds up a hand to stop the blood fae. "I want the scar. How else will other shifters know to keep their paws off what's mine?"

Godsdamn, I love when she's possessive.

I beam at her, proud as hell when the others finally spot the injury on my neck, too. "Don't worry, baby. They'll know I'm yours."

Everett sighs. "I will never fucking understand shifters wanting to scar their mates."

"That's because elementals are holier-than-thou wimps," I supply, still on Cloud Nine from two days in heaven with my mate.

But our keeper frowns, glancing around like she's looking for something we can't see.

"Where's Crypt?"

"His markings were glowing, so I assume his disappearance has to do with Limbo," Silas says, nudging Everett aside to kiss Maven's temple and gently check her neck to see how it's healing. "You should eat real food. Brigid is making—"

"I heard that," my mom calls from the distant kitchen. "Even if we're family now, it's Commander Decimus or Bael's Mom to you."

I laugh and lead them into the sweet-smelling kitchen, where my caster dad Ivan is carefully decorating cupcakes with Bran at the table. My mom is helping Oscar mix what appears to be a batch of brownies.

It never gets less funny to see that short commander next to my dad, who's my height.

As soon as my mom spots me, she quirks a knowing brow and waves me over until I follow her out of the kitchen and into one of their spare bathrooms down another hall. She pulls three extra-strength packs of rut suppressants out of the medicine cabinet and slaps them into my hand, shaking her head at me.

"For gods' sakes, use these next time. Your poor mate," she hisses quietly enough that I know only Oscar can overhear from the kitchen.

"Oh, my gods." I try to shove them back at her. "Look, it was just bad timing."

"Bad timing? No, that's called not using common fucking sense. You don't just spring that on someone—*especially* not a non-shifter! If Oscar had caught me off guard like that before we were bonded, I would have thrown his ass into the Divide myself," she scoffs. "I'm surprised your mate didn't kick you out and—"

She cuts off, eyes widening as they land on my neck for the first time. "Oh. Gods."

I can't help the elated smile that breaks free on my face. "Yeah. It's official."

I could almost swear my mom's eye waters with emotion for a second before she sniffs in a no-nonsense way.

"Liquid silver? Brutal, but it's also kind of...touching."

"Brutally touching is Maven's specialty," I grin.

My mom snorts and then gets serious, studying me. "You seem... different. Something about your dragon. My own inner dragon noticed it immediately."

I shrug. "Just having a good day."

She hums. I know she doesn't buy it, but she gets business-like quickly. "You two missed New Year's with the family. The rest of your quintet was certainly welcome, and all went well, but you'll have to apologize to Quinn. She was in tears that *Uncle Baelfire's Ninja Mate* wasn't around."

"Sorry about missing that."

She rolls her eye. "No, you're not."

I grin. "You're right. I'm really not."

"Don't look so smug. You also missed a bunch of assholes trying to break into our territory."

My smile fades. "Shit."

"Yeah, shit. They came close to breaking through the wards until Declan rained fire down on them. That Douglas boy was there and insisted he just wanted to speak with the *telum*. I told him to go eat shit," she adds haughtily. "Still cannot believe he was stupid enough to try invading *our* territory. Although I admit...it was a close call for Declan."

I pick up on Maven's subtle footfalls and glance over as she walks into the hall with the bathroom. She looks at my mom, her brow furrowing as she clearly heard that last part.

"Let me guess. Bounty hunters."

My mom nods.

Maven's lips press together. "I'm sorry I led them here. I doubt they've given up, so we'll need to leave soon." My mom starts to protest, but Maven quickly adds, "We have another mark to get to, anyway."

The commander sighs. "All right. Like I said, all my kids like to fly the coop before I'm ready for it. But before you leave…remember I wanted to show you something the other night? I would still like to show you."

"Lead the way."

Maven and I follow my mom as she leads us past the kitchen and toward what my family has always jokingly called the War Room but is really the commander's office. Silas and Everett fall into step with us quickly. We step into the spacious room, which is mainly filled with a massive table painted with a sprawling map of the world.

Only right now, it's also covered in a shit-ton of little game board-like pieces and erasable marker drawings.

I frown when I see a cluster of five white pieces inside my parents' land on the map. One of them is marked "*telum.*"

"Is that us?" I ask.

My mom nods and starts to say something else, but Crypt steps out of fucking nowhere and promptly dips Maven, kissing her deeply like he just got back from war.

Although, I guess with his curse, maybe he did. There's a spray of blood on his boots, not to mention a bloodied rip in the calf area of his pants. His markings are glowing faintly.

There's my girl, he says telepathically, grinning as they straighten.

He tosses me a testy look, his purple gaze flicking briefly between the matching mating marks healing on both my and Maven's necks before he speaks through the bond again.

I considered all kinds of uses for dragon leather over the last couple of days. But seeing as how I possibly drove your dragon a bit mad in Limbo, we'll call it even.

Thanks, buddy, I tease.

He rolls his eyes. *We'll make friendship bracelets later, right before we make an Eiffel Tower with Maven.*

An Eiffel…? Oh—got it.

I'm down if she is, I grin.

Maven is clearly confused about what we're talking about, which reminds me that there are gaps in her knowledge about the mortal realm. There's a big chance she's never heard of the Eiffel Tower.

Hellion, that's when we're on either end of you and– I start to explain telepathically.

"Oh, my gods. Baelfire Finbar Decimus, why didn't you tell me about this?" my mom demands, looking between us…because we've clearly been having a totally silent, telepathic conversation.

Oops.

"I knew your dragon was different—it's because your curse is gone. You're bonded?" she demands, looking at Maven in fascination. "How is that possible?"

"Because we're fucking perfect together," I say confidently at the exact same time Maven mutters, "Because the gods are playing games."

Games? What is she talking about?

My mom obviously has questions, but when Maven changes the subject, pointing out the dark marker on the board and asking if it represents the Nether, the commander focuses.

"Yes. As you can see, ever since Del Mar's death, it has grown steadily to encompass more land area. The human government is now in full crisis mode with their military on standby past these markers," she points at a few dots on the map and then gestures at a few other green markers on the West Coast. "These are cities where emergency aid is available for those evacuating from the East Coast."

We all examine the map. Silas tips his head, motioning at Alaska.

"You have the Sanctuary marked."

"After the bounty hunter massacre there, it made the news in a big way," she sighs. "Hard to keep such a place secret with that level of resources sent from the Legacy Council." Then she looks at Maven, pointing at clusters of orange and blue markers, respectively. "These are Remitters. These are Reformists."

I blink as I take in what she's saying. "Holy shit. All of the little blue Reformists are still on the East Coast. Why haven't they evacuated?"

"They're waiting on a decision. *My* decision, based on whatever Maven tells me she needs."

Hold the fucking phone. I gawk at my mom. "You're a Reformist?"

"Bael, honey, I love you, but how the hell did you not put that together?" She shakes her head. "You've seen the fights I've had with the legacy government. You know how messed up the system is and how corrupt things have become. Of course, I want to find something better—and I think your incredible mate is the gateway to change we've been waiting for."

We all look at Maven, but she's studying the map with a cunning eye. I can practically see the plans spinning inside her pretty head. She points at blue markers in Nebraska.

"This cluster. It's the Bairds, isn't it?"

My mom nods.

"There's a lot more blue on the map than I expected. How are there so many Reformists?" Maven asks.

"With the rising political tensions, legacies have been joining the cause in droves—but so have many humans. They can tell that something big is about to happen, especially because two large rumors have been circulating. One rumor is that the Nether is about to be unleashed on the mortal world. The other is that humans from the Nether are about to finally escape. So…which should I tell them it is?"

Maven meets my mom's eye, considering. "You're showing me this to express that…I have your support."

My mom smiles. "Not just mine. A great deal of support from even the unlikeliest of people, should you need it."

"I thought everyone feared the *telum*. From what I'm told, I've been in prophecies for a long time. I'm supposed to bring about the end of times and a lot of death and suffering."

The commander shrugs one shoulder. "Prophecies are fluid. They change and can even be avoided altogether. We all thought the *telum* would be some faceless, unspeakable evil spreading plagues and destruction wherever it went. Instead, it's *you*. The abducted girl I researched fifteen years ago, who survived in hell and came here for a damn good reason. I know you have a plan. I also know that the Nether has grown wildly unstable. Many people are terrified—"

"They should be," Maven asserts quietly, looking at the Nether on the map. "Not succeeding in my plan would result in all the horrors in the prophecies. Which is exactly why I won't fail."

She straightens her shoulders, looking at my mom again. "Are there capable Reformists who can mobilize quickly for a fight?"

"Yes."

"How quickly?"

My mom tips her head from side to side. "Given all the casters who may be capable of transportation, I would bet they can gather within an hour if the destination is anywhere along the Divide."

"Good. If we need them, Baelfire will call you. All other Reformists who aren't fit to fight shadow fiends should retreat to the west with everyone else."

My mother smiles. "I'm glad to hear that. This is the start of something new. Even if it gets messy, I believe it will be worth it— and it's about damn time something changed. I've seen far too many horrors at the Divide to think this endless cycle of legacies living and dying young could possibly be the gods' ideal plan."

Maven grumbles under her breath about the gods and then pauses. "You said you researched me."

"I did."

"Were there any records of me being selected as a saint at birth?"

Oh, fuck. Does she think Everett's theory might be right?

Come to think of it, maybe he *is* right. I mean, she stabbed a fucking wraith with a bone, and it hurt the damn thing even without being blessed. I can't think of another explanation for that.

It's a big question, and we all look at the commander in the room.

My mom frowns, brow furrowing around the strap of her eye patch. "It's possible records like that exist, but I have no access to temple data. Not to mention, living saints are notoriously under-recorded. Why do you ask?"

Maven fidgets with her gloves, blowing a strand of dark hair out of her face. "No reason. Out of curiosity, can we count on help from any of the saints out there? There's a high chance more wraiths will break loose once the Divide is weak enough, and only casters possessing holy magic can take them out."

If they're anything like that motherfucker Gideon, that's a horrific thought that makes me grimace.

My mother makes a face. "I doubt it. Saints are frustratingly hard to pinpoint—they're famously into giving without getting any recognition and tend to fall off the radar of any government entity entirely to carry out their gods-given missions until they choose to show up again. They're also pacifists who wouldn't want to engage in combat. It doesn't help that any holy magic is untraceable, even for someone like Douglas."

Perhaps that explains our prophetess friend slipping past Silas's magic wards after First Placement, Crypt muses telepathically.

Silas frowns. *Just because someone's magic is untraceable does not mean they are. My wards would have stopped a typical prophetess. It still makes no sense how she was able to get into our apartment.*

Maybe your magic's just not as impressive as you think, I tease.

Or maybe Maven is right, Everett sends through the bond, frowning at the map as he adjusts one of his sleeves repetitively. *Maybe some of the things that have happened to us have to do with the will of the gods.*

Those meddling fuckers, Maven grumbles telepathically.

Snowdrop, he groans. *You know what? Maybe they are messing with us just because you blaspheme so much.*

Maven ignores him as my mom makes me promise that I will stay in touch with her—since, according to Maven, all the shit that's about to happen is about to happen really damn quickly.

Maven and my mom continue to talk as Crypt begins putting back several of the little pieces he removed from the board when no one was watching. He also returns the packets of suppressants that he apparently swiped from my back pocket out of boredom during this little meeting.

Fucking pickpocket.

Either use those or invite me in to at least watch next time, he sends just to me.

I'm about to tell him there's no fucking way he's going to ever see me in a rut with my mate, but I pause. With how far gone I was, it honestly would've been weirdly reassuring to know he was there if Maven *did* have to put me in stasis.

Maybe, I reply telepathically.

Maven finishes speaking with my mom and announces that we'll make any necessary preparations and leave tonight for Baltimore for her final "mark."

As in, Natalya fucking Genovese.

36

EVERETT

I can't say I mind waiting in the car for hours when Maven is sitting in the passenger seat beside me in that tight black crop top, gloves, and dark leggings. A jacket waits for her at her feet, but I'm purposely keeping the vehicle toasty just so I can have this view.

It's before dawn. We're in an unmarked SUV parked down the street from the luxurious safehouse where Maven thinks Natalya is hiding out, based on Engela's detailed letter.

Baltimore is practically abandoned, with all the buildings on the historic roads left lightless. At first glance, the emptiness might seem like it's just because it's the early hours—but nobody else is parked out here on the street overnight. This is typically when humans would be getting up and leaving early for work to get ahead of city traffic, but the roads are empty.

A light snow flurry settles on the defrosting windshield as Silas and Baelfire talk quietly in the back seat. Crypt is unseen but probably hanging around in here somewhere, if he's not busy eating the dreams of anyone who ignored the evacuation warning and stayed in Baltimore.

The Garnet Wizard mentioned you bought something from him for an empath years ago, Maven muses through the bond just to me.

I tense. What else did that old eccentric tell her? If he brought up the whole thing with Silas—

It was for your sister, right? She glances at me.

My keeper is always so sharp. I nod.

That's a rare gift, she notes.

I make a face. *Not sure she'd call it that.*

You seem protective of her.

I am, I admit. *She went through a lot as a kid. Had it much tougher than I did. As an empath, she experienced everyone else's emotions constantly, even when she was a baby. Empaths tend to overload and get severe panic attacks. Most of the legacy community accepts that and has been raising awareness about it for years to end the negative stigma about empaths being weak, but my parents never got the memo. They punished her anytime she couldn't handle everything she felt from others, which was way too fucking much in that house. So, as soon as I had the means to step in, I did.*

Maven studies me, her expression soft. *You keep saying you're not worthy of me. That's bullshit. The reverse is true.*

I'm about to argue when Crypt appears suddenly in the backseat between Baelfire and Silas, making them both swear in surprise. The incubus leans forward to peer between Maven and me, his piercings glinting in the dim light from the dash.

"I'm fucking bored."

"Stakeouts aren't known for being exciting," I grumble.

"Yes, except for the fact that we have the sexiest woman alive with us."

"Not alive," Maven corrects without missing a beat, squinting through the windshield even though nothing is happening at the safehouse.

"Yet you have an aura, like all living things."

"But no fucking heartbeat, like all dead things."

He grins. "Very well, then—the sexiest revenant in the world."

"I'm the only one, so that checks out," she shrugs. "Silas, has anyone tripped the undetectable wards you set around the premises?"

"Not yet, *sangfluir*."

My phone buzzes in my pocket. I check it to see another text from Ian and squint to read without my glasses.

> Everything's in place.

I type a reply.

> Even the transportation?

> Yup. No eyes on any of it. Smooth AF from here on. You're welcome for being the best in the business. Sending you the invoice. Btw one of your polar bear dogs shit on my carpet so I'm billing you for that too.

I roll my eyes and pocket my phone, tuning in to realize that Baelfire is now arguing with Crypt about some past birthday.

"...and you were twelve, meaning you're seven years older than me, which makes you twenty-eight. If what you said about other stewards of Limbo kicking the can at thirty is true, that gives you about two more yea—"

"I lied about being twelve," Crypt drawls.

"What the fuck? Why?"

"You were a dyslexic little five-year-old who confidently told me the legal drinking age was 'one-two.' You'd caught me drinking from your parents' hidden liquor stash, so I played along and said I was that age. None of you ever bothered asking again, and I obviously didn't and still don't fucking care."

Silas frowns. "You're not the oldest?"

"Everett is the oldest," Maven offers.

Baelfire frowns. "How the hell did you know that before us?"

"Like I said, Kenzie stalked you four online. Apparently, her sleuthing is more solid than your ability to have a single conversation without arguing over the span of nearly two decades."

"Damn," Baelfire shakes his head. "I would've sworn on my family name that Crypt was seven years older than us."

Our keeper makes a face. "Us? You're twenty-one."

"Yeah, like you."

She shakes her head.

He frowns. "Twenty-two?"

"Twenty-three as of two days ago," she corrects.

What?

We all turn to glower at her at the same time.

"Do you truly mean to say that we just barely missed your birthday, and you chose not to fucking *tell us?*" Silas demands.

Maven looks at each of our pissed-off faces and smooths her gloves.

"No?" she tries like that might be the right answer.

Godsdamn it.

"We could have celebrated with you," I gripe. "Why didn't you tell us?"

"I forgot," she shrugs. "Besides, birthdays celebrate another year of life, which isn't applicable here. I only keep track of my age because Lillian made a big deal out of it. She liked to make me feel as human as possible and insisted on singing to me on the same day every year." She pauses, her expression turning wistful. "I…miss her voice."

We fall quiet at that, and then Baelfire sighs.

"Well, I can't wait to meet this Lillian, but from now on, we are fucking celebrating your birthday, got it? As a matter of fact, the second all this shit wraps up, and the humans are safely in the mortal realm, I'm planning a party so we can spoil the hell out of you."

The Nightmare Prince leans forward again to grin deviously at Maven. "But for tonight, I believe twenty-three birthday orgasms are in order."

She chokes. "Twenty-three? Hell no. That's not even poss—"

Silas tenses as red magic flares around his blackened fingertips.

"Someone just tripped the perimeter ward entering the safehouse from the south."

We're all immediately ready for action, following Maven's plan. Crypt disappears. Baelfire exits the car to stroll toward the rowhouse we're targeting. I turn off the car to follow him while Maven and Silas split off to try deactivating wards in the basement entry.

We all have talismans Silas made to keep Natalya out of our heads. He claims they'll work well for the next two hours before the magic tapers off. After that, Natalya will be able to sense our proximity from our thoughts alone.

As Baelfire and I near the front of the rowhouse, Silas updates us through the bond.

We got into the basement.

Nice. Let's see if our Angel of Death was right about this bitch hiring a bunch of fire elementals, Baelfire says cheerfully.

The cocky shifter has been in a damn good mood ever since he finally bonded with Maven. For once, I understand him.

I stand back and watch Bael kick down the front door of the fancy rowhouse to storm inside. Immediately, fire engulfs him, shattering windows as it explodes throughout the first floor. Security alarms begin to peel through the otherwise silent streets. I glimpse Baelfire snap a fire elemental's spine through one of the front windows. His clothes have burned off, but of course, the fireproof brute is unharmed.

The once-luxurious rowhouse starts to go up in smoke. I take a deep breath and send a massive wave of snow into the building, putting out the worst of the fire as steam hisses all around.

No one upstairs, Crypt updates. *Well, no one alive, at least. It seems Natalya's been draining any human stragglers she's come across.*

You got in? I frown. *Why don't they have dreamcatchers set up?*

That is the question, isn't it? Gods above, that alarm is irritating.

Baelfire finishes with the last elemental as I walk into the ruined rowhouse.

Silas, Boo? Where's that update? the dragon checks telepathically.

It's quiet for long enough that I start to get concerned before Maven replies, her voice urgent.

Our target isn't here. Abort.

Fuck. I immediately turn toward the stairs leading down toward the basement where they're supposed to be, but Baelfire stops me.

"She said abort. Come on."

"But—"

Get the fuck out of here, Maven reiterates. *She set traps. It's empty down here except for a hairpin hex we just triggered.*

What the hell is that? I demand.

Baelfire and I abandon the smoky building, backing away on the road as we wait and watch. The blaring security alarm abruptly cuts off, most likely courtesy of our incubus.

Think of it as a mine. Only if one of us steps out of place without carefully diffusing it, the hex will dismember us, Silas supplies in a strained voice. *Maven's destructive magic will only set it off.*

Fuck. That's one of the ways Maven can permanently be killed. Obviously, Natalya knows that and planned for it.

I grit my teeth as Baelfire paces up and down the road, swearing viciously as he drags a hand through his hair.

For one moment, I'm pissed off—and then the sound of a gunshot goes off at the same time a bullet lodges in my stomach. I grip the gushing injury and stagger back as more gunshots ring out. Baelfire tackles me to the ground, rolling and dragging me until we're in a small alleyway between buildings where the falling snow is building up. No bullets are flying here.

"Shit," I hiss, freezing over the injury to stop the gushing blood. Aggravating heat spreads from the bullet, slowly morphing into pain as my system catches up with the impact.

It fucking hurts. How did Maven brush off getting shot by bounty hunters like it was nothing?

It's an ambush out here, I warn the others.

"Stay here, Snowflake," Baelfire says before rushing back out into the street, which is now filled with the clatter of gunshots and shouting.

The damn shifter is going to get himself killed.

At least, that's what I think until I hear the unmistakable, ear-splitting roar of Baelfire's dragon. I wince when my ears start to ring. Any stragglers asleep in all of Baltimore are wide awake now if their eardrums didn't just fucking burst.

Getting to my feet, I lean against the brick alley wall, wiping my bloodied hand on my now-ruined coat.

Crypt? Do you have eyes on what's happening? I check.

All the lackeys once at Everbound are here for a party. They also appear to have a Void on the way. Still no sign of the immortal blood-guzzling bitch.

Damn it.

Everyone knows about Voids. They're rare and don't fit into a House. They absorb magic, their presence nulling any existing enchantment—meaning the talismans Silas spelled will be useless once the Void gets close enough.

Maven? I press, anxious as I peek around the corner in time to see Baelfire's massive golden beast step on a group of screaming legacies in the dim light of early dawn.

Silas is almost done, she answers finally.

I hear the rustle of fabric behind me and turn in time to impale a knife-wielding siren through the chest with a saber of ice. He falls. I summon another blade as I slip out of the alley, still clutching my stomach where the bullet burns under the soothing frost.

Luckily for me, Baelfire makes one hell of an ally now that he and his dragon aren't playing tug-of-war with his brain. He snarls and bends his neck down to snap a leopard shifter in half, flinging the other half into a trio of casters launching spells at him.

A few of their spells bounce off his golden scales, but a summoned magical weapon lodges under one of Bael's wings. He hisses and opens his mouth, his long neck glowing with molten royal blue light from the inside out as he prepares to burn them to ash.

But we're not here to burn down Baltimore. I lift my hand to send a wave of ice spikes into the casters before they see me coming, leaving them impaled high above the ground before I turn to freeze another.

And another.

The threats keep coming as legacies pour out of massive vans that screech to a stop down the street. Others arrive in bright flashes of transportation magic, while more come running from gods know where, armed to the teeth for this obvious ambush.

I only realize Crypt is helping with the fight when I turn to defend myself against two vampires and see that they're both ripping into each other's skin, hissing and cackling like killing each other is the most fun they've ever had while blood starts to drip out of their ears.

Some other legacies are turning on each other, but as I look around, I realize just how fucking outnumbered we are now.

Maven was right. Natalya prepared for us. All of these well-trained legacies were lying in wait—and now bounty hunters are joining the fray, their hellhounds at their sides as they take aim.

I lift my hands to raise an ice shield against a spray of bullets before sending another solid wave of ice and freezing a nearby siren just as she begins to sing. Baelfire snarls at some other attack and sweeps his tail through the growing sea of enemies. Crypt continues to send maniacal, homicidal chaos throughout the crowd.

But it still seems like we'll be lucky to make it out of this with all our limbs attached.

Amid the flashes of magic, snarling shifters, deafening gunshots, and howls of hellhounds, a dark cold sweeps through the street, which has become a battlefield. I tense until I see Maven stalking out of the ruined, smoking rowhouse with daggers in both hands, her hair tied up, looking every bit as deadly as she did in that photo on the news.

Especially because she's smirking like she *actually* stumbled across a party and not an oversized attack.

"The *telum!*" a nearby vampire shouts. "Atta–"

One of her daggers plants itself in his throat. I grimace as his head falls back at an unnatural angle.

As soon as they know my keeper is here, all forces target her. She deflects several blasts of magic, rolls away from a shifter, rips out an elemental's heart, and kills off a hellhound within a matter of seconds.

It's impossible *not* to watch as the woman who owns my heart and soul steps into the slaughter like she owns the damn place. The way she moves with lethal agility and kills as naturally as breathing is both spellbinding and fucking terrifying.

Or maybe the terrifying part is her smile...except I really like watching Maven enjoy herself.

"Arati, bless my beautiful maniac," I breathe.

37

EVERETT

ON YOUR RIGHT, Silas warns just in time for me to turn and freeze a hellhound.

The fight continues, but with Maven and Silas now in the mix, it starts to lean in our favor—until I hear Silas swear nearby over the loud fight.

A necromantic spell he's casting fizzles out as he tries to dodge a coyote shifter. Its claws still slice shallowly through his chest. He falls back, rolling away from the shifter until I stab it with my ice saber and kick it aside.

"Two types of magic, and you're still useless," I huff.

He glares at me, red irises blazing. "Only with a Void nearby."

Shit. I almost forgot about the Void.

I help him stand, and we turn to watch a tall, thin woman with completely whited-out eyes walk into the street. All magic dies within a few yards of her. She's getting closer to where Maven is gleefully slaughtering our enemies with crackling explosions of dark magic—but before we can warn our keeper, Crypt blurs into existence behind the Void and snaps her neck.

Okay, then. That problem was solved way easier than I thought.

Except then, Crypt's voice comes urgently through the bond.

Our pretty berserker has come out to play.

As soon as he points it out, I can see it, too. The way Maven is tearing through the decreasing enemies has changed completely. Her movements are just as brutal but far less calculated and precise. She still sweeps through the legacies and hellhounds like death itself— only now she's completely wild, flinging herself into each new threat with a deranged, breathtaking bloodlust evident in every movement.

She's too far gone to notice when two bullets hit her.

Or when a hellhound clamps its jaw around her thigh, tearing at her flesh.

Fuck, Baelfire swears through the bond. *She's going to get herself killed.*

Baelfire's dragon slices through the hellhound latched onto our keeper with one massive claw. The dragon's tail wraps around the berserker, trying to prevent her from diving back into the fight. But he roars in shock and pain when more dark magic explodes from her body, crackling over his tail and sending the massive beast staggering in agony.

Our berserking keeper immediately darts back into the massacre. Silas and I race after her, using magic and ice to blast enemies away from our out-of-control keeper before they can harm her. She rips out hearts, tears hellhounds to pieces with her magic, and sends crackling waves of her uniquely unholy ability through anything living that she sees, leaving a path of blood and excessive gore in her wake.

Unstoppable and fueled by death. The perfect weapon.

Except if we're not careful, she can be killed permanently.

We cannot let her expire here, Silas grits through the bond as he takes down a powerful caster. Blood is dripping from his nose, but he ignores it. *Natalya knows the ways to kill a revenant and will have passed those methods on to her army. If Maven expires, she will be vulnerable to being ripped to shreds or burned to ash while unconscious.*

I swear when another bullet grazes my right arm. Turning around, I send a blast of ice into any enemies racing after us to make sure no one attacks from behind.

Baelfire's dragon roars and crushes more legacies before he

speaks telepathically. *During training, she said the only way to snap her out of this is by expiring, but I'm not fucking hurting her.*

I've got a better idea, Crypt says.

Just as I turn back around, he drops out of Limbo—directly onto Maven's back.

Oh, fuck. The berserker is going to rip him limb from limb, just like she's done to everything else that has made the mistake of getting too close to her.

Crackling black magic blooms around the death-craving revenant as she tries to attack Crypt, but even though he must be in agony, the incubus reaches down to cradle Maven's head. He grimaces, swearing viciously as his markings light up brightly.

Silas and I move to shield the two of them from any more threats. Luckily, the fight is waning as many opponents have started to run from the terrifying revenant. The few who remain are primarily focused on the biggest target—Baelfire. Silas and I take care of any legacies or hellhounds who approach as Crypt tries like hell to use his sleep-inducing ability on the berserker.

Her dark magic finally dissipates. I risk a glance over my shoulder, relieved to see that Maven is blessedly unconscious.

"Thank the gods," I mutter.

Silas sends some necromantic spell at two wolf shifters racing toward us, but his gaze slips to the sky.

"Those godsdamned humans and their love of drama," he scowls.

Glancing up, I swear.

A news helicopter is hovering high in the sky, getting footage of the fight in the street below. Baelfire snarls and pauses in chasing enemies away to shoot a warning column of blinding blue fire into the air. It's nowhere near close enough to endanger the idiot humans looking for a scoop, but it does seem to frighten the pilot into his good senses because the helicopter slowly backs off.

Not nearly as many enemies remain now, and the ones that do are attacking Baelfire. I let Silas stay on guard and crouch beside

Maven, who is sleeping on the black pavement of the blood-soaked street.

Crypt looks exhausted as he finally pulls his hands away from her head, wiping sweat off his brow. His leather jacket is missing, and he has a nasty-looking cut on one forearm that's struggling to heal.

"Scyntyche's scythe, our girl is strong," he mutters. "That took nearly everything I had."

"Let's hope she wakes up as Maven instead of the thing that did all of this," I say, turning to survey the dying aftermath of the battle.

But then I freeze.

Natalya Genovese is standing at the end of the blood-and-corpse-filled street, dressed in a shimmering cut-out dress like she was just about to hit her favorite high-end club. Her auburn hair is brighter under the rising dawn as her glowing blue gaze falls to Maven, still unconscious on the ground.

Silas spots her, too, and swears. "She can't get into our heads, so why are her eyes glowing?"

Shit, Baelfire says through the bond. *This is so fucking creepy.*

Not willing to take my eyes off Maven's final immortal target, I use my peripheries to see what he's talking about. The remaining legacies who were just retreating are now approaching, their movements and steps in perfect synchrony.

A dozen or so casters raise their hands at the same time. The handful of remaining shifters howl, snarl, hiss, or roar at once. Three bounty hunters cock their guns and take aim simultaneously.

They're like puppets now. Completely under the vampyr's control.

All at once, perfectly coordinated attacks surge around us. I throw a thick ice shield around Maven just as Crypt leaps away, drawing out his enchanted sword to attack the nearest enemy. Baelfire swivels, his neck swinging low as he goes right for Natalya—but just as he opens his mouth to breathe fire, one of the mind-controlled bounty hunters fires off a tranquilizer that tags the beast in the roof of his mouth.

He roars, shuddering as he crashes into the row of historic Baltimore houses. I'm so busy freezing anything that comes close to my shielded keeper that I don't see the toppling building beside me until it's too late.

"Shit," I swear.

I try to roll and end up buried in debris up to my neck, weight crushing my chest. Pain lights up my right arm.

Broken. Great.

I try struggling, but I'm completely pinned as the others fight the creepily coordinated attacks of Natalya's puppets. Baelfire has lost his dragon form and is passed out from the tranquilizer. Crypt and Silas try to keep the mind-controlled legacies away from Maven's icy enclosure. But Silas's magic is flagging, and as I watch, Crypt is tackled from behind by a fucking bear shifter.

Meanwhile, Natalya Genovese uses her vamp speed to dart to where I'm trying to summon ice—but I'm also running out of steam. I can't breathe under this heavy mass of bricks and shit.

Natalya shows off her fangs as she examines me, preening like the well-dressed predator she is. "Why can't I get into your handsome head?"

I've never been so grateful for Silas's magic. If we survive this, I'll even thank him.

The immortal reaches down, her hand wrapping around my neck. I choke in pain as she pulls me out of the crushing debris like it weighs nothing to her—but then, in a blindingly fast move, she pins me to the asphalt with my hands over my head. Struggling against her is like fighting against steel bands.

Fucking vampyr strength.

Natalya's blue eyes still glow, her pupils like hungry pinpricks as she bares her fangs at me again, this time with a carnal smile. Somewhere in the fight, I hear a loud crack—

Like ice breaking.

Like someone just got through Maven's shield.

Maven? I send through the bond, alarmed as I struggle.

I try to send a spike of ice up beside my head to stab Natalya, but she's too fast and dodges the spike with ease.

"Worry not, I'll let my new friends rip that hideous revenant of yours to shreds," she purrs. "It won't be long now, and I just cannot stand getting my hands dirty when they could be so much more *pleasantly* occupied."

I strain away from her, bending my neck desperately to see if Maven is okay—but the bitch takes the opportunity to lick my neck.

Dear gods, that is fucking repulsive.

I gag and try to freeze her, but the glaze of ice barely encompasses Natalya before she breaks out of it as easily as a snake shedding its skin. Proof that I'm tapped out from the fight.

"Get the fuck *off* of me," I grit out.

From somewhere beyond this horrific moment, I hear Silas shout before it gets quiet.

Really damn quiet.

Natalya has the audacity to fucking *giggle*, batting her eyes at me. "I think I'll keep you alive. I've always wanted to play with a Frost. Now that your brothers have fallen and I've won, let's take a look at how your keeper looks in pieces, shall we?"

She darts upright, pulling me with her. I struggle to keep my footing, looking around desperately for Maven.

I don't see her, but I do see why it's quiet.

The rest of Natalya's puppets are now dead, their corpses joining the countless others on the street. The only people left standing are Silas and Crypt, but just barely. Both of them look like injury-riddled shit as they turn to face us.

Just as Natalya hisses in displeased anger, Maven blurs to a stop in front of us, moving quicker than a shifter. The vampyr drops me, reaching for Maven with an infuriated shriek.

Maven moves faster. She sidesteps the immortal, ducks under another attack, reaches around Natalya's head, and—

Rips it clean off.

"That's for Amato," she mutters as the immortal falls.

I watch in disgusted, morbid fascination as my keeper drops the head before reaching down and searching Natalya's headless corpse. She removes a choker necklace from some hidden pocket inside the cut-out dress's skirt, sets it on the asphalt, and wastes no time driving Pierce into it.

As the pendant shatters, I realize it was etherium.

Immediately, the ground rumbles like there's a distant earthquake. The dawn seems to dim, and snow begins to fall lightly from clouds that have steadily crept into the sky during the ambush. Everything feels darker—almost less colorful, somehow.

The Nether is creeping into the mortal realm even more.

"Snowdrop," I breathe in relief, kicking aside the shattered etherium necklace to wrap her in my arms.

Well—arm. The broken one isn't moving very well.

Maven hugs me back weakly before pulling away, her breaths labored. She grimaces. "Her life force is really fucking potent."

Shit. "Silas—"

"On it," he says, pulling the briefcase out of his pocket void and quickly handing Maven one of the clear etherium pieces.

She grimaces and whispers the strange words until the stone darkens. Silas accepts it and places it with the other two for safekeeping until our keeper needs them later. For a moment, the four of us stand beaten, bloodied, and exhausted in the aftermath of the brutal fight.

Until I notice Silas visibly flinch, closing his eyes as he becomes even paler than usual.

"You good?" I frown.

"There are many ghosts here. Scyntyche is reaping," he murmurs hoarsely.

A chill rolls over my back as I glance around. Of course, I see nothing because I'm not a fucking necromancer, but knowing the goddess of death, fate, time, and so much else is nearby is…chilling.

Baelfire coughs nearby. We all look over as he sits up and yanks the tranquilizer out of his mouth with a grimace. The shifter's face lights up when he sees the four of us before he notices the headless immortal.

"Holy fuck. We did it!"

"Maven did it," I correct, glancing up at the sky when I hear another helicopter approaching. "We can't stick around here, Snowdrop."

She doesn't respond, her eyes closed as if in concentration.

Or—shit, is she in pain?

"Darling?" Crypt checks, stepping over a couple of bodies to cradle her face. His markings glow softly, but he ignores them. "Maven?"

"What's going on?" Baelfire demands, hauling his ass up to approach. As usual, he's butt-ass naked after a shift, streaked in ash and dirt.

Maven's lashes flutter open, relief stark on her face as she looks at the four of us. Her voice has a surprisingly emotional rasp to it. "It worked. The humans can leave the Nether."

"How do you know for sure?" I frown, reaching out to brush dirt from her jaw.

"Felix has a piece of etherium that I marked with a beacon spell before I left the Nether. He just activated it. I'll transport us to where my spell was set off." She takes a deep breath. "And when we get there, the exodus won't be far behind."

38

SILAS

THE SKY over North Carolina is a thick blanket of turbulent dark clouds as far as the eye can see while I heal Everett's broken arm—the last of our significant injuries.

The white-haired elemental sits on an old stone bench in the cemetery where we appeared when Maven transported us after the ambush. This cemetery is connected to a massive, empty field of dirt and brambles on the brink of the encroaching Divide.

The Divide itself lurks along one side of the cemetery and field, a towering wall of perturbing dark gray, like a misty veil.

I can sense it even from here. The powerful, old magic humming in the air, now barely keeping the Nether at bay.

Maven stands waiting for the caster named Felix where we first appeared. Crypt waits next to her, smoking *reverium* and ignoring his glowing markings.

Meanwhile, Baelfire paces nearby as he waits for his phone call to be answered. He's dressed in spare clothes, which I'm now thanking all six gods that I tossed into my void pouch at some juncture—otherwise, all the poor humans escaping the Nether would be greeted by the idiot's bare ass.

"Mom?" he checks when Brigid Decimus picks up the phone. I can't hear her on the other end, but he breathes in relief. "Yeah, we did. No, I'm good—we are all. Yeah, it got pretty fucking rough. What do you mean, footage? Oh, shit, I didn't realize they filmed that." He listens for a moment and then grunts. "You're right. Maven wants any willing Reformists here as soon as fucking possible for when the shadow fiends start to pour out. I'll send you the coordinates."

As he talks, I finish with Everett's arm and straighten, grimacing at my sore muscles. Our entire quintet is sore and exhausted. We've been patching ourselves up as best we can while we wait, but we'll require serious time to recover and rest once this is over.

Earlier, Maven insisted I feed on her to heal the others in any way they need. The intoxicating flavor of her blood has only deepened, becoming richer and even more addictive as she has grown stronger with the completion of our quintet.

It was truthfully a challenge to stop drinking from her pretty neck.

Baelfire hangs up and moves closer to our waiting keeper. "My mom said the Reformist aid will be here within thirty minutes."

Maven glances over her shoulder. Like the rest of us, she is still dirty from the ambush. Yet somehow, the rough look is incredibly flattering on her—her dark hair tied in a ponytail, her olive skin smudged with dirt and blood, the flash of those cunning eyes.

My keeper will forever take my breath away.

"That's fast," she replies to Baelfire.

"They kinda started prepping when they saw us on the news," he shrugs, pocketing his phone.

As if his words summoned it, we all hear a helicopter in the distance.

"Why does that thing seem to be looking for us?" Maven asks.

"It's a news helicopter. Humans want to see what's going on. I wouldn't be surprised if they tried to land and interview you," Everett grumbles.

She pulls a face. "Gag me with a knife."

Crypt laughs. "But darling, I have something far more enjoyable for you to gag on."

I roll my eyes. Our keeper grins and starts to say something, but we all snap to attention when a flash of green light is followed by a figure stepping into the cemetery from the Divide.

It's a thin young man, possibly Everett or Crypt's age. He has brown hair, pale skin, dark circles under his hazel eyes, and only one arm, which holds an almost laughable makeshift weapon of a piece of etherium affixed to a stick. His haggard clothing looks like something a medieval peasant would wear.

Still, his voice is strong when he greets Maven without his expression changing. "You did it."

"You doubted me?"

His attention slips to the world behind us, and his strange, Maven-like composure slips momentarily as his voice cracks. "Gods. This is the mortal realm? It's...it's so *colorful*. And bright."

"It's a fucking cemetery on a dark and cloudy day," Baelfire points out.

That draws the caster's attention to us, and he blinks, recomposing himself. "Who are these guys?"

"Felix, this is my quintet," Maven says breezily, motioning to each of us. "Silas, Baelfire, Everett, and Crypt. Guys, this is Felix."

His eyes widen slightly like he doesn't want to show too much emotion. "These are your gods-selected matches? My gods, these poor men."

Crypt's eyes narrow. "Did you just insult my keeper?"

Felix coughs, glancing at Maven. "That one looks like he wants to kill me."

"He will if you answer wrong," she grins at him.

Baelfire huffs. *Quit giving him your smiles,* he says through the bond. *Those are mine, Boo.*

So jealous, she teases.

Meanwhile, Felix flinches back. "Did...did you just fucking *smile?*"

She shrugs. "We can show emotions here."

"Sure, but...it's *you*. That just seems wrong. Not to mention, you seem way too chatty for the *telum* I know." He squints hard at her eyes. "But your pupils are round. How are you not a changeling?"

Maven regards Felix seriously. "Where are the humans? Is the plan going smoothly?"

The caster quickly replaces his poker face and turns business-like, explaining that the frightened humans who have escaped and been on the run for over a day are about to breach the Divide. He just needs to set up one more spell on this end to make passing through more bearable for them since their weak constitutions put them at risk of succumbing to the gods-placed ward.

He also says that monsters won't be far behind the escaping humans but that Lillian is at the back of the massive group, helping to fend off any dangers that may chase after them.

I frown. "Does Lillian possess magic to fend off dangers?"

Felix shakes his head. "She's just capable and selfless."

"Just like my mate," Bael grins. "All right, let's get this show on the road. How can we help?"

I meet Everett's eye. He nods and steps away to make a call. Our brief planning session should help immensely once the humans are through, but in the interest of getting them here, I step forward to address Felix.

"Teach me the spell you're using. I'll help you set it up on this side."

He hesitates. "It's a complicated spell—"

I level him with a look that makes him cut off. "Don't presume to underestimate me."

He finally notices my pointed ears. "Oh—shit. You're a blood fae. Um, okay, if you want my blood—"

Maven rolls her eyes and steps to my side, tilting her head to the left to offer her neck. My mouth waters immediately, and I hold back a moan of delight when my fangs first pierce her skin there, my arms wrapping around her on instinct.

A gratifying rush of delicious power sweeps through me as I swallow, drawing again as my heart pounds euphorically. I can practically feel the bond between Maven and I shudder with our combined pleasure.

You're taking too much, Everett grumbles through the bond.

I release Maven's neck, licking away the last precious remnants of her blood from the tiny fang pricks on her neck as my body buzzes with power and intimate hunger. She meets my eye as I pull away, and I smirk at the way she's practically eye-fucking me here in the cemetery.

When I turn back to Felix, he's turned around entirely like he's trying not to witness something inappropriate.

"I can help now," I inform him, walking past him to the edge of the gray veil that is the Divide.

The caster is clearly still uncomfortable from the display of feeding as he describes a waypoint spell I've never heard of before. As I help him lay the runes and recite the needed incantations to stretch the waypoint all along this section of the Divide—from the cemetery through the field—I note that although he does seem a bit enfeebled from growing up in the Nether, he has an impressive grasp of magic and especially of fae-specific incantations.

Out of curiosity, once the waypoint spell has been laid and hums to life before us, I turn and arch a brow at him.

"À bheil linguam matris ah'gad?"

Meaning, *Do you speak my mother tongue?*

His eyes light up, and he tames a smile. *"Anns antiquo dòigh, tha."*

In the ancient way, yes.

Interesting.

Before I can ask more, Felix says he needs to go back and guide the first humans through the Divide so the others can follow. He slips into the dark wall of gray at the waypoint we established, and I return to Maven and the others.

We wait.

And wait.

At long last, the bright light of a transportation spell appears in the field beside the cemetery—a group of Reformists, judging by the blue they're wearing and the smiles on their faces when they see my quintet.

But the brightest smile of all is Kenzie Baird's as she rushes into the cemetery, squealing like this is the best day of her life and not a tenuous escape plan that will almost certainly end in a fight with shadow fiends.

"Maven fucking Oakley! *Surprise!*"

Maven blinks rapidly as her friend goes to hug her, but Crypt holds up an arm to block the lioness shifter. That doesn't dampen Kenzie's spirit. She bounces on her tiptoes in excitement as more Reformists transport into the nearby field.

"Are you so surprised? You look so surprised and also *super* covered in blood, which I'm learning is just an official look for you. Ta-da! I joined the Reformists. I mean, for a while there, I kept asking my parents if they were anti-legacy activists, and they kept saying no. But then they told me all about this movement and how it fully supports you, and I was like, well, then of *course* I'll join. Oh, fuck— is that where the humans are going to enter?" she asks, pointing at the massive glowing spell designating the waypoint.

Maven nods.

Kenzie squeals again. "Oh, my gods! This is so exciting and also kind of terrifying and—"

"Is it safe for you to be here?" Maven frowns.

"Pfft—fuck safe. Have those humans been safe? No. And I might not be a full-blown shifter thanks to my curse, but I can fucking help however I can, so don't even say I can't."

"I didn't mean that. I'm just surprised. In a good way," Maven tacks on, smiling at Kenzie.

Kenzie beams and then blinks multiple times over her shoulder at us. "Damn, you all look awful. I mean, I saw that you guys were in a horrible fight live on the news a little bit ago, but it's *way* worse in person."

"Thanks for that, Baird," Everett rolls his eyes.

Maven glances at the field next to us where Reformists are gathering and frowns. "Is that Harlow Carter?"

"Yep! She's a Reformist now. So are most of the asscasters who survived the shit that went down at Everbound. I guess it makes sense that they're on board with reforming the system since the system is kind of rough on their survival chances at the moment," Kenzie grimaces, blowing a strand of pale curly hair out of her face. Her face lights up, and she waves at Vivienne and Luka, who have just arrived with one of the other transporting casters. "My quintet joined, too, by the way."

As she chats off my keeper's ear, I frown when I sense something appear in one of my hands, buzzing like a phone that needs to be answered.

When I raise the Scarab-shaped amulet, tingling with familiar magic, I understand immediately and answer the communications spell placed on it.

"You truly are old-fashioned," I sigh, stepping away from the others for privacy. I wander through old gravestones, gazing at the stormy sky overhead and wondering if it's an omen. "You do know phones exist now, don't you?"

The Garnet Wizard's voice is muffled because of the spell, cutting out now and then. "Enough cheek. I have a message for your keeper."

When I pass by an old, fading statue of the goddess Syntyche, a cloak concealing her face and her scythe propped over one shoulder, I can't help the shiver that rolls over me.

"Then why not send this to her?" I ask.

"Don't be daft. You know that I know your magic well enough to send you a communication anywhere in the world. I barely know your keeper's magic well enough—and this message could not be missed, for it is quite important."

He cuts out for a moment. I frown. "Repeat that."

"I said, tell your keeper that Zuma's paramour left the Sanctuary without permission, and she followed him despite my trying to stop her. I have sent acolytes out looking, so they should be found swiftly."

I pause. "He left without permission? How? The wards should completely prevent that."

"I am investigating how this happened. Just tell your keeper at once."

The Scarab amulet vanishes.

I sigh. Ever the eccentric.

I move back toward Maven, intent on sharing the update—but just as I approach her, the glowing waypoint flashes on our side of the Divide, lighting up the gray wall throughout the cemetery and field. Everyone present, including my quintet and the Reformists, goes still and quiet as we watch the first of the humans escape the Nether.

They're all haggard, barefoot, gray-skinned, dressed in rags, and streaked with dirt and sweat as they venture into the field. And they're all women and children. With a start, I realize the humans have sent their most vulnerable first to get them away from danger the fastest. Pregnant women, wide-eyed, terrified children, and other trembling humans make their way out of the Divide.

Many burst into tears.

Others collapse as if the journey to get here took all their strength.

It's a surprisingly touching sight. At once, the present Reformists, including Kenzie and her quintet, hurry to help. They support the fallen humans and offer words of comfort, welcoming them to the mortal realm.

Unfortunately, many of the malnourished escapees are bone-thin. Others have visible wounds. They need the supplies and other aid.

When I glance at Everett again, he nods.

It will all arrive soon, he says through the bond.

Maven tips her head. *What will arrive soon?*

I didn't mean to send that to you, he says sheepishly.

Her eyes narrow. He fidgets with his sleeve, a flush crawling over his cheeks.

Aid, I inform her finally. *When you wished to know what we were up to, that was it—planning resources and assistance for the humans once they are safely in this world. Emergency medical help. Food. Temporary housing. Transportation to safety away from the Divide and the legacy government.*

Maven stares at me and then at Everett, Crypt, and Baelfire. *You guys were...planning more help for the Nether humans?*

We all nod.

She looks away, a smile brushing over her face and vanishing just as quickly as she tries to tame her emotion. I suspect our keeper speaks through the bond because she doesn't trust her voice to remain steady.

Gods. You're all such fucking softies. But...thank you.

Crypt leans over to kiss her temple. *You can thank us properly later when we give you those twenty-three orgasms.*

That's way too many fucking orgasms, she argues. Then she pauses, tipping her head. *Isn't it?*

Only one way to know for sure, Baelfire grins. *We'll keep a scoreboard and everything. Whoever contributes the most to your birthday orgasms wins—*

A howl in the distance makes us all tense. Even the Reformists in the nearby field go still, recognizing the approach of hellhounds. The Nether humans are pouring through the waypoint now, rushing into freedom by the hundreds, but some of them slow in alarm when they hear the hellhounds braying.

Maven swears and storms out of the cemetery toward the howling. We follow her, passing by many tearful, awe-struck humans from the Nether until we near a small forest at the edge of the barren field.

A hellhound leaps out from the trees. I lift my hand to rip it in half with blood magic, but then a voice firmly says, "*Heel.*"

Douglas emerges from the forest along with a handful of other bounty hunters and their hellish dogs. Baelfire growls while Crypt's markings light up ominously.

But Douglas ignores them, looking behind us at the humans fleeing into the mortal realm.

Then he studies Maven, debating. "We'll help."

"What?" one of the other bounty hunters snaps angrily. "She's the fucking *telum*. We're supposed to kill her!"

"Try," Crypt warns darkly, smiling without humor.

Douglas shakes his head, still holding Maven's stare. "This is why I wanted to question you, but now it's fucking obvious that the rumors were right for once. So. Will you accept more help?"

"How about an apology for hunting us like dogs first?" I point out dryly.

Douglas snorts. "Apologies are worth shit. Action is all that matters."

Maven smirks. "I knew I liked you."

Baelfire sighs, dropping his head forward. *Raincloud, are you fucking trying to make us jealous?*

The other irritated bounty hunter swears angrily, having had enough. He takes aim at Maven—but just as I notice and step in front of her, Douglas turns and promptly shoots his comrade in the leg.

The other bounty hunter goes down with a sharp cry. His pet hellhound bares its teeth at Douglas, but Douglas's massive black hellhound snarls menacingly, snapping its teeth close enough to the other pet that it whines and yields.

Douglas looks at the other hunters. "Now, does anyone else feel like being a fucking moron, or are we going to help these people escape the Nether?"

The others don't argue.

"Good. When shadow fiends escape, you have dibs," Maven says decisively before turning to walk back to the waypoint where the humans are still emerging into the mortal world in droves.

Douglas makes a face as he and the other bounty hunters fall into step with us. "You can't call dibs for someone else, you fucking—"

"Stop there, or I'll have to disappoint my keeper by slaughtering you and your friends," Crypt says in a too-eager tone.

The bounty hunter glares at the incubus. "You're lucky I haven't ended your miserable fucking existence for killing my dad."

"Your dad," Crypt parrots distractedly, clearly bored of the conversation as he busies himself with checking out Maven's incredible ass in her tight dark leggings as she walks ahead of us.

It would be a lie if I claimed I wasn't just doing the same thing.

"How do you not fucking remember?" Asher Douglas snaps at Crypt. His fist clenches white around his gun as his hellhound walks obediently behind him.

The Nightmare Prince shrugs. "I kill a lot of people. Try being more specific."

"You drowned him in his own blood, you sick motherfucking freak."

"Hmm. Drowned in blood. Oh—right, him," Crypt nods, finally checking back into the conversation, grinning as if they're discussing a fond memory. Then he levels Asher with a hard stare. "That bloke was abusing his wife in a sickening number of ways. He more than deserved it."

"No shit. That's why I vowed to put a bullet in his head—then you had to go and fucking steal the chance from me," Asher mutters.

My brows go up. What an unexpected response.

Crypt says something flippant in reply to the hunter, but my attention turns to Maven again as I finally have a moment to relate to her the message I received.

My mentor told me Zuma and her lover left the Sanctuary, I tell her in fae through the bond.

She stiffens but continues walking. *Why did he let them leave?*

He didn't.

Maven is quiet for a long moment, thinking. *Wherever Engela is shouldn't matter.*

My attention latches onto the Divide where the humans are emerging. The gray wall is wavering and shaky, as if its instability has only worsened since we've been here.

What happens if the Divide falls before you can restabilize it, my blood blossom? I ask.

Then I fail. I can only weaken and stabilize it—it can't be rebuilt from nothing.

Then, where Engela is does *matter. Because if anything happens to her*

— I begin, frowning as I realize that elemental is the only thing standing between Maven fulfilling her purpose as a revenant.

Maven looks over her shoulder at me briefly, her dark eyes determined. *The humans need to get through the Divide. That's our top priority. As soon as they are through, we're taking the etherium filled with the life forces of the Immortal Quintet to the nearest temple, which is twenty minutes away. Any priest or priestess can bless the stones the way we need to finish refortifying the Divide. We can do this.*

As always, her fierce determination leaves me breathless.

As we near the cemetery, the bounty hunters break off to help the arriving humans. Many are in terrible condition, so it's a relief when I finally see several ambulances drive onto the far end of the field from an old dirt road. More vehicles also begin to arrive, the drivers rushing to open the backs of their vans to offer water bottles, food, and other emergency aid to the countless wide-eyed, filthy humans who just escaped captivity. Others offer jackets and gloves for the cold.

I don't miss the relief in Maven's expression as she witnesses all the help gathering for those she just freed.

She cares deeply for these poor humans.

And as I watch hundreds more stream into the mortal world, I can see why. They're a stark contrast to legacies, who believe the weak should be culled. Instead, I watch as the humans prioritize the weakest and most vulnerable among themselves, supporting one another and ensuring those who need help the most receive it first.

Though these people appear haunted and frightened by this new world, and although they most carefully conceal their emotions just as Felix and Maven do, their eyes are still full of great hope. Many whisper quiet, genuine thanks, while others fall to pray to the gods in gratitude.

Fascinating. These humans have none of the powerful abilities that my quintet possesses, yet they emanate quiet strength and resilience. All the suffering they've gone through, and not a drop of bitterness toward the gods.

Reaching out to squeeze Maven's hand, I join the Reformists in welcoming the Nether humans into their new lives.

39

MAVEN

NEARLY AN HOUR HAS PASSED. Humans are still arriving from the Nether, but now a far more organized system is in place to get them helped and situated.

All thanks to my quintet members.

I can only assume Everett funded all of this as I watch more vans arrive to transport yet another massive group of shell-shocked Nether humans to safety far away from the unstable Divide. Others are being treated for dire injuries, or they're hesitantly accepting food and water with trembling hands, confounded by the hospitality that has greeted them here.

It will take time for them to adapt to freedom in this world.

But gods—they're here.

It's working.

I'm finally fulfilling my blood oath.

So why can't I shake the dread rising in my gut?

As I remain on the lookout for danger and any sign of Lillian arriving through the waypoint, another group of humans passes me. When one of them sees me, he whispers to the others that I'm Amadeus's daughter and quickly bows his head in respect. The others follow suit, a strange mix of gratitude and terror as they hurry away from me.

A badly bruised girl pauses in following after them, clutching her bleeding elbow. Like the other Nether humans, it looks as if the color has been bled from her, so her big blue eyes are more of a gray. She can't be older than ten and looks at me with moisture on her hollow cheeks.

"Thank you," she says quietly.

Crying still makes me really fucking uncomfortable, but I offer a smile. "Stay right here."

I hurry to one of the nearby supply crates brought by the vans earlier and return to her with a roll of bandages. Grateful for my gloves since they provide a buffer against skin contact, I quickly wrap her injury.

"Is...is Amadeus really your father?" she whispers.

"No." I meet her eye briefly. "My father was a human named Pietro Amato."

She watches as I finish bandaging her arm. As with most people from the Nether, her expression is guarded as if, aside from the tears that escape, she's afraid of showing how she feels. Probably because in the Nether, excessive emotions end with getting devoured by the Undead.

She sniffles slightly. "S—someone told me the *telum* is a monster. But...I think you're so pretty."

I study her, noticing the way she's hugging herself and shivering. "Thanks. And I think you're freezing. Go get warmed up, all right?"

She thanks me again and hurries to follow a cluster of other humans, wrapping herself in an emergency blanket. Fewer humans are crowding around the supply vans now as the exodus finally seems to slow.

I tuck the remaining bandages in the pocket of the hoodie I'm wearing, which Silas grabbed from his pocket void and gave to me earlier. Glancing nearby, I watch as Crypt cheers up a group of several sullen, wide-eyed children. He hands them blankets and leads them across the giant field toward one of the food-distributing trucks. Everett, Baelfire, and Silas are also in the midst of the exodus, directing and helping wherever they can.

Watching my quintet like this makes that same fluttery sensation rise in my stomach—that tender, consuming feeling I have tried and failed to fight whenever I'm around them.

There's just something so *right* about being bound to all of them now. A completeness I've never experienced before, like something that was always meant to be a part of me is now finally in place.

It's a bizarrely incredible feeling.

But still, as that unspeakable emotion mixes with my growing apprehension, I turn again to frown at the Divide.

With how weak it is right now, thin enough that even humans can pass through with some magical assistance, I expected to fight off constant surges as the humans escaped.

So why the hell hasn't an attack happened yet?

I don't realize Felix has emerged from the Divide again until he clears his throat beside me.

"There are monsters on their way. And shadow fiends."

I nod, still frowning. "Odd that they haven't come sooner."

Felix opens his mouth to say something else, but Kenzie skips up to us, her light corkscrew curls bouncing in a high ponytail. Her nose is slightly pink from the cold despite the fluffy light blue jacket she's sporting alongside tight, shimmering green leggings.

"Okay, just for the record, this is completely fulfilling my lifelong dream of being a tour guide. I mean, I'm not *really* giving a tour, but sort of because so far, I've explained to about thirty different people that the trees are green and my eyes are blue. Are there just no colors in the Nether? Because they're all blown away by them. And they're all so incredibly *nice*. I mean, I want to wrap up every single person popping out of the Nether with a massive hug and cry for them for a little while because it's clear they've been through terrible shit—but *gods*, I am so glad I get to be here to help any little way I can," she gushes.

"I'm glad you're here, too," I grin.

I would never say it out loud, but I've really missed this bubbly lioness shifter.

Her gaze darts to Felix, and she smiles brightly. "Hi there! I'm

Kenzie. Lion shifter. Artist. Retired slut extraordinaire—unless you ask anyone in my quintet," she winks. "What's your name?"

He fumbles. "Um...I'm, uh..."

Then he looks wide-eyed at me like he needs help. I arch a brow, not sure why he's glitching.

"This is Felix. I've known him for years. He helped orchestrate the exodus."

Kenzie grins. "Oh! Are you like, May's oldest friend?"

"Not friend," I correct. "More like...distant accomplice."

She laughs at me and tells Felix she's glad to meet him. Then she excuses herself to help Vivienne since the petite little air elemental is trying to support a full-grown human man who seems to have twisted his ankle during the humans' escape.

As soon as Kenzie bounces away, the one-armed caster swallows thickly.

"Gods."

"She's a whirlwind, but I'll kill to protect her any day," I shrug.

Except when Felix continues to gawk after Kenzie, I realize he's not just baffled by her unparalleled ability to shoot words out of her mouth in rapid succession.

No, he's...starstruck.

"Does—does she need any help?" he asks hopefully. "With anything? At all?"

"I'm sure her matches will help her if she does."

His face falls, and he clears his throat. "Oh, right. She mentioned already having a quintet."

"Yes. An incomplete one." I squint at Felix, considering him. "Come to think of it, they're missing a caster."

He's still busy staring after Kenzie when cold creeps down my spine. I snap to attention when my senses fly into high alert, all of my instincts sharpening. My gaze slips to the towering, hazy gray of the Divide.

Shadow fiends. I can sense them coming—a *lot* of them.

Too many.

I swear and remove my gloves, slipping them into the waist of my leggings as I make the infernal symbol with my hands and close my eyes. Breathing out the forbidden words, I feel my pulse start to slow.

Boo? What are you doing? Baelfire checks telepathically.

An instant later, I sense Crypt beside me. "Trying to see ahead, love?"

Stop bothering her. She needs focus for that spell, Silas asserts through the bond.

Everett says something, too, but his voice fades as darkness creeps in. My breathing stops. For a moment, I can feel death draw close around me, almost like a brush of cold fingers along the skin of my face. My focus drops to the shadow heart in my chest as I prepare to tap into Amadeus's abilities to see what the fuck is going on.

But when I try, it's like I've pulled on the wrong loose string. Instead of flashes of the future, dark malice reverberates throughout my mind as his deep, rumbling voice sweeps through my mind.

Daughter. Your dreams betrayed your betrayal.

I can't breathe. Tendrils of dread wrap around me, cutting off my oxygen as fear coagulates inside my chest.

I fight against a feeling like sinking into oblivion, struggling against this dark link as the shadow heart inside of me clenches, shuddering in response to the Entity's control.

Until I feel something else yank on me—no, *four* other somethings. They pull at my soul obsessively, warming the emptiness inside my chest.

I finally break free of the link with a sharp gasp, my eyes flying open to see that Baelfire is holding me in his arms. The others are gathered around with pinched foreheads.

"Fuck, Raincloud. Are you okay?" Bael asks. "What just happened?"

I'm disoriented and squirm until he sets me down. He doesn't let me go entirely since I'm still unsteady, but I ignore the lingering weakness from the ritual and look at each of my matches in turn.

"Maven?" Everett asks softly, peering into my eyes. "Talk to us."

The dread that has been haunting me since we arrived here for the exodus grips my throat tightly.

"A fight is on its way. We—"

I shake my head hard, looking around for Felix. He's a couple of yards away, frowning at us in concern, but snaps to attention when I catch his eye.

"Tell whatever humans remain in the Divide to get out of there *now*. Amadeus—" My voice breaks, so I retry in a whisper. "He knows about the exodus. His forces are on the way to stop it."

My matches swear. Felix nods and takes off toward the waypoint, shouting at the arriving humans to hurry before he slips back into the Divide to hurry along anyone remaining.

My pulse continues to pound. "Silas, tell the bounty hunters the fight is about to begin. They need to be ready at the waypoint. Baelfire, work with the Reformists. Crypt—"

"I'm staying with you, love," he says firmly, violet eyes blazing.

"Whatever hell is about to break loose, we'll stay at your side," Everett agrees.

At the end of the field, the Divide wavers before terribly shrill, otherworldly shrieks echo through the cold air—the sounds of a massive surge of fiends approaching.

The fleeing Nether humans know the sound too well and scramble as one great mass toward the back of the field, clearing much of it in record time. Bounty hunters and Reformists quickly mobilize, their attention on the glowing waypoint spell as they prepare for whatever is about to come through it.

For a moment, it's like the stormy sky itself is holding its breath.

And then hell barrels through the Divide and into this world.

Various monsters, banshees, ghouls, wendigos, Undead, basilisks, and other horrors pour into the field with roars and screams that split eardrums. Two massive harbingers appear, their spider-like legs piercing the dirt as they shriek in harmony, lacing the air with their deadly songs. Reformists and bounty hunters immediately leap into action, launching their attacks as the battle to defend the Nether humans begins—but my stomach plummets when I see how many of the fiends continue to arrive.

Amadeus figured out my gambit. This is his move. A planned attack.

My horror is temporarily eclipsed by shock when Baelfire uses his shifter speed to bolt across the field—right into the middle of a horde of Undead. Before any of them can try to bite him, he bursts into a bright explosion of royal blue flames, shifting and leaving behind a wake of burning, screaming shadow fiends. A golden dragon is suddenly on the field, his deafening roar splitting the air. Molten blue fire spews from his mouth, sending a row of enemies up in flames.

Gods. That's my mate.

Damn straight, Baelfire replies through the bond that I didn't realize I spoke through.

"Maven." Everett gets my attention by gently tipping my chin to meet his pale blue gaze.

I realize Silas has already rushed to join the fight. Crypt is beside us, his markings glowing.

Taking a deep breath, I force myself to focus. Ultimately, it doesn't matter what Amadeus does or doesn't know. If we push back these forces, I can still refortify the Divide and keep the humans and the rest of the mortal world safe from his grasp.

Determination blazes through me as I take in the battle quickly evolving before our eyes. The Reformists are fighting fiercely, as are the bounty hunters. The field is filled with flashes of magic and fighting shifters. Elementals cut down fiends with their elements, and all types of siphons take down opponents. Meanwhile, Baelfire is burning another line through the field as a buffer against the onslaught of shadow fiends.

But when I see two glowing skeletons dressed in ceremonial attire step through the waypoint in the distance, I swear.

Liches.

The only one of Amadeus's Undead that can wield magic after death—and they're fucking powerful.

Withdrawing daggers from their hiding places, I roll my shoulders before racing into the battle with Crypt and Everett on either side of me. Already, I can sense the irresistible weight of death in the air as my blood begins to rush with readiness for the delicious chaos of a frenzied battle.

I race to leap up onto a ghoul, slicing Pierce through his neck. As he falls, I roll and take down a banshee, then several Undead in quick succession. Twirling Pierce in my hand, a grin stretches over my face.

This is a fight I can handle. I was made for brutality like this.

I am nothing but deadly calm.

No—I'm more than that. Much more.

And as soon as this is over, the Divide is restabilized, and the dust begins to settle, my mission will be over. Then, finally, I'll be able to focus on my newlybound quintet and give them every part of myself until I fade away.

We just have to survive this first.

40

MAVEN

GODS, I love combat.

Ice explodes to my left, freezing a section of shadow fiends solid. Crypt swings his enchanted sword, beheading a monstrous vampire before he drives it through the stomach of another lumbering ghoul. A bright flash of Silas's unmistakable blood magic catches my eye in the distance. I hear Baelfire's dragon roar just before the great beast leaps into the sky, its majestic wings sending powerful gusts of air down onto the battlefield.

Fighting alongside my quintet is glorious.

Baelfire laughs through the bond, the sound like cheer itself. *You're so fucking unhinged and cute, hellion. I love it.*

Enough with the L-word. And I'm not cute, I correct, slicing through several more Undead.

Sexy as sin itself? Crypt suggests through the bond.

Temptation personified, Silas tacks on.

Everett's internal voice is exasperated. *You horny idiots are going to get yourselves killed. We're all right as long as we agree that Maven is attractive to a ludicrously unholy degree. Now get your heads out of your asses and focus.*

Lightning crackles through the sky high above as the storm that has been threatening finally breaks above the raging fight.

Amadeus can't keep sending forces forever, I tell them through the bond as I use dark magic to incapacitate a wendigo before beheading it. *If we drive them back into the Divide, I can get to the nearest temple and start refortifying the—*

I cut off when a blast of spine-tingling magic sends me flying backward. I crash into a pile of dismembered Undead, smacking my head on something as my ears ring. Blinking and rolling to my side, I realize that attack came from one of the liches. He's spotted me and is crossing through the battle, his glowing red eyes like miniature fires inside that fleshless skull.

Crypt and Everett are at my side immediately. Crypt helps me stand. He stares down the approaching lich while Everett checks my head for damage. This time, when the lich sends a blast of its magic toward us, I lift my hands to rip through it with my own magic.

I barely register the chilling hiss of a nearby basilisk before the shadowy serpent sinks its fangs into Crypt's leg. He swears and turns to slice at it with his sword, but a rotting Undead barrels into him, knocking him to the ground. His scuffle distracts me for a fraction of a second—

And when the lich hurls a cutting spell toward me with blinding speed, Everett leaps in front of me.

He cries out, collapsing. I swear, dropping to the ground to dodge another attack spell as I turn Everett toward me.

Shit. His face is covered in blood.

He was hit hard.

Cutting spells are simple. They function just like blades, and now my ice elemental looks like someone cut a long gash from one of his hips, diagonally through his chest, and up over half of his face, passing over his eye all the way up to his left temple. Blood drips freely from the long wound as he hisses in pain, squinting the eye that the slash crosses over.

Everett's eye isn't gone, thank the fucking universe—but the rest of the cut is deep. He's losing blood quickly. When he tries to move, he chokes on the pain.

Seeing my beautiful match in agony floods me with rage.

Looking up, I deflect another attack spell just in time, dipping into the life forces rushing inside my veins. I grit my teeth and fire off several brutal attack spells toward the lich to ward it away and buy time.

Everett sputters, struggling like he's trying to get up and help before abruptly blacking out. Blood stains his white hair, matting it as his breathing turns labored.

"Everett?" I whisper, voice trembling.

Shaking with anger, I check the fray around us to see if any threats have noticed that we're vulnerable. I need to use what magic I can and bandage him here before he bleeds out.

Then I'll need to get him out of the battle so Silas can heal him later, far better than I can.

But I can barely think through the anger crowding my brain. I loathe that my elemental is bleeding in my arms, motionless.

Stupid fucking lich.

Blood blossom? Silas checks in fae inside my head.

Everett will need healing soon, I send back, rage making my voice shake even telepathically.

Crypt appears, making me realize he slipped into Limbo to handle his previous scuffle. His silver-flecked violet gaze drops to Everett and the long gash across his torso and face.

My incubus's markings light up as he meets my eye. He must see the pure fury there because he glances up at the lich, who is back on his feet and heading toward us again as if killing me is his one and only mission.

It very well might be.

"Tell me what you need," Crypt murmurs.

My hands shake as I try to wipe blood out of Everett's eyes. His breathing is growing even weaker.

"Bring me his head," I grit, looking back at my Nightmare Prince.

His lips curl up maniacally. "Done. I'll be back soon, darling."

He vanishes. I glance around again to ensure we aren't about to be killed before I focus on patching Everett before he bleeds out.

Revenant magic destroys, and necromancy can't heal the living, so I'm left with my weak grasp of common magic abilities as I struggle to minimize the worst of his deep wound. I can't get it to close, but I manage to slow the bleeding. It's better than nothing.

Pulling out the roll of bandages, I pause to send another blast of dark magic out around us, bringing down an approaching ghoul and a shrieking banshee.

As I begin wrapping clean bandages around the worst of the damage to the side of Everett's face, he grimaces again, rousing.

He opens his other eye, gazing up at me in pained, disoriented confusion. Then his unwrapped eye widens, and he lifts an arm to freeze a banshee I didn't sense coming behind me.

Somewhere overhead, Baelfire roars again before thunder rocks the heavens, barely audible over the deafening battle around us. Ash rains slowly down, along with small flurries of snow. Screams surround us, the grunts and cries and wonderfully morbid sounds of a battle in full swing.

For a fraction of a second, I plead with the universe to keep my other matches unharmed—along with Kenzie and our other allies.

"Come on," I say urgently, helping Everett get to his feet. "We need to get you out of this."

"I can handle it," he argues, lifting his hand to send a massive shard of ice through a Nether vampire when it moves toward us, splitting it in half. But he stumbles, clutching at his still-bleeding chest.

Silas? I check, looking for him in the raging battle surrounding us.

I'll be right—

He cuts off with a swear, and although I can't see where he is in the chaotic flurry of monsters, shadow fiends, Reformists, hellhounds, and bounty hunters, I know he has his hands full.

I just need to get Everett out of here before he gets killed. Then we can drive this shitstorm back, and I'll take care of the Divide.

For several harrowing minutes, Everett leans on me, still using his powers as we fight to make headway through the bloodbath surrounding us. He's weak and clearly in a lot of pain—and not the fun kind. He's trying like hell not to show it.

Meanwhile, I'm trying to stop anything attacking us without killing it—because the last fucking thing I need is to lose control and kill my beautiful ice elemental myself.

Pain blooms inside my chest, so sharp and unexpected that I gasp. It's severe enough that for a fraction of a second, I assume I've been hit by some spell or stabbed with an adamantine blade.

But then I recognize the cold sweeping over me. That empty, shadowy link.

Fuck. No.

Not right now. *Not right now.*

I fight it, trying to breathe through the pain as my vision blurs. Only this time, I don't expire.

Instead, I hear him again, clear as day inside my head.

You were what I made you to be. A masterpiece. A scourge. Even in your betrayal, you honored me.

What the fuck is he talking about, and why is he talking about me in the past sense like this is a eulogy? I grit my teeth through the pain, distantly aware that Everett is freezing anything that comes near and repeating my name in alarm.

Here is your elucidation. The time has come.

For a moment, the battle before me cuts out as a vision sweeps through me. I find myself watching a scene unfold—a moment that Amadeus is sending through his link to me.

But it doesn't feel like a vision of the future.

What I'm about to see is happening right now.

I recognize Engela Zuma as she runs through an empty street in some abandoned city on the East Coast. The elemental looks uncharacteristically frightened and is covered in blood. She sends a blast of power behind her before rounding the corner onto a new street—where Bertram waits.

But instead of a lover's reunion, he darts forward with unparalleled speed and buries his teeth in Engela's neck, ripping her throat out.

Horror floods me as I realize what's happening. The twin demons' words swim in my head.

A tricky legacy. A secret mission from the citadel.

Oh, my gods. When Amadeus learned about my gambit, he decided to outmaneuver me.

And he hired...fucking Bertram.

The vision wavers as Bertram removes the bracelet from Engela's pocket, setting it on the asphalt. He pulls out a knife and poses it above the etherium.

Just as the knife falls, Amadeus's voice echoes through my head one final time.

Your purpose is fulfilled, daughter. May the Beyond embrace you.

No.

This can't fucking happen. I absolutely *cannot* let this—

The etherium shatters, and the vision dissipates. A cold unlike anything I've ever experienced sweeps through my system. I'm so numb that I don't even realize I've hit the ground until I roll over and stare at the billowing winter sky streaked with flashes of lightning.

What just happened? Where are you, sangfluir? Silas's voice demands in my head.

Distantly, I can still hear the screams and mayhem of the fight. But I feel nothing. I'm...going. This is it. The end of my purpose, and therefore, the end of me.

Fuck.

"Maven!"

Everett's shout seems so far away, but suddenly, I'm cradled in his arms with his beautiful, half-bandaged face above me. The ash and blood streaking his skin are in sharp contrast with his soft, blue, panicked eyes.

"No, no, no, no. Breathe. Damn it, why aren't you fucking breathing? Don't you dare—"

My hearing cuts out. Everything is fading to nothingness, including me.

All along, I knew there would be no happy ending for me. I can't even fully blame the gods because I chose this fate. But that doesn't stop the useless tears that prick my eyes as I struggle to drag in just one more breath—because this is really not fucking fair to *them*. Their pain wasn't in my godsdamned plan.

I just needed more time with them.

Vaguely, I'm aware of Crypt and Baelfire frantically trying to speak to me through our bond, but I shut all four of my quintet members off telepathically. I'm sure permanent death hurts like a bitch. They shouldn't have to go through it with me, even distantly.

Everett is shaking now, shouting something at me. I missed when it happened, but he's created a thick shield of ice around us as he tries to get a response out of me. His agonized expression finally drags me back just enough that I can whisper hoarsely.

"Find Lillian. Make sure she survives."

"Stop. Don't do this. The whole final wish thing—I can't handle this. Just keep breathing and…and…" His voice breaks, and he shakes his head helplessly. "Don't leave me. Dear gods on high, *please* don't leave me."

I want to hug him and promise that things will be okay, but I can't lie: we're fucked. Without Engela's life force propping it up, the Divide has officially fallen and the rest of Amadeus's forces will break through as he goes on to conquer the mortal realm. I have failed epically, but I won't even be around to take it on the chin the way I deserve.

Moisture trickles over my temples as I fight like hell for another breath. "I need you to do something for me."

Everett's own tears drip, leaving clean streaks through the ash and dampening the bandages over one half of his face. He gently touches my face with trembling fingers, but his normally chill body temperature doesn't even register to my nearly lifeless remains.

"Anything. Anything for you," he whispers.

"Take care of the others for me." I swallow and shut my eyes. "Please."

"You'll take care of them. You'll stay. I'll find a way to fix this—

godsdamn it, there has to be a way to fucking *fix* this if you just keep breathing and—"

"Everett."

He buries his face in my neck, sobs wracking his shoulders. I can barely hear him when he speaks.

"Okay. Okay, I…I promise."

Whatever else happens after I'm gone, I trust this beautiful snow angel. If I had a heart, it would belong to him—to *all* of them. I don't even know how to express the newfound, overwhelming, unspeakable pain inside my hollow chest until the quiet words are already leaving my lips.

"I love you."

Damn it. I was so right to be terrified of this consuming emotion. It's destroying me. Still, what a shame it is that I won't get to explore this beautiful destruction with them.

Something stutters and then evaporates inside my chest—and at once, I feel the bonds snap.

I thought I knew suffering before, but I had no idea agony like this existed.

Everett cries out. Far overhead, a roar of pure draconic anguish splits the air, so loud that even my malfunctioning ears ache. I can no longer sense the others trying to reach me telepathically. I can no longer sense *anything*, but I know they're hurting.

It makes me despise the gods even more. How dare they give me this quintet just to take it away?

"Stupid fucking gods," I choke as everything goes dark.

Yet even as my not-life fades away at last, I hear it. The smooth, quiet voice of a woman who sounds almost…amused.

"Quite the finale. Come along now, Maven."

A strange whistle fills the air, and for the first time in countless deaths, my soul is reaped.

41

MAVEN

Gentle warmth permeates my body. I open my eyes and stare at a rich blue sky filled with dancing constellations. Sunlight glows around me, highlighting golden flowers and long strands of grass that wave slightly in a soft breeze, brushing against me.

I feel strange. Not only because I don't know where the fuck I am, but also because...

I'm not sure *who* I am.

Sitting up, I take stock of my surroundings. To my left is an orchard filled with trees hanging with some kind of spiral fruit I can't put a name to. Tiny, faintly glowing winged figures flit about. I watch as a massive elk with silver fur and golden antlers ambles peacefully through the orchard, golden flowers blooming wherever it steps.

To my right is a picturesque cottage with a gold-thatched roof, a blooming garden, and oversized butterflies everywhere. It's so bizarrely idyllic that it takes me a moment of staring before I realize a young man is lounging on a massive flower in the garden, reading from a leather-bound grimoire.

His hair is white, the top tied up in a knot and the rest shorn. I think his face is handsome, but what the hell do I know? I can't remember anything to compare it to. His skin is a pale sage green, and he wears multiple necklaces, bracelets, rings, earrings, and a shiny septum piercing studded with emeralds.

When I catch the man's attention, his face lights up. He stands and drops the grimoire. It hovers safely to settle on the flower, which closes around it and disappears into the ground.

Pretty sure that's not fucking normal.

But again, no memories for comparison. So whatever.

"At last! You're awake," he says with a brilliant smile as he approaches.

No shit. "I don't remember anything."

"Ah. That would be a side effect of apotheosis. I'm afraid that turning into one of us has a learning curve—but don't worry, I expect your memories will start to return soon after your mother arrives. I've already sent a magical summons announcing that you're conscious."

My mother?

I don't understand, but I glance down for the first time to see that I'm wearing a plain white dress with no sleeves. No shoes, no jewelry, nothing of note on my entire person—except for the tip of a scar that appears to run down the center of my chest. I stare at it because something about it feels wrong. Like it should be different.

Or more like something is…absent.

"I feel strange," I repeat aloud.

"Again, another result of your arrival here."

"Which is where, exactly?"

The man smiles gently, offering a hand to help me stand up. I start to accept, but when his fingers come near mine, I jerk my hand away. I can't explain why the idea of touching him makes my nerves clench, especially because nothing else about him makes me feel uneasy, but I opt to stand without his assistance.

"Your rightful home," he replies to my question, gesturing at our ethereal surroundings. "And you've certainly earned it. The others

have had so many *opinions* ever since you entered the mortal world
—especially our dear queen. But I want you to know that I, for one,
am exceedingly pleased that you qualified."

I stare at him deadpan and wait, because surely he knows how
vague and unhelpful that was.

The man throws his head back with a bright laugh. "My word,
you really do take after her! How amusing. Forgive me—you
deserve an introduction. My name is Koa. You could call me Uncle
Koa, if you like, for I am the lover of your aunt."

Yikes. I was not a fan of that last sentence.

I still don't know what's happening, but I do know one thing:
with every second that passes, I'm starting to feel torn. Because
while this place is gorgeous, and I feel oddly safe and at ease…some-
thing still feels odd.

I frown at the dancing stars in the sky. "I'm missing something
important."

Or is it multiple somethings? My chest aches, so I rub the scar
there.

"Your memories," Koa suggests with another kind smile. "But as
I said, those will return in short order. Your soul has been through so
much that it is only natural that you will need time to settle in this
plane of existence. For now, please come with me. We're all so eager
to greet you, dear Maven—we've watched your progress, after all,
and it's been nearly three millennia since we welcomed a new
goddess to Paradise."

New goddess? I don't need memories to instinctively know that
idea repels me.

"Fuck, no. Hard pass."

A tinkling laugh nearby makes us both turn, and I watch as a
woman in a flowing white dress approaches. Her golden hair falls in
cascades well past her hips. The closer she gets, the more I can see
that her eyes are a bizarre kaleidoscope of swirling colors, constantly
shifting through the full spectrum of the rainbow.

She's almost nauseatingly beautiful, yet also oddly familiar. Have
I ever seen her face before?

"You've never seen my face, my fearless one," she replies to my thoughts matter-of-factly. "I'm afraid I had to have some method of disguise in the mortal realm."

I stare at the woman for another second and then glance at Koa. "You summoned her?"

Meaning...this is my mother?

"No. He summoned me," another woman's voice says from behind me.

And I *know* this voice because, with a jolt, I remember hearing it when everything else faded to black. Memories of who and what I was begin returning to me, so by the time I turn to face the owner of that voice, I'm not surprised to see the Reaper herself push back the hood of her cloak.

Tall, dressed in swirling shadows, with dark hair and pitch-black eyes. Skin so pale, she could be a fresh corpse. A massive, wicked-looking scythe rests on one of the goddess's shoulders as she stares back at me without a change in her expression—

Until her lips curl up slowly in a chilling smile.

Something about her face also feels like I should know it.

Things click together as more memories rush to the surface. With a start, I realize Syntyche's face is so fucking familiar because I've seen it in mirrors countless times.

Because I look exactly like her.

Because she's my mother.

Thank you for reading *Twisted Soul!*
I promise that the fourth and final book of Cursed Legacies will have answers and, eventually, a happily ever after.

In the meantime, I really do apologize for the cliffhanger. Kind of.
What can I say? This was always intended in Maven's story.

If you're enjoying the series, feel free to share your review for *Twisted Soul* on Amazon or Goodreads for others.

If you want to join a Facebook reader page to chat about the Cursed Legacies series and other why choose romances, join Morgan B. Lee's Why Choose Fiends.

Want to get notified about new releases and signed copies? Join Morgan B Lee's newsletter here.

Thanks for reading

ABOUT THE AUTHOR

Morgan is a certified nerd who loves long bubble baths and big, bad, sexy cinnamon roll book boyfriends. When she's not busy reading spice or lint-rolling cat hair off of her yoga pants, she works a day job while daydreaming about the before-mentioned cinnamon roll book boyfriends.

To find out about upcoming releases or signed copies, join her mailing list at https://prodigious-knitter-8903.ck.page/48d02b6fe8.

24173473R00226